Cricket Maxfield had a hell of a hand. Her confidence made that clear.

And right now, she was looking like *far* too much of a winner.

Lucky for him, around the time he'd escalated the betting, he'd been *sure* she would win.

He'd *wanted* her to win.

"I guess that makes you my ranch hand," she said. "Don't worry. I'm a very good boss."

Now, Jackson did not want a boss. Not at his job, and not in his bedroom. But her words sent a streak of fire through his blood. Not because he wanted her in charge. But because he wanted to show her what a boss looked like.

Cricket was...

A nuisance. If anything.

That he had any awareness of her at all was problematic enough. Much less that he had any awareness of her as a woman. But once this evening was over, he could forget all about ever being tempted to look down her dress during a game of cards.

"Oh, I'm sure you are, sugar."

"I'm your boss. Not your *sugar*."

* * *

***The Rancher's Wager* by Maisey Yates is part of the Gold Valley Vineyards series.**

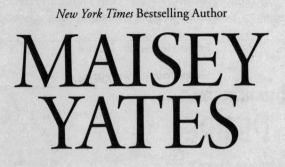

New York Times Bestselling Author

MAISEY YATES

The Rancher's Wager
&
Take Me, Cowboy

HARLEQUIN
DESIRE

⊞ HARLEQUIN®
DESIRE™

Recycling programs
for this product may
not exist in your area.

ISBN-13: 978-1-335-25092-6

The Rancher's Wager & Take Me, Cowboy

Copyright © 2021 by Harlequin Books S.A.

The Rancher's Wager
Copyright © 2021 by Maisey Yates

Take Me, Cowboy
First published in 2016. This edition published in 2021.
Copyright © 2016 by Maisey Yates

This edition published by arrangement with Harlequin Books S.A.

For questions and comments about the quality of this book,
please contact us at CustomerService@Harlequin.com.

Harlequin Enterprises ULC
22 Adelaide St. West, 40th Floor
Toronto, Ontario M5H 4E3, Canada
www.Harlequin.com

Printed in U.S.A.

CONTENTS

THE RANCHER'S WAGER

Chapter 1

Cricket Maxfield had won any number of specious prizes in the game of life. From being born youngest in her family, barely rating a passing glance from either of her parents and being left to essentially do as she pleased, to being the only Maxfield sister born with both pigeon feet *and* buck teeth.

The latter was largely solved by braces, the former was mostly dealt with by casts on her feet when she was a baby.

She hardly walked turned in at all anymore.

All the way to a decrepit ranch that had been buried in her father's portfolio, discovered after his disgrace, and unwanted by anyone else in her family.

She had a feeling, though, that she was about to win the strangest prize of all—six feet and four inches of big, rock solid cowboy.

She couldn't have planned it better if she'd tried.

Oh, *he* didn't think he was going to lose. She knew he didn't. Because he had been betting like a fool all the way through this hand, and he had no idea that she had just gotten the absolute best hand possible.

No. He was playing like a man with a full house or a straight flush.

But she was a woman with a *royal* flush.

This final hand was always the most interesting part of this charity fundraiser, and it was the first year that Cricket had ever been in the hot seat for Battle of the Gold Valley Stars charity poker tournament.

This was the grudge game. This was the game for spectators.

Huge amounts of money had already been counted and distributed in previous rounds, all of it donated by businesses as each player had fought tooth and nail against each other, pouring cash into a pot for the sole purpose of giving back to the community. Now came the part where things got interesting.

Rivals tried to get back bits of their own, as hotly contested items that had been tussled over at rummage sales, and family heirlooms that had gone back and forth in this game for decades, were all put in the pot.

Cricket was currently wearing an oversized black leather jacket with fringes—won in the previous round from Elliott Johns, the guy who ran a water filtration company in the area. She also had an oversized black cowboy hat that she had already won from her current target. It was resting low on her head, and smelled vaguely of sweat, which was unnerving, since smelling Jackson's sweat made her feel strange. Just the idea of it.

It was a bit like that feeling she'd gotten when she was a child, and had been tempted to do something she knew she shouldn't. A strange tingling low in her stomach, that then went lower and spread down her thighs, making her feel restless and strange. She shifted in her chair, her dress slippery on the material of the seat. Another specious prize. A hand-me-down red gown originally worn by her sister Emerson to this event.

Cricket's fidgeting was just anticipation. And being so close to Jackson Cooper.

A man she usually avoided.

From afar, she had made a study of the Cooper family over the years. Something she was embarrassed to admit.

She had gotten to know Jackson's brother, Creed, a little better over the past few months, since he'd become her brother-in-law. She'd acted shocked and appalled and said any number of things about her sister Wren when she found herself involved with a Cooper. It had gone way past involved now, and they were married with a baby. And Cricket had sworn to Wren, up and down, that hardheaded, irritating, stubborn cowboys would never ever be her type.

Cricket was a liar.

Jackson made her feel strange…but he was also the only one of the Coopers who could answer the questions she needed answered.

Because of Wren, she couldn't really talk to Creed. And she didn't really want to talk to the youngest Cooper either, even though Honey was closer to Cricket's age. She'd never found the other girl approachable.

In some ways, Cricket was jealous of her.

Honey was a country girl. A tough cowgirl. And

she just seemed to fit with her family. In a way Cricket did not.

Case in point, Cricket had never really had much of anything to do with the family winery. But she was a fantastic card player. And with their father officially out of commission—having been exiled in disgrace, and for good reason—Cricket had been nominated by her sisters to take his place.

And Cricket was about to take it all.

"I'll raise you," she said.

Oh yes, it was time. In that pot were a great many things she was interested in. Jackson's cufflinks. His watch. A pony from his ranch.

She'd only had to offer a diamond bracelet—wasn't hers anyway—a case of Maxfield reserve wines, and the dollar from her father's very first sale, which still hung in his vacant office, framed on the wall. Something that Jackson said he was going to give to his father.

The Maxfield and Cooper families were rivals from way back, though that rivalry had been dented some by her sister marrying Creed.

Still, sitting here across from a Cooper brought out her competitive spirit. Especially because right along with that competitive spirit, Jackson also brought out that complicated sensation she could honestly say she wasn't a fan of.

And now it was right down to the final bet.

"I bet myself," she said.

"Excuse me?"

"I bet myself. I will work for Cowboy Wines for free for thirty days."

His brows shot upward. "That's pretty rich."

"You afraid?"

He snorted. "I'll see you. And raise you. I'll work at Maxfield Vineyards for thirty days."

"No," she said. "The winery doesn't need you. You'll work at my ranch for thirty days. And sleep in the bunkhouse." She desperately needed a ranch hand. And she knew that Jackson Cooper knew what he was doing when it came to horses.

Cricket wanted as far away from the uppity confines of her upbringing as possible. And this ranch was her one way to get there.

"And if I lose…"

"You'll work at Cowboy Wines, in the tasting room. Dressed up in cowgirl boots and a miniskirt and serving our guests."

He was trying to scare her or humiliate her. But she'd grown up with James Maxfield. She'd been made to feel small and sad and unwanted for years. It was only recently she'd started to suspect why her father had treated her that way. But after a lifetime of humiliation, a miniskirt and waiting tables wouldn't defeat her. "Deal."

And she wouldn't lose. She wanted his forfeit and wasn't worried at all about her own.

She needed Jackson on her ranch. Unfortunately, she was all stalled out. Didn't quite know where to begin. That's where Jackson would come in handy.

And then there was that *other* matter.

And so she waited.

"You look awfully confident," he said.

"Oh I am."

He laid down his cards, that handsome mouth turning upward into a smile.

The smile of a man who had never lost much of anything in his life.

Oh how she would enjoy showing him what a foolish mistake that smile was.

Because not only had he lost. He had lost to her. A woman at least ten years younger than him, a woman she knew he didn't think of as wise. A woman she knew he thought of as not much of anything special.

He'd made that clear the few times they'd seen each other since they'd become kind of, sort of family.

Dismissive. Obnoxious.

"I hate to be a cliché. But read 'em and weep, cowboy."

Cricket Maxfield had a hell of a hand. And her confidence made that clear. Poor little thing didn't think she needed a poker face if she had a hand that could win.

But he knew better.

She was sitting there with his hat on her head, oversized and over her eyes, and an unlit cigar in her mouth.

A mouth that was disconcertingly red tonight, as she had clearly conceded to allowing her sister Emerson to make her up for the occasion. That bulky, fringed leather jacket should have looked ridiculous, but over that red dress, cut scandalously low, giving a tantalizing wedge of scarlet along with pale, creamy cleavage, she was looking not ridiculous at all.

And right now, she was looking like *far* too much of a winner.

Lucky for him, around the time he'd escalated the betting, he'd been sure she would win.

He'd *wanted* her to win.

"I guess that makes you my ranch hand," she said. "Don't worry. I'm a very good boss."

Now, Jackson did not want a boss. Not at his job, and not in his bedroom. But her words sent a streak of fire through his blood. Not because he wanted her in charge. But because he wanted to show her what a boss looked like.

Cricket was…

A nuisance. If anything.

That he had any awareness of her at all was problematic enough. Much less that he had any awareness of her as a woman. But that was just because of what she was wearing. The truth of the matter was, Cricket would turn back into the little pumpkin she usually was once this evening was over and he could forget all about the fact that he had ever been tempted to look down her dress during a game of cards.

"Oh, I'm sure you are, sugar."

"I'm your boss. Not your *sugar*."

"I wasn't aware that you winning me in a game of cards gave you the right to tell me how to talk."

"If I'm your boss, then I definitely have the right to tell you how to talk."

"Seems like a gray area to me." He waited for a moment, let the word roll around on his tongue, savoring it so he could really, really give himself all the anticipation he was due. "Sugar."

"We're going to have to work on your attitude. You're insubordinate."

"Again," he said, offering her a smile. "I don't recall promising a specific attitude."

There was activity going on around him. The small crowd watching the game was cheering, enjoying the way this rivalry was playing out in front of them. He couldn't blame them. If the situation wasn't at his expense, then he would have probably been smirking and enjoying himself along with the rest of the audience, watching the idiot who had lost to the little girl with the cigar.

He might have lost the hand, but he had a feeling he'd win the game.

And it was hardly dirty poker. Cricket had started it, after all.

She was in over her head, and he knew it.

When he'd heard that James Maxfield owned the property next to his, Jackson had figured he'd swoop in and buy it now that ownership of the man's properties had reverted to his family. But then Cricket had grandly taken control of the land—with great proclamation, per Jackson's brother, that she was going to be a rancher.

But Jackson knew there was no way in hell Cricket had the chops to start and run a ranch. It was hard enough when you had experience. She had none. And he knew she had some of her dad's money, but it wasn't going to be an endless well.

She was out of her league.

And a month spent as her ranch hand was more than enough time to show her that.

"Also, you should bring my pony," she said.

She was placated by the pony. He was going to end up getting that pony back. He knew it down in his bones. Because in the end, Cricket had not one idea of the amount of work that went into having animals. No idea the amount of work that went into working a ranch. Working the land.

She was stubborn and obstinate, and different than her sisters.

Their families might be big rivals, but they all worked in the same industry. He'd watched Cricket grow up. He had a fair idea of her personality. And he also had a fair idea of just how privileged the Maxfield family was.

They had a massive spread, worked by employees.

Any vision she had of ranching was bound to be romanticized.

He knew better.

He knew people looked at him and figured he was just another guy who'd grown up with a silver spoon in his mouth. Well, not literally. They didn't look at him and think that. He looked like a cowboy. But the fact was, he had grown up in a family that was well-off. At least, for most of his life. He was still old enough to remember when they had struggled.

He knew his younger brother didn't remember much of that time, and their youngest sister, Honey, didn't remember it at all. But Jackson did. He also knew Cricket had never known a moment of financial struggle in all her life. It wasn't that he thought she was stupid. She wasn't. She was bright and sharp, and a bit fierce.

He had always found her fascinating, especially in contrast with the rest of her family. Even before it had turned out her father was a criminal and a sexual predator, Jackson had always found the Maxfields to be a strange and fascinating family. So different from his own. There had always been tension between James Maxfield and his wife. Wren and Emerson had always seemed like perfect Stepford children from an extremely warped, upper-class neighborhood, cookies from the same cutter.

But not Cricket.

She had never been at the forefront of any of the events they had put on at the winery. And though Maxfield Vineyards and Cowboy Wines might have been rivals, they often attended each other's events. Professional courtesy, and all of that. And scoping out the competition. So he'd seen Cricket many times over the years. Usually skulking in the background, but then, when she got older, not there at all. One time, three years ago or so—she must've been eighteen—she'd been out on a swing in the yard, wearing a white dress he was almost certain she didn't want to be wearing. It had been dark out there, and inside, the Maxfield event room had been all lit up.

She was just lit up by the moon.

She had looked completely separate. Alone. And he'd felt some kind of sympathy for her. It was strange, and a foreign feeling for him. Because he wasn't an overly sympathetic kind of guy. But the girl was a square peg, no denying it. And in his opinion—particularly at the time—it wasn't round holes she needed to fit into. Just a family of assholes.

Now, he had changed his opinion on Wren and Emerson in the time since.

But his general opinion of Cricket's family, of her father, had certainly been correct. And just because he now thought Wren and Emerson were decent people... they were still so different from their sister. So different—it was the strangest thing.

But Cricket wasn't so different from her family that she would simply be able to step into ranching life. And he'd be right on hand to show her just how much work it was. He wouldn't have to do anything. Wouldn't have to sabotage her in any way.

She just needed a dose of reality.

And then she'd be willing to sell him that property.

He'd bought his own ranch and transitioned from working the one at Cowboy Wines after his mother died. And yes, he had people who helped him, so they would cover the slack of him not being there.

And that was the thing. Ranching never took time off. That was something he understood, and well.

"Report for work first thing on Monday," Cricket said. "And bring a sleeping bag. I don't have any extra and the bunkhouse gets cold."

She did not shake his hand. Instead, she clamped down on that unlit cigar, scrunched up her nose, grabbed the brim of the black cowboy hat and tipped it.

And right then, he vowed that no matter that Cricket had won the pot, he was going to win the whole damn thing.

Whatever that looked like.

"You *what*?"

Cricket looked at Emerson, keeping her expression as sanguine as possible. She wasn't going to get into the details of any of this with her sisters. Not now. Not just yet.

"Well, you would have known if you would have gone."

"I'm a whale," Emerson said, gesturing to her nine-months-pregnant stomach. "And my ankles were so swollen, I couldn't get my shoes on. So I didn't go."

"And I didn't tell her," Wren said, grinning. "Because I wanted her to hear it directly from Cricket's mouth."

"I won him in a poker game," Cricket said. "I won him fair and square, and now he has to come work on my ranch."

Triumph surged through her again. Her plan was working out perfectly, and she had a handle on it. All of it.

"Your ranch."

"And I won a pony," Cricket said, grinning with glee. "Why are you looking at me like that?"

"Because," Emerson said. "Jackson Cooper is a tool."

"So is Creed Cooper, but Wren married him." Cricket's teeth ground together as she said that. The whole thing with Wren and Creed had come as a shock, and like with all things Cooper-related, Cricket had kept that shock completely to herself, but she was still struggling with it a bit. "Come to that, your husband is kind of a tool," Cricket said to Emerson. "Just not to you. Also, I'm not *marrying* Jackson, I'm just having him work for me. For free."

She was practiced at pretending she didn't think much of Jackson. But this conversation pushed her thoughts in strange directions. Directions she'd been actively avoiding for months now.

"All right, I have to hand it to you, it's a little bit brilliant."

"I'm just happy to see you're doing something," Wren said. "Unfortunate double entendres aside. We've been worried about you."

"I know you have. For more than a year now. But you are both too afraid to say anything to me."

They didn't know how to talk to her. That was the truth. They might never admit it, but Cricket knew it. Fair enough, she often didn't know how to talk to them either.

"We never know what's going to make you run further and faster," Emerson said. "I'm sorry. But you know... You're not a little kid anymore. But I think it's easy for us to think of you that way. There's no reason for that."

"Glad to know that I'm finally getting a little respect."

"I did question your sanity when you asked to take on the ranch."

"It's paid for. I mean, there's definitely a lot of work to be done on it, but there was no reason to just let it sit there going to seed. And this is something I've always wanted. My own place. Wine isn't my thing and it never has been. I know you're shocked to hear that."

"Yeah, not so much," Emerson said.

"We're just different," Cricket said.

Honestly, she and her sisters couldn't be any more different if they tried. Emerson was curvy—though sporting an extra curve right now—and absolutely beautiful, like a bombshell. Wren was sleek and sophisticated. Cricket had always felt extremely out of place at Maxfield events. It was like her sisters just knew something. Innately. Like being beautiful was part of their intrinsic makeup in a way it would never be for Cricket. And she had never really cared about being beautiful, which was another thing that had made her feel like the cuckoo in the nest.

So she just hadn't tried. Emerson and Wren had. They'd tried so hard to earn Jameson Maxfield's approval. Cricket had hidden instead. Had flown under the radar straight into obscurity.

She could remember, far too clearly, asking her father about college four years ago.

"You didn't particularly apply yourself in school, did you?"

"I..."

"What would you want to do?"

She'd been stumped by that. *"I don't know. I need to go so that I can figure it out..."*

"Emerson and Wren contributed to the winery with their degrees. Is that what you plan to do?"

There had been no college for Cricket.

She knew her dad could afford it. It wasn't about the expense. It was about her value.

Both of her parents had always been so distant to her. And it wasn't until later that she'd started to understand why.

Started to suspect she was not James Maxfield's daughter...

Well, the suspicion had made her feel like she made some sense. That her differences made sense. There were things that hurt about the idea, and badly. But she'd put those things in their place.

She'd had no choice.

"I appreciate it. I do."

"And whatever you think about our husbands," Emerson said, "they're both cowboys, and they would be happy to help you with the ranch."

"I know that. And when I've exhausted my free Cooper labor, I may take them up on it. But for now, I'll solve my own problem."

"Well done, Cricket," Emerson said, sounding slightly defeated. "I can't even see my toes."

"You're not supposed to," Wren said.

Wren's baby was three months old now, and of course, her slim figure had already gone right back into place. But even slightly built Wren had been distressed about the size of her stomach at this stage in her pregnancy.

It was weird to see her sisters so settled in domesticity. Having babies and all of that. They had never seemed particularly domesticated to Cricket, but they had fallen in love, and that had changed them both. Not in a bad way. In fact, they both seemed happier. Steadier and more sure of themselves. But that didn't make any of that racket seem appealing to Cricket.

Who just wanted…to be free.

To not feel any of the overwhelming pressure to fit into anything other than the life she chose for herself.

Maybe she'd wanted something else when she'd been young and silly and hadn't understood herself or her life.

She was the awkward sister. The ugly sister, really. She didn't mind at all about her looks. She was tall, and she was thin, and her curves weren't anything to write home about. But while that seemed elegant and refined on Wren, with her somewhat bony shoulders and knees, Cricket had always just thought her thinness seemed unfortunate on her. Her cheekbones were sharp, and she had freckles. Her top lip was just a little bit more full than the bottom one, and even though she'd had braces to solve the buck teeth situation, the gap between her two front teeth hadn't closed entirely, and it remained.

Her features were… Well, they were strong. And like everything else about her, kind of a love or hate situation.

Cricket didn't much care how she looked. She cared about what she could do. She was good at riding horses. She could run fast; she was strong. Her hair was a little bit wild, but she didn't much mind. No, she didn't mind at all. Because it made her look like she was moving. Made her look like she was busy. And that was what she liked.

That was the thing. As much as the Coopers were supposed to be rivals of her family, in some ways, she could identify a little bit more closely with them than she did with the Maxfields. They had country roots and sensibilities. That was what she understood.

It was what she connected with.

Country strong was hard to break. And that was what Cricket wanted to be.

It was what she was.

"I plan on making good use of Mr. Jackson Cooper," Cricket said triumphantly, immediately picturing the man, his broad shoulders and large hands.

Good for work.

And a good place to start when it came to figuring out how to…how to broach the topic of what she thought might be true between them.

"Yes indeed," she said to herself.

Her sisters exchanged a glance. "Just be careful."

"Why?"

"The Coopers are a whole thing," Wren said.

Cricket blinked. "I don't understand what you mean."

"You start talking about making full use of Cooper men, and I'll tell you, it gives me ideas," Wren said.

Cricket still didn't get it.

"Sex, Cricket," Wren said. "Some people might think you mean sex."

Cricket was suddenly made of heat and horror. "No! No. Not at all. Never. How could you... Look, Wren, I'm not you. When I finally do decide to take on a man, and I'm going to need to get my actual life in order a whole hell of a lot better before I do, it is not going to be... He's *old*."

Among other things.

Wren laughed. "Right. So old. Like two whole years older than my husband."

Cricket sniffed. "And I'm several years younger than you."

Wren seem to take that as a square insult, her lips snapping shut.

Fine. Cricket wasn't old enough to take age commentary as that deep of a wound yet.

"This is strictly a business arrangement," she said. A fluttering grew and expanded in her chest. Evidence of her dishonesty. "He's going to help me with my ranch. And that's it."

"If you say so."

"I absolutely do."

"The one thing I know about you, Cricket. When you set your mind to something, you do see it done."

And what she had her mind set to, was finding out for sure if she wasn't a Maxfield at all...

And hiring Jackson Cooper was the best way to do that.

Chapter 2

The place was a mess.

To call it a ranch was a stretch. The house was…
It was damn near falling apart. The porch was sloping on one side. He didn't want the place for its current assets, though.

He wanted it for the location.

This property was the best and only way for him to
increase his spread, and that was what he needed to
do. He wasn't going to spend his life working on his
father's legacy.

He wasn't his father.

And when that screen door opened, and Cricket
came out, she looked like the feral pirate queen of a
sinking ship.

She had a hat on over frizzy blond curls, and a
tight white tank top and denim shorts. She also had

on cowgirl boots. She was quite unintentionally the very image of a sexy, tousled cowgirl, and he knew that she hadn't done that on purpose. Not at all.

Her legs were long, endless. Her curves were slight, but they were ripe. She had no makeup on her face, but she was damn pretty. Unique looking, that was for sure. But he liked her look, he found. At least, he had been liking it more and more lately, which he didn't really care to dive into.

He wasn't here to look. He was here to educate.

In such a way that she might realize the subject matter was not for her.

"Reporting for duty," he said.

"Excellent," she responded, grinning.

"So what is it you had in mind, because this is way more than a month's worth of work, I can already tell."

She looked immediately crestfallen and he had to wonder if she was going to make it easy for him. "Why? What do you see?"

"You're liable to fall right through that porch if somebody doesn't get in there and reinforce it. I have some concerns. Are you living in this heap?"

"Yes," she said. "It's fine. I just avoid the saggy boards over there."

"Cricket," he said. "You're about to slide through the whole damn thing."

"I won't."

"Okay. Maybe you won't, because you probably don't weigh a buck and a quarter soaking wet. Somebody like me is going to fall right through."

"Well, sounds basically like the equivalent of a cowboy moat to me. And I may be okay with that."

"You got something against cowboys? Because it

seems to me that you need one to get this place going."
He looked around and affected an expression he hoped
looked something like overwhelmed.

He'd never been overwhelmed a day in his life.

"You might need more than one cowboy, realisti-
cally," he added.

"Nothing *against*. Just don't need one in my house."

"I also suspect that isn't true. Because I'm thinking
you probably need some things fixed in there."

She looked stubborn for a moment. But under that
he could see…she was wary and he wasn't sure why.
He'd never given her a reason to be wary. "Well, maybe
a few things. But I can call someone else out for that."

"Why?" he asked. "You've got me."

Her eyes narrowed. "You know how to repair
things?"

"I sure as hell do."

"Well… All right. I'll let you come take a look then."

"Lead the way. Point out the mushy boards."

He walked up the steps and through the front door,
into the tiny, shabby entryway.

Cricket held her arms out. "Well, this is it." She
smiled. "What do you think? Just kidding. I don't care."

He looked around, turning in a circle. "It's…some-
thing, Cricket."

To tell the truth, the little farmhouse wasn't so bad.
It was worn with years, and a bit shabby, but it was
definitely repairable.

What he couldn't imagine was a girl like Cricket—
who'd grown up in a monstrosity of a mansion that
was doing a poor imitation of a Tuscan villa—settling
into it.

"I thought so. It's a ranch. I feel like… That's what I feel like I want to do. Wine's not really for me."

"Yeah, I noticed you were never all that into any of the Maxfield events."

But there was a lot of ground between not wanting to be part of the winery and wanting to run a ranch. She might not know it yet, but he did.

He'd spent years working the ranch at Cowboy Wines. Years. Pouring blood and sweat into his father's land. His father's legacy.

Until he'd found out the truth about Cash Cooper. And then he'd just…

He'd wanted his own.

Now, he still worked at the winery. He wouldn't cause a rift. His mother wouldn't have wanted that. She'd spent years working to make sure she kept the family together at the expense of her own happiness and he wouldn't be the one to wreck that.

But he didn't have to make his father's life his own.

"No, I was really not," she said. "And this has always been kind of my dream. So…"

"Why ranching?"

Her expression suddenly went shy, then sharp. "I don't know. I feel like it's in my blood. Which is weird, because my family doesn't do it. Is that how you feel? Like ranching is in your blood?"

He shifted. Shrugged. "Can't say as I know. It's just something I do. I can't see doing any different."

"Yeah. That's exactly it. Except, it wasn't just right there for me, so I had to figure out what that meant. What it might mean for me that I dreamed about having my own little house out in the middle of… Well, just like this. A field all around. I want horses."

"How are you going to make money? Are you breeding horses?"

"Well…"

"Cattle?" He didn't wait for her to respond. "Dairy or meat? Have you thought about dealing with slaughtering cows? With getting to the nearest USDA station and the cost of it all?"

"I…"

"If you decide to do horses are you going to keep studs or have sperm brought in?"

"Well," she sputtered again.

"Doing produce? More of a farm? Have you thought about CBD? That's a growing industry."

"The thing is," she sputtered, her manner that of a wet hen. "I haven't exactly decided. I don't really know what I want to do with the place. But I kind of feel like until I get a bit more… Until I get it into shape, I'm not going to know."

"I don't know how that's going to work," he said, like he was honestly doing her a favor. The girl had no idea what she was getting herself into. She'd be in water five feet high and rising. Before she knew it, she'd be in over her pretty head.

This was practically a rescue mission.

Yeah, don't go that far. You're being a dick. Own it.

Sure, he'd own it.

Like he'd own this ranch in the end.

But Cricket suffered from the overconfidence of the young and inexperienced. Jackson Cooper hadn't been young or inexperienced for a long time. The problem with someone like Cricket was she was sure she knew exactly what was happening, exactly what she was doing, and she was also certain no one could possibly know better than her.

"I mean, I'll be honest," she said. "I don't know if I have the fortitude to do beef. But it seems to me that the overhead with horses is really high."

"Horses are expensive. Getting into good ones… That's pricey. But it might be more what you're looking for. Breeding good horses."

"Maybe that's it." That she seemed to be considering anything he said shocked him. "I'll think about it. I'll spend some time reading." She sighed. "Fundamentally, I have time. This place is paid for. And I have some reserves."

"From your dad's estate?"

"Pretty much. I sold my stake in the winery. I wanted out. I wanted to…follow my own path, and I knew I wanted out. So… I sold my stake. I got some cash."

"And you're using me for slave labor."

"Well, since I had the opportunity, that just seems like good business. Why pay for something when you can get it for free?"

"Let's start with the house," he said, walking from the little sitting room into the kitchen. There were spiderwebs in the corner. "Have you cleaned?"

"A little," she said.

He said nothing, he just kept on looking. At the dust, the peeling paint.

She wrinkled her nose. "Okay. I'm not really used to doing any of my own cleaning. I'm not opposed to it. There's nothing wrong with being prepared. It's just… I haven't really done it, so I don't really think of everything. And I hate that, because I don't feel like I'm a spoiled rich girl, but I guess to an extent I am. I feel like I *can* do all these things, but I never have. It's all based on… Well, basically nothing. Just my feelings about the fact that I can do this. But that has to mean something. Right?"

Granted, he was here to try and give her advice. Advice that would discourage her from all this. The truth. He was here to give her the truth, but she was suddenly looking at him like he might contain the answers to the mysteries of the universe, and he had no idea why.

He didn't like it either.

"I don't know," he said. "But I do know that it is always a good time to learn to take care of your own damn self. So go get a broom and clear your cobwebs. I'm going to evaluate." He began to walk the perimeter of the room, making note of places where it felt like there might be water damage. Right by the sink. He wasn't surprised. It was an old farmhouse, and it was easy to believe it hadn't been worked on at all, judging by the rest of the place.

He was surprised when Cricket did what he asked, and went into the small pantry, grabbed a broom and began to harass the spiders in the corners.

"Granted," she said. "I can keep the spiders."

"I would've thought you and spiders were natural enemies."

"Why?"

"Don't they eat crickets?"

She rolled her eyes. "Funny."

Her name was just another thing that didn't quite fit with the rest of the Maxfields. A name with bounce and humor. And he didn't think anyone in her family had an ounce of either. "Why did they name you Cricket?"

"Why is your sister named *Honey*?"

"Well, that's easy. Mom picked it, and my dad agreed because it was so sweet to finally have a girl."

She frowned. "He sounds nice."

That was the problem. Cash Cooper was nice. A good father in many ways. It would have been easier if he was an out-and-out asshole. He wasn't. Jackson resented him plenty sometimes, carried a lot of anger toward him.

But Honey adored him. Creed had been so mired in his own issues he'd never gotten to know their mother as an adult the way Jackson had, and she'd certainly never confided in Creed.

Jackson was the only one who knew.

"He has his moments," he said. "I mean, he's a crusty old man."

"Yeah, well, James Maxfield is a little more than crusty."

James Maxfield had been unveiled as an unrepentant sexual predator. One who'd gotten a girl pregnant and cast her aside, left her a shell of herself after a mental breakdown. A man who'd blackmailed any number of employees who'd felt harassed by him. A serial cheater, liar and all-around asshole.

Cash might have his flaws, but he wasn't that.

"Right. Sorry." Then, he did feel bad, because she looked so lost.

And the way she looked reminded him of how he'd felt when his mother had died. It had been…a hell of a thing to lose her. The entire family had done what they could to stay strong in the aftermath and they had each other. But he remembered that feeling. Cricket was hollow-eyed, and he had to wonder if James's behav-

ior was as shocking to her as it had been to her sisters.
It hadn't shocked him. The way his father had always
carried a grudge against James Maxfield had made
Jackson suspect there was a very serious reason for it.
Of course, there would be. His father wasn't the kind
of man who disliked somebody just because.

"It's okay. So, how did your dad get interested in
wine? You know, since he was a cowboy first."

Jackson peeked under the sink, frowning when he
saw water. Then he turned on the water so that he could
try and figure out the exact source of the leak. "Well,
he didn't like your dad. And I think his aim was more
or less to try and prove that he could do exactly what
your dad did. But better."

"That's a pretty powerful dislike. To do something
just to prove you can. I mean, I respect it. That's exactly
the kind of thing I can understand. Needing to prove
yourself that much. It makes perfect sense to me."

"A little bit vindictive, are you, Cricket?"

She shrugged. "I think so. I mean, in seventh grade
Billy O'Connor made fun of my buck teeth, and then
I got braces, and two years later I made him think I
wanted to go to a school dance with him, only so I
could turn him down."

"That's pretty stone cold."

"He shouldn't of made fun of my teeth. Did you
have buck teeth?"

He frowned. "No."

"Did Honey?"

"If so, I don't recall."

"Oh. Well, I do. And no one else in my family does.
I think that's kind of weird."

"Families are different."

"Of course. I'm not saying they aren't. I'm just… I dunno. Sometimes I try to see something in common with my sisters, and I just can't. But I don't know. That feeling kind of goes away here. Spiders or not."

"Well, good to know." He knelt down, had a good look at the pipe. "I have some plumber's tape in the truck. But I'm going to need to go get a part from town to actually fix this."

"Can I go with you?"

"Sure," he said.

"Great." He headed back out toward the truck, and he could practically hear her holding something back. "Yes?"

"It just occurred to me that maybe I should go out to the bunkhouse with you. Show you around."

"Okay." He looked at her. "Are you really going to make me sleep in the bunkhouse?"

If he were another kind of man he'd sneak across the field and into his own house. But he was honorable with his dishonor. They'd had a bet.

He was sticking to it.

"Absolutely. It was part of our bet. You're going to be my ranch hand."

She didn't elaborate. Didn't offer any sort of reasoning behind why she needed him here. He just had a feeling it amused her.

Cricket was a bloodthirsty little thing.

He had to grudgingly respect that.

She led the way down a trail that had been worn into the grass, and he followed. And groaned when the very rustic-looking house came into view. "You're not serious."

"I am absolutely serious. What's wrong with it?"

"If the house is dilapidated, how bad is this going to be?"

She kicked open the door, and inside was... Well, pretty much nothing. There were bunks, but they looked like they were moldier than not.

"Cricket," he said.

He'd slept in worse, that was for damn sure. But not for as long as a month.

"Okay," she relented. "All right, I have a better idea. You can sleep in the house."

The look he gave her was full of skepticism, but his skepticism wasn't her problem. She was enjoying talking to him. Trying to get a sense of what he thought. What he knew. If they were *alike*.

And when he had talked about his dad...

She had wanted to know more. She was jealous. Because her own father had never cared for her at all. What would it have been like to grow up on the ranch? To have a place where she belonged. It had actually become something of a cherished fantasy.

The idea that James Maxfield wasn't her father. The idea that she made sense.

"Sleep in the house."

"Yes. There's an extra bedroom."

"Great."

They went back toward the house, him with his sleeping bag in tow.

"There's a quilt," she said.

"Is it full of dust?"

"Don't be silly." She waved her hand. "I beat the blankets out. I looked that up online. I've got this, I really do."

"Right."

"This place wasn't totally unoccupied until recently. The older lady who lived in it passed away. I don't really know why my dad owned it. He wasn't charging her very much in rent, which honestly doesn't seem like him. It leads me to believe that one of his business managers must've bought it and he didn't remember. Or even know. That does sound like my dad. He doesn't really notice people."

It was weird to call James Maxfield her dad. She had suspected he wasn't for at least six months. Not since she found out that the reason for the feud between the Coopers and the Maxfields was that her mother had once been in love with Cash Cooper.

It had all made so much sense then.

Her mother hadn't felt like she could get married to Cash, because he was penniless. And so, she had chosen to marry James Maxfield, and signed on for a life of misery. But Cricket had long suspected that the reason *she* existed, the reason she was a late-in-life child, was not because her parents had suddenly found a way to rekindle their romance ten years after her sisters were born. No.

It made much more sense to her that her mother had gone straight back into the arms of Cash.

It was just Cricket wanted to tread lightly in finding out the truth. Because his wife had passed away not that long ago, and she imagined it would be very painful for Creed, Jackson or Honey to accept that their father had had an affair.

From her point of view, it was pretty romantic. But then, her father wasn't heroic to her. Cash seemed much nicer. Though, she knew the Coopers loved their mother very much, and she'd seemed like a nice woman. Cricket didn't like the idea that Cash might have done her wrong.

For all that Cricket could see the affair as a forbidden romance, she imagined the Cooper children wouldn't view it in quite the same way.

So she had to tread carefully. Treading carefully wasn't her strong point. Never had been.

She tramped up the steps again. And Jackson cursed sharply. She turned just in time to see his foot go through the second step.

The only problem with all of her theories had been Jackson. And the way she'd felt about him for the last ten years. And the way her suspicions had forced her to...

Well it was a relief, really. She'd *always* hated how Jackson made her feel. Like her heart was too big for her chest and her breath was too big for her lungs. She'd felt connected to him, from the first moment she'd laid eyes on him, and she'd hated it. Especially as she'd gotten older and seen how badly a relationship could hurt a woman. Her parents' marriage was toxic. She'd never wanted anything like that, but her heart had attached itself to Jackson all the same.

That connection had made a strange, dizzying sort of sense when she'd realized. When she'd figured it out. Because, of course.

Of course she wasn't so foolish as to fall in love with him.

Of course love at first sight wasn't real, especially not as a kid.

Of course that connection was something else.

Of course.

Cricket didn't trade in uncertainty. And for years, the intensity of the emotions she'd felt around Jackson Cooper had felt *uncertain*.

It was a relief to find certainty.

It was.

"I've never had that problem," she said.

"Like I said. Not more than a buck twenty-five soaking wet."

"Can't help it." She scampered the rest of the way up the steps and into the house. He followed her, and she noticed that he didn't lighten his footsteps at all to make allowances for the fact that some of the boards were iffy. He got what he got. If he ended up severing a tendon it wasn't her fault.

"Thank you for the wild goose chase around your property."

"No, that wasn't a goose chase. We'll goose chase later. There's a pond."

"Do geese favor a pond?" he asked.

"Mine do."

"You have geese?"

"A few domestic. One Canada goose. He has a broken wing. It's flipped kind of upside down. He can't fly."

He frowned. "You have a Canada goose?"

"I do. His name is Goose."

"Creative."

She arched a brow. "Do you have a problem with a Canada goose?"

"No. Not at all. But you can't exactly make a ranch off of them."

"I'm not suggesting that it be a *goose ranch*. But my

point is that tomorrow we'll go on an actual tour. No drama. This was just a walkabout."

"I can't believe you were going to throw me in the bunkhouse without ever having looked at it."

She shrugged. "I figured you're tough. And you can take it."

"I could sleep there."

"This will be more comfortable," she said. "Just down the hall."

She didn't really want to alienate him. She also didn't quite know how to wrangle him. She had a feeling that if she suddenly started being extra nice to him, he would only be more suspicious than not. So she was trying to be measured in her interactions with him. She had to...get to a place where she could talk to him. Where they had a little bit of trust. Perhaps like training a dog. She'd done that. That she understood. She might not have any experience with men, but she did know animals pretty well. Her dad might have spent a lot of years ignoring her, but she also hadn't been denied much. And when she'd asked for animals, she'd gotten them. She'd had several dogs growing up, and still had her favorite old ranch dog, Pete.

Perhaps Jackson would be like Pete.

If only she knew how to cook. Then she could feed him. Dogs really responded well to food as an incentive. Perhaps men did too.

She'd heard that. That old-fashioned saying about the way to a man's heart being through his stomach. Not that she wanted Jackson's heart.

Well, she sort of did. She needed him to feel *something* for her. Some sort of connection. Without that, he would just think she was crazy and reject everything she had to say. Without that, he might just think she was trying to ruin his family. And that wasn't it. Not at all. She had no designs on causing any kind of trouble in his family.

But her own family was broken. Smashed all to pieces. And her place, it had never been secure. She wanted to find her place.

She pushed the door open to the small bedroom. The bed was tiny, shoved into a corner, brass rails surrounding a thin mattress that might just as likely be stuffed with corn husks as anything. The quilt that was placed over the top of it was threadbare and worn.

"It's simple," she said. "But hopefully adequate."

"Adequate." He set his sleeping bag down, and looked around. "It'll do just fine."

"Yeah. I suppose." He looked absurd, too tall and too broad for the space. His feet were going to stick through the rails at the end of the bed. And the little lace curtains behind him... Well, they seemed absolutely ridiculous.

The sun shone through the window, catching his face, highlighting the stubble on his jaw. His hair was dark, his eyes a startling blue. The same color as the bluebonnets on the quilt fabric. She didn't look like him. Not even a little bit. Her eyes were somewhere between pine cone brown and green, depending on how the sun shone. Her hair was light. But his sister had lighter hair. He was so tall. Cricket was fairly tall for a woman. About an inch above average. He was... massive. His hands were bigger, his shoulders muscular. His chest broad. He looked like a man who did hard labor all day, every day.

She felt a strange sort of cracking expansion happening in her chest.

Then he turned and looked out the window, squinting against the sun, and something in her stomach leaped. And fear gripped her.

He was just very handsome.

Of course he was. It was one of those things that was indisputable. And her feeling about that was…pride. She could see that now.

She was…proud of him.

When she was twelve years old, she'd realized it. The girls in her class were all giggling over Ryan Anderson and his floppy blond hair and she'd been fixed on Jackson Cooper. She'd been a little embarrassed about it. She'd told no one.

She knew she was a girl and he was a man and there was no way they could ever…

She'd never been silly enough or brave enough to write about him in her diary. To have a diary *at all*. But she'd thought of him every night and wove stories where they could be together, on a ranch.

Him all rugged and handsome and her riding a horse right alongside him. There had been freedom in those fantasies. In this idea that her place in the world, her real and rightful place, was alongside this forbidden man whose family her father hated.

She'd never let on how much it bothered her that Wren had swooped in and taken up with Creed. Cricket had been the one full of forbidden desire for years and years.

Wren had gone and made a Cooper and a Maxfield hooking up a thing of no particular consequence.

But now Cricket knew there was consequence after

all. And anyway, she'd been twelve when she'd imagined her place by Jackson. When she'd imagined fitting into a life with him.

And it made sense now. That mystical feeling of connection, the idea that she would fit in with his life, with his family… He was her half brother. Of course. Their connection finally made sense.

A twelve-year-old couldn't be in love. The truth was just that the connection she'd felt to him had gotten muddled because she hadn't known.

It was pride she felt for him. That was all. A desperate longing for a place where she fit.

That was all it was.

That was all it could be. All it could ever be.

Get a grip, Cricket.

"Well."

"Did you still want to go to the store?"

"You know. I was actually thinking I might whip up some food. Some dinner. So why don't you go to the plumber, and I'll handle all that here."

"You cook?"

"Of course I do," she lied.

She had either been going down to town and getting a burger for dinner or eating frozen pizza for weeks now. But he didn't need to know that.

"All right. I'll see you in a bit."

"See you in a bit," she repeated decisively. He walked out, and suddenly it was easier to breathe. He walked out, and suddenly, everything inside her chest eased.

She scurried back into the kitchen, and opened up the fridge. Wren had brought her some groceries, and she'd been ignoring them. But now, staring at the leafy greens and wrapped steaks, she felt that she had to figure something out. She picked up the phone and called her sister.

"How do you cook?"

"That is a broad question," Wren said.

"Well. You gave me all this food. And I don't know what to do with any of it. And I just told Jackson that I would cook dinner."

"You're going to cook him dinner? Honestly, Cricket, are you sure you don't have some kind of crush on him?"

That would have been a horrifying thing for her sister to ask six months ago.

It was worse now.

"I do not," she said ferociously, ignoring the tightening in her stomach. "I don't. That would be…ridiculous."

"All right. I'll walk you through… What were you thinking you were going to do?"

"Make steak."

"Right. Fantastic. What else did I get you?"

"I don't know. Green stuff. Green beans."

"Okay. I will walk you through very simple pan-fried steak and green beans. Do you have potatoes? I'm pretty sure I brought you potatoes."

"Meat and potatoes," Cricket said. "Perfect."

And in the end, she barely broke a sweat over the whole thing and managed to put together something that smelled pretty darn decent.

"Thank you," she said to her sister.

"Seriously. Are you okay? Because I feel like this is the most we've talked in…ever."

"I don't know," Cricket said. "I mean, I know I'm

okay. I just don't really know how to explain us not talking. Except… I spent a lot of years hiding. Running as fast as I could through childhood. Through that house. I hated it there. I always did. I never felt at home. I never felt like one of you. I don't want to be mean, but nothing with James really surprised me." She couldn't quite bring herself to call him Dad. "He wasn't cruel to me, nothing like that. It's just that he didn't care about me at all, and there was something in that way that he dismissed everything I was that… Nobody ever saw me—and it wasn't your job to. I was a kid and you were teenagers, and then you were having lives. You went off to school. I didn't do that."

"You could have."

"Maybe," Cricket said. "But I didn't know what I wanted anyway. I guess that's the thing. I've never fit. And I've been searching for the place where I do. I think I might've found it."

She might have found her family.

"And now it feels… I don't know, I feel more like talking."

Because even if Cash Cooper was her real father, her mother, Wren and Emerson were still her family. But if her suspicions were right, Cricket could finally disavow that piece of herself that had never really fit. It would all suddenly make sense.

"I can understand that. I always felt like I was being wedged into a life that I didn't fully want. I embraced it, and I care about the winery—I'm happy to work on it now—but, you know, I'm working toward my architectural engineering degree because it's something I always wanted. But I always knew I couldn't because

Dad didn't want me to do it, because it wasn't useful to him."

"Believe me," Cricket said. "I do understand that being in his sights wasn't necessarily better. I really do."

"I know. It's not a competition. A tough childhood is a tough childhood. Whether you're in a nice house, whether your dad pays attention to you… Doesn't really matter. It is what it is. I mean, we were better off than a lot of people. But it doesn't take away the things that weren't great."

"I know. Anyway. I… I think I'm going to be happier."

"I'm happier," Wren said. "I think Emerson and I weren't really that much different than you, when you think about it. We started our own lives. Really and truly. And even though we are still maintaining our stakes in the wineries, we have more than that. We *are* more than that. The winery was never for you. And it's a good thing that you're finding the thing that you want."

Cricket nodded, and then after exchanging farewells, hung up the phone. Just in time for Jackson to return with a whole bag full of supplies. He had his cowboy hat on, his jacket. He was such a striking figure. Because he was an emblem. Of what she wanted. Of the life she was hoping to find.

Because he represented something that fit. That was it. That was all it could be, and she had to really know that, understand it.

Had to understand what the extra thump of her heart meant. The jitter in her stomach.

She had to.

She had no choice.

"Smells good," he said.

Deep pride swelled in her chest. "Really?" She cleared her throat. "I mean. Sure. Impossible to mess up a decent steak."

Except she had a feeling it was very possible and if she hadn't been receiving instructions the entire time, she would've definitely done so.

"Well, I didn't realize I would be receiving payment in the form of steak."

"I do try. Food first," she said. "Then you can get to the plumbing." She served their plates and sat across from him. In the tiny kitchen, it felt incredibly…domestic.

It was such a world apart from the life she usually lived. She'd grown up with a grand banquet hall set for every dinner. Her dad all the way down at one end away from the rest of them. This little square table with peeling red paint felt homey in a way dinners never had. And Jackson smelled like soap and skin, close enough for her to get the scent. It was simple. Down-home and perfect in a way she'd always wanted things to be.

There had been a time when she'd dreamed of this. Sitting at a table with Jackson. Asking about his day, having him ask about hers.

Her Jackson fantasies had run the gamut over the years, but they'd always led to one conclusion. The only place for her was beside him.

That had terrified her before six months ago, because—as she'd gotten older—she'd realized what her feelings must mean, and she'd been unhappy with them. Ready to perform an exorcism, in all honesty.

She didn't want to get married and be miserable like her mother was.

It had been a relief to discover the real truth behind her feelings.

"What were your dinners like growing up?" she asked.

She was hungry. But not for steak. She wanted to know him. His family. What his life was like, and how hers might have been.

"Well, something like this. I mean, we started with a house that was pretty similar to this. It expanded as time went on."

"And that changed things? I mean, for all of you?"

"I guess so. I'm probably the only one who really remembers the change. Who really remembers what it was like before. Or… I don't know. Creed probably does to an extent. Not Honey, though."

"Right." So that wouldn't have been different. If she had grown up with them, she would have been like Honey. She wouldn't have known what it was like to have normal family meals around the table. She knew that being wealthy was a privilege. It wasn't that. It was easy to romanticize things you didn't have. Easy to look at them in a simple way. She knew that too.

She wasn't stupid.

She'd spent a lot of time by herself. And as a result, she'd spent a lot of time thinking. She thought a lot about the way other people lived. The way families looked on TV. And while she knew there were other struggles involved in their lives, she also knew that some of the good things they showed on sitcoms were real.

"So you got a big table, probably then," she said.

"What does the size of the table have to do with anything?"

"You know, on TV," Cricket said. "When everybody sits around this little, cheerful table. Just like this. And they have some kind of casserole. It's always casserole. And I don't even know anyone who's ever eaten a casserole."

"Yeah, can't say as I've had a lot of casserole experience myself."

"Well, there's always a casserole, and they're all sitting together, and reaching for the dishes, and talking. And we didn't have a table like that. It was big and long, this banquet hall. As if there were fifty of us, but there wasn't. And my dad would always sit down at his end, miles away. And that's just… It's a metaphor. Really. For my family. All spread out, all engaged in their own thing and not paying attention to each other. Oftentimes we would even have different food. We had a chef. And we could basically put in an order for whatever we wanted at the beginning of the week. We would sit there in the same room and basically all be… separate. And sometimes I just wanted a small table. Because I thought that would fix things."

"Well, we might've gotten a bigger table, but we all sat down at one together."

"Oh," she said, feeling wistful. "You all really love each other."

"You love your sisters," he said, and she noticed he skimmed over her question.

"I do," she said. She looked up at him, taking a chance at meeting his gaze. "My siblings are the most important people in my life."

His lips curved upward, and something in her stom-

ach shivered. She didn't like it. She didn't like the feeling at all.

"Well, I… Anyway. I don't know. I'm just curious.
About how other people grew up."

"Did you go over to anyone's house when you were
a kid?"

"Not really. My sisters went to private school. They
were away from home a lot. They sent me away for a
while, but I hated it. I wanted a family, and being at
school with strangers didn't help at all. Dorm rooms
and formal dining halls and all of that. I just ended up
walking the grounds alone. They brought me back.
They enrolled me in a school in Gold Valley. But they
didn't really want me associating with any of the local
people. So I had friends. But only at school. My parents didn't let them come over. They didn't let me go
over there. The stupid thing is, I'm not sure my dad
would have actually known what I was doing if I hadn't
asked for permission. But I've never really known how
to live."

Except, she was deceiving Jackson a little bit. And
that made her feel… Well, that made her feel margin-
ally guilty. It wasn't the most honorable thing, but her
deception was all in service to something bigger.

She looked at him, and the sense of intensity, of
longing, grew. She couldn't feel bad. Not now. She
wanted him here. She needed him here. And some
part of her knew that. On a deep, cellular level. She
knew that.

"Anyway. I'm just kind of making up for lost time.
For things I didn't have."

"So, you got yourself a little kitchen table."

"Yeah. And you're the first person to sit with me here."

He looked a little uncomfortable with that statement. Cleared his throat. She blinked, wondering what he thought she meant. And then she realized her words could be misconstrued.

"Only that…"

She must've sounded panicked, because he held her gaze, his expression steady then. "No drama."

"Right." His words made her feel immediately soothed and she didn't really know why.

She'd first felt this weird sort of connection to him years ago. He hadn't been as broad then as he was now. He'd been lean and rangy, and very different from his brother, Creed, who was often at winery events, fulfilling much the same job as her sister. Jackson wasn't a salesman. He wasn't the kind of guy who was in the front of the house. Much like her. He was behind the scenes. It was also very clear that Jackson was an integral part of his family in a way that Cricket had never felt like she was.

Jackson very clearly had a firm hand in everything.

He wore his authority with ease. It was so different from the way her father was. James blustered about, ordering employees around. All Jackson had to do was walk into a room. She had seen him helping with setup at different community parties on more than one occasion. He was a man who led by example. He was a man, she had always thought, to be admired.

And she had. She admired him greatly.

Wherever Jackson was, her eyes seemed to find him.

It was hard to explain how it had felt to find out there was a high probability he was her half brother.

It had been the death of a dream she'd told herself had never been real.

But it had felt like a real, actual death. Before, she might have pretended she knew he was off limits, but apparently part of her had always secretly hoped…

That connection was so powerful. That sense of need she felt when she saw him.

And the connection had only grown and intensified as she had gotten older.

As she began to realize just how much of a misfit she was with her family.

So really, finding out about her mother and his father…it made sense. And she shouldn't be sad.

"I'll help clean up," he said.

"You don't have to do that."

"You said yourself you don't know how to clean. Anyway, there's no dishwasher here."

He took her plate, which was empty, went over to the sink and started running water. She could only stare at his broad back, at the way he worked, smoothly and capably.

And then she realized she was staring at the back of him while he washed dishes with her mouth dropped open. Like he was performing some kind of Herculean effort, rather than just scrubbing a couple of dinner plates and a pan.

She scrambled to her feet and looked around the tidy kitchen. There wasn't really much to do. Not after the spiders had already been chased away and the cobwebs had been dealt with. She grabbed the broom again and began to sweep the floor, even though there was no dirt on it.

But she needed to do something, and she wasn't going to go stand over by the sink.

"Cricket," he said. "Why don't you dry?"

Well, apparently, she was going to go stand by him.

She moved over to the sink, and he thrust a dish towel in her direction. She grabbed it, her fingertips brushing his. His hands were rough.

She'd never touched him before.

She'd dreamed about it.

About his hands.

She hadn't known just how rough they would be.

She felt the lingering echo of that touch and she did her best to try and ignore it. He was warm too. She could feel heat radiating from his body as she stood beside him. Her shoulder vibrating with it as they stood with just an inch between them while she dried the dishes that he set on the side of the sink.

She looked over at him, and he turned his head. Then she immediately looked back down at the dish in her hand. She was acting weird. And he must realize that. He must know that things were weird. But she imagined he had no idea why.

She could tell him. She could tell him right now.

You don't even know why. Do you get what you're doing?

This wasn't the reaction a woman should have to her half brother.

A pit of despair grew in her stomach.

She was supposed to know better. She was supposed to have fixed this.

No. She couldn't tell him her suspicions yet. It would only cause problems. It would only... It would ruin things. Everything. She couldn't take a chance on springing all this on him too soon.

So instead, she cleared her throat, mirroring the same gesture he'd done only a moment before, and carried the plates to their rightful spot in the kitchen.

"Well, I'm going to head to bed," he said, turning and gripping the edge of the counter. The muscles in his forearms flexed, and she made a study of the red paint on the tabletop. Of all the places that it was chipping and wrinkling.

"It's early," she said.

"Not really."

Then he brushed past her and left her standing in the kitchen. The room suddenly felt much larger without him standing in it. And that left her with a whole lot of questions she couldn't quite form. And even if she could, she wasn't sure she wanted to know the answers.

Chapter 3

This was Jackson's favorite part of the day. When the sun hadn't risen yet, and he put the coffee on. As strong as he could make it. When the world outside was quiet, and still. When the whole day had a wealth of possibilities in it.

Once upon a time, he'd spent mornings like this with his mother at the kitchen table. His father wasn't one to enjoy mornings. A rancher he was, but he also was always half stumbling out the door after the first rays of light had begun to filter over the mountains, his coffee in a to-go cup, his eyes bleary.

Not Jackson. And not his mom. Four o'clock had been his wake-up time for as long as he could remember. Plenty of time to get a jump on the day. To plan everything that needed to be done. To do it without all the damn people cluttering up the world. Let them sleep.

Those times had become especially precious when his mother had been ill.

He had lived in his own place at that point. But he still worked the family ranch. He got up, he drove over, he sat with his mother and had coffee. And then he went out to work the ranch.

In the years since, he had begun to exclusively work his own place. His father had enough hands on deck to handle the family place without Jackson. And anyway, once his mother had been gone, there had been no real reason to stay. There had been no one to have coffee with in the morning.

Jackson had realized at that time that the only reason he had stayed was that he was hanging on to something in his past that he had known wouldn't last forever.

And once she was gone, it had been time for him to move on too.

Anyway. His father was still barely dragging his ass out of bed and making it out to work on time.

Jackson didn't mind having coffee alone.

He walked down the hall, taking note of each squeaking board as he went into the kitchen and started the pot of coffee. This was not the kind of coffee maker he was accustomed to. But in truth, he could make coffee anytime, anywhere. He could MacGyver coffee with nothing but a tin can, a cheesecloth and a campfire. He could do what needed to be done. He could make this little plastic job work. But he preferred his programmable machine at home. Which had everything waiting for him as soon as his feet hit the ground.

He might enjoy this hour of the day, but there was

nothing wrong with wanting everything to be in its place, and as easy as possible. At least, not to his mind.

He thanked the good Lord that Cricket had coffee, and got it all started, his mood lifting immediately as the sound of the water beginning to heat filled the room, as the scent of the freshly ground beans hit him.

He really did love mornings.

He had a feeling Cricket didn't. Because she wasn't up. That actually suited him just fine.

He still couldn't figure out what the hell she actually wanted.

For a woman who said she couldn't wait to run a ranch, she really didn't seem to have a concept of what it took. And then there had been the way she'd behaved last night.

Like you don't know what it is?

Dammit. It really wasn't worth examining. He had been sure that when she wasn't in that dress, when she was back to being the Cricket he had known since she was awkward and had those buck teeth she'd been talking about earlier—which he did remember—those feelings of lust that he'd felt the night of the poker game would vanish.

But the problem was, now he'd seen the potential in Cricket. And he didn't much like it.

He wasn't a man for relationships. He had arrangements. Satisfying, adult relationships with women his age who, for whatever reason, didn't want relationships either. Divorcées, single mothers, busy women who traveled through in a group of friends, or with a bachelorette party. City girls looking for flings with a cowboy.

Yeah, he was down for all that.

But not young, earnest looking girls who had roots in this valley as deep as it was possible to have, who had already been wounded by her father, and who clearly had issues. Daddy issues.

That made him grimace. He supposed being a bit more than a decade older than her put him squarely in the territory of daddy issues.

And what did that make him?

Just a man, he had a feeling. Men were basic. And while he prided himself on maybe not being as basic as some of them, the fact of the matter was… He wasn't any different. He liked arrangements because he liked sex. And he didn't go without.

Come to think of it, though, he'd been without for a while.

He'd had to increasingly spend more time at the vineyard. Their father hadn't really gotten better since their mother had died, he'd only gotten worse. He was withdrawn. And he wasn't functioning in quite the same way that he used to.

Which pissed off Jackson, since he wasn't quite sure why his dad had fallen apart so much, all things considered. But the blowback was hitting the vineyard, and it was hitting Honey, and Jackson didn't want that to happen.

He had no idea how to fix it. Not when he had never really reconciled his own grief, or the accompanying anger at his dad.

His mother had been the single most important person in his life.

She had been a strong woman. And she'd sacrificed

everything for Jackson. Everything. He hadn't realized just how much until he'd gotten older. And he'd never had the chance to repay her. He'd been planning on it.

But there hadn't been enough time.

Grief about all that was always close at hand. But here in the silence of the morning, he could remember his mother as she'd been.

And he felt a little closer to her, instead of impossibly far.

He waited until he had his first sip of coffee. A smile touched his lips and he looked out into the yard. Everything was quiet. There were still stars in the sky. Then, once the caffeine had begun to do its work, he decided it was time to make his move. He went down the hall, doing nothing to modify the sound of his steps, and threw open the door to Cricket's bedroom.

"Get up, princess. There's chorin' to do."

"Mfffmmmmmgh."

"What's that?"

The indignant figure in the bed moved, then sat up. It was dark, but he could see that her pajamas consisted of a white T-shirt. And he wondered if there was anything else. Or if she was bare underneath that thing. Then he quickly turned his focus away from that.

"Go away!"

"It's time to start doing work."

"It's…" She whipped her head around to look out the window. "It's midnight."

"It is 4:30."

"Basically midnight."

"Not in my world. And not in your world either.

Not if you want to be a rancher. I thought this was in your blood?"

He couldn't see her face. Obscured as it was by the fact that the light was off. And she was lucky. Because if he'd been in a really mean mood, he might have turned it on. But while he enjoyed harassing Cricket, there was no real reason to poke at her quite that much.

"I think sleep might be in my blood at this hour of the day."

"Too bad. If you have animals, you're going to have to get up and take care of them."

"I…"

"Sorry. That's how it works. You gotta get up early to be ready to work."

"That seems obscene."

"I grant you, I like an earlier morning than most."

"Go away. Morning people are suspicious."

"I made coffee."

She made a rumbling sound again.

"I'm going to go into the kitchen and pour you a cup. Don't make me come back in here and wake you up."

He turned around and walked down the hall. He did not need to see her get out of bed. He did not need to answer any of the questions he had about what she was or wasn't wearing under that T-shirt.

He didn't like the whole thing. This whole sudden, errant attraction to Cricket. It could definitely be argued that it would be a fine enough thing in theory. Because it wasn't like they weren't both adult people, even if he was a bit older. But he couldn't give her anything. And that… That didn't seem fair. She was young and scrappy and trying to make it on her own, and the last thing he wanted to do was…

Well, none of it bore thinking about because he was a grown man. And thinking a woman was pretty didn't mean acting on anything.

He wouldn't do it. Most especially because he was here to talk her out of her ranch. He had his limits.

He got a small, chipped mug out of the cupboard and poured some coffee in it. Just in time for Cricket to appear, in what he thought might be the same T-shirt, her blond hair resting on top of her head in a messy knot, jeans and a pair of boots.

"Good morning," she groused.

"You said you wanted to be a cowgirl."

He handed the coffee mug over to her.

"I was unaware that being my own boss would involve being woken up at a specific time. Hey. I'm your boss. You're not my boss."

"Yes. But the land waits for no one, Cricket. That's your first lesson in being a real, bona fide rancher."

"I don't like it."

"Doesn't matter. Why do you love the idea of being a rancher?"

"I don't know," she said.

"You have to do better than that."

"I feel… I don't know. I feel weird and wrong most of the time. I feel like I don't fit. But outdoors, I always felt like maybe I belonged. You know, I was better at riding horses, at dealing with bugs and dirt and all of that kind of stuff than my sisters. It was something I was just naturally more comfortable with. And maybe that's not right or fair. Maybe that's a little bit smug.

To like something simply because I was better at it, when I couldn't be better at school, or being pretty."

"Better at being pretty?"

"Oh, come on. Wren and Emerson are naturally elegant and completely and totally perfect in every way."

"They're perfect when it comes to their particular kind of pretty, I'll give them that. And I'm not going to say people don't tend to have their favorite kind of flower. But all flowers are pretty."

"Surely not all of them."

"You're messing with my metaphor."

"It's too early for metaphors."

"It's never too early. Drink your coffee."

He didn't know why he felt the need to be nice to her. It was just that she seemed…utterly lost. He related to the feeling. He supposed that in some ways, losing whatever connection with her father that she'd had—though she claimed that it wasn't a very deep one—was a lot like a death.

And he knew what it was like to lose a parent. It was hard. It had left him feeling… Honestly, he hadn't known what to do after his mother had died. He hadn't been ready for it. No one was ever ready. But he had felt deeply and profoundly unprepared for the way the grief had rocked his life. For all the things he'd left unsolved and unsaid. For all the regret he felt on her behalf.

He knew she'd felt stuck in a loveless marriage. Even though she'd loved their family. Loved the kids.

Sometimes he felt…responsible for her unhappiness.

His dad was mired in grief, as if she'd been the love of his life, but sometimes Jackson thought the real reason his dad was mired in grief was that he'd known they *weren't* the loves of each other's lives and they'd trapped each other.

Sometimes, as a family they'd been so happy...

It didn't matter. All he knew was there was something in Cricket that he recognized. Didn't matter that she was a completely different creature than him. He knew what she was feeling.

And he might resent the position he found himself in, but honor prevented him from backing out. Anyway, now that he was here, he wanted to help her.

She sat at the table, her shoulders hunched up by her ears, and sipped her coffee a bit too slowly for his taste. He liked a leisurely morning, but you needed to get yourself out of bed a bit earlier if you were going to be that sluggish with it. Granted, they didn't actually have specific chores. But this was her lesson. Her lesson in ranching. And if she really thought she was going to do it... Well, then she had better get used to this.

He didn't think she would, though.

In fact, he had a feeling he was a step closer to being able to make his move than he'd thought he'd be at this point.

"Come on, little Cricket," he said as soon as she had drained the last drop of her coffee.

"I'm not little," she said.

"You are to me."

"I'm quite tall," she sniffed.

He looked down at the top of her head. "Again. Not to me."

"Well, you're ridiculous. Height runs in your family," she commented.

"Honey is short."

"But you and Creed are very tall."

"Yes," he agreed.

She seemed suddenly renewed, and he opened the front door and held it for her, and she went past him, going straight down the steps. "What are we going to do?"

"Well, why don't we start by looking at your pastures and your fencing. Then we're going to take a look at the barns and see what kind of shape they're in."

"That's all a very good idea," she said.

"Well, that is why you hired me. Or rather, won me."

"Yes," she said, frowning. "I suppose you are the expert."

"Say that again?"

"You're the expert," she said, but this time angrily.

"Just remember that."

He opened the door to his truck.

"What are you doing?"

"I figured we'd drive."

She got in, grumbling the whole way. They started driving out on one of the access roads that went toward the back end of the property. They would start there, and work their way back. At that point, the sky was beginning to lighten, and turn a bluish gray. The mountains were like sloping ink spills bleeding down into the fields. It was a beautiful piece of land. Hell, if Cricket didn't want to keep it, he'd be happy to add it to his own portfolio.

"Except," she said. "You do kind of have to admit that there is no actual reason for us to be up this early since there are no animals."

"Again," he said. "Practice. And also to give you a little dose of reality."

"You think I need a dose of reality?"

"Before you go committing to having lots of animals, I do think you probably need to have an understanding of what you might be in for."

"Bully for me."

"Yeah, well. You chose me to be your consultant."

"Ranch hand," she corrected.

"Yeah, who's calling the shots?"

She sputtered. But at that point, he put the truck in Park and got out. "Oh boy," he said, going up to the edge of one of the fences. It was light enough to see now, now that the sun was rising, the sunlight spilling rapidly over the landscape. "This fence is a mess. You're going to have a lot of work ahead of you."

"Well, we need a crew."

"We're going to have to figure out your budget."

"Don't talk to me like I'm a child. I do understand that. I know I haven't lived on my own, and I know that I come from money, but I also know there has to be money. Don't worry. Like I said, I sold my stake in the vineyard. So I have a bit of cash."

"Great. You're going to need quite a lot of cash."

"I'm sure you have an idea of how much a winery like Maxfield Vineyards is worth."

"True." Cricket was probably a fairly rich woman at this point. Even selling a quarter stake would've probably netted her quite a lot. "But it still wouldn't hurt you to have training. There may be an emergency, and you may not be able to get someone out here in time. What's going to happen if part of your fence comes down and you've got horses everywhere? You're going to have to know how to solve some of your own problems. Fortunately, I have tools. This," he said, indicating the whole fence line, "is going to be a hassle. And you're right. We're going to need to get a crew out here. But we can start it together."

"That sounds unpleasant."

"No, sweetheart. It's ranch work." He handed her a hammer and a pair of wire cutters. "Living the dream."

Cricket was exhausted and sore by noon. But at least then Jackson produced beer and sandwiches, and she found herself sitting happily on the tailgate of his truck, eating and watching as he continued to work. He never stopped.

"All right," he said, "let's head to the barn."

"We're not done?"

"Nope. And this is ranch work when you haven't got any animals. I'm just letting you know what you're in for."

"I feel like you're trying to actively discourage me."

He lifted a shoulder. "If you can be discouraged from being a rancher, then you should be."

"What does that mean?"

"That it's a hard life that often produces very little profit. And if you don't love it, you should do something else."

"Why would you say that?"

"Because it's the kind of thing that needs to be said, Cricket. If the work doesn't deter you… Then it doesn't. But you know, you could still live here without being a rancher. You could lease the fields to someone. Or you could sell up, get yourself a nice farmhouse and a couple of chickens."

"I don't want to do that," she said, feeling resolute. "I want to have my own life. My own land."

That statement was clarifying.

Because honestly, he had worked her ragged enough today that she had begun to question some things. And yeah, she was having to admit that she was a little sheltered. That she hadn't done all that much work in her life. She had done a lot of running around in the country, and she had managed to equate that with doing this kind of work. But it wasn't the same.

She just wished that she could do things half as effortlessly as he could. His body was a machine. Every muscle, every movement contributing to the other. She felt like she was all thumbs. That it took her five hits of the hammer to create the same kind of movement he got out of one. He was more efficient, more precise… It was frustrating. Maddening, even.

Though watching him was…

Well, she was learning a lot. She felt her cheeks get prickly. But she chose not to think too much about that and got into the cab of the truck with him as they drove to the barn.

He parked in front of the old, run-down building, and the two of them got out.

He walked over and pushed the door open, muscles straining. And yet again, she realized she was standing there gaping at the back of Jackson Cooper.

She mobilized herself, scampering through the open doorway as soon as it was wide enough for her to get through.

He came in behind her, and she could feel him. It was the strangest thing. Like there was energy crackling between them. It was more than just his body heat; it was something else.

She turned, and was looking up underneath his jaw. At the square line there, the stubble on his chin, his lips.

His lips were really very compelling. They were turned down slightly, naturally, which gave him a bit of a grim look. An intensity. That was one of the things that had always fascinated her about him. That quiet, brooding intensity. Something she did not have in common with him at all, because there was very little about her that was brooding. She wasn't quiet, she just avoided things by choice.

She took a step away from him and moved deeper into the barn. "Well," she said. "This is it."

He made an amused sound. "Not much," he said. "Is it?"

"No. I mean, all of it can be revamped." She looked at him sharply. "I know that it costs money."

"I know you do."

"Well, you do a lot of lecturing. So I can't exactly be sure."

He walked past her, and she noticed, not for the first time, that he had a very particular scent to him. His skin and soap and the wild. The pine from the trees, and a bit of the earth. "This could be a decent facility, with some upkeep. Don't get me wrong. I'm not trying to discourage you. I promise."

"Well, that's good to know," she said.

"There is a whole lot of moldy hay in here, though.

We need to get it cleaned out. Why don't you grab a shovel?"

"More chores?"

"Yes," he said. "Actually, thinking of it as chores is kind of counterproductive. It's part of the gig. Part of life. Everything in life that you care about, whether it's your house or the land, has to be taken care of by somebody. I understand on the Maxfield family spread that somebody else does a lot of the caretaking. At our place, the Coopers do the caretaking."

"And you're currently caretaking your own ranch?"

"Obviously I have help," he said. "Which is good for you. Because if I didn't, I wouldn't be here."

"Right, right."

"Grab a shovel."

That was how she found herself feeling sweaty and indignant, moving great piles of moldy hay out into the bed of his truck.

"It will make decent enough compost. But you don't want it in here," he said.

"It smells," she said.

"A whole lot of things about ranch life smell."

"I don't mind it," she said, resolute.

"Sure."

"I really don't. I was just saying."

He arched a brow, half of his lips curving up into a smile. "You do a lot of questioning for somebody who just knows, and is fine with everything."

Her cheeks burned. She didn't really know why. "I'm fine," she said, stepping into the corner and grabbing another shovelful of that vile hay.

"Yeah, you seem totally fine."

"It's just a lot to learn. I'm happy to. I want to. That really is why I…" Except that would be a lie. She was about to finish the sentence with *it was why I wanted you here*. But it wasn't why. The words caught in her throat, and then her gaze caught his and held. She couldn't seem to look away. And he didn't look away either. He was close.

Closer than she had realized a moment ago. Or maybe the space around them had shrunk. She didn't know which. Except, of course that was impossible. But there was something about his nearness that felt impossible all on its own. Like she had been dropped onto an alien planet, into an alien body.

But there was no guide for how this should feel. Living with this man who had captivated her for the better part of a decade. This man who was so unlike anyone she'd ever known, and who she didn't really know, but who felt like he might be the answer to *something* all the same.

This was not what she'd dreamed about. But…she had to make what she was feeling something else because the only other option was for everything she'd suspected to be nothing and she couldn't bear that either.

To have her life just be the same.

To have her whole self just be the same as she'd always been.

His gaze flickered downward, and she realized that he was looking at her mouth. And that was when the tension in her stomach twisted, making her organs roll. Causing her heart to stutter.

And suddenly, her mouth felt like it was on fire. She

was just so very aware of it. Had never, in all her life, been quite so conscious of the fact that she had lips.

But she was now.

Because he had looked at them. Because he was standing there, so close. Because they were sharing this space, sharing the air. Because he fascinated her in a way no one else had.

Because he had the answers.

Her heart started racing.

No.

No.

She had never been this close to him. And last night his hands had brushed hers and now he was standing right there. She knew she had to think of him differently now, and not as a man, like she'd always seen him. But she couldn't make him that. She just couldn't. Couldn't force her body to acknowledge what her brain suspected, no matter what she'd tried to tell herself about their connection.

He was there. And she *wanted*.

It couldn't be.

But then the light went on in those eyes, and even she could recognize the expression there, because she'd eaten dinner with the man last night.

Hunger.

And she felt it. She felt an answering appetite low and deep.

He moved, and she didn't know if it was toward her or away from her, because she dropped her shovel and ran out of the barn.

Ran.

Like the devil and all of hell was coming after her.

Ran and didn't look back. Ran past his truck, through the fence, and out into the middle of the field. She stopped, panting, her forehead damp with sweat. She planted her hands on her knees, and only then did she realize what she'd done.

She had run from him.

He must think she was insane. She was acting insane. Except...

Why?

The word was more a groan in her soul than a real, actual word. A deep, enduring sadness that made her feel like she might be crushed with it.

It wasn't fair. It just wasn't fair. How in all the world was he...

The one man, the *only* man, that she had ever felt this for?

She was sick. There was something wrong with her.

You always knew there was something wrong with you.

Yes, but she hadn't thought *this*.

She made a rough sound of distress. Out loud, and she didn't care if it carried all the way back to the barn. She couldn't care.

She looked around suddenly, wildly, to see if he was behind her. He wasn't.

Why was this happening to her? She had thought she had finally been on her way to finding her place. She had been resolute in winning over Jackson, in getting to know him so she could approach him about their potential connection...

And what if he had been moving toward her? What if he had been about to kiss her?

Well, then everything was ruined. Absolutely everything.

Cricket wasn't one to cry. She wasn't one to give in to despair. But she wanted to now. Yes, she did. She wanted to now because she had thought she'd found a way out. She had thought she'd found a way to change her life. To change everything. But she hadn't. She was just weird, awkward Cricket, who would never find a place that felt comfortable.

Because this certainly wasn't comfortable. This was an abomination.

And you're not a baby. You're going to figure out how to face him, apologize and get your head on straight.

Yes, but she couldn't face him now. So she spent about an hour picking through the field and ignoring the fact that she was going to have to face him eventually. And when she finally went back to the barn, his truck was gone, and so was he.

And it left Cricket to wonder if she had hallucinated the whole thing.

Chapter 4

Jackson had decided to go to town to get some things for the ranch, and check on his own spread. Anyway, a drive to town was good for a little bit of self castigation. Obviously, he had terrified Cricket earlier when he'd moved in on her. He could pretend that he hadn't been about to kiss her. But he had been. And he knew better. Earlier, he had decided that he wouldn't. But for a minute there, she had seemed like she wanted him to, and his reasoning had gotten lost.

He hadn't felt like an ass for having ulterior motives for agreeing to the bet, knowing he'd lose. Knowing it would put him in a prime position to convince her to sell. Until now.

Because one thing he wouldn't do was get into a personal relationship with her while trying to get her land.

That was a step too far.

He had thought about going after her, but he had figured it would only create more problems. She had run for a reason, after all. It was pretty clear she didn't want him to go after her.

Now, of all the reactions he'd had from women he'd made a move on, running full tilt the other direction wasn't one of them. Sure, sometimes they might decide they weren't into it, and then all it took was a simple no thanks. He wasn't a man to push himself on anyone. And anyway, he didn't have to.

But Cricket had run like he might. And that made him wonder things about her. And he didn't want to wonder about her. Not any more than he already did.

He also figured that while he was out, he should go and check in on his father. Honey still lived at the ranch, and he knew she took on a fair amount of responsibility. Probably more than she should. It suited him that she was relatively sheltered, he had to admit.

And that got him right back into guilty thoughts and feelings about Cricket. She and Honey were roughly the same age. And if a man his age made a move on Honey, she wouldn't be the one running away. *He* would, with Jackson right after him.

He maneuvered his truck down the driveway, up to the winery show room. The place was no less grand to him now than it had been when he was a boy. It always would be. But he would also always picture his mother standing there, waiting with a smile. No matter how many years she was gone, that's what he would see.

But she wasn't there. It was Honey.

"What brings you around?" his sister asked, pushing the door open to the tasting room. "Aren't you in indentured servitude to Cricket Maxfield currently?"

"Currently."

"Honestly, I'm glad you lost the bet. I can't imagine having her working the tasting room."

"What do you have against Cricket?"

Honey shrugged. "I just don't really know her. Anyway, she's not all that friendly."

He frowned. "She's not particularly unfriendly."

"I don't know. She's weird. Don't you think?"

He thought about all the things Cricket had said. About feeling out of place. And that his sister's take, that she was weird, made him feel…

Sorry for her, he supposed.

"That's not a very nice thing to say."

"Since when do you care?"

"I don't."

"You must, a little."

He shrugged. "She's a nice kid. Anyway, I feel bad for all of them."

"Maybe someday I'll get there. I still can't believe Creed married Wren."

"You like Wren."

"I know. But… Isn't it weird? Switching allegiance like that."

"The problem was James."

"I don't know. I think it's deeper than that. Dad really…"

"Dad's not perfect," he said. "Dad's feelings on something don't have to be the final say."

"I know that."

Poor Honey had only been a teenager when their mother had died. And Jackson felt like she had thrown herself in a relationship with their dad even deeper, trying to please him much more than she would have if that hadn't happened. There was no gray area with Honey when it came to Cash Cooper. While Jackson's relationship with him came with about fifty shades of it.

"Speaking of Dad," Jackson said. "Is he around?"

"Yeah, he's just back in the office."

The main office for the winery was at the back of the tasting room.

"You have any groups coming today?"

"A couple. Stick around, it's a bachelorette party."

And he found he had no interest at all. He found he was soured on the thought of it. Maybe his reaction had something to do with a woman running flat away from him not that long ago.

Or maybe it had something to do with Cricket herself, and her deep, seeking eyes. And that pretty mouth of hers.

Well.

He waved a hand toward his sister, then walked back to the office, his boots making a hard sound against the reclaimed barn wood floor. He knocked once, then opened the door without waiting for his dad to respond.

"The prodigal has returned," Cash said.

"Just to check in," Jackson grunted.

"Jericho came by yesterday and made it sound like you are pretty busy with your new boss."

"Yeah," Jackson said. "Jericho can shut it." Jericho was basically another brother to Jackson. They had grown up thick as thieves, and had started their own ranches about the same time. Like a brother, Jericho could also be a spectacular pain in his butt.

"Why exactly are you here?"

"I came to check in on you. I don't like being away for so long."

"You don't sound happy about it."

"What's going on, Dad? Look, I've never called you out. Not once. Not in front of Creed, and not in front of Honey, and I won't. Not even in front of Jericho. You might not be his dad, but he looks up to you. But I was closer to Mom, and I know that… I know that you're grieving. I believe that. But I don't get exactly what you're grieving. Because I don't think she was the love of your life."

"Jackson…"

"I know that things weren't always great with you."

"I loved your mother."

Jackson paused, a muscle jumping in his jaw. He wasn't going to argue with his dad about what he felt or didn't. "I'm sure you did. But enough that you're still nonfunctional five years later?"

He sighed. "It's complicated."

"I'm sure it is."

"You've never loved a woman in all your life, Jackson, let alone two. So what would you know about the kinds of things that I've been through?"

Jackson's senses sharpened. "Two?"

"I'm not going to discuss it with you. All I can tell you is nothing in my life has been right since I lost your mother. There are a variety of reasons for it. And maybe you're right, but to me it's not so simple. And maybe you don't think I deserve to have the grief and regret that I do. But I do. You know what's worse than grieving the love of your life? I think it might be grieving a person you wronged."

"What exactly…"

"Not up for discussion. Why don't you get on back to the Maxfield property? Used to be you were all so against them."

"*You* were against them," Jackson said.

His father cleared his throat. "Yeah. I was."

"Not anymore?"

"James was the problem."

"I figured as much."

"Turns out he was a problem for everyone."

"Again, not a surprise."

Though, Jackson wondered if her dad's problems had been a bigger surprise to Cricket than she let on, and if that was maybe part of *her* problem.

He had no idea what his problem was. Why was he overthinking every interaction with Cricket? He didn't overthink anything. If anything, he tended to under-think. He was a man of action. If there was something to be done, he liked to get it done. But maybe that was the problem. He couldn't quite figure out Cricket's aim in having him work at the ranch. Yes, she needed some guidance, but she often seemed to bristle beneath it, and she seemed more interested in him as a person then she did in his ranching expertise half the time.

But then, when he'd nearly kissed her, she'd run away. He would have thought that if there was a moti-vation, her having a crush would make sense.

Still, he preferred to take his chances with Cricket than trying to stand here and reason with his father. Trying to understand his father. "I'll see you around. Just… Why don't you go to the bar tonight or some-thing? Do something. Honey shouldn't have to cook you dinner every night."

"She doesn't have to. I could easily get food from the winery."

"She doesn't want you to do that. She wants you to take better care of yourself. And you not doing it is keeping her here."

"Didn't keep you here."

"Yeah, well, I don't feel responsible for a stubborn old man. And she does."

He put his hat on his head and walked out of his dad's office. Honey was standing in the middle of the room, and Jericho was there too.

"Don't you have your own place?" he asked his friend.

Jericho grinned. That particular grin of his, the one he got when he wasn't being genuinely friendly. "Yeah. I do. Just came to see how everyone was faring. Saw your truck, and thought I'd see how you were doing with your life as a ranch hand."

"What is it exactly that you find that so funny?"

"Because long as I've known you, you've never taken orders from anyone. And I hear you're taking orders from her."

"Not exactly."

"And sleeping in a bunkhouse," Honey said. "If I recall the terms of the bet correctly."

"Turns out the bunkhouse was in disrepair. I'm sleeping inside."

That earned him openmouthed stares from both Jericho and Honey.

"Really?" Jericho asked, a dark brow lifting.

"Really," he said, giving his friend a flat look.

Jericho frowned. "I didn't take you for a cradle robber."

"I'm not." He shoved his discomfort aside, shoved

the memory of a couple hours ago aside. "Anyway, I didn't take you for a busybody."

"Well, it's not every day my best friend is suitably lowered to such a position. I'd be lying if I said I wasn't enjoying it."

"Some friend."

"I never claimed to be a *good* friend, just the best one you have."

"No kidding," Honey said. "Just an exasperating one. Anyway, I have work to do, unlike you two lazy cowboys. I actually still work here."

"And the place is hopping," Jericho said, looking around the empty space.

"I have a bachelorette party coming in twenty minutes. And no, I've decided neither of you can stay. I can't bear watching you go for the low-hanging fruit. I'd like to have more respect for you."

"I never pick low-hanging fruit," Jericho said. "The sweetest ones are at the top of the tree."

"Well, put up your ladder somewhere else, cowboy. Because you're not picking off this one." She made a shooing motion with her hands. "The ladies deserve to have a party in peace."

Both he and Jericho allowed Honey to kick them out of the room, and he walked out toward his truck with his friend. "What were you really doing here?"

"I… I have a meeting with your dad."

"You have a meeting with my dad?"

"Yes. About the vineyard."

"Really?"

"You and Creed are silent partners. At least, more or less these days. Your dad is… Well, he's not enjoying this as much as he used to. He wants to get out of it."

"Are you buying my dad out?"

"Talking about it."

For some reason, that bothered Jackson. "You didn't think to talk to me about it?"

"It's a business deal, Jackson. I don't have to talk to you about my business."

Jackson knew that Jericho had been very successful with investments. His friend was a rancher, but he was a great deal more than that. Successful, extremely so, and not because he sat on his hands, or did things with caution.

"No. But you are my friend."

"Yes. I'm talking to you now. But I figured I would have a conversation with your father before I did that. I haven't finalized anything yet."

"What's the deal?"

"I'm buying half. And I'm going to transition to running the day-to-day."

"That means you're buying Honey's portion."

"She hasn't come into it yet. Because of her age. So yes."

"She's going to be…"

"She should be free of this. Don't you think?"

"Now you're going to tell me that you have nothing but my sister's best interest at heart?"

Jericho shook his head. "No. But I care about her too. I'm not just acting without thought."

Jackson shook his head. "She's going to kick you in the nuts."

"She might. Like I said. It's business. It's not personal."

"It kind of has to be personal. Given that our relationship is personal."

"If it were personal, I would be buying him out for a good deal. I'm not. I'm overpaying."

"Well, at least there's that."

His dad hadn't told Jackson, of course. Bottom line, there had been a wedge between his parents whether his dad was ever going to address it or not, and by default Jackson had ended up on his mother's team. They had all rallied when they'd needed to. His dad had been there for his mom. He couldn't fault him for that. No. If only it were more straightforward. If only things had been toxic. Because if they had been toxic then Jackson could have disavowed his dad. If his father hadn't been there for his mother, then Jackson could easily cut his father out of his life.

But it was never going to be that simple. His dad wasn't a bad man. But as far as Jackson could tell he'd been a bad husband.

He'd also been there when it had counted.

"Look, I gotta get back to work. I'll see you around."

Jackson got into his truck, leaving Jericho standing there, leaving his conflicted feelings there at Cowboy Wines, because it was easier than staying and confronting them. Honestly, dealing with Cricket was much easier than all of this.

Chapter 5

Cricket was bound and determined to pretend that nothing had happened earlier. Though, when Jackson arrived in his truck, she was a little bit chagrined. She had hoped that she might get a small reprieve. After all, he hadn't said why he'd left, and it was entirely possible that he figured, since she had run away from him like someone not thinking straight, he had every right to back out of their agreement. But no, he was back.

She flung open the door to the house, and stood there with a grin fixed permanently on her face. A grin that dared him to comment.

He got a couple of paper bags out of the truck, and held them. Standing there staring at her.

"Glad you're back," she said.

"Yeah," he said. "I'm ready to fix the sink."

"Well great," she said.

"Yeah, I said I would."

He slammed the door of the truck shut and began to walk toward her. She scampered back through the entryway, but still stood there, with her hand on the door. She didn't want to look like she was running scared. Not again. She needed to get a grip. That was the thing. She needed to stop acting this way.

"I really appreciate it."

"Yeah, I mean, you said."

He brushed past her, and she held her breath. Because she didn't want to smell him. Didn't want to get the impression of his scent again, because it did weird things to her insides and she heavily resented all the weird things Jackson did to her insides. She couldn't think about it right now though. Because she had to act… She had to act like everything was okay. She just really desperately needed to pretend like everything that happened earlier hadn't happened.

He set the bags on the table and she stood in the doorway, watching as he got out pipes and tape and tools.

"Do you want to learn something?"

"Well, you are ever the teacher."

They had found a way back to their earlier rapport, so there was that.

"That I am."

"Where's the water shut off, Cricket?"

"I don't know that," she said.

He shook his head. "Well, we're going to have to turn the water off or we're going to end up with a flood."

"Okay. Maybe it's… Maybe it's in one of the cabinets."

"The water shut off is in the cabinet."

"No, I mean the instructions. There's some paperwork that has information on the house. In this cabinet." She walked past him and reached up into a cabinet that was full of papers. She didn't have enough dishes or utensils to bother moving them. She had plenty of space in the kitchen that they could stay right there. She pulled out the paperwork and spread it out on the table, rifling through the sheets, but he had already walked out of the room. She heard the door shut, and a few moments later he was back.

"Found it."

"How?"

"Logic. Experience," he said. "Anyway. It's fine now."

"I should probably know where the water shut off is," she said, still standing there holding the papers.

"I'll show you afterward." He got down underneath the sink, tools in hand, and began to dismember things.

"Can I hand you stuff?"

"Sure."

They set up an assembly line, where he asked for things, and she handed them to him. When he was done, he would give it back, and she would put it on the table.

Things felt not quite so fraught. And it was easy for her to forget that earlier today had gone so horribly wrong.

"Come down here," he said.

She started. "What?"

"I want to show you something."

Slowly, cautiously, she knelt down beside him. It wasn't him she was afraid of. It was herself. He wasn't the one who knew why earlier was such a disaster, and he probably didn't even…well, she hadn't stayed to find out if he'd even been leaning in toward her. It was all in her head, that was the thing. So she resolutely got down next to him and made a valiant attempt at not breathing the same air, since that had caused her some serious problems earlier.

"What are you showing me?"

"I'm going to have you fit the pipe."

"Oh…okay."

He handed her a wrench. "Lean in and tighten it right here."

She leaned in and she couldn't help but breathe. And when she did…

When she did, she was overwhelmed by him.

Why did he have to smell so good? Why was he so compelling? She looked at the square line of his jaw, the straight blade of his nose. The intensity in those eyes. Those eyes that had always been so fascinating to her.

It *had been* a crush but now it *couldn't* be.

It couldn't be.

It couldn't be.

She still couldn't breathe.

She looked down. But then… She could feel him looking at her, and she couldn't keep herself from looking back.

And when she did, he was so close. His eyes so intent on hers. She had run away earlier. And she had been smart to do that. She had needed to do that.

She should run. She should run. She should move away. Because this was wrong. And it was crazy. *She* was crazy.

And for some reason—anger, rebellion against what she was feeling—she didn't run. Instead, she leaned forward.

Instead, she closed the distance between them.

She was going to prove, once and for all, that she did not want him.

This would disgust her.

It would burn all those feelings to the ground.

And for the first time in her life, Cricket's lips touched another person's.

Because she was sure she'd find that once she kissed him, once she took the mystery out of it all she'd be disgusted. She had to be, right? Because surely, *surely*, nature would take care of this and she'd recoil in horror when their mouths met.

As soon as her lips touched his, though, she knew she was wrong.

It was like a flash bomb had gone off inside of her stomach.

And Cricket ignited.

He moved, large, rough hands cupping her face, holding her steady as he consumed her. His whiskers were rough, his mouth hot. He smelled like heaven.

She was shaking. Guilt warred with desire as her mind went blank of everything. Of what she should be doing. Of who he was. Who she was. And what she suspected. It was all gone. There was nothing left but the intense sensation of being touched by him, kissed by him.

How had this happened?

How had she… How had she ended up desiring him?

You don't know? As if it hasn't been halfway to a crush all this time?

She'd been fascinated by him but she'd never called it that. She'd been interested in him, intrigued by him, but she'd never…

And then she'd found out about their parents and… and…she'd thought what she'd been feeling was something else.

She didn't know anything.

She'd moved to this ranch convinced that she was finally figuring things out. Finally making a move toward having a life that she wanted. But here she was, drowning in confusion. Drowning in desire. A desire she had no business feeling. Not at all. Here she was, making the biggest mess of everything that she could possibly make.

She was less certain now than she'd been before. Less of anything, less of everything. And more too.

Jackson Cooper. This is Jackson Cooper.

And he's probably your half brother.

She jerked herself away from him, gasping. "No."

"Cricket, it's okay," he said. "You don't have to run away."

"No," she said. "I might."

"You don't need to be afraid of me."

"It's not you I'm afraid of."

"What?"

"It's me," she said. And much to her horror, tears sprang to her eyes. And they started to fall before she could even consider holding them back. Cricket didn't cry. And here she was, weeping like an inconsolable child in front of Jackson. He must think she was insane. She thought she was insane.

"What is it?"

"It's us," she said. "Jackson," she said. "I think you might be my brother."

Chapter 6

Jackson was on his feet and halfway across the room as soon as that last word came out of Cricket's mouth.

He didn't know what the hell she was on, but she was wrong.

He knew that down to his soul.

He had a sister. He knew what that felt like. This did not feel brotherly at all. Not in the least. Absolutely nothing about what he felt for Cricket could fall under the heading of familial. She was a beguiling little minx who had essentially been a source of irritation for him for the last several years, and then had turned into a wholly irritating, and far too attractive, woman.

Then she'd kissed him. And now she was telling him that she thought she was his sister.

"You better explain yourself, and quick."

"I just… I found out something about our parents.

My mother and your father… They used to be… Did you ever wonder why your father hated mine so much? I mean, beyond the fact that James is a real piece of work, there had to be something else. And I knew there had to be. Well, my mother started talking about it more. And since she and my father got divorced… Well, she told us. She told us that she used to be with your father. She was in love with him, but he was poor, and she chose to marry James instead. Why am I so much younger than my sisters? It doesn't make any sense. I don't fit with them. I fit with you."

"Cricket," he said. "You are not my sister."

"I pretty much have to be," she said.

"You pretty much don't," he said. "There is no way, no way in hell, that you could possibly be my sister."

"Why not? I think it makes plenty of sense. Seems to me that it's reasonable enough."

"There is nothing reasonable about any of this."

"I have always…thought that I didn't fit. And I think this is why."

"So why did you psychotically decide to kiss me?"

"To prove it would be gross!"

The way his blood was burning through his veins made a mockery of that statement. He just stared at her.

"Hey," she groused. "*You* almost kissed me earlier. Why do you think I ran away? It's wrong, Jackson. And I was just trying to make it right and now I messed it all up!"

"Get in the truck."

"What?" she squeaked.

"Get in the truck. There's one person who can settle this."

"I mean," she said, using that same arch, certain tone

she'd used many times she'd been certain, but wrong, in the time he'd known her, "there are DNA tests that can settle it. Many men in labs could settle it…"

"We're talking to my father."

"Oh…"

"I'm going to have him tell you, once and for all, you couldn't be his daughter."

"I…"

"Did you talk to your mother?" he asked.

"I… No. I didn't ask her directly. But you have to understand that she… It took her so long to tell me any of the specifics about her life. About her relationship with your dad. We're not really all that close. And I just didn't… Talking to her won't mean a lot to me. I won't believe that it's true."

"I'm sure that if you told her you were considering jumping my bones, she might give you the straight answer."

"Don't say that. Anyway, I never said I wanted to do that. I just kissed you."

"You're not in high school, Cricket, when does it end with just a kiss?"

"Well." She didn't know what to say to that, and it was clear. And he was being mean, but he…

Hell. His father had cheated on his mother…

Would it really surprise you?

He didn't think Cricket was his sister. End of story. He knew too much about women and chemistry to think it, even for a moment.

His certainty in his libido was sound.

His certainty in his father? Less so. And even though he knew Cricket had the wrong end of the stick here, he was worried that one piece of it might be true.

He had enough of a hard time with his old man without having to believe he'd been unfaithful to his mother.

"Get in the truck," he said. "I'm not repeating myself again."

They marched out to the truck, and he jerked the passenger side door open for her.

"Thank you," she said softly.

"No problem."

He started the truck and pulled out of the driveway much faster than necessary. "Why didn't you tell me? Why didn't you tell me right away when you had a suspicion?"

"Because. Because I knew that… It doesn't bother me to think about my mom cheating on my dad. I wouldn't blame her. I think she loved your dad, and she made a terrible mistake. And I can see how… When someone gets under your skin, Jackson, it's not that easy to get rid of them. I can understand that."

"Can you?"

"Yes," she said, filled with fury. "I can. I don't judge my mom. Except… Except on behalf of yours. Because I know how much you love your mom. And she was a lovely woman from what I remember. And she's gone, and I just didn't want to… I wanted to get to know you better first. I wanted to figure out the whole situation."

"Why didn't you just ask Creed?"

"I'm not even that close with Wren and Emerson. I'd like to be closer. But… That's the thing. We're not a normal family, and we never have been. They're close with each other because they're close in age. Because they had more in common in their upbringing. I'm different. I always have been. So I'm not just magically close with Creed because he married my sister. I'm not even magically close to my sister."

"What? You thought you'd become magically close to me?"

She made a sputtering sound. "I've always... I... I don't know. Forget it."

He thought back to how she'd trailed after him. Like a damn puppy when she'd been young. Had she thought he was her brother even then? No, she'd said that it only occurred to her recently. And all his thoughts, all his intentions toward buying her ranch, everything...just kind of faded away.

Because handling this was what mattered.

Settling it was what mattered.

He pulled up to the winery and saw that there was still a light on in the tasting room. He was sure that his dad was still in there.

"Come on."

"Okay," she said, clearly filled with trepidation.

He gripped her arm, and propelled her forward.

"Can you not touch me?" she said, jerking her arm out of his hold. She was as disgusted by the whole thing as he was.

Except.

Except, the problem was his body wasn't all that disgusted.

His blood was on fire from that kiss. And while there had been a momentary dampening caused by the shock of what she'd said, it had not created in him an instant disgust.

They needed to get this settled.

He needed her to be as sure as he was that there wasn't any truth to her suspicions at all.

Fact was, he was sure he had more experience than Cricket when it came to sex. So maybe she was naive enough to think they could be related, but he was not confused about connections, chemistry and attraction.

And he knew what was happening here.

None of it was familial.

He opened the door to the tasting room and walked in. Cash Cooper was standing at the back of the room, examining the stock.

"Dad," he said. "We need to talk."

His father turned, shock registering on his face when he saw Cricket standing there. "What can I do for you?"

"Oh…" Cricket started to fidget. "I just had a question to ask."

"What's that, young lady?"

"Well, I kind of need to know if I'm… If I'm your daughter."

It had happened. *It had happened.*

She was standing there in front of Cash Cooper, and she was asking him if she was his daughter. Except now… She hoped that it wasn't true.

Because Jackson was in her blood. And she…she wanted him. And she had been so sure she could overcome that. That she could put all these feelings in their proper place, but she hadn't managed to do it. She didn't know if she ever could. She just didn't know. She had tried. She had tried, and it had ended with her kissing him on the floor of her kitchen.

Everything was a disaster. It was an absolute and total disaster. But then it had been from moment one, hadn't it? Because there were only two scenarios here.

One, she was hopelessly and utterly attracted to Jackson Cooper who was unobtainable in every way, who would never want her, and who would never keep her even if he enjoyed kissing her, and she was just out of place in her family because she was.

Or the second one, which was that she was unforgivably, irrevocably attracted to her half brother.

No, she couldn't win.

"What made you think that, young lady?" Cash asked.

And he was so kind, it made her heart ache. It made her chest feel like it was being cracked in two, because James certainly wouldn't have been this nice. She wanted Cash to be her father, but she did not want Jackson to be her brother, and she didn't think that there was...

There was just nothing.

"My mother told me. She told me she was in love with you. She told me that she married James Maxfield and it was the wrong choice. And I've just never felt like I belonged. I've never felt like I fit. When she said that it all made a lot of sense. That... That maybe I'm not a Maxfield, and that's why I don't fit. That maybe I was supposed to be here the whole time. Because I want to be a rancher. I don't want to spend my life in a stuffy winery. Because I want different things and I look different and I act different and I... I just thought maybe that was why."

"Cricket," Cash said, and his voice was so kind and gentle she thought she might break apart. "I'm not your father."

She wanted to cry. In despair, with relief.

Jackson wasn't her brother.

He wasn't her brother. So that was… There was that.

Beside her, she heard him let out a huge sigh of relief. And that brought a skeptical look from Cash, but he didn't say anything. Then he looked back at Cricket. "I did love your mother." Then he turned to Jackson. "I… That was the problem, Jackson," he said. "I loved Lucinda. And I never quite got over it. You know… You know that your mother and I got married because she was pregnant with you. I acted rashly because I was heartbroken. She and I both paid for it for years. We tried. And we love you kids. With everything. I cared for her. I cared for her a whole hell of a lot. But you know what makes me the most sorry? That I could never be the husband she needed. That she died being with someone who always had feelings for someone else. That's what kills me."

Cricket felt guilty. Standing there listening to this.

It was clearly a private conversation, one that needed to happen without her presence. But here she was.

All because she had been…

Because she had been so desperate to fix this thing inside of her.

What was wrong with her? Something was wrong with her. And there always had been something wrong, and this was just further evidence of it.

A tear slid down her cheek and she felt horrified. Horrified to be displaying this kind of emotion in front of not just Jackson but Cash. This man who wasn't her father, who should feel nothing for her at all.

"You look like your mother," he said softly.

She hadn't expected that. It was like an arrow to the heart.

"No, I don't," Cricket said. "My mom is elegant.

And pretty. And her hair never…does this," she said, gesturing to her curls.

"She used to be like you, Cricket. And she was my first love. Just like I was hers. But love wasn't enough. Not for her. That's fine."

"It wasn't fine though, was it? She was miserable. She was absolutely miserable being married to him. I hope you weren't miserable."

"I wasn't miserable," he said. "I think I might've made my wife miserable. But I wasn't. Still, I have a lot of regrets."

"My father doesn't have any. His only regret is that he's lost everything. He doesn't care about anything or anyone else. When I say everything, I don't mean us. James Maxfield never cared about a damn thing. And he's…he's my father."

Sadness settled deep in her stomach. Because for just a little while she had hoped. She had really, genuinely hoped…

"Did you ever cheat on Mom?" Jackson's voice was granite.

"No," Cash said, addressing his son. "I swear it. I swear to you I never did."

"Well then. I guess that answers all those questions."

"I'm not sure if I should apologize or not," Cash said.

Cricket shook her head. "I should. I assumed something about you that wasn't fair. And I did it because I… I'm not happy with my family. I'm not happy with my place in it. But that's just the way it is. There's no answer for it. So… So. That's it."

Then, she turned and ran out of the tasting room,

back to the truck. She leaned against the door, breathing hard.

She was doing so much running.

And all she could think was—what a mess she'd made out of everything. She'd revealed to Jackson that she was interested in him, revealed that she had suspected he was her half brother... Every single thing that she'd been so bound and determined to have control over, she had gone and just made a huge mess of. He was never supposed to know that she was attracted to him. And she was supposed to time this whole thing... better. But did it even matter?

He came out a few moments later, looking like thunder. And she knew that the truth didn't matter. She had managed to absolutely and totally... She felt stupid. And small. And wrong.

Every bad thing she had ever felt, it was magnified now.

"I can walk..."

"You cannot walk. Get in the damn truck."

She didn't even argue, because she felt too guilty. Too bad. So she got into the truck, and they made the drive back to the ranch in total silence.

She was going to send him away. Send him back to his place, because there was just no... There was no point in anything. She wasn't a rancher. It wasn't in her blood. She had spun herself all manner of fantasies about Jackson Cooper when she was a girl, when she didn't know anything about anything. And then, when her family had imploded, she had spun different fantasies altogether. She had watched her beautiful, elegant sisters win over handsome cowboys, and Cricket had realized that her own darkest, most cherished secret—

the thing that she had lied about for years—would never come true. Because Wren had gotten the interest of Creed, and Wren was...well, she was beautiful.

Elegant and sophisticated and refined and everything Cricket could never be.

And not only was Cricket too young for Jackson to ever evince an interest in, she was also just... She was just her. And so yes, it had been convenient to weave a new fantasy. About all the reasons why she might feel wrong. All the reasons why she might have felt connected to Jackson, ways that explained away the feelings that she had, but that would still mean he mattered.

She stumbled out of the truck when they got to the house.

"Jackson..."

He rounded the front of the truck quickly, his eyes filled with liquid fire. "First things first," he said.

And before she could react, before she could open her mouth or say anything, his lips were on hers. And he was kissing her again. Deep and hard and longer than the first time. There was rage in this kiss. An intensity that she had never known a kiss could possess.

Wrong.

Small.

Ugly.

All the words that she felt inside—all the words she had used to describe herself—slowly began to fall away, each pass of his mouth over hers stripping them back. Creating something new inside of her. Something different. Something she had never experienced before. Like an avalanche. One of need and desire and hope.

It was the hope that stunned her. Suddenly that yawning, cavernous thing in her chest was filled with light. Suddenly it was lifting her, propelling her forward. Up on her toes and more firmly into his arms.

He angled his head, his tongue passing over hers.

And she felt right.

Because this had been the feeling all along. That first connection that she'd felt to him. When she had first known what it meant that she would be a woman some day, and that she would want to be in the arms of a man, and that she was certain that man was Jackson Cooper. In that one blinding moment he had taken everything that felt wrong and turned it around.

Because he had kissed her.

She wasn't wrong about that. He was kissing her, and he was doing it with just as much passion as she felt inside of her for him. And if he felt that, then she wasn't wrong.

She hadn't been wrong.

Life had been wrong.

And she had altered her expectations, changed what she felt to make it easier to digest. She had been trying to create a story that was easier to live with.

One where her father didn't love her because she wasn't his.

One where her mother found her difficult because Cricket was a reminder of sins.

One where she was so different from her sisters because they were only half of each other.

And one where Jackson mattered not because she had an unobtainable crush, but because he was her long-lost brother.

One where she wanted to be a rancher because she came from a family of them, not just because she did.

But this was proof.

That she had her own dreams just because.

That she was herself, wholly and singularly, for better or for worse. That she wanted him, maybe because—like ranching—he was too big, too unobtainable and too impossible to have.

Maybe that's who she was.

A pioneer. A person who saw what was possible and asked for that little bit more.

A person who looked around and said this doesn't have to be just enough, I can have more, I can have better.

Maybe that was who she was.

It was a revelation. Just like his arms, just like his mouth.

But then, just as suddenly as he kissed her, he was pulling away.

"That had to happen. Because I had to… I couldn't leave it at that last one. Not with what you said."

Cricket launched herself back into his arms. Because she didn't want to be anywhere else. Because she wanted to feel. All these things that he and he alone had made her feel for all these years.

It was done. That was the beauty of it. The beauty of having made such a damn fool of herself already. There was no going back. There was nothing to protect.

The crushing reality was that James Maxfield might be her father. Or he might not be. But the one thing that mattered most was that Jackson *wasn't* her brother.

Her long-held crush had no doubt been revealed by her earlier actions, but that was freedom in many ways. She had wanted him—she had wanted this—for so long, and there was no reason to not simply…take it now. None at all.

So she did. She drank deeply from his mouth like she was a dying woman and he was the source of life-giving water.

His whiskers were rough beneath her palms, where she grabbed hold of his face and stretched up as hard as she could, on her toes, kissing him with all the breath she had in her.

"What exactly do you want?" he said, large hands grabbing her hips and setting her back on the ground. "Because you've got to know, little Cricket, that you're playing with fire here. I don't want you to get burned."

She scoffed. "I'm not afraid of fire."

"You're not?"

She tilted her face upward. "I'm not afraid of anything."

"You're trembling."

"Yeah, that happens sometimes, when a woman is turned on, didn't you know?" She spoke with a bravado she didn't necessarily feel.

"You might have to educate me on the subject."

"I'm not afraid of anything, do you know why? Because… I already can't have the approval of my family. And you know, I was really scared of what it meant that I wanted you, suspecting what I did. I was really scared to look foolish, but you know what? I did. I do. So where is there to go from here? I guess I could fear for my own physical safety, but I don't. Not when you hold me. I spent my whole life wanting things I couldn't have. Wanting my parents to care about me in a way that they didn't. Wanting to fit in a way that I couldn't. Wanting to be part of a family that I wasn't." She felt like it was the better part of valor to maybe not mention that wanting him was part of what she'd been denied for all this time. She might not have a whole lot of pride, but she had a little, and she was going to protect it.

"I'm tired of that. No, I'm not afraid of this. I'm not afraid of you. I'm just afraid of living more of the same."

"Marriage is not for me," he said. "Just right up front. Relationships aren't for me."

"That's real flattering, cowboy, but did I propose?"

"I'm just getting that out there, Cricket, because I can't ignore the fact that you had a hell of a day, and from the sounds of things, a hell of a few weeks. On top of that, you are younger than me. And I just need to make sure that we are both completely aware of what this is."

"I want you. I'm very tired of not having the things I want."

"Seems fair."

It was deeper than that. But it wasn't really his business. She had a feeling, though, that Jackson Cooper was a mountain she had to climb if she was ever going to figure out what lay on the other side of him. On the other side of this. Because honestly, the weirdness of the last few months was all bound up in him, and before that, years of a crush that had quite overtaken her life.

So, there was no magical, mystical connection to the Cooper family.

But Jackson was still a thing. And that needed to be sorted out before she could be the new Cricket. This woman who was going to make a way apart from her family. This woman she wanted desperately to be. Needed to be.

He was so tall and strong and beautiful. And she

had no idea what he was getting out of this. But that wasn't her concern. Her concern was...*her*.

It didn't matter what anybody else thought. Didn't matter what anybody else wanted from her, what they thought of her. It didn't matter what he thought. She had been dragged into Cash Cooper's very own tasting room, and she had accused him of cheating on his wife. Had asked if *he was her father*. She had reached the height of humiliation. So she was all in on this, because there was nothing left to protect or destroy.

She was Cricket, reduced.

And she wanted to build herself back up again.

"I'm tired of talking," she said.

Talking wasn't her thing. She had spent so many years just off on her own, daydreaming about the life she might have someday. She had done more talking with him over the last week than she had ever done with anyone, really. She didn't want to talk. She just wanted him.

"Suit yourself."

That was how she found herself being lifted off the ground, his large hand on her ass, around her back, as he picked her up and kissed her, hard and deep. She could feel his body, firm and insistent against hers, evidence of his arousal. And it thrilled her. Thrilled her down to her soul. To know that he wanted her the same as she wanted him. To know that, of all the mistakes she'd made, and all the things she might have done wrong today, she hadn't dampened his desire for her.

He did want her.

He did.

His kiss was wild now, far beyond anything she'd ever fantasized about. She'd done a lot of fantasizing about Jackson Cooper, but it had been gauzy, and it hadn't been half so physical. She hadn't really known about the heat of another person's body pressed against hers, the rough feeling of his whiskers, the firmness of his mouth. That slick friction of his tongue against hers. The way their breaths would mingle, the way she could feel his heart raging through his chest and against hers. Those rough hands, moving over the fabric of her T-shirt, and then under it, against her skin. His body was so very hard.

No, she hadn't counted on this. The intensity of it. The reality of it. It was blindingly brilliant and beautiful, and was making her into a version of herself she hadn't known was possible—a wild creature, which in many ways she'd always been, but with aim, with purpose.

Because her wildness was pouring out of her and over him. She didn't feel embarrassed. Didn't feel nervous.

There was no inhibition at all. She bit his bottom lip and he growled. And she didn't know why she'd done it, only that it had felt right. And she didn't question it. Didn't question anything. This felt natural. This felt right in a way that nothing else ever had in her entire life. He felt right, fitted against her, the softness of her body seemingly made for the hardness of his, and she couldn't recall a time when she had ever felt so…right. So real. So complete.

So certain that the things about her that were different were what made it all so good.

For all her life she'd felt like the lone misfit toy on an island of beauties, and now, she didn't feel misfit at all.

No, she fit just right.

He carried her up the front steps, stumbled slightly on a board, then braced her hard against the door, and she gasped. His erection pressed firmly between her thighs, hitting her right where she was the neediest for him. At the place where she was desperate with longing.

He rocked against her, growling as he took the kiss deeper. She gasped, letting her head fall back, arching into him, rubbing her breasts against his chest, reveling in how sensitive she was.

She had been so ashamed, so embarrassed of her every desire for a great many years—to feel a total lack of that shame was a revelation she hadn't known she'd been waiting for.

He pushed the door open, then propelled them both down the hall and toward his bedroom. Toward the little twin bed there.

She doubted he fit on it by himself, she had no idea how the two of them were going to fit. But her bed wasn't any larger.

He didn't seem concerned at all. Just like a loose board hadn't caused him to make a false move, the bed size didn't do it either.

With knowing, competent hands, he pulled her top off over her head, and with one deft motion took her bra with it.

She was standing there, totally topless in a pair of jeans, and mesmerized by the look of abject hunger in his eyes.

He wanted her. More than a little. He wanted her, and it was obvious.

And she, with all her slight curves and frizzy hair, felt desired. Felt beautiful.

She closed the space between them, pushing her hands beneath his shirt, loving the feel of his hard muscles, the rough hair that covered his hot skin. She'd never thought much about sex in general. Only sex with *him*. But he was far and beyond anything she'd ever fantasized about. Far and beyond anything she'd ever dreamed she might have.

She pushed his shirt up and over his head, revealing his body. So much more beautiful and perfect than she could have ever imagined. That broad chest, lean waist and perfectly defined muscles. He was all things masculine and glorious, and everything feminine within her bloomed with glee.

And suddenly, she wanted to cry. Because Cricket Maxfield never got what she wanted. Cricket Maxfield never got the best or the brightest. She had the leftovers of her family's gene pool. She wasn't brilliant or beautiful, particularly ambitious. She wasn't the one the sun shined down on with favor.

But she had wanted Jackson Cooper for as long as she'd known what it meant to want, and she was getting him.

Whatever happened after this didn't really matter.

Because this was the most perfect moment she'd ever felt. Ever experienced.

Oh, she'd tried to pretend that her feelings for him could be something other than this, but they couldn't be. This was the connection. For her, this was what it was. What it always would be.

"What?" he asked.

"You are just stunning," she said.

He laughed. Honest to God. A chuckle rumbling in his chest. And then she found herself caught up in those big, strong arms, her bare breasts brushing against his hot, rough skin.

"Well I'm glad you think so."

She found herself being kissed again, and all the while his hands worked on getting rid of her jeans, her panties, socks and shoes.

Until she found herself stretched across the bed with his big body over the top of hers. She completely naked, he still in his jeans. The denim was rough between her thighs, the delicate skin there scraped by the raw material. And she could feel him, right there, so hard and insistent and...

She ached.

And he just kept on kissing her. And kissing her. He shifted slightly, putting one hand between her thighs, finding her slick and wet, each pass of his fingertips over that sensitized bundle of nerves creating a white, electric heat that nearly left her blinded.

She had never felt anything like this before. And yes, she'd put her own hand between her legs plenty of times, but it wasn't like this. His skin was rough, and she had no control over how fast he worked, how slow. How much time he took. And when he pushed a finger inside of her before drawing her wetness back out over the source of her desire, she gasped. He did it again, and again, adding a second finger to the first, until she was sobbing. Until she was begging. For what, she didn't even know.

She fumbled for the front of his pants, tried to get his jeans open.

He chuckled. Husky and knowing.

"Not yet," he said. "I'm not done with you."

He dropped off the bed and she found herself being

dragged to the edge of the mattress. Her thighs draped over his shoulders, the heart of her completely open to him.

"Jackson," she said, her voice trembling.

She might be a virgin, but she wasn't innocent. In that she fully knew all the things men and women did to each other. Her sisters had never been particularly shy about their sex lives, or their desires. And beyond that, she hadn't kept herself sheltered in terms of what she watched or read.

But having a man right there, looking at her, with no way to hide herself, that was a different proposition altogether than simply knowing. And when his mouth touched her, she jumped back, only to find herself pinned firmly against his face, his strong arms wrapped around her thighs, holding her there.

She wiggled as he lapped at her, as he tasted her like she was a decadent dessert.

"Jackson," she said, a feeling like flying building in her stomach, making her certain that she was no longer being held to the bed, but somewhere among the stars.

She couldn't breathe.

She didn't want to. She just wanted this. Forever. Him. His hands. His strength. His mouth.

The pleasure she felt wove around all those things and created the magic tapestry that wrapped itself around her, cocooning her, making her feel safe even as she was brought to the edge of an intensity like she had never known before.

She rocked her hips in time with the motion, and when he pushed two fingers inside of her again, she broke apart. Her internal muscles squeezing around his fingers as he worked them in and out of her body. As he continued to tease her with the flat of his tongue.

She was left desperate and panting, begging for more.

"There's more," he said, his voice rough. "Don't worry."

He stood, and she watched transfixed as he undid his jeans, lowering the zipper slowly, the strong column of his arousal coming into view.

And he was… Well, much larger than she had imagined. Not that she had a great frame of reference. Or a very good idea of scale. But he was as beautiful as he was intimidating. And he was a lot of both.

Everything about his body was glorious. Strong and well defined and damn near miraculous.

And she didn't have time to cling to her worry, because then he was positioning himself at the edge of the bed again, wrapping his arms around her thighs, this time lifting her hips up off the mattress as he positioned himself at the entrance of her body, and thrust home.

The pain nearly blinded her.

She cried out, hand scrabbling for purchase, but she couldn't reach any part of him. And she wanted to hold on to him, wanted to dig her nails into his skin to keep herself from crawling out of her own.

His eyes widened, and for the first time, he looked truly at sea.

He adjusted their positions, bringing her legs around so that her feet were pointed toward the end of the bed, bringing himself onto the mattress the right way, still inside of her, but over her now, and she gripped his shoulders, squeezing her eyes shut tight.

"Cricket," he growled.

"Don't stop," she begged. "It's already done."

"Cricket…"

"Just please don't stop." And then, she opened her eyes, grabbed his face and kissed him.

And that seemed to work.

She could feel his control begin to unravel as he started to move slowly at first, gently even, until the pain began to recede. Until it was replaced with a full, complicated pleasure that made her want to cry as well as scream with desire.

She began to move her hips in time with his, as they found a rhythm that pleased them both. As they found each other.

And then, he took control, his movements no longer measured, his skin slapping against hers. The primal edge to their joining so much more than she had ever imagined it could be. So much better.

Desire built inside of her until she was trembling again, like she had done outside, like she had done after their kiss. He reached between their bodies, moved his fingers along the sides of where they joined, then back upward, pinching her gently as he thrust in, and light—bright and brilliant—flashed behind her eyes, pleasure breaking over her like a wave.

It was unlike any reality she'd ever known. Deep and unending as she pulsed around him. And he thrust inside of her, once, twice more, and on a growl gave himself up to his own pleasure.

She felt rocked. Stunned. The aftershocks of everything that had just happened continuing to move through her, little tremors of need that caused her to cling to him with each passing ripple.

"Well," he said. "You should've told me."

"Oh, about being a virgin?"

"Hell yes," he said.

"I figured that was pretty evident."

"Not evident enough, Cricket," he said.

"Well. It wasn't really any of your business."

"It was exactly my business."

"I didn't want it to be. I just wanted it for me. Please don't ruin it by lecturing me or scolding me or yelling at me, because I just don't care about your opinion, okay? It was good." She let herself fall backward onto the bed, her head resting against the pillow. "It was good, and that's all I care about."

"Cricket... I shouldn't stay."

"Why?" She scrambled into a seated position, leaving herself completely uncovered. She didn't know why she was so at ease being naked in front of him. It felt right though. Natural. In a way that being clothed in many other situations never had. She felt... Well, she felt essentially Cricket. Like the baseline nature of who she was was completely and totally reinforced by this. Like the essence that made her her, that had always felt wrong and out of place, suddenly fit. In this house, in this bed. With this man. And, she didn't see any point in feeling regretful or shy. In apologizing to him for the fact that she'd been a virgin.

Really, if it didn't bother her, it shouldn't bother him.

"Because there are things you don't know about why I agreed to come and work here."

"You lost a bet, cowboy. Seems pretty straightforward to me. Though, the bet had nothing to do with this, so don't go and try to cheapen it now."

"I'm not going to," he said, his eyes level. "Cricket, why do you think I bet myself as your ranch hand?"

"You thought you were going to win."

"No. I thought I was going to lose. I *knew* I was going to lose. Your level of bravado was not that of a woman who had an iffy hand."

"How…" She felt utterly aghast. "How can that be?"

"It just is, sweetheart. I knew for a fact that you were going to win, and I agreed to these terms because I wanted to be here. Because I wanted to… I wanted to show you that you didn't have the chops to be a rancher."

"You what?"

"I wanted to talk you out of it. Because I wanted to buy this place."

She frowned. "You… You were tricking me?"

"Yes. Though, in fairness, I never lied to you, not once. I never lied about how much work it takes to run a place like this. Everything I said to you was the absolute truth. The morning wake-up time was real. The amount of work and money and time that is going to be needed for this place is all real. And nothing I said to you was off base there. But I certainly didn't do anything to encourage you. Not really. Because what I wanted was for you to give up and throw in the towel, and for me to be there ready to buy you out."

"Jackson…"

"Yeah. And now I feel like an ass. Because I didn't know that all this was going on. That you thought we might be related. And I…"

"So wait a minute, were you going to…seduce me to try to get the ranch away from me?"

"No."

"Just please tell me this was real. If nothing else, Jackson, just tell me this was real."

"It was real. But that doesn't mean it can be anything but tonight."

"Why not?"

"Because it's a disaster. Because I'm not the kind of man who can give you what you want. You've already been hurt by too many people in your life, Cricket, and I don't want to be another one."

"Well, too bad. Because this is hurtful."

"I'm sorry about that. I didn't want to hurt you."

"No. You just wanted to crush my dreams and make me think that I wasn't up to them, and then buy my dream piece of property out from under me. Jackson, you did want to hurt me. It was just that you didn't know me, so you didn't particularly care. And if you feel guilty now, it's only because you've seen what a pathetic human being I am, and I was a virgin on top of it."

"I don't pity you."

"Then what is it?"

"Having seen you naked, having been inside of you, I can't take advantage of you. Okay? Because yeah, I can stand here and justify my actions, and say that I didn't lie to you like that makes it all okay, but I know it's not, Cricket. I know it was a shady thing to do. And the fact of the matter is, I could ignore what a shady thing it was when I wasn't personally involved with you, but after tonight I think it's pretty safe to say that personal involvement has happened. From dragging you in front of my dad to getting into bed with you."

"Well, then how can you stand there and say it can't be anything else? If we are already personally involved…"

"It's a mess."

"Oh, no argument here. Believe me. I've been pretty much mired in the mess this whole time." She let out an exasperated sigh. "Don't you know that I have had a crush on you the size of the Willamette River for… I don't know, years? So finding out that you were possibly my brother was about the worst thing I could think of. Do you have any idea what it's like to spend years lusting after somebody, and then find that you might share a dad? It was horrifying. I'm sorry, but I needed to know, and then once I did know… I needed to be with you. Because I felt so wrong, in so many ways, for so many years—I think this had to happen for me to…get over it. To start feeling some things that are…a little bit more normal. Like, believe me, none of this was how I saw…the hookup between us going. But that whole trying to get my ranch thing… That was pretty awful. And, you know, not something I thought you would do."

"Cricket, I didn't know you had a crush on me. But I'd venture to say that you might have a slightly better view of me than is realistic. I'm just who I am. I'm not a particularly bad man, but I'm not a really great one either."

"Why my ranch?"

"I'm right next door. It just makes sense. If I want to expand…"

"Why do you need to expand?"

"It's what people do."

"I mean, to what end? For more money?"

"No," he said. "For more of something that's mine."

"Oh. Well, I mean I understand that. Wanting something that's yours. But this ranch is mine. And you can't have it. And I don't really care how hard it's going to

be to make it work. It's going to be mine. You under-
estimated me. You had no idea about everything that
was going on in here." She tapped her temple. "Honestly, it's been a wasteland of horror for the past…six
months at least. So, don't go trying to scare me away."

"I'm going back to my place tonight. Let's just…
cool off."

She sputtered. "I don't want to cool off."

"I need to."

She stared at him. "We had a deal," she said. "And
none of that's changed because of what just happened
tonight. Are you the kind of man who backs out of
the deal?"

"Things have…"

"Changed for you. Because you were lying to me.
But I was never lying. I was always being honest,
and…"

"Except for the part where you thought that I was
your brother, and you figured that you needed to… I
don't know, what were you trying to do exactly?"

"Get close to you, enough that I could say, 'Do you
suppose it's possible your father cheated on your late
mother, and he is perhaps my dad?'" He barely moved,
but a muscle in his cheek flinched. "Yeah," she said.
"Exactly. It's awful. And there's really no good way
to approach it. At least, not one I could think of. And
believe me, I tried. I tried to think of something better than that. So yes, I guess I had ulterior motives
too, but I also just want to run my ranch. And I need
your help. And you promised me thirty days. Staying
here. Free labor."

"You're in my bed."

"So, you have a couple options. You get back in bed

with me, you go to the bunkhouse with the spiders, or you go to my bed, where I may just end up."

He sighed heavily, then came back down onto the mattress. "You don't know what you're playing with here, little Cricket."

"There's only one way I'm going to find out, though, isn't there? By continuing to play."

She took a deep breath, focusing on the tenderness in her chest. "In all honesty, Jackson, I am just really sick to death of feeling like I'm fundamentally wrong. And this felt right. So…why don't we just keep on?"

"I lied to you," he said.

"Yeah. But so what? I mean, we're not friends. You lost a bet. End of story. You're not my family, so we don't have some kind of mystical connection like I thought we might. We are not…anything. So what does it matter? Your plan would've only worked if you could have talked me out of my dream, and quite frankly, if you could have talked me out of it, I would've deserved what I got."

"Is that really what you think?"

"Yes. As it is, you were never even close to making me second-guess it. Because you know what's harder than figuring out how to do chores and work a ranch? Growing up in a mausoleum. An altar to your father, when you don't even like or respect the man. Being made to feel like you have to fit in, when you don't particularly want to, or see the benefit of it. Yeah. That's hard. And, well… I decided not to do it. I decided to figure this out. So I did. So I took it upon myself to figure this out. A few early mornings weren't going to scare me off."

"You're a whole thing, aren't you, Cricket?"

"Not by choice. It just kind of seems to be the way I am."

He lay down next to her, and gathered her up against his body. She put her hand on his chest, tracing shapes over the broad expanse of muscle. "You seem like a man who might be able to handle a whole thing. And you kinda make me feel like less of one. Or at least like…this might be the place for it."

"Sure, if you want to play… You know I'm here to play. But playing is all I got."

"That's okay. I'm trying to figure out my life. I'm trying to figure out what I want to be. Who I am. What it means… James is my father, most likely."

"Are you going to ask your mother directly about it?"

She nodded. "I am. Because I need to know the truth. I'm afraid this is probably it."

"Sometimes, you have to contend with things you don't like about your parents. And I grant you, your dad is a hell of a lot worse than mine."

"Your dad seems… Well, I mean, to me he really seems not bad at all."

"He's not, I suppose. But his relationship with my mom… I wouldn't have been surprised if he'd cheated."

"I'm sorry."

"None of it's your fault."

"Well. I kind of put you in an awkward situation tonight."

He shrugged. "My dad's own behavior actually put him in that situation."

"For what it's worth… I used to look at your family and think… Well, I really wished that I could be part of it."

"I guess that's the thing, then. I never wished that I was part of your family. I suppose that's the difference."

"Yeah, there is imperfect, and there's dysfunctional. Believe me, there's kind of an important distinction between the two."

"We might be skirting the edge of dysfunctional, here," he said.

"Yeah, but I think we can both handle it. And we're not dragging anyone else into it."

He huffed. "True."

"Might as well enjoy this. I have twenty-one days left of indentured servitude from you."

And then suddenly she found herself pinned to the mattress, his large body over hers, his eyes glittering. "Might as well," he growled.

And then, they were done talking for the rest of the night.

Chapter 7

Jackson felt like an ass. He should have left last night when he'd said that he would, but Cricket had looked at him like she was a wounded puppy, and he couldn't bring himself to do it. Still, there hadn't been much of an excuse to stay. Except that he was weak. And human, and basically just a man. And she had presented a temptation he couldn't turn away from.

Though it wasn't just being a man, that was the thing, because if it was, then it would've been about her just being a woman, and fundamentally, he could have turned down any other woman. It was Cricket that was the problem. Cricket was a damn problem.

He was marinating on that as he drove into town for more lumber the next day. She had been up early, at the crack of dawn, without so much as a complaint, while he had been the one who'd had a hell of a time getting his ass out of bed. He was driving back out toward Cricket's spread when he noticed his brother's truck in the oncoming traffic lane. Creed waved his hand, and Jackson found the nearest turnaround and followed his brother, both of them parking by the side of the road. It wasn't extraordinarily unusual to randomly run into his brother about town. Gold Valley was a small enough place. And they were off running similar errands, considering they were both ranchers. They had the same haunts, the same basic routines.

"Fancy meeting you here," he said.

"Likewise," Creed said. "I was figuring on coming out to see you today anyway."

"Oh?"

"Yeah. My wife has been after me to check in on you."

"Why?" Jackson asked.

"Just to make sure nothing untoward is happening between you and her little sister."

Jackson kept his face flat and immovable as stone. "Is that so?"

"Yeah. She told me that Cricket called her the other night inquiring about how to make steak. Because she was cooking for you. And that got Wren stirred up."

"I fail to see what your wife's feelings have to do with me."

"Well, the funny thing is, then I went by the winery this morning, and I talked to Dad, he said that you and Cricket stormed the place last night, and she demanded to know if he was her father."

"Oh."

"And that you said it was really important to know for sure."

"Look, she had a valid suspicion."

"Why? Dad was crazy about Mom. He would never have cheated on her."

Jackson's frustration finally boiled over. Maybe it was Cricket and all the nonsense with her, or just the vast unfairness of his brother's complete and total obliviousness over something Jackson had borne the weight of for years. Whatever the reason, he was at the end of his patience.

"Are you blind, Creed? Dad was not crazy about Mom."

"The hell you talking about? He's been deep in the throes of grief for her for…five years. Completely messed up. Not right at all. You can't tell me that's a man who was not crazy about his wife."

"He's a man who was crazy with guilt." Jackson let out a harsh breath. "Look, I was closer to Mom than you."

"I…feel bad about that. But I was pretty deep in some of my own stuff there for a while."

"I know. It wasn't a criticism. I'm just saying… Believe me, what Cricket thought was valid enough. Did you ever wonder why Dad hated James Maxfield so much? Not just because he's a prick."

"Yeah, I mean it crossed my mind a time or two."

"Dad was in love with *his* wife. Always. And I think, whatever he felt for Mom never overshadowed what he felt for her. It wasn't… It was never fair. Ever. It's not just grief that has Dad a mess. He has a mountain of regret. And he should."

Creed huffed out a breath. "That doesn't make any sense. Why would Mom… Why would she be with him?"

"Why do you think? They stayed together for the kids." He looked at his brother. "That would be us."

"Why did they get married in the first place?"

Jackson sighed and shifted his weight. "Me. She was pregnant with me. Haven't you ever done that math? I have. And anyway, I don't have to rely on math. She told me. I thought… Damn, you know, I thought we had this great, happy family. And then I found out… Not so much. A forced family, and then they tried to… Honey was their attempt at making things better. But that doesn't work. Or at least, it rarely does. Anyway. That's what everything was about with Cricket. She suspected, given that she, like our sister, is a late in life baby… That maybe she was the product of an affair. An affair her mother had always wanted to have. But no. Dad said no."

"Oh. Well, that is entirely different from what Wren was afraid was going on. And I can't say I could really figure out what I thought was happening…" Creed stared past him, off at the thick grove of pine trees that lined the highway. "I don't know what to make of any of this. I… I didn't know that Mom and Dad…"

"They didn't want us to know."

"Why did Mom tell you?" Creed sounded hurt. Jackson didn't have the capacity to deal with his brother's hurt. Not now.

"She had to tell someone. She was lonely. And…"

"Dad was there for her though. He was. He didn't leave. And if he didn't have an affair…"

"You're a married man, Creed, don't tell me you wouldn't feel a difference between being the love of your wife's life, or knowing there was someone else out there that she wanted first."

"Right. But you know..." Creed chuckled. "Wren and I got married because of her pregnancy."

"Given your background, I understand that."

He nodded. "But it's not why we stayed together."

"Yeah, but I think it was why Mom and Dad stayed together."

"Well, I just pulled you over to give you a hard time, I didn't figure you'd give me this depressing as hell story."

"I'm just explaining the last twenty-four hours, which believe me, have been a little weird for me too."

"Well, be careful with her. Wren is really worried."

It was Jackson's turn to stare at the trees.

He could feel his brother's eyes burning into the side of his face. "If you're sleeping with my sister-in-law... I might have to punch you. I'd rather not."

"I'll be careful with her."

"That's not a denial."

"Can't give you a denial."

"Really? Really. *Really? Cricket. Really.*"

He shot his brother a look. "Say it one more time."

"So...she thought you were her half brother, and somehow you ended up... You know what. I don't want to know." Creed lifted his hands and took a step back. "The less I know the better, because I'm going to have to explain it to Wren. And I don't want to be the keeper of that information, because God knows I love my wife, but she is the kind of woman to shoot the messenger. And I like all my body parts where they are."

"So do I."

"And *really* don't let Holden find out." Creed's brother-in-law, married to Emerson, the middle Maxfield sister.

"Why is that?"

"My loyalty is torn. You're my brother. Holden…
Well, his loyalty is in one place firmly. And, also, I get
the feeling he's done some things."

"Look, nothing happened that Cricket didn't want."

"I'm confident in that. I'm still confident it won't
matter to Wren."

"Just let us sort it out."

"I can't keep secrets from her. But I can keep her
busy." Creed grinned.

"Great. Do that. And keep this to yourself. What's
going on with me and Cricket is nobody's business
but ours."

"I just don't get why. I mean, she's cute enough,
sure. But…"

Jackson felt a violent surge of…protectiveness? He
didn't even know. Just something primal and overly
irritable. He couldn't explain what appealed about
Cricket. It was not simple. But… She was special, and
when he saw her as something other than an adver-
sary to be defeated, he could truly see that. She was
tough. And beautiful. Naive in some ways, sure, but
in others… Like a person outside age or time. Not like
anyone or anything he'd ever known. He came back
to that vision he'd had of her the first time he'd rolled
up to the ranch.

When he thought of her as a feral pirate queen on the
deck of her ship. And he should have known then. She
wasn't a woman to take prisoners, and neither would
she be one to negotiate. She wasn't going to give up on
what she wanted half so easily as he had hoped. And
now, he didn't even want her to. Because somewhere
in all of this, he'd begun to root for her. He wanted her

to win. That vulnerable, delicate piece of herself only he'd seen was something he wanted to protect now, not exploit.

"Don't worry about me. And don't worry about Cricket. She can more than handle herself."

And he was...well, dammit all, he was going to help her.

Jackson had been gone for most of the day, and it was probably for the best, Cricket had to concede. She wished he was in bed with her instead of seeing to ranch chores. But the ranch chores were important and all. It was kind of the whole point of having him on the property. But now she wanted the point to be more of him in her bed, and honestly, who could blame her? Having an orgasm was a lot more fun than doing chores.

But...she also needed to do something other than chores today. Which was how she found herself driving to Maxfield Vineyards.

She usually avoided the place as much as humanly possible. But it was weird. Today, with a bit of distance from her family, from everything that they were, and all the pain and isolation she had experienced growing up here... She was not feeling trapped by it. It felt... better. She felt able to appreciate the beauty of it. The rolling vineyards, the vast, Tuscan-style villa. The elaborate pavilions and tasting rooms. It was a beautiful facility, when she wasn't a prisoner.

"Prisoner" wasn't really fair. But she had felt trapped in her circumstances, that was for sure. And now that she had another place to be, now that she had...

Honestly, had a night with Jackson changed her so

much? She looked the same. She had checked herself over in the mirror this morning just to see if this change was visible, that shift that had taken place inside of her last night. But as far as she could tell it wasn't. She took a breath, and put her car in Park, right in the circular drive just in front of the massive entry to her family home. A place that had never, ever felt like home to her. But she didn't have the same knot of dread that she used to have when James was in residence, didn't have the same feeling of discomfort. So there was that.

She knocked, because she didn't live here anymore, and when one of the members of the staff opened the door, she was led in as politely as if she were a guest.

She stood in the foyer, waiting for her mother to appear.

When she did, Cricket could only stare. Her mom was still every inch the lady of the manor, even though the circumstances at the manor had changed pretty drastically.

"Cricket," Lucinda said, smiling brightly. "What brings you by?"

"I… I really need to talk to you. About…" She took a breath. "I spoke to Cash Cooper last night."

"Oh," her mom said, faltering.

"I asked him if he was… If he was my father."

"Cricket…"

"I know that you are in love with him. And I know that he was in love with you. And I know you didn't marry him because you chose money over love. I just thought that maybe…"

"He's not your father."

"That's what he said."

Her mom looked…embarrassed. "Was he…"

"He wasn't mad. I mean, not much. Jackson was kind of mad, but… I don't know. I was just embarrassed. But I really thought… There's something wrong with me? I think? Because I'm not like anyone in this family, and I just thought that maybe I would fit better with the Coopers. And I thought that after I found out that you were in love with him…"

"I was always in love with him. I always will be. I gave things up, Cricket. For a life that I thought would make me happy. But I was very foolish. I was very wrong. And it has taken me all this time to be able to admit it. All this time to be able to understand. Just how… Just how wrong I was. I thought this house could take the place of love. I thought money could do it. And then I thought social standing, because Cash managed to go and make all that money, just to show me what I was missing. I won't tell you I wasn't tempted by him. I won't tell you *we* never were. There were times… We had opportunity, and it was hard. Because I remembered what it was like with him. And it wasn't… I shouldn't tell you all of this. You don't want to know about my love affairs, I'm sure."

Cricket didn't really, it was true. But she could be a whole lot more understanding about them now that she'd experienced a bit of it herself. Would it be like that with Jackson? Forever and ever? Staring at him from across crowded rooms and knowing how it was? If he married someone else… Would she still always remember what it was like to have his hands on her body? What if she married another man?

Frankly, she couldn't imagine it. She didn't really have dreams of being a wife and mother. She had always had dreams about him.

"But you didn't. That's the important part."

"No."

"And did you… With anyone else?"

"No."

"So James Maxfield is my father." It wasn't a question, but a heavy confirmation.

"Yes."

"Okay." Cricket turned, her chest feeling weighted with answers. The fact was, she hadn't wanted to ask her mother before because she had been afraid that this was the answer. And it turned out…it was. There was nothing half so romantic as a hidden family out there waiting for her. Nothing half so wonderful as an explanation for why she was the way she was.

She just was.

And she was going to have to find a way to cope with that, to understand herself.

To be okay with that.

"He said that…" She took a breath. "Cash said that I looked like you." She turned around again to face her mother, looked at her smooth, unlined skin, her sleek blond hair. "I don't see how. He said I reminded him of you."

Her mother's expression became soft. Wistful. "Because back then I did. You're probably the most like me, Cricket, of any of the girls. I was wild, and I was headstrong, and I couldn't be told a damn thing. I made a sport out of daring him. Of pushing him. I felt like I was meant for bigger and better things than I could get in Gold Valley. Bigger and better things than he could give me. And I would yell that at him. I would tell him that if he really wanted me, if he really loved me, then he would figure out a way to give me the kinds of things I wanted. Because you see… I really believed that the man who would make me happy would come with all the things I wanted, and I didn't think about the kinds of things I would give to him. And that was how I ended up in a one-sided marriage where I didn't ask any questions, and I just took everything that came my way. I didn't have dreams of my own. Not beyond what I could have. And when I realized that I was stuck with a man who didn't love me, with a man who wasn't faithful to me… I had you girls. And I wouldn't do anything that might jeopardize my having you. And he used the three of you to threaten me." She closed her eyes. "I'll be completely honest, half the time the only thing that kept me away from Cash Cooper was knowing that if your father found out he would do his best to make sure I never saw you again."

"I'm sorry, Mom," Cricket said. "And I'm sorry I never realized how unhappy you were here."

"Yes, well. I'm the one who made this place." She looked around. "It was my prison. And I built it for myself, and locked myself inside. And you right with me. I never felt like I had a right to offer you any comfort."

Cricket didn't know what to say. Except… She remembered what Jackson had asked her, that first day he had come to her house. "Can I ask… Why did you name me Cricket?"

Her mom smiled. "Because it reminded me of who I used to be. A hot summer night sitting outside and listening to the crickets. Of simpler things and simpler times. And by then I knew… I knew I wasn't ever going to find happiness here. The only happiness I had was you girls, and I didn't… I was distant, because I let my guilt and my fears determine how we connected.

I'm sorry for that. I really am. The divorce—this has been like a slow waking up. I'm not liking everything that I'm seeing around me. My own flaws. My own… failings in all of this."

"James Maxfield is kind of an evil bastard."

"Well, there was a time when I was suited to him. And that doesn't fill me with any great joy."

"I don't understand how you could… I don't want to pile anything on, Mom, and for the most part, I just think… We were all victims of his. But one thing I don't understand is how you could marry him knowing that you loved Cash."

"Cash didn't come after me. He let me marry him. And up until the wedding I imagined him riding up on a white horse and taking me away from it all. I really did. I thought he would rescue me. And he didn't. Instead he found someone else, and they had children right away. Much faster than your father and I did. And I threw myself into loving the money. If Cash hadn't gotten married, I don't think my marriage to your father would've lasted. But my other option was gone."

"Have you ever thought that…now it might not be?"

She smiled sadly. "He's a proud man. I don't think he would have me. I can't say that I blame him."

"I don't think you can know that. Unless you try. And don't you think we all deserve a chance at being happy? Whatever that looks like?"

"I know that you do. I think for me it might be too late."

Cricket left her mom's house with a lot to think about. And she wasn't sure that she liked any of it. It sounded to her like her mother's relationship with Cash had been more than a little dysfunctional. And she couldn't deny that her mom had a decent sized stake in the way things had gone. But she also didn't see the point in the two of them continuing to be sad forever. They both clearly had feelings for each other that they hadn't resolved. But one thing Cricket couldn't imagine was…

She could never marry another man.

The conversation with her mom had solidified that thought. Not after Jackson. She couldn't have another man's children. Chances were, she would grow old with her ranch. But at least she would have her own dreams.

When she pulled up to the house, he was on the porch, hammering boards in place. Each swing of his hammer was hard and decisive, every muscle and tendon in his body working harmoniously toward its goal. He was a thing of beauty. And the porch was… It was practically brand-new. In the few hours since she'd left, he had transformed the place. It was no longer sinking, no longer looking dilapidated. It was incredible. And it was all him.

He was incredible.

Her heart lifted in her chest, and she felt… She didn't really know. Renewed in some ways. Her mother's story was tragic, but it was also a reminder that there was no circumstance Cricket could simply sit back and accept.

She was James Maxfield's daughter. That hadn't been her choice. But everything she did with her life… that was her choice. James didn't own her. Didn't have a claim on her. She was Cricket. Named after the simple summer nights her mother loved and remembered. After a time in her life that had been special to her. After memories that had mattered. And Cricket was made of those things as much as she was her father's DNA.

It made her feel rooted, grounded to this place, and certain of her decisions. Much more so than she had ever been before.

"Horses," she said as soon as she got out of the truck.

"Excuse me?" Jackson looked up, his gaze meeting hers, sending her stomach into a freefall.

"Horses," she reiterated. "I want to breed horses. That's what this ranch is going to be. I've decided. I want to start right away."

"We're going to have to build stables."

"Then let's work out a budget. And I can find a contractor. I know it might take some time, but I'm willing. Because my life is going to be what I want it to be. It doesn't matter what my DNA is. I talked to my mother today. James is my father. For sure and for certain. But that's not even really the biggest thing. My mom lived a life that she didn't love for years because she felt trapped in it. Because she felt like she didn't have a choice. I never want to feel like I don't have a choice. I'm not one determined thing because I'm James's daughter, and not Cash's. I'm not anything but what I decide to be."

"Good for you."

She pointed her index finger at him. "But you can't have my ranch."

"That's okay."

"And you still have to finish out the terms of the bet. I'm not going to have you back out early, just because you can't do your whole secret…thing. I have nothing but your own honor as a man to hold you to it."

"You got me."

"And I want to keep sleeping with you," she said, suddenly resolute in that decision too. "Until this is over."

"You sure?"

"I'm sure. I'm building my life. And this is who I am. I don't sit back having crushes on men and not saying anything. I don't just dream about having a ranch. I'm going to have all those things."

"And then at the end of the thirty days?"

That made her chest feel sore. But she was resolute either way.

"You go your way. I'll go mine."

And she wasn't going to worry about all the things he could and couldn't give her. She was going to focus on what she could do. Who she could be. What she could give to herself.

Because she would never be her mother. A passive participant in her own life.

No.

She was the one who decided.

Nobody else. She would have a ranch, and a man. And sure, it would be temporary. But it would be hers. The start of something.

And she was so very ready for her life to begin.

Chapter 8

The crew had started work on Cricket's stables. It was weird, now that his focus had shifted. He actually wanted her enterprise to be a success. And that meant looking at things from an entirely different point of view. That meant teaching her about ranching, rather than just making overarching statements and watching her stumble around. It meant bringing her alongside him for repairs, not just to show her how hard it was, but to show her that she could. And with each improvement on the property, he saw her become more firmly rooted in her sense of who she was, and there was a great sense of accomplishment inside of him that he couldn't quite explain. Except that... Except that he'd felt useless to fix the sadness that he saw inside of his mother, and being able to do something to give Cricket a better life did something to help heal that sense of failure.

Somewhere in the back of his mind, he always thought that if his mother had gotten better, maybe he would have helped her leave his father. Given her a place to stay, proved to her that it didn't matter whether they were together like a traditional family. What really mattered was her happiness. She didn't need to stay. Not for him. But he'd never said it to her. She'd died before he ever could. Before he'd gotten his own place up and running. And maybe part of him had still been working toward that with wanting to expand to Cricket's property. But he didn't need to do that now. What he could do was help Cricket find her way to a dream.

And then maybe that would help put something to rights in his own life. Cricket wasn't out with him today, she was off bustling around the house. He told her he would check in on the building site, and then he was going to drive up to the upper pasture, and get the lay of things. It really was a beautiful property.

He thought back to what she'd asked, if ranching was in his blood, as he stood out in the middle of the bright, patchwork field, filled with brilliant green mixed with patches of dark olive and backed by rich pine. As he looked at the sprigs of yellow that clustered around the perimeter interwoven with waving fire-colored Indian paintbrush and dappled orange fritillaria, at the pale blue sky that would be a richer blue come the height of summer, he knew the answer was... It was deeper than blood. It was down in his bones. He was part of the land, and it was part of him. Something that went further than want.

And he'd never thought about it that way before. Only when Cricket had asked, did that thought grow into a feeling.

And he understood. He understood why she wanted this. Why she was here. It was true. When it was part of you, it simply was. Nothing you could do about it.

He heard the sound of a truck engine and turned, and there was Cricket, rumbling up the dirt road, driving that big beast of hers.

That was another thing that was getting down into his blood. Because he hadn't just been helping her on the property.

No.

They'd spent long nights in beds that were too small, exploring, tasting, and he loved to say that he was teaching her there as much as he was around the ranch, but it was more than that. Because Cricket was a whole new landscape, one he'd never seen or explored or imagined before. She was strong, and she was energetic.

She had no limit as far as he could tell. Nothing embarrassed her.

Rather, she touched and tasted with full enthusiasm, never shying away from anything. That wild girl he'd seen out on the swing at the Maxfield Vineyards brought that sense of the unrestrained into the bedroom, and there were no lessons involved in any of it. No. He was just on the ride. At the mercy of it. And he loved every minute.

He gritted his teeth. There was no getting attached to it.

Why not?

He pushed that thought aside. Cricket got out of the truck, wearing a white tank top and tight jeans, holding a blanket and a picnic basket. And she looked like far too much of a temptation for him to handle.

And hell, she wasn't a temptation he had to resist over the last couple of weeks, so why should he start now? He crossed the distance between them, and wrapped his arms around her slender waist, pulled her into his arms and planted a kiss on her lips.

"What are you doing?"

"I brought lunch," she said, a pleased smile curving her lips. "I've been practicing being a good pioneer woman. I made bread, I cooked a ham and I've made sandwiches."

"You really made bread?"

"Yes," she said, her face shining with triumph. "And two of the four loaves turned out. So, you have sandwiches."

"Cricket, that was awfully nice of you."

"I know," she said. "And often I'm not very nice, so it surprised me too."

"You're plenty nice."

Or at least, her particular brand of sharpness was nice for him. Didn't really matter either way.

She spread the blanket out in the meadow and took a seat, and he stared at her, the golden glow of the sun shining on her face. And he couldn't figure out quite why she'd done it. Quite why she'd given him this. He couldn't recall anyone else doing similar for him. Sure, his mom cooked for them. But… She was his mom. Family.

Cricket wasn't family.

She wasn't beholden to him in any way. He'd lost a bet to her. That was why he was here. And his education hadn't included cooking. She had just done this. Just because.

And it did something to his chest that made him

want to growl, because he wasn't a sentimental man. And he didn't concern himself much with things like this. But it was…unexpected, and it was a hell of a lot more than he'd ever wanted or gotten from another person.

It shocked him how good everything she made was. Though he supposed it probably shouldn't surprise him. Everything Cricket set her mind to she did with her whole self. And it didn't mean she couldn't fail, but she was determined enough that he had a feeling she would have baked ten loaves of bread in order to present him with just one. Because what she wanted, she went and got. And that was something. It was really something.

He liked to watch Cricket eat, among the many things he enjoyed about her. Because she did that with the same level of ferocity and intensity she did everything else. She was sitting on the blanket with her elbows propped up on her knees, her sandwich gripped tightly in her hands. She had brought cans of Coke for the two of them, and when she had eaten about half of her sandwich, she brushed her hands off and picked up the Coke, tipping it back like a beer.

She looked over at him. "What?"

"What?" he repeated.

"You're staring at me."

"You're pretty." That made him sound like a dumb high school boy. Come to that, he kind of felt like one.

But Cricket blushed. Cricket, tough little thing that she was, blushed, and he found that was all the payment he needed for the worse moment of feeling like an idiot. Something he wasn't accustomed to.

"Well," Cricket said. "So are you."

"Really?"

"Yeah. I mean, I've always thought so."

"Yeah," he said. "You mentioned something about that." He wasn't sure he wanted to know. Because already he felt some kind of strange obligation to her. Deeper than his obligation to any other woman he'd ever had a physical relationship with. And he wasn't sure he wanted to dig in any deeper, but sitting there under that brilliant blue sky, eating her homemade bread and ham sandwich, he didn't know if there was any other option but to dig in. He didn't know how *not* to be involved with her, and it was absurd. It had started with a bet, an assumption on her part that they might be related, a nefarious plan on his part to talk her into selling him her ranch…

But maybe that was it. The whole thing was so bizarre—how could they come away from it with neutral feelings about each other? Maybe it was impossible. Maybe the only option in a situation like this was to develop some kind of attachment. Maybe it was the only way.

"I'm pretty sneaky," Cricket said. "I mean, I'm used to hiding what I feel from people. And you were no exception. I mean, the way that I felt about you. I would just tell my sisters that I thought cowboys were annoying. And that I didn't want anything to do with any of them. It was a pretty convincing ruse, if I say so myself. Plus, I knew you were way off limits. A thousand years older than me."

"Hey. Not a thousand."

"Well, it seemed like it at the time. The gap feels a lot smaller now." She smiled. "Oh, I didn't like any of the boys at school. None of them. But how could I, when I already liked a man? And a Cooper at that. I knew nobody would understand. But nobody understood me, so that didn't really bother me. And so I just…kept it a secret. And then I was so mad when Wren hooked up with your brother, because I felt for so long that being attracted to you was this great, impossible thing, another sort of deeply rooted difference in who I was. In my genetic makeup versus the rest of my family. And then she got to Creed before I could get to you. Honestly. It was an insult. But still, when she told me that I would maybe find my own cowboy… I played it off. I told her no. That I didn't want anything to do with a man like Creed, and I didn't. I just wanted you. So it feels right, you know? To start this new phase of my life with you… Though I'm not asking you for anything. I promise."

"Well, happy to help."

Except it made him feel… He didn't even know. It kind of made him angry, because she was the younger one. She was the one without experience, and she made him feel like he had no idea what he was doing. It didn't seem right. That was all.

He should be the one who knew what he was doing. He should be the one who had total confidence in everything taking place between them. But he couldn't say that he did. He couldn't give a reason. Couldn't give a speech about what he was doing here. He had written it off as being male and basic and taking the sex that was on offer, but he knew that wasn't true. It wasn't how he did things. It wasn't how he looked at women. And he had been telling himself a story, all this time. Cricket's story made a lot more sense, and had a purpose behind it. And he just… He just wanted to touch her. It was a hell of a thing.

"You know, the way you were talking to your dad that day… Tell me about your mom. I mean, tell me about all that. Because you know about my dad, and you know all about my mom…"

"They were obligated to be together. And it was primarily because of me," he said. Because he might as well tell her. She was right. He'd had a front row seat to all of her issues. He'd talked to Creed about it, sure. But Cricket? She could hear it all. Because she didn't have a connection to the family, so why not? It was a safer place. This moment out here in the meadow.

"One day when I was sixteen, she was crying. Then I asked her what was wrong. We were the two that got up early. And we used to spend mornings together. I loved that. So I would have all this extra time with her. And one morning, I asked her what was wrong. And it was like everything I ever thought about my life broke to pieces. My father married her because she was pregnant. My father was in love with another woman. He'd told my mother that. Before they got married. He was honest, if nothing else. And she thought that he'd fall in love with her. But instead, it had just become years of the two of them stuck. Because they had a family. Because they had a business. Because they had all these things that were obligated to come before having feelings. Before love.

"And you know, I'm not over-bothered by my dad anymore. I think that was enough for him. He couldn't have your mom, so he made himself a life he enjoyed. But I'm not sure my mother ever got to fall in love with anyone. Not for real. Not and have them love her back. She was just stuck. With a partner, sure. And when she was sick… I can't fault my dad for how he

was. He *was* a partner. He cared for her. And he stayed
with her. And you know, plenty of marriages that are
founded on love, they don't end up that way. Somebody gets sick and they go through a years-long battle, and the other person leaps. It's too much for them.
And sometimes I wonder if maybe my dad not being
in love with her made him more able to take care of
her during that time. It's complicated as hell. Because
there was a very real partnership between the two of
them, but sometimes it made my mother feel broken,
and I will never not feel responsible for that. Like I
should've found some way to fix it."

"They made their choices," Cricket said. "That's
what I'm realizing about my mother. For all her own
misery, for all that I feel bad for her sometimes, for all
that my father was an unforgivable asshole, my mom
made her choices. She wanted money. And she thought
that would be enough. She wanted to have things, and
thought that would transcend love, but it didn't. And
then she didn't leave. She stayed. Because she was
afraid. And all her reasons, they were real enough, but
they were still excuses. Even if they were pretty valid
ones. My mom stayed with James for us. Because she
was afraid that he would find a way to take us from
her. But she also could've had the fight. She weighed
her options. And she chose."

"I have some sympathy for that," he said. "If she
thought she couldn't win…"

"It was still a choice. Just like your mother had one.
It's not like it was the 1800s. They could've gotten a
divorce. They could have. Nobody had to be unhappy.
They sat there in rules they made for themselves, and
lived lives they made for themselves, prison walls they

decided were okay. That isn't your fault, and it isn't mine."

"Yeah, but on the other side, now your mom has a chance to make something new. Mine doesn't. It's a hell of a thing."

"I know." She shook her head. "I'm not saying it would've been easy. I'm just saying you can't take their choices and blame yourself for them."

"You're twenty-two years old."

"Yeah. And you're what? Thirty-four? Thirty-five? So what? I'm not stupid. I've had a lot of time to think. That's what comes of being the isolated, odd one out in your family. You have way too much time to think. And believe me, I've had tons. I don't need experience to have figured that out."

"So you have the whole world all figured out, do you?"

"I mean, I'm not gonna say the whole world. But maybe my piece of it."

This girl. This woman. She didn't know when to question or doubt. She dove headlong into everything. Bets at a poker table, wild conclusions and into his bed. And he just…he liked that about her.

"Bold claim, little Cricket."

"I don't know, things make more sense now than they ever have. I didn't think that was possible. I just walked through the messiest, weirdest time of my life. And it's really not so bad. And yeah, I basically do have it all sorted out."

He wrapped his arms around her, and pulled her on top of him, laying them both back on the blanket. He looked into her earnest face, and desire stirred in his body. "You have everything figured out, is that it?"

"Basically. The mysteries of sex are even solved."

"Every last one?" he pressed.

He didn't know why he needed this right now, but he did. It was deeper than lust, that was the problem. He couldn't write it off as simply basic desire. He'd wanted to. He'd tried to. But it was so much more than that. That was the thing. With her, it always would be. And whatever was happening between the two of them, she didn't have to be here. They didn't have to be here. They were choosing it, out here under the unending sky. With the land and the ranch in their blood, and his need for her pumping hot and insistent through his body.

"Bet you can't teach me anything," he said, his voice rough.

And Cricket, true to form, sat up, her thighs on either side of him, and stripped her white tank top up over her head without pause. She was wearing a plain, matching bra, her lean, athletic body a sight to behold. "Is that a *bet* bet, cowboy?"

"Sure."

"You know, historically, you lose bets with me."

"Yeah. I feel like a real loser right now." With her sweet ass perched on top of him, and all her beauty blocking out the sun.

"Well."

"Just remember that there are some bets I lose on purpose." He gripped her hips, sliding his hands up to her slim waist, then up further still, brushing his thumbs over her breasts. Then he reached around and unhooked her bra, flinging it off somewhere in the grass.

She made a small sound that might have been indignant, but he didn't much care. Because she was bare and gorgeous and perfect and he was dying for a taste.

He pressed his palm firmly against the center of her back and brought her down toward him, toward his mouth. He sucked one perfect, ripe bud between his lips, and the cry that escaped her lips wasn't indignant this time. Not at all. It was one of pleasure, one of desire, and he reveled in it. She wrenched his shirt over his head, wiggling away from him as she did. And he pinned her down on her back, her arms up over her head, and kissed her deep.

"Little Crickets with smart mouths get themselves in trouble," he said.

A challenge glimmered in her eyes. "Do we? I sure hope so."

"Do you?"

"Yes. I lack discipline."

"Is that so?"

"I've mostly been neglected. I need a firm hand."

"I could probably provide you with one."

"So many promises. And yet..."

He growled, unsnapped her jeans, unzipped them and pushed them down her thighs, and she helped eagerly. Then she wiggled downward, kissing his chest, his stomach, still on her back beneath him as she undid his pants and freed him. She peered up at him, squeezing his length and making a sound of purely feminine satisfaction.

"You're really kind of a work of art," she said, leaning forward and rubbing her cheek against him. He could honestly say a woman had never done that. And the look on her face made him so hard he thought he might burst.

She shoved lightly, and he moved, going onto his back as she bit her lip and looked down at him. Then she knelt over him, taking him slowly into her mouth, the sweet, wet heat an assault on his senses. She tortured him. And she wasn't practiced or knowing or anything like that. Didn't have a parade of well coordinated tricks, but she made up for it with enthusiasm. Pure and simple. She was a woman in full enjoyment of his body, and he didn't think he'd ever experienced anything quite like that. And hell, looking at her, at the elegant line of her spine, her ass up in the air as she pleasured him, was something more powerful than he'd ever experienced.

This moment was free of obligation. Something in his chest began to unravel, as if each pass of her tongue, each movement of her mouth over his body, was working to loosen something inside him, unraveling something he hadn't been aware was there.

Who knew that sandwiches and a blow job out in the middle of a field would be enough to make a man almost believe in romance? He sure as hell hadn't. But it was something. *She* was something. Far and away beyond anything he'd ever known or experienced or figured he might want to understand.

Cricket.

She pleasured him until he thought he couldn't take it anymore. Then he reached in his back pocket, grabbed his wallet and took out the condom, tearing it open and guiding her up his body as he sheathed himself with one practiced hand.

She seated herself on top of him and took him inside of her slowly, achingly so, her mouth dropping open, her head falling back. She flexed her hips, a ragged sound on her lips, and then she began to move, slowly at first. Then more quickly. But it still wasn't enough for him. He grabbed on to her hips, moved her up and down over his body, driving them both crazy. Pushing them both until she cried out her pleasure. And then he reversed their positions, pounding into her, unable to hold himself back any longer. It was primal and urgent, and exactly what he needed to compound that strange unraveling in his chest. Only then, she opened her eyes and met his.

And he couldn't breathe. Not then. Just as his climax took him over, he was lost. In Cricket. In the look of wonder on her face, the absolute trust there. He was her first lover. The only man who had ever touched her like this. He was bound up in all of the strange things she'd been going through for all this time, and he didn't want to be even more turned on by that, but he was. And he lost himself then, just went over the edge, growling out her name as she cried out his and convulsed around him. As she stared up at him, the look of absolute contentment in her eyes undid him. She didn't know better. Didn't know a different man.

He had taken her crush and used it to his advantage.

He had taken her inexperience as a rancher, as a poker player, and had used it to his advantage there too.

He felt… Well, he felt like shit, actually. Because there was something in him that knew instinctively he could never answer the depth of longing in her eyes. There was something in him that knew he had bound her to him. Her childish feelings, her awakening desire—she would feel connected to him in a way she shouldn't. That was a fact. That was the problem. And he would… He would what? Take her away from this place that she was turning into her own? Away from this life she was making and into his? He would just be another man taking a woman's dreams and putting them underneath his own.

They would be done at the end of the month. That was the deal. And whatever possibilities he felt out here in the wilderness… They just weren't to be.

That was good. It was right that he knew that, felt that. Everything would go back to the way it had been, when all this was said and done. That was for the best. Because he wouldn't be able to give Cricket what she wanted. Not really. And when she realized that, then they would both be trapped in the exact same hell their parents had been trapped in.

And he wouldn't have that.

Not ever.

But he didn't say anything. Instead, he kissed her forehead, and she snuggled against him. And right out there in the open, completely naked, the two of them fell asleep.

What happened at the end of the wager was a problem for their future selves. Because right now, they had this.

And Jackson's last thought before he drifted out of consciousness was that he couldn't remember the last time he'd felt quite this content.

Chapter 9

It was the thirtieth day.

Cricket hadn't had the heart to ask if he would be staying the entire day, or leaving right away, or… She didn't know. And she was afraid to find out exactly what the answer was.

She was a coward.

She desperately wanted this to keep on going. She desperately wanted him to stay with her.

Right. So you're going to beg him to stay in your little ranch house? And for what? You're trying to find your own way…

No. She couldn't beg him to stay.

But they woke up the morning of the thirtieth day in the same bed just as they had every morning since they'd begun sleeping together, and he had gone out to work the same as he had from the beginning.

And so when he returned that evening, dirty and disheveled, she breathed out a sigh of relief.

Maybe he wasn't ready for things to change either. Maybe things wouldn't change. Maybe it would all stay the same, just for a little while. Maybe they could put off all the hard conversations for another time. They could say goodbye another day. She had cooked. Just in case. And she had been rewarded. It was funny, how much she enjoyed cooking. And she would have been more annoyed about the fact that she liked such a traditionally feminine pursuit, except that he seemed to enjoy it so much, and he appreciated it. She thought back to the day she'd made bread and brought out ham sandwiches. Oh yes, he'd appreciated that a whole lot. She felt a dreamy smile cross her face when she thought about it. These times with Jackson had been... Well, they'd been everything.

He'd been everything she'd ever fantasized about.

She knew this moment was supposed to be about moving on. About moving into the next phase of her life, but...

No. It doesn't bear thinking about.

Except, he was here.

And she kept thinking that, even as they each built hamburgers out of the ingredients she had laid out.

"Jackson," she said softly as they finished eating. "How was your day?"

"Good. And yours?"

"Good and—"

She cut herself off. Because she didn't care. She didn't want to have this conversation. She really didn't. She didn't want to talk at all. Because her insides were jumbled up and everything hurt. Because this was the last day, and she didn't know how to ask him if he would stay. She didn't know how to explain to herself, in a way that made her not feel silly, why she might ask him to stay.

Because I want to marry him.

And I want to have his children.

Because I would be his ranch wife in this house or any house.

Because he was her dream. And that was the bottom line.

She was young, and she was supposed to go out and live. She knew that. She wasn't supposed to want a man she had been completely hopeless over since she was twelve. She was supposed to experience more. Have more lovers. Travel. Something.

But she just didn't want to.

And she had the sick, terrible feeling that—much like her mother—there was really only one man for her, and there would never be anything that would take away her feelings. So she didn't want to waste time talking.

She flung herself into his arms, climbing up on the same chair as him, her legs on either side of his, the heart of her right up against where he was rapidly growing hard. And she kissed him. Kissed him until she thought she might die. Kissed him because she thought if she *didn't* she might die.

He stole her oxygen and became it all at once, and she couldn't have explained that feeling if she'd been put before a firing squad. She had never thought in terms of fate. She had always believed she was a pragmatist. But he felt like fate. This moment felt like fate. And she really couldn't deny it. Didn't really want to. Didn't want it to end.

He stood up from the chair, and he swept their plates to the side, breaking them on the floor. "I owe you a set of dishes," he said roughly.

"I don't care," she said.

Oh she *really* didn't care. Because she just wanted him, wanted this. And nothing else mattered. Not plates, not anything. And she gave thanks that she had worn a dress, which she so rarely did, because it made everything easily accessible for him. Because then he had his hands at her hips. Had his fingers between her thighs, stroking her, stoking the fires of her desire. This was like madness. This was like every fantasy she'd ever had.

And she had a terrible feeling that it had been love she'd been feeling from the very beginning. Love and fate—and that was why. That was why it had been him from the time she was twelve years old. And it didn't matter how much she wanted to deny it. It simply was. It simply, simply was. But he was here. He was here.

And he had broken dishes and cleared the table and was kissing her on top of it.

This table that had been an emblem of everything she'd been missing.

And she'd thought what she'd wanted had been some generic idea of a sitcom family. And she'd tried to shoehorn Jackson into that picture. But that wasn't what she'd wanted. It hadn't been quiet dinners that she was missing. It had been him. Just him. It wasn't an aching for domesticity that she felt that first night they'd sat down to dinner together, it was a life spent with him. It had been things shared with this man that had called to her from the very first time she'd ever seen him.

It didn't matter if the idea was crazy. It didn't matter if she was younger than he was. It didn't matter if she was just starting out. Because she knew.

He'd made fun of her the other day, when she'd said she'd understood all these things, but she did. She understood this. Now, suddenly, in his arms—she understood.

She loved him.

And that was all there was to it.

She loved him and she wanted to be with him. And whatever else she needed to experience, it didn't matter. Because this was the one thing her heart and her body had known from the beginning. A lifetime spent feeling like she might always have to be second best, not quite so spectacular as her sisters, had seen her trying to find another explanation for how she felt. To find a way to protect her heart. But there was no protecting it, not now. She felt exposed. Cut open. She couldn't hide or protect herself even if she wanted to. So she didn't try. She surrendered to this madness between them.

And then he was inside of her, the table hitting up against the wall with each and every thrust. And he was amazing. In every way. And she let herself feel it. All of it. The love she felt for him expanding, growing in her chest, so much so that she thought she might burst. So much so that she nearly wept, and when her orgasm finally broke over her, she did. She shook and cried and held him, as his own release took him over.

And when it was done, he stood, and she just lay there, wrecked. The dishes on the floor a metaphor for her body.

"I…"

"Jackson," she said, at the same time.

"Cricket, this has been… It's been… The bet's over."

She just lay there, frozen, her arms spread wide, like

a butterfly that had been pinned in place in a collection, unable to move, her back against the table.

"Are you leaving?"

"It's the end of the bet," he said again.

"Day thirty," she said. "You almost left me that first night too. Why don't you just…not."

His eyes looked tormented then, pained. "I should have left you then. That's the thing. Better late than never."

"No…"

"But it has to be some time. I've got a ranch. I've got a life, and so do you."

"Well, maybe don't leave me with my fucking dinner plates on the floor, you asshole," she said.

He didn't flinch. Instead, he righted his clothing and went over to the corner, grabbed the broom and the dustpan. His actions reminded her so much of the first night he'd been here, when he had fixed things and she had swept, that she nearly cried. And she just lay there, naked, while he swept up the glass on the floor, but left all the pieces of her heart.

"If you ever need anything—if, when the horses come, you need something… You just let me know, Cricket."

"No," she said.

Because what she wanted from him, he wasn't going to give.

The words were lumped in her throat, and she couldn't bring herself to ask for them. And when he left her house, and she was there, nothing but misery, she had to wonder if she had changed at all.

Because she hadn't said what needed to be said. She

hadn't. She'd just left it all there, in her chest, afraid of rejection.

What was the point? What was the point of any of it if she hadn't gotten strong enough to say what she needed?

What was the damn point?

But she didn't go after him. And for the next several days, she did nothing at all. Until she started to realize that something wasn't right. Not just the loneliness or her heart. She was pretty upset by Jackson leaving, and by his not coming back, but not enough to screw with her cycle. And when she showed up at her sister Emerson's house, practically shivering from the cold and clutching a bag that contained a pregnancy test, she was in a daze.

"What are you doing here?"

"I couldn't go to Wren. Because she is married to Creed."

"Yes," Emerson said, stepping back away from the door. "She is."

Cricket stepped inside, and held up the test.

Emerson touched her stomach. "I'm actually good. But is there something you need to tell me?"

"Yes," Cricket said. "I mean, maybe. I need to use your bathroom."

"You know you can."

"Please don't tell anybody," Cricket said.

"I won't."

She went into the bathroom, and didn't come out for way longer than the prescribed number of minutes. It didn't take long for Emerson to knock.

"I feel like your lack of communication indicates the test results were not what you wanted." Her sister's voice was soft through the door.

"No," Cricket said. But even as she said that, she didn't feel like it was true. She wasn't devastated. She wasn't even sad. It felt…right somehow. That there was no way she was going to get out of a relationship with Jackson without keeping something of him.

Without being changed.

"Honey," Emerson said. "Open the door."

And Cricket did, knowing she must look every inch the bedraggled insect her name suggested she might be.

"Whatever you need. I'm not here to judge. If you need a ride to anywhere, if you need me to provide you with an alibi while you collect a weapon to go kill someone…"

"No," Cricket said.

"No to…"

"Any of those things. I'm fine. I mean, I will be. I've just got to…tell him."

"And by him, do I take it you mean Jackson Cooper?"

"The very same. And I didn't want Wren to tell Creed to kill him."

"Well, I'm fixing to tell Holden to kill him, so all you're really doing is sparing Creed's conscience."

"Please don't kill him. I've got to tell him."

"Sure."

"I'm not upset."

"You look upset."

"Well we're not really…together anymore. So that kind of sucks."

"Well, you don't need him. You've got us. Whatever you want to do, you've got us."

"I want to have a baby," Cricket said. "And I didn't think I did. But now that it's happening… I mean, I guess it's not a bad thing that I'm not horrendously unhappy about it."

"Yeah," Emerson said. "I guess so."

"I just need...to see him. Before anything else."

Emerson had been protective, but Cricket managed to extricate herself from her sister and get herself on her way to Jackson's place. She had never been there before, and she was stunned by how impressive the modern ranch house was. All black windows, reddish wood siding and charcoal paint. An extraordinary collection of shapes and angles. So very different from the classic little farmhouse she had.

They were so different.

But...

At their core, they had plenty in common.

There was a reason they were in this situation, after all. Chemistry, for sure, but more than that.

She would never forget that day they had spent out on the picnic blanket. He might have been stern and cold the last time they made love. The last time she'd seen him, but that wasn't the sum total of what they were as a couple.

A couple.

But they had never been that, had they? They'd been two people bonded together by a bed, by her pain and...

And glimmers of his. Which he had shared, but so sparingly. And she knew there was more to him. She did. Knew there was more to who he was and everything that he carried around inside of him, even if she didn't know quite all what it was.

But this was the time, she supposed. This was where the rubber met the road and the...well, the positive pregnancy test met with their present reality.

She took a deep breath and got out of her truck, making her way up the paved walk that led to the large, flat entryway. The door was huge, and it made Cricket feel tiny. She stood there and took a breath, trying not to be reminded of feeling tiny in other circumstances. Standing outside the door to her father's office. Sitting way down at the end of a long banquet table, feeling lost in the family villa.

No, this was different. Because she was standing there a changed woman from who she'd been back then. When she'd just been a girl. When she hadn't known who she was or what she wanted. When he called her little Cricket, it wasn't a bad thing. And she didn't mind. When he said it, it somehow made her feel special, protected. And right now, she was protecting a life inside of her. And that made her feel strangely powerful. Renewed and changed.

She'd never really thought about being a mother. And in fact, in passing, had thought she wouldn't be. After all, her own experiences with family hadn't been any good. But she didn't feel tied to that. Not now. Not anymore. Whatever the Maxfields were, it didn't make Cricket Maxfield one of them. It didn't mean she had to repeat their legacy over and over again. Somehow, that little inner boosting helped buoy her on, and she raised her hand and knocked on the solid oak door. She shook her hand out, because it hurt. And she wasn't even sure it had made a sound in the gigantic space.

But then, the door opened, and she jumped back. Because there he was, standing in the doorway wearing a tight black T-shirt, jeans and a black cowboy hat. And he looked…well, amazing.

"Hi," she said.

"Cricket," he responded. "What are you doing here?"

"Well, that's not the friendliest greeting."

"Sorry. Do you want to come in?"

"Probably should."

He opened the door, and let her into the room made of the same wood as the exterior of the house, glossy black details punctuating the rustic look, making it feel somehow modern. The room was huge, square, with a ceiling so tall it brought her back to that place of smallness.

Of course, Jackson and all his height contributed to that, as well.

"We need to talk," she said. "The way you left me… I wanted you to stay."

"Yes, and I explained that I couldn't." His jaw was tight, his expression firm.

"Yeah, and you didn't give me a good reason. So I'd like to hear it. I really would."

Before she told him what she had to say, she wanted to know what he might say to her without that information.

"It's complicated."

"No. Complicated is having a crush on a man for years, then finding out he might be your half brother, then wanting to sleep with him anyway. Then finding out he's not your half brother and sleeping with him for the duration of a thirty-day wager. That's complicated. So, we've been through complicated already, so whatever else you have on your mind, whatever else you have to tell me, is not going to touch that. I think we can figure it out. Trust me when I say I'm pretty resilient."

"All right, Cricket," he said. "You really want to have this conversation?"

"Yes. I do."

"I don't want to get married. I mean, what's the point? It just two people being tied together for no particular reason that I can see."

"So, why does there have to be marriage? Why can't we just be together?"

"I would never want to be responsible for not loving someone enough. For doing to them what my father did to my mother. And at the end of the day, whether I admire or look up to him or not, I'm Cash Cooper's son."

"And I'm James Maxfield's daughter, but I'm not going to sexually harass anyone. I'm not going to treat my kids like an afterthought and my wife…well, husband, like a trophy. It doesn't matter whose son you are. What matters is what kind of man you are. And that's your choice."

"Okay then, it's my choice not to put myself in a position where I could hurt someone that way."

"So you don't think you could love me."

She stared at him, willing herself not to break his gaze. Not to be a wimp. She would brazen this out. She just would.

"It's not you."

"Oh, it's not you, it's me. Very original. You know, Jackson, I expected better from you. Better from us. For us. We are not like anyone else. So don't be a cliché now."

"I'm not trying to hurt you…"

"Another good one. Who writes your dialogue? Because it's not very good."

"I'm sorry."

"And I'm pregnant."

Chapter 10

Jackson felt like a bomb had been dropped in the middle of his living room. It was like watching a horror movie. Looking back on the last few weeks. Sitting there, wanting to tell the idiot not to go into that house, but he'd gone in anyway. And now here he was. Exactly the thing he'd been trying to avoid.

She was pregnant.

That was absolutely everything that he hadn't wanted to happen.

"When did you find out?"

"Literally an hour ago? I went to my sister's house—not the one who is married to your brother—and then I came straight here."

"What the hell are we going to do?"

"Well, the unfortunate thing is I was kinda hoping you would have something better to say than what you just did."

"You understand that we can't get married."

"Well, fantastic," Cricket said. "I figure I'll just find another man to marry, then."

"You damn well will not."

"But you don't want to marry me. Then maybe somebody should. Because maybe I care about that kind of thing." She took a big, deep breath. "Maybe I care about tradition and I don't want my child to be a bastard. Did you ever think about that?"

"Well, do you?"

"No. What I care about is the fact that you're being ridiculous. We are good together."

"And this is exactly the kind of thing I wanted to avoid. This obligation. This idea that two people have to be together. For the sake of the child. Do you know what it does to a child, Cricket? I was worried about you. About what I might do to you if I couldn't be what you needed… But a kid. Dammit, that kid is basically me. You know what it's like to find out you're the unhappy glue that held your parents together for better or for worse? Mostly worse?"

"We already talked about this. It's all about choices and—"

"But I've seen what it does. If I committed to that, if I committed to you… I would never let you leave."

"Great. I don't want to leave," she said. "I want to be with you. I want to stay with you. Why is that bad? Why would it be so wrong?"

"I don't love you," he said, the words scraping his throat raw, and he knew they felt wrong. He knew they *were* wrong. But he couldn't find any other words. Couldn't figure out what else to say, what else might come from that hammering feeling in his chest.

"What if I said I loved you?"

"That's what we can't do, Cricket. We cannot have that. We would make each other miserable. I would make you miserable."

"I want to be with you. I'm choosing that. What about my choice? Maybe I want to be with you even if I would be sorry that you didn't love me. Maybe I'd rather be with you than not."

"Cricket…"

"No. Be honest. Be honest about what you want and what you don't want, Jackson. But don't blame it on me, and don't blame it on your need to protect me. Because that's not what's happening here. You're not protecting me. You're…protecting yourself. I'm standing here, and I'm not scared. I'm not scared to love you. I'm not scared to have this baby. And you know what? I'm not scared to do it alone, either. I would rather not. I mean, flat out, I'd rather not. But that's just because I'd rather share my life with you. Because I have never felt so happy as I did living in that farmhouse with you. And so I would weather anything to figure out how we could work. You're the one who doesn't want to. And I can't quite figure out why.

"You think because I'm young, because I was inexperienced, that I can't understand what I want. But I do, Jackson. I do. I have always known what I wanted. A place in this world where I fit, and to be with you. It seems to me that what you're after is a life where you won't regret anything. And I don't think anyone can guarantee you that, Jackson, I really don't. We could be together, for better or worse, like you said. And maybe sometimes it would be worse. But I think it would still be a better kind of worse than being apart."

"Because you don't know what that looks like. Not really. I do. I watched my mom… I watched her wish for another life. And I was the cause of her not having it."

"So, we can get married. And if you were miserable, we could get divorced."

"Cricket…"

"No, really, what's your problem? You're afraid of what? You're afraid of failing? Because we're not trapped. We wouldn't be. It would be up to us. But you're afraid of something. Otherwise…this would be a different conversation. You're acting like I didn't grow up around a dysfunctional marriage. So why don't you stop hiding behind the one you grew up around. I thought cowboys were supposed to be brave."

Her words were like a dagger through his heart. He did feel like a coward. He felt like the worst kind of coward, standing there and offering her absolutely nothing. Standing there and failing her, except…

He knew what he knew.

He knew what it was to be a child who had been part of a marriage of obligation. More than that, he knew what it was to be the child who'd caused it. And maybe Creed had been willing to do that to be with his kid, but his brother had been through something entirely different. His brother had been barred from seeing his child.

His child.

So Jackson was going to live in a different house than his kid?

This was why they'd done it. He could understand it. That was the thing. Standing there staring at her, and the enticement of the future they could have…

But Cricket hadn't said she loved him.

She was standing there, asking for something that would make their lives easier on a surface level. The thing that so many people did. To try and make a family for a child.

But he knew that beneath the surface of the happiest-looking nuclear family there could be rot and decay. A kind of desperate sadness that nobody saw but the people on the inside of the arrangement.

And whatever he was, he didn't want to be her obligation. Whatever he was, he didn't want to be her regret.

You're protecting yourself...

How? He didn't feel protected. Not now. What he felt was angry. Infuriated and just damn helpless.

He hadn't done any different than his parents. And that was a galling thing. But he would do different now. He would. He would do better, for them both.

"Do you even want to be this baby's father?"

"I'll be a father. If I made a kid, I'm going to take care of the kid."

"It's a shame you can't feel a little bit of that for me."

"Whether you see it or not, Cricket, this is me caring."

"No, I don't see it," she said, her tone as icy as her expression.

"We'll find a way through this."

"To what? Coparenting? Sharing custody? Will we trade our kid back and forth in the parking lot of the grocery store?"

He didn't like anything about the future she painted with those words. He didn't like any of this. What he wanted to do was grab her and pull her up against him, pick her up in his arms and carry her upstairs and make her his.

He wanted to keep her.

And she would stay.

For the child.

And he would still be that obligation he'd always been.

He gritted his teeth, shoved that aside. "Whatever you need."

"Except a husband."

"It's better."

"Well, if you say so. But if I were you, I don't know that I'd lay a bet on it. Since you'd only lose. Because you know what, I got the better hand." She stopped and looked at him, her expression almost pitying. "The thing is, Jackson. You keep thinking that you know exactly how this is going to play out. You keep thinking that you know better than me. Even from the beginning. When I won, you felt like you had another plan, and so you didn't really lose. But you did, though, didn't you? I got my way. So if I were you, I would maybe try to figure out what all I know that you don't."

And then Cricket left.

Turned and left him there, driving off in her great truck down the hill, taking some piece of him with her. But she didn't understand. She didn't understand that this was how it had to be. Because in her mind she could will all these things into fitting together, and he knew better. He'd spent his life as an obligation.

But now he was standing there, feeling like he'd cut his own heart out of his chest, and he knew he was a liar.

He couldn't love her…

He already did.

And he was every bit the coward she had accused him of being.

Cricket didn't go back to the ranch. She couldn't. Instead, she went to Emerson's. And it didn't take long for Wren to show up. At this point, there was no protecting Jackson from the wrath of her brothers-in-law. And Cricket didn't intend to try. She was too angry at him. He was being…ridiculous.

He didn't have a damn good reason for any of this.

Cricket had never sulked so hard in her life. But she was doing her best to work a groove into her sister's overstuffed, white fluffy beanbag chair with the weight of her indignant sighs.

"So, when do we get the whole story?" Emerson asked.

It all came pouring out of Cricket, from her lifelong crush to their love affair, to the half brother thing, and all the way to what had just happened at his place.

"Well," Wren said. "Creed is going to kill him."

"I know," Cricket said. "It's why I went to Emerson first. Because I didn't really want him to die. I'm feeling more flexible on that subject right at the moment."

"So he said he can't love you?"

"Yes. He did. And you know what, if I believed it… then maybe I would think he was doing the right thing. But I don't believe it. I do think he can love me. I really do. I think he might love me already. And I think he's being afraid."

"Well," Wren said, "love makes fools out of men. Trust me."

"Even Creed?"

"Oh, Creed was the *worst*," Wren said.

"No," Emerson said, "I think Holden was the worst. I told him that I loved him and he lost his mind."

"Yeah, Creed was not exactly receptive to me loving him either."

"Oh," Cricket said, frowning.

"What?" Wren asked.

"I didn't exactly tell him that I loved him."

"Really?" Emerson asked. "But you do, right? I mean, you have for years."

"I… Yes. But I…wanted to see what he would say, and I didn't want to…"

"Cricket," Wren said gently. "I'd like to kill him. With my bare hands. If he didn't think that he could give you something real he never should've touched you."

"No. I told him it was okay. He was honest with me. He was upfront. He was. He never lied to me. It's just… I thought I could be with him and then move on. I thought I could be with him and then make it part of a phase that I moved past. But I couldn't. I was lying to myself. He was never a phase. He was always fate."

"Then you need to tell him."

"He *humiliated me*."

"Yeah. And…sometimes we have to be fools for love."

"I don't like that at all."

"I don't either," Wren said. "But I love my husband. And I would debase myself for him a thousand times to keep him. But he doesn't make me. Maybe the real problem is that Jackson needs to know how you feel. The Coopers are… They're hard men. And I don't know all of Jackson's issues. But I do know what it looks like when a Cooper runs scared."

"So what? I don't wait for him to come to me? I don't…wait for him to say it first?"

"You can. But I think you have a good head on your shoulders, Cricket. And you always have," Emerson said. "You know who you are. And it would be great if relationships could be fifty-fifty, but they can't be. Everybody has to give everything they've got all the time, and sometimes you're going to have to be the one carrying your partner. No, it should never look like Mom and Dad's marriage. Where one of them dies emotionally, without any kind of love or support. But sometimes you have to be the first one who's willing to break. The first one who's willing to be vulnerable. And it might be tough, but it's best. Because otherwise you end up in a stalemate forever, and nobody wins."

"Maybe it's just a bad hand. All around."

"No. Don't say that. Look, he's a good man, and you're a good woman. And I don't believe for a minute that the two of you can't find a way to make something together."

"But…"

"It sucks," Emerson said, "but anything that matters is tough sometimes. The only person who ever has it easy in a relationship is someone like Dad. Someone who doesn't care enough to be hurt. Who doesn't care enough about someone else's feelings."

Those words resonated inside of Cricket and sank down deep. She had always wanted to be protected, but being part of her family, in the way that she had wanted to be…it had been a bigger risk than she was willing to take. It hadn't mattered enough. It hadn't mattered enough because she hadn't aspired to the kind of life her mother and father had anyway. So contorting herself to become part of it had seemed the opposite of a good idea. But Jackson... He was different. The life they could have—she could see it. She ached for it. A life together, one with their child. And that hadn't been her fantasy. She had thought about Jackson, about having him. Not about domestic bliss or anything of that kind. But she wanted it. It was a future that burned bright and hot in her mind. A future that mattered.

Because she loved him.

And where in the world did pride fit in with love? She *couldn't* protect herself.

That was what he was doing. Whether he would admit it or not, that was what he was doing. And she wasn't going to do that. She wasn't going to sacrifice love on the altar of her own pride. Because this was deeper than that. It was in her bones, in her blood. Like the land. Like ranching.

Some things simply were.

And for her, loving Jackson was one of those things. And she was going to fight for it. Fight for him.

Because her life mattered too much to let someone like James Maxfield twist her sense of who she was enough to prevent her from being happy even when he wasn't around. And it was the same for Jackson, whether he knew it or not. His parents' mistakes didn't get to decide what he was.

She burrowed out from the large poof she'd been sitting on. "All right," she said. "I'm going to tell him that I love him."

"A good idea. Maybe not at nine o'clock at night, though," Emerson said.

"Why not?"

"Formulate a plan. You got this. But it wouldn't hurt to take some time with it."

Cricket nodded. "Okay. Time."

And that was when she did start to form a plan.

"I'm going to need to borrow your dress again," she said to Emerson.

"Whatever you need."

Chapter 11

Jackson was no stranger to grief. But what surprised him this time was that the situation with Cricket felt more like death than he'd anticipated anything like this could feel. He had reached the end of his rope and he knew he had two options. Reach for the bottle of whiskey, or reach for his car keys. He opted for the car keys, and found himself driving down from the ranch and heading to where his father was, at the tasting room, and that was how Jackson ended up pounding on the door. He knew he'd woken up the old man, but he didn't really care.

"Jackson? Is everything all right?" Cash asked, tying his robe hastily as he pulled open the door.

"Cricket is pregnant," Jackson said.

"Well hell," Cash said. "You really did need to know who her father was."

"I told you I did."

"You didn't waste any time."

"It was inevitable. But it doesn't matter. I need to know something else from you, and I need to know it now. Why did you marry Mom if you couldn't love her? Why did you do it for me? Because you know what, it doesn't feel very good to be the reason your parents are miserable. To be the reason that they're together. To know that you're why they are not happy."

"You were never why we weren't happy," Cash said. Then he sighed wearily. "Come in."

Jackson stepped inside, enveloped by the sense of strangeness he always felt when he entered his childhood home. He had sat at the dining table countless times with his mother. He had opened Christmas presents in the corner, right there by the fireplace where the tree always was. He had read to his mother while she lay on the couch, while she wasn't well. While he was losing her, watching as she slipped away.

He couldn't be in here and not…feel.

"You need to understand that we weren't unhappy," Cash said. "Not always. Just like we weren't happy always. And look, the pain that your mother felt, that was my fault. We had a bad fight. Must've been…fifteen, sixteen years in, and she told me how much she hated the winery, and at that point, it had made us so much money, it felt like the best thing I'd ever done. But she said it just reminded her that my whole life was built on the foundation of trying to win back another woman."

Cash shook his head. "And I… I let that sit inside me. I let that fester. And I figured… It would've been a lot easier to be married to Lucinda Maxfield. But I know better than that. I mean, I know better than to believe that being with Lucinda would've fixed all my problems. Because you can't compare a childish infatuation to a marriage that spans decades. You just can't do it. Every what-if supposition your mother and I ever had about if we hadn't been together... We were never with anyone else for all those years. I didn't have children with anyone else. The stresses and pressures that time in a family put on you can't be compared to anything else. We grew up with each other, for better or worse. We changed together, in sickness and health. We were part of each other."

"You were together because you felt obligated," Jackson said.

"Is that a bad thing?"

"Yes. You should be with someone because...hell, because you love them."

"Where the hell did you get the idea that love didn't come with obligation? Loving a child is full of obligation. A marriage is filled with obligation. *Obligation* is not a bad word. It's bad people that turn away from it, don't you think?"

"I can't say that I ever thought of it that way."

"We weren't perfect. We weren't blissfully, perfectly happy. And I carry so much guilt for all my feelings. For the kind of husband I wasn't. It's not that I couldn't have loved her, it's that I chose—*we* chose—to let certain things affect what we believed. To let certain feelings grow rotten and determine how much and how little we could feel and forgive."

"When she told me that you only got married because she was pregnant with me—"

"Maybe," his dad said. "Maybe that's true. But she doesn't know that. Not even I know that. We could say that, shout it at each other at the worst of times, and we certainly did. But that doesn't make it true. That doesn't make it a sure thing that we can know. We loved each other then."

"Well, you were only with mom because Lucinda Maxfield married James."

"This is the problem," Cash said. "I don't know the way things would've gone, or could've gone if we'd done things differently. If we'd been less stubborn. Less self-righteous. But we weren't. And that's my burden. It's not yours or anyone else's, and she shouldn't have put it on you. But there's a lot of things I shouldn't have put on her... You shouldn't have been the person she had to talk to. But the problem is—this is all 'should have,' 'could have.' And you drive yourself crazy with it, Jackson. Believe me. I've done it. For years and years, I've done it. And most of all since she passed."

"Why since then?"

"I told you. Guilt. And regret. Because at the end of the day, I loved your mother very much. And what I didn't do was show it. Because I kept expecting it to feel the same as something I felt when I was young, something I felt that was impossible and painful, and wonderful in its way..." He shook his head. "And then, I wonder what could have been between us now and that makes the regret even worse. Because I can hear her in my head, saying I was just waiting for her to die so I could be with the person I really wanted. But that's not the truth of it. It just isn't."

Jackson let out a long, slow breath and rocked back on his heels. He didn't know what the hell to do with any of this. Cricket looked at him and talked about fate. She had talked about him and her as if they were something preordained. And his dad was making this all sound a lot like choice. And a whole collection of hard ones at that.

But something else Cricket said burned bright inside of him.

They weren't their parents.

And they weren't. It was true.

Because Jackson didn't feel conflicted or confused about whether or not he should be with Cricket because he had feelings for someone else. He'd never had feelings for anyone like he did for Cricket. And he wasn't young and naive. But what he was, was damn tired of feeling like a sacrifice. And if he was truly honest with himself, he was angry at his mother. Because she'd made him feel that way. Whether she'd meant to or not. And hearing his dad say he wished she hadn't dumped that on Jackson gave voice to all these things he'd tried not to think about.

"You know, son," Cash said. "She was sick, not a saint. A wonderful woman to be sure, but flawed like any of us. I know she didn't mean to hurt you. But the fact of the matter is…she did. Doesn't mean she didn't love you."

"I know," Jackson said.

"For what it's worth, she would've walked into fire for you. Marrying me was only a hardship for part of the time."

"Do you regret the way things happened?"

"I regret the way I handled them. I regret that I didn't find a way to be a better husband. I've never regretted you. I've never regretted the life your mother and I built together. But I didn't let go of the past the way I should have, because your vows say you forsake all others. And I never cheated, but I kept that desire and those memories in a special place inside myself. You make choices every day, Jackson. And I don't know that you'll ever be able to live a life with no regrets, but you should make sure you live a life that's honest. Those games we all played, they were games. And games don't amount to much. Nothing more than needless heartache, anyway."

"I don't want to feel like she has to marry me."

"She seems like a modern enough girl."

"I told her I wouldn't marry her."

"Well hell, boy," Cash said. "I didn't raise you to wimp out on your responsibilities."

"I'm not. I'm trying to make sure she doesn't see me as another responsibility."

"Well, ask her if she does. Don't just try to protect yourself. Ask her how she feels."

"How will she know?"

"How will she know?" Cash repeated. "You want too much. You're going to have to trust her. You're going to have to believe her. Trust would've gone a long way in fixing my marriage. Trust, faith and honesty. If I could do more of any three things, it would be those. And we would've had a different life."

Jackson loved Cricket. He did. He was sure of that, standing there in this house filled with all these memories. All those weighted, hurtful memories that had seen him silently carrying around a whole lot of baggage he hadn't realized was there.

And she had been right. He was protecting himself. Because the burden of feeling like an obligation to his mother, a debt that he'd never been able to repay, haunted him. And the last thing he wanted was to be that burden for Cricket.

But he would have to ask. And he would have to trust.

And he would have to hope that…well, that Cricket really did know everything. And that she had faith in all those things she'd shouted at him before she left.

She was right. He'd lost the bet.

But it was one he was glad to lose.

The next morning, when Cricket opened her door wearing that red dress from the poker tournament, that oversized leather jacket, cowboy hat, but no cigar, Jackson was standing there. He looked haunted, like a man possessed. Like a man who hadn't slept all night.

"What are you doing here?"

"What are *you* doing?"

"Well, obviously I was on my way to stage a very serious scheme."

"Very obviously. Do you have a pistol on you?"

"No pistol." Her heart hammered, hard, as she looked up at him. As she tried not to hope what his presence meant.

"I fold," he said.

"You…what?"

"I fold, Cricket. I'm done. I surrender to this, to you. And you're right. I was afraid. I was a coward. A damn coward. Because I didn't want to face the fact that I wasn't really afraid of being my father, I was afraid of being my mother. Sitting all bitter and hollow at my kitchen table and telling my teenage child I was only in a marriage for their sake. That there was no love. No, the real thing I was afraid of was being the one who felt unloved. Because I have to tell you, when my mom said all that to me, that's how I felt. Like a burden and an obligation that she should never have had to take on. And I couldn't stand being that for the rest of my life. Not with you. But I love you, Cricket. And I'm willing to be that. I'm willing to do anything if it means being with you, having you. I'm willing to be an obligation, and to earn your love later. I know you want to be free. I know you want to start a life, and I know that having a child right now, and settling down with me, doesn't have much of anything to do with that. But I think…this is fate. And far be it from me to go against her."

"Jackson," she whispered, her heart expanding in her chest. "You're not a burden to me. I went to my sister's house last night and I complained to her about how you rejected me. And then they asked me if I told you that I loved you, and I realized that I hadn't. That was me protecting myself. I wanted to know what you felt, what you thought, before I put myself out there. It was easy to talk about marriage, and so much harder to talk about my heart. Because I've never done it. I've never seriously talked to anyone about how I felt. Except for you. And I've done more of that over the past month than ever in my life. Told you more about who I am, what hurt me, and what made me who I am. The bottom line is, above all else, and with everything else shoved aside, I love you. I have loved you for years. And I would want to be with you, pregnant or not. It was just the thing that got me up the mountain. It was just the thing that forced me to be as brave as I was, and even then, I wasn't all that brave. So I didn't really have a right to yell at you."

"You had plenty of right."

"Jackson," she whispered. "I really, really love you. And I have never wanted much of anything in my whole life enough to fight for it. Except for you. Only you. I can't imagine another person, another feeling, another anything that would ever be worth all this hassle. You're not an obligation. You're my inevitability."

"Cricket Maxfield," he said, wrapping his arms around her waist and looking at her, square in the eye. "You're the surprise I didn't see coming. Little Cricket, you're the thing I've been missing. I didn't know the right place to look to fill the hole in my heart. But you've known all along. You are wiser than me. Smarter than me. Braver than me. And I am going to love you today, and every day after. I don't care if some days are hard. I don't care if there are sleepless nights, or if I have to move out of my house and into your farmhouse. Because nothing matters but you. And that's… My dad said to me, that obligation and love often go together, and I expect that he's right. Love is what makes you want to fulfill that obligation. But this is different. Everything else feels like an obligation. You feel like breathing. And that's as deep as I can explain it."

"Is it in your blood?" she asked, her voice a whisper.

"Yes," he responded. "It's in my blood. My bones. My heart."

"Mine too."

And then he kissed her, and she couldn't think anymore. Couldn't breathe. She could only feel. And somehow, she knew she felt the same thing he did. Somehow, she knew that in this moment they were one. And it wasn't a pregnancy or marriage vows that would make it so. They could never have parted even if they'd wanted to. Because it was too late. The chips had already gone down. The game was over.

And in the end, they had both won.

Cricket Maxfield had won any number of specious prizes in her life. And she had often felt uncertain about her place in the world. But the biggest and best prize she'd ever won was loving Jackson Cooper and having him love her back. And if all the years of feeling misfit and frizzy and gap-toothed and like she didn't belong was what it had taken for her to get here, then she counted them all worth it.

She wouldn't change a single thing, not about herself, not about anything. Because it had brought her here. To this man, to his arms.

And that was truly the greatest prize of all.

* * * * *

In Gold Valley, Oregon, lasting love is only a happily-ever-after away. Don't miss any of Maisey Yates's Gold Valley tales, available now!

Gold Valley Vineyards

Rancher's Wild Secret
Claiming the Rancher's Heir
The Rancher's Wager

Gold Valley

A Tall, Dark Cowboy Christmas
Unbroken Cowboy
Cowboy to the Core
Untamed Cowboy
Smooth-Talking Cowboy
Cowboy Christmas Redemption

TAKE ME, COWBOY

Chapter 1

When Anna Brown walked into Ace's bar, she was contemplating whether or not she could get away with murdering her older brothers.

That's really nice that the invitation includes a plus one. You know you can't bring your socket wrench.

She wanted to punch Daniel in his smug face for that one. She had been flattered when she'd received her invitation to the community charity event that the West family hosted every year. A lot less so when Daniel and Mark had gotten ahold of it and decided it was the funniest thing in the world to imagine her trying to get a date to the coveted fund-raiser.

Because apparently the idea of her having a date at all was the pinnacle of comedic genius.

I can get a date, jackasses.

You want to make a bet?

Sure. It's your money.

That exchange had seemed both enraging and empowering about an hour ago. Now she was feeling both humiliated and a little bit uncertain. The fact that she had bet on her dating prowess was…well, embarrassing didn't even begin to describe it. But on top of that, she was a little concerned that she had no prowess to speak of.

It had been longer than she wanted to admit since she'd actually had a date. In fact, it was entirely possible that she had never technically been on one. That quick roll in the literal hay with Corbin Martin hadn't exactly been a date per se.

And it hadn't led to anything, either. Since she had done a wonderful job of smashing his ego with a hammer the next day at school when she'd told her best friend, Chase, about Corbin's…limitations.

Yeah, her sexual debut had also been the final curtain.

But if men weren't such whiny babies, maybe that wouldn't have been the case. Also, maybe if Corbin had been able to prove to her that sex was worth the trouble, she would view it differently.

But he hadn't. So she didn't.

And now she needed a date.

She stalked across the room, heading toward the table that she and Chase, and often his brother, Sam, occupied on Friday nights. The lighting was dim, so she knew someone was sitting there but couldn't make out which McCormack brother it was.

She hoped it was Chase. Because as long as she'd known Sam, she still had a hard time making conversation with him.

Talking wasn't really his thing.

She moved closer, and the man at the table tilted his head up. Sam. Dammit. Drinking a beer and looking grumpy, which was pretty much par for the course with him. But Chase was nowhere to be seen.

"Hi," she said, plopping down in the chair beside him. "Bad day?"

"A day."

"Right." At least when it came to Sam, she knew the difficult-conversation thing had nothing to do with her. That was all him.

She tapped the top of her knee, looking around the bar, trying to decide if she was going to get up and order a drink or wait for someone to come to the table. She allowed her gaze to drift across the bar, and her attention was caught by the figure of a man in the corner, black cowboy hat on his head, his face shrouded by the dim light. A woman was standing in front of him looking up at his face like he was her every birthday wish come true.

For a moment the sight of the man standing there struck her completely dumb. Broad shoulders, broad chest, strong-looking hands. The kind of hands that made her wonder if she needed to investigate the potential fuss of sex again.

He leaned up against the wall, his forearm above his head. He said something and the little blonde he was talking to practically shimmered with excitement. Anna wondered what that was like. To be the focus of a man's attention like that. To have him look at you like a sex object instead of a drinking buddy.

For a moment she envied the woman standing there, who could absolutely get a date if she wanted one. Who would know what to wear and how to act if she were invited to a fancy gala whatever.

That woman would know what to do if the guy wanted to take her home after the date and get naked. She wouldn't be awkward and make jokes and laugh when he got naked because there were all these feelings that were so…so weird she didn't know how else to react.

With a man like that one…well, she doubted she would laugh. He would be all lean muscle and wicked smiles. He would look at her and she would… Okay, even in fantasy she didn't know. But she felt hot. Very, very hot.

But in a flash, that hot feeling turned into utter horror. Because the man shifted, pushing his hat back on his head and angling slightly toward Anna, a light from above catching his angular features and illuminating his face. He changed then, from a fantasy to flesh and blood. And she realized exactly who she had just been checking out.

Chase McCormack. Her best friend in the entire world. The man she had spent years training herself to never, ever have feelings below the belt for.

She blinked rapidly, squeezing her hands into fists and trying to calm the fluttering in her stomach. "I'm going to get a drink," she said, looking at Sam. *And talk to Ace about the damn lighting in here.* "Did you want something?"

He lifted his brow, and his bottle of beer. "I'm covered."

Her heart was still pounding a little heavier than usual when she reached the bar and signaled Ace, the establishment's owner, to ask for whatever pale ale he had on tap.

And her heart stopped altogether when she heard a deep voice from behind her.

"Why don't you make that two."

She whisked around and came face-to-chest with Chase. A man whose presence should be commonplace, and usually was. She was just in a weird place, thanks to high-pressure invitations and idiot brothers.

"Pale ale," she said, taking a step back and looking up at his face. A face that should also be commonplace. But it was just so very symmetrical. Square jaw, straight nose, strong brows and dark eyes that were so direct they bordered on obscene. Like they were looking straight through your clothes or something. Not that he would ever want to look through hers. Not that she would want him to. She was too smart for that.

"That's kind of an unusual order for you," she continued, more to remind herself of who he was than to actually make commentary on his beverage choices. To remind herself that she knew him better than she knew herself. To do whatever she could to put that temporary moment of insanity when she'd spotted him in the corner out of her mind.

"I'm feeling adventurous," he said, lifting one corner of his mouth, the lopsided grin disrupting the symmetry she had been admiring earlier and somehow making him look all the more compelling for it.

"Come on, McCormack. Adventurous is bungee jumping from Multnomah Falls. Adventurous is not trying a new beer."

"Says the expert in adventure?"

"I'm an expert in a couple of things. Beer and motor oil being at the top of the list."

"Then I won't challenge you."

"Probably for the best. I'm feeling a little bit blood-thirsty tonight." She pressed her hands onto the bar top and leaned forward, watching as Ace went to get their drinks. "So. Why aren't you still talking to short, blonde and stacked over there?"

He chuckled and it settled oddly inside her chest, rattling around before skittering down her spine. "Not really all that interested."

"You seemed interested to me."

"Well," he said, "I'm not."

"That's inconsistent," she said.

"Okay, I'll bite," he said, regarding her a little more closely than she would like. "Why are you in the mood to cause death and dismemberment?"

"Do I seem that feral?"

"Completely. Why?"

"The same reason I usually am," she said.

"Your brothers."

"You're fast, I like that."

Ace returned to their end of the bar and passed two pints toward them. "Do you want to open a tab?"

"Sure," she said. "On him." She gestured to Chase.

Ace smiled in return. "You look nice tonight, Anna."

"I look…the same as I always do," she said, glancing down at her worn gray T-shirt and no-fuss jeans.

He winked. "Exactly."

She looked up at Chase, who was staring at the bartender, his expression unreadable. Then she looked back at Ace.

Ace was pretty hot, really. In that bearded, flannel-wearing way. Lumbersexual, or so she had overheard some college girls saying the other night as they giggled over him. Maybe *he* would want to be her date. Of course, easy compliments and charm aside, he also had his pick of any woman who turned up in his bar. And Anna was never anyone's pick.

She let go of her fleeting Ace fantasy pretty quickly.

Chase grabbed the beer from the counter and handed one to her. She was careful not to let their fingers brush as she took it from him. That type of avoidance was second nature to her. Hazards of spending the years since adolescence feeling electricity when Chase got too close, and pretending she didn't.

"We should go back and sit with Sam," she suggested. "He looks lonely."

Chase laughed. "You and I both know he's no such thing. I think he would rather sit there alone."

"Well, if he wants to be alone, then he can stay at home and drink."

"He probably would if I didn't force him to come out. But if I didn't do that, he would fuse to the furniture and then I would have all of that to deal with."

They walked back over to the table, and gradually, her heart rate returned to normal. She was relieved that the initial weirdness she had felt upon his arrival was receding.

"Hi, Sam," Chase said, taking his seat beside his brother. Sam grunted in response. "We were just talking about the hazards of you turning into a hermit."

"Am I not a convincing hermit already?" he asked. "Do I need to make my disdain for mankind a little less subtle?"

"That might help," Chase said.

"I might just go play a game of darts instead. I'll catch up with you in a minute." Sam took a long drink of his beer and stood, leaving the bottle on the table as he made his way over to the dartboard across the bar.

Silence settled between Chase and herself. Why was this suddenly weird? Why was Anna suddenly conscious of the way his throat moved when he swallowed a sip of beer, of the shift in his forearms as he set the bottle back down on the table? Of just how masculine a sound he made when he cleared his throat?

She was suddenly even conscious of the way he breathed.

She leaned back in her chair, lifting her beer to her lips and surveying the scene around them.

It was Friday night, so most of the town of Copper Ridge, Oregon, was hanging out, drowning the last vestiges of the workweek in booze. It was not the end of the workweek for Anna. Farmers and ranchers didn't take time off, so neither did she. She had to be on hand to make repairs when necessary, especially right now, since she was just getting her own garage off the ground.

She'd just recently quit her job at Jake's in order to open her own shop specializing in heavy equipment, which really was how she found herself in the position she was in right now. Invited to the charity gala thing and embroiled in a bet on whether or not she could get a date.

"So why exactly do you want to kill your brothers today?" Chase asked, startling her out of her thoughts.

"Various reasons." She didn't know why, but something stopped her from wanting to tell him exactly what was going on. Maybe because it was humiliating. Yes, it was definitely humiliating.

"Sure. But that's every day. Why specifically do you want to kill them today?"

She took a deep breath, keeping her eyes fixed on the fishing boat that was mounted to the wall opposite her, and very determinedly not looking at Chase. "Because. They bet that I couldn't get a date to this thing I'm invited to and I bet them that I could." She thought about the woman he'd been talking to a moment ago. A woman so different from herself they might as well be different species. "And right about now I'm afraid they're right."

Chase was doing his best to process his best friend's statement. It was difficult, though. Daniel and Mark had solid asshole tendencies when it came to Anna—that much he knew—but this was pretty low even for them.

He studied Anna's profile, her dark hair pulled back into a braid, her gray T-shirt that was streaked with oil. He watched as she raised her bottle of beer to her lips. She had oil on her hands, too. Beneath her fingernails. Anna wasn't the kind of girl who attracted a lot of male attention. But he kind of figured that was her choice.

She wasn't conventionally beautiful. Mostly because of the motor oil. But that didn't mean that getting a date should be impossible for her.

"Why don't you think you can get a date?"

She snorted, looking over at him, one dark brow raised. "Um." She waved a hand up and down, indicating her body. "Because of all of this."

He took a moment to look at *all of that*. Really look.

Like he was a man and she was a woman. Which they were, but not in a conventional sense. Not to each other. He'd looked at her almost every day for the past fifteen years, so it was difficult to imagine seeing her for the first time. But just then, he tried.

She had a nice nose. And her lips were full, nicely shaped, her top lip a little fuller than her bottom lip, which was unique and sort of…not sexy, because it was Anna. But interesting.

"A little elbow grease and that cleans right off," he said. "Anyway, men are pretty simple."

She frowned. "What does that mean?"

"Exactly what it sounds like. You don't have to do much to get male attention if you want it. Give a guy what he's after…"

"Okay, that's just insulting. You're saying that I can get a guy because men just want to get laid? So it doesn't matter if I'm a wrench-toting troll?"

"You are not a wrench-toting troll. You're a wrench-toting woman who could easily bludgeon me to death, and I am aware of that. Which means I need to choose my next words a little more carefully."

Those full lips thinned into a dangerous line, her green eyes glittering dangerously. "Why don't you do that, Chase."

He cleared his throat. "I'm just saying, if you want a date, you can get one."

"By unzipping my coveralls down to my belly button?"

He tipped his beer bottle back, taking a larger swallow than he intended to, coughing as it went down wrong. He did not need to picture the visual she had just handed to him. But he was a man, so he did.

It was damned unsettling. His best friend, bare beneath a pair of coveralls unfastened so that a very generous wedge of skin was revealed all the way down...

And he was done with that. He didn't think of Anna that way. Not at all. They'd been friends since they were freshmen in high school and he'd navigated teenage boy hormones without lingering too long on thoughts of her breasts.

He was thirty years old, and he could have sex whenever he damn well pleased. Breasts were no longer mysterious to him. He wasn't going to go pondering the mysteries of *her* breasts now.

"It couldn't hurt, Anna," he said, his words containing a little more bite than he would like them to. But he was unsettled.

"Okay, I'll keep that in mind. But barring that, do you have any other suggestions? Because I think I'm going to be expected to wear something fancy, and I don't own anything fancy. And it's obvious that Mark and Daniel think I suck at being a girl."

"That's not true. And anyway, why do you care what they—or anyone else—think?"

"Because. I've got this new business..."

"And anyone who brings their heavy equipment to you for a tune-up won't care whether or not you can walk in high heels."

"But I don't want to show up at these things looking..." She sighed. "Chase, the bottom line is I've spent a long time not fitting in. And people here are nice to me. I mean, now that I'm not in school. People in school sucked. But I get that I don't fit. And I'm tired of it. Honestly, I wouldn't care about my brothers if there wasn't so much...truth to the teasing."

"They do suck. They're awful. So why does it matter what they think?"

"Because," she said. "It just does. I'm that poor Anna Brown with no mom to teach her the right way to do things and I'm just…tired of it. I don't want to be poor Anna Brown. I want to be Anna Brown, heavy equipment mechanic who can wear coveralls and walk in heels."

"Not at the same time, I wouldn't think."

She shot him a deadly glare. "I don't fail," she said, her eyes glinting in the dim bar light. "I won't fail at this."

"You're not in remote danger of failing. Now, what's the mystery event that has you thinking about high heels?" he asked.

Copper Ridge wasn't exactly a societal epicenter. Nestled between the evergreen mountains and a steel-gray sea on the Oregon Coast, there were probably more deer than people in the small town. There were only so many events in existence. And there was a good chance she was making a mountain out of a small-town molehill, and none of it would be that big of a deal.

"That charity thing that the West family has every year," she mumbled. "Gala Under the Stars or whatever."

The West family's annual fund-raising event for schools. It was a weekend event, with the town's top earners coming to a small black-tie get-together on the West property.

The McCormacks had been founding members of the community of Copper Ridge back in the 1800s. Their forge had been used by everyone in town and in the neighboring communities. But as the economy had changed, so had the success of the business.

They'd been hanging on by their fingernails when Chase's parents had been killed in an accident when he was in high school. They'd still gotten an invitation to the gala. But Chase had thrown it on top of the never-ending pile of mail and bills that he couldn't bring himself to look through and forgotten about it.

Until some woman—probably an assistant to the West family—had called him one year when he hadn't bothered to RSVP. He had been…well, he'd been less than polite.

Dealing with a damned crisis here, so sorry I can't go to your party.

Unsurprisingly, he hadn't gotten any invitations after that. And he hadn't really thought much about it since.

Until now.

He and Sam had managed to keep the operation and properties afloat, but he wanted more. He needed it.

The ranch had animals, but that wasn't the source of their income. The forge was the heart of the ranch, where they did premium custom metal-and-leatherwork. On top of that, there were outbuildings on the property they rented out—including the shop they leased to Anna. They had built things back up since their parents had died, but it still wasn't enough, not to Chase.

He had promised his father he would take an interest in the family legacy. That he would build for the McCormacks, not just for himself. Chase had promised he wouldn't let his dad down. He'd had to make those promises at a grave site because before the accident he'd been a hotheaded jackass who'd thought he was too big for the family legacy.

But even if his father never knew, Chase had sworn it. And so he'd see it done.

In order to expand McCormack Iron Works, the heart and soul of their ranch, to bring it back to what it had been, they needed interest. Investments.

Chase had always had a good business mind, and early on he'd imagined he would go to school away from Copper Ridge. Get a degree. Find work in the city. Then everything had changed. Then it hadn't been about Chase McCormack anymore. It had been about the McCormack legacy.

School had become out of the question. Leaving had been out of the question. But now he saw where he and Sam were failing, and he could see how to turn the tide.

He'd spent a lot of late nights figuring out exactly how to expand as the demand for handmade items had gone down. Finding ways to convince people that highly customized iron details for homes and businesses, and handmade leather bridles and saddles, were worth paying more for.

Finding ways to push harder, to innovate and modernize while staying true to the family name. While actively butting up against Sam and his refusal to go out and make that happen. Sam, who was so talented he didn't have to pound horseshoe nails if he didn't want to. Sam, who could forget gates and scrollwork on staircases and be selling his artwork for a small fortune. Sam, who resisted change like it was the black plague.

He would kill for an invitation to the Wests' event. Well, not kill. But possibly engage in nefarious activities or the trading of sexual favors. And Anna had an invitation.

"You get to bring a date?" he asked.

"That's what I've been saying," she said. "Of course, it all depends on whether or not I can actually acquire one."

Anna needed a date; he wanted to have a chance to talk to Nathan West. In the grand tradition of their friendship, they both filled the gaps in each other's lives. This was—in his opinion—perfect.

"I'll be your date," he said.

She snorted. "Yeah, right. Daniel and Mark will never believe that."

She had a point. The two of them had been friends forever. And with a bet on the table her brothers would never believe that he had suddenly decided to go out with her because his feelings had randomly changed.

"Okay. Maybe that's true." That frown was back. "Not because there's something wrong with you," he continued, trying to dig himself out of the pit he'd just thrown himself into, "but because it's a little too convenient."

"Okay, that's better."

"But what if we made it clear that things had changed between us?"

"What do you mean?"

"I mean…what if…we built up the change? Showed people that our relationship was evolving."

She gave him a fierce side-eye. "I'm not your type." He thought back to the blonde he'd been talking to only twenty minutes earlier. Tight dress cut up to the tops of her thighs, long, wavy hair and the kind of smile that invited you right on in. Curves that had probably wrecked more men than windy Highway 101. She was his type.

And she wasn't Anna. Barefaced, scowling with a figure that was slightly more…subtle. He cleared his throat. "You could be. A little less grease, a little more lipstick."

Her top lip curled. "So the ninth circle of hell basically."

"What were you planning on wearing to the fundraiser?"

She shifted uncomfortably in her seat. "I have black jeans. But… I mean, I guess I could go to the mall in Tolowa and get a dress."

"That isn't going to work."

"Why not?"

"What kind of dress would you buy?" he asked.

"Something floral? Kind of…down to the knee?"

He pinched the bridge of his nose. "You're not Scarlett O'Hara," he said, knowing that with her love of old movies, Anna would appreciate the reference. "You aren't going dressed in the drapes."

Anna scowled. "Why the hell do you know so much about women's clothes?"

"Because I spend a lot of time taking them off my dates."

That shut her up. Her pale cheeks flamed and she looked away from him, and that response stirred… well, it stirred something in his gut he wished would go the hell away.

"Why do *you* want to go anyway?" she asked, still not looking at him.

"I want to talk to Nathan West and the other businessmen there about investment opportunities. I want to prove that Sam and I are the kind of people that can move in their circles. The kind of people they want to do business with."

"And you have to put on a suit and hobnob at a gala to do that?"

"The fact is, I don't get chances like this very often, Anna. I didn't get an invitation. And I need one. Plus, if you take me, you'll win your bet."

"Unless Dan and Mark tell me you don't count."

"Loophole. If they never said you couldn't recruit a date, you're fine."

"It violates the spirit of the bet."

"It doesn't have to," he insisted. "Anyway, by the time I'm through with you, you'll be able to get any date you want."

She blinked. "Are you... Are you Henry Higginsing me?"

He had only a vague knowledge of the old movie *My Fair Lady*, but he was pretty sure that was the reference. A man who took a grubby flower girl and turned her into the talk of the town. "Yes," he said thoughtfully. "Yes, I am. Take me up on this, Anna Brown, and I will turn you into a woman."

Chapter 2

Anna just about laughed herself off her chair. "You're going to make me a…a…a woman?"

"Why is that funny?"

"What about it *isn't* funny?"

"I'm offering to help you."

"You're offering to help me be something that I am by birth. I mean, Chase, I get that women are kind of your thing, but that's pretty arrogant. Even with all things considered."

"Okay, obviously I'm not going to make you a woman." Something about the way he said the phrase this time hit her in an entirely different way. Made her think about *other* applications that phrase occasionally had. Things she needed to never, ever, ever, ever think about in connection with Chase.

If she valued her sanity and their friendship.

She cleared her throat, suddenly aware that it was dry and scratchy. "Obviously."

"I just meant that you need help getting a date, and I need to go to this party. And you said that you were concerned about your appearance in the community."

"Right." He wasn't wrong. The thing was, she knew that whether or not she could blend in at an event like this didn't matter at all to how well her business did. Nobody cared if their mechanic knew which shade of lipstick she should wear. But that wasn't the point.

She—her family collectively—was the town charity case. Living on the edge of the community in a run-down house, raised by a single father who was in over his head, who spent his days at the mill. Her older brothers had been in charge of taking care of her, and they had done so. But, of course, they were also older brothers. Which meant they had tormented her while feeding and clothing her. Anyway, she didn't exactly blame them.

It wasn't like the two of them had wanted to raise a sister when they would rather be out raising hell.

Especially a sister who was committed to driving them crazy.

She loved her brothers. But that didn't mean they always had an easy relationship. It didn't mean they didn't hurt her by accident when they teased her about things. She acted invulnerable, so they assumed that she was.

But now, beneath her coveralls and engine grease, she was starting to feel a little bit battered. It was difficult to walk around with a *screw you* attitude barely covering a raw wound. Because eventually that shield started to wear down. Especially when people were used to being able to lob pretty intense rocks at that shield.

That was her life. It was either pity or a kind of merciless camaraderie that had no softness to it. Her dad, her brothers, all the guy friends she had...

And she couldn't really blame them. She had never behaved in a way that would demonstrate she needed any softness. In fact, a few months ago, a few weeks ago even, the idea would have been unthinkable to her.

But there was something about this invitation. Something about imagining herself in yet another situation where she was forced to deflect good-natured comments about her appearance, about the fact that she was more like a guy than the roughest cowboys in town. Yeah, there was something about that thought that had made her want to curl into a ball and never unfurl.

Then, even if it was unintentional, her brothers had piled on. It had hurt her feelings. Which meant she had reacted in anger, naturally. So now she had a bet. A bet, and her best friend looking at her with laser focus after having just promised he would make her a woman.

"Why do you care?" He was pressing, and she wanted to hit him now.

Which kind of summed up why she was in this position in the first place.

She swallowed hard. "Maybe I just want to surprise people. Isn't that enough?"

"You came from nothing. You started your own business with no support from your father. You're a female mechanic. I would say that you're surprising as hell."

"Well, I want to add another dimension to that. Okay?"

"Okay," he said. "Multidimensional Anna. That seems like a good idea to me."

"Where do we start?"

"With you not falling off your chair laughing at me because I've offered to make you a woman."

A giggle rose in her throat again. Hysteria. She was verging on hysteria. Because this was uncomfortable and sincere. She hated both of those things. "I'm sorry. I can't. You can't say that to me and expect me not to choke."

He looked at her again, his dark eyes intense. "Is it a problem, Anna? The idea that I might make you a woman."

He purposefully made his voice deeper. Purposefully added a kind of provocative inflection to the words. She knew he was kidding. Still, it made her chest tighten. Made her heart flutter a little bit.

Wow. How *annoying*. She hadn't had a relapse of Chase Underpants Feelings this bad in a long time.

Apparently she still hadn't recovered from her earlier bit of mistaken identity. She really needed to recover. And he needed to stop being… Chase. If at all possible.

"Is it a problem for *you*?" she asked.

"What?"

"The idea that I might make you a soprano?"

He chuckled. "You probably want to hold off on threats of castration when you're at a fancy party."

"We aren't at one right now."

She was her own worst enemy. Everything that she had just been silently complaining about, she was doing right now. Throwing out barbs the moment she got uncomfortable, because it kept people from seeing what was actually happening inside of her.

Yes, but you really need to keep Chase from seeing that you fluttered internally over something he said.

Yes. Good point.

She noticed that he was looking past her now, and she followed his line of sight. He was looking at that blonde again. "Regrets, Chase?"

He winced, looking back at her. "No."

"So. I assume that to get a guy to come up and hit on me in a bar, I have to put on a dress that is essentially a red ACE bandage sprinkled with glitter?"

He hesitated. "It's more than that."

"What?"

"Well, for a start, there's not looking at a man like you want to dismember him."

She rolled her eyes. "I don't."

"You aren't exactly approachable, Anna."

"That isn't true." She liked to play darts, and hang out, and talk about sports. What wasn't approachable about that?

"I've seen men try to talk to you," Chase continued. "You shut them down pretty quick. For example—" he barreled on before she could interrupt him "—Ace Thompson paid you a compliment back at the bar."

"Ace Thompson compliments everything with boobs."

"And a couple of weeks ago there was a guy in here that tried to buy you a drink. You told him you could buy your own."

"I *can*," she said, "and he was a stranger."

"He was flirting with you."

She thought back on that night, that guy. *Damn.* He

had been flirting. "Well, he should get better at it. I'm not going to reward mediocrity. If I can't tell you're flirting, you aren't doing a very good job."

"Part of the problem is you don't think male attention is being directed at you when it actually is."

She looked back over at the shimmery blonde. "Why would any male attention be directed at me when *that's* over there?"

Chase leaned in, his expression taking on a conspiratorial quality that did…things to her insides. "Here's the thing about a girl like that. She knows she looks good. She assumes that men are looking at her. She assumes that if a man talks to her, that means he wants her."

She took a breath, trying to ease the tightness in her chest. "And that's not…a turnoff?"

"No way." He smiled, a sort of lazy half smile. "Confidence is sexy."

He kind of proved that rule. The thought made her bristle.

"All right. So far with our lessons I've learned that I should unzip my coveralls and as long as I'm confident it will be okay."

"You forgot not looking like you want to stab someone."

"Okay. Confident, nonstabby, showing my boobs."

Chase choked on his beer. "That's a good place to start," he said, setting the bottle down. "Do you want to go play darts? I want to go play darts."

"I thought we were having female lessons."

"Rain check," he said. "How about tomorrow I come by the shop and we get started. I think I'm going to need a lesson plan."

* * *

Chase hadn't exactly excelled in school, unless it was at driving his teachers to drink. So why exactly he had decided he needed a lesson plan to teach Anna how to be a woman, he didn't know.

All he knew was that somewhere around the time they started discussing her boobs last night he had become unable to process thoughts normally. He didn't like that. He didn't like it at all. He did not like the fact that he had been forced to consider her breasts more than once in a single hour. He did not like the fact that he was facing down the possibility of thinking about them a few more times over the next few weeks.

But then, that was the game.

Not only was he teaching her how to blend in at a function like this, he was pretending to be her date.

So there was more than one level of hell to deal with. Perfect.

He cleared his throat, walking down the front porch of the farmhouse that he shared with his brother, making his way across the property toward the shop that Anna was renting and using as her business.

It was after five, so she should be knocking off by now. A good time for the two of them to meet.

He looked down at the piece of lined yellow paper in his hand. His lesson plan.

Then he pressed on, his boots crunching on the gravel as he made his way to the rustic wood building. He inhaled deeply, the last gasp of winter riding over the top of the spring air, mixing with the salt from the sea, giving it a crisp bite unique to Copper Ridge.

He relished this. The small moment of clarity be-

She looked as though he had just suggested she eat a handful of bees. "Do we really need to do that?"

"Yeah, we *really* need to do that. You won't just have a date for the charity event. You're going to have a date every so often until then."

She looked skeptical. "That seems…excessive."

"You want people to believe this. You don't want people to think I'm going because of a bet. You don't want your brothers to think for one moment that they might be right."

"Well, they're going to think it for a few moments at least."

"True. I mean, they are going to be suspicious. But we can make this look real. It isn't going to be that hard. We already hang out most weekends."

"Sure," she said, "but you go home with other girls at the end of the night."

Those words struck him down. "Yes, I guess I do."

"You won't be able to do that now," she pointed out.

"Why not?" he asked.

"Because if I were with you and you went home with another woman, I would castrate you with nothing but my car keys and a bottle of whiskey."

He had no doubt about that. "At least you'd give me some whiskey."

"Hell no. The whiskey would be for me."

"But we're not really together," he said.

"Sure, Chase, but the entire town knows that if any man were to cheat on me, I would castrate him with my car keys, because I don't take crap from anyone. So if they're going to believe that we're together, you're going to have to look like you're being faithful to me."

"That's fine." It wasn't all that fine. He didn't do

celibacy. Never had. Not from the moment he'd discovered that women were God's greatest invention.

"No booty calls," she said, her tone stern.

"Wait a second. I can't even call a woman to hook up in private?"

"No. You can't. Because then *she* would know. I have pride. I mean, right now, standing here in this garage taking lessons from you on how to conform to my own gender's beauty standards, it's definitely marginal, but I have it."

"It isn't like you really know any of the girls that I…"

"Neither do you," she said.

"This isn't about me. It's about you. Now, I got you some things. But I left them in the house. And you are going to have to…hose off before you put them on."

She blinked, her expression almost comical. "Did you buy me clothes?"

He'd taken a long lunch and gone down to Main Street, popping into one of the ridiculously expensive shops that—in his mind—were mostly for tourists, and had found her a dress he thought would work.

"Yeah, I bought you clothes. Because we both know you can't actually wear this out tonight."

"We're going out *tonight*?"

"Hell yeah. I'm taking you somewhere fancy."

"My fancy threshold is very low. If I have to go eat tiny food on a stick sometime next month, I'm going to need actual sustenance in every other meal until then."

He chuckled, trying to imagine Anna coping with miniature food. "Beaches. I'm taking you to Beaches."

She screwed up her face slightly. "We don't go there."

"No, we haven't gone there. We go to Ace's. We

shoot pool, we order fried crap and we split the tab. Because we're friends. And that's what friends do. Friends don't go out to Beaches, not just the two of them. But lovers do."

She looked at him owlishly. "Right. I suppose they do."

"And when all this is finished, the entire town of Copper Ridge is going to think that we're lovers."

Chapter 3

Anna was reeling slightly by the time she walked up the front porch and into Chase's house. The entire town was going to think that they were...*lovers*. She had never had a lover. At least, she would never characterize the guy she'd slept with as a lover. He was an unfortunate incident. But fortunately, her hymen was the only casualty. Her heart had remained intact, and she was otherwise uninjured. Or pleasured.

Lovers.

That word sounded...well, like it came from some old movie or something. Which under normal circumstances she was a big fan of. In this circumstance, it just made her feel...like her insides were vibrating. She didn't like it.

Chase lived in the old family home on the property. It was a large, log cabin–style house with warm, honey-colored wood and a green metal roof designed to withstand all kinds of weather. Wrought-iron details on the porch and the door were a testament to his and Sam's craftsmanship. There were people who would pay millions for a home like this. But Sam and Chase had made it this beautiful on their own.

Chase always kept the home admirably clean considering he was a bachelor. She imagined that the other house on the property, the smaller one inhabited by Sam, wasn't quite as well kept. But she also imagined that Sam didn't have the same amount of guests over that Chase did. And by *guests*, she meant female companions. Which he would be cut off from for the next few weeks.

Some small, mean part of her took a little bit of joy in that.

Because you don't like the idea of other women touching him. It doesn't matter how long it's been going on, or how many women there are, you still don't like it.

She sniffed, cutting off that line of thinking. She was just a crabby bitch who was enjoying the idea of him being celibate and suffering a bit. That was all.

"Okay, where are my…girlie things?"

"You aren't even going to look at them until you scrub that grease off."

"And how am I supposed to do that? Are you going to hose me off?"

He clenched his jaw. "No. You can use my shower."

She took a deep breath, trying to dispel the slight fluttering in her stomach. She had never used Chase's shower before. She assumed countless women before her had. When he brought them up here, took their clothes off for them. And probably joined them.

She wasn't going to think about that.

"Okay."

She knew where his shower was, of course. Because she had been inside his bedroom casually, countless times. It had never mattered before. Before, she had never been about to get naked.

She banished that thought as she walked up the stairs and down the hall to his room. His room was... well, it was very well-appointed, but then again, obviously designed to house guests of the female variety. The bed was large and full of plush pillows. A soft-looking green throw was folded up at the foot of it. An overstuffed chair was in the corner, another blanket draped over the back.

She doubted the explosion of comfort and cozy was for Chase's benefit.

She tamped that thought down, continuing on through the bathroom door, then locking it for good measure. Not that he would walk in. And he was the only person in the house.

Still, she felt insecure without the lock flipped. She took a deep breath, stripped off her coveralls, then the clothes she had on beneath them, and started the shower. Speaking of things that were designed to be shared...

It was enclosed in glass, and she had a feeling that with the door open it was right in the line of sight from the bed. Inside was red tile, and a bench seat that... She wasn't even going to think what that could be used for.

She turned and looked in the mirror. She was grubby. More than grubby. She had grease all over her face, all up under her fingernails.

Thankfully, Chase had some orange-and-pumice

cleaner right there on his sink. So she was able to start scrubbing at her hands while the water warmed up.

Steam filled the air and she stepped inside the shower, letting the hot spray cascade over her skin.

It was a *massaging* showerhead. A nice one. She did not have a nice massaging showerhead in her little rental house down in town. Next on her list of Ways She Was Changing Her Life would be to get her own house. With one of these.

She rolled her shoulders beneath the spray and sighed. The water droplets almost felt like fingers moving over her tight muscles. And, suddenly, it was all too easy to imagine a man standing behind her, working at her muscles with his strong hands.

She closed her eyes, letting her head fall back, her mouth going slack. She didn't even have the strength to fight the fantasy, God help her. She'd been edgy and aroused for the past twenty-four hours, no denying it. So this little moment to let herself fantasize… she just needed it.

Then she realized exactly whose hands she was picturing.

Chase's. Tall and strong behind her, his hands moving over her skin, down lower to the slight dip in her spine, just above the curve of her behind…

She grabbed hold of the sponge hanging behind her and began to drag it ferociously over her skin, only belatedly realizing that this was probably what he used to wash himself.

"He uses it to wash his balls," she said into the space. Hoping that that would disgust her. It really should disgust her.

It did not disgust her.

She put the scrubber back, taking a little shower gel and squeezing it into the palm of her hand. Okay, so she would smell like a playboy for a day. It wasn't the end of the world. She started to rub the slick soap over her flesh, ignoring the images of Chase that were trying to intrude.

She was being a crazy person. She had showered at friends' houses before, and never imagined that they were in the shower stall with her.

But ever since last night in the bar, her equilibrium had been off where Chase was concerned. Her control was being sorely tested. She was decidedly unstoked about it.

She shut the water off and got out of the shower, grabbing a towel off the rack and drying her skin with more ferocity than was strictly necessary. Almost as though she was trying to punish her wicked, wicked skin for imagining what it might be like to be touched by her best friend.

But that would be crazy.

Except she felt a little crazy.

She looked around the room. And realized that her stupid friend, who had not wanted her to touch the nice clothing he had bought her, had left her without anything to wear. She couldn't put her sweaty, grease-covered clothes back on. That would negate the entire shower.

She let out an exasperated breath, not entirely certain what she should do.

"Chase?" she called.

She didn't hear anything.

"Chase?" She raised the volume this time.

Still no answer.

"Butthead," she muttered, walking over to the door and tapping the doorknob, trying to decide what her next move was.

She was being ridiculous. Just because she was having an increase of weird, borderline sexual thoughts about him, did not mean he was having them about her. She twisted the knob, undoing the lock as she did, and opened the door a crack. "Chase!"

The door to the bedroom swung open, and Chase walked in, carrying one of those plastic bags fancy dresses were stored in and a pair of shoes.

"I don't have clothes," she hissed through the crack in the door.

"Sorry," he said, looking stricken. At least, she thought he looked stricken.

She opened the door slightly wider, extending her arm outside. "Give them to me."

He crossed the room, walking over to the bathroom door. "You're going to have to open the door wider than that."

She already felt exposed. There was nothing between them. Nothing but some air and the towel she was clutching to her naked body. Well, and most of the door. But she still felt exposed.

Still, he was not going to fit that bag through the crack.

She opened the door slightly wider, then grabbed hold of the bag in his hand and jerked it back through. "I'll get the shoes later," she called through the door.

She dropped the towel and unzipped the bag, staring at the contents with no small amount of horror. There was…underwear inside of it. Underwear that Chase had purchased for her.

Which meant he had somehow managed to look at her breasts and evaluate their size. Not to mention her ass. And ass size.

She grabbed the pair of panties that were attached to a little hanger. Oh, they had no ass. So she supposed the size of hers didn't matter much.

She swallowed hard, taking hold of the soft material and rubbing her thumb over it. He would know exactly what she was wearing beneath the dress. Would know just how little that was.

He isn't going to think about it. Because he doesn't think about you that way.

He never had. He never would. And it was a damn good thing. Because where would they be if either of them acted on an attraction between them?

Up shit creek without a paddle or a friendship.

No, thank you. She was never going to touch him. She'd made that decision a long time ago. For a lot of reasons that were as valid today as they had been the very first time he'd ever made her stomach jump when she looked at him.

She was never going to encourage or act on the attraction that she occasionally felt for Chase. But she would take his expertise in sexual politics and use it to her advantage.

Oh, but those panties.

The bra wasn't really any less unsettling. Though at least it wasn't missing large swathes of fabric.

Still, it was very thin. And she had a feeling that a cool ocean breeze would reveal the shape of her nipples to all and sundry.

Then again, maybe it was time all and sundry got

a look at her nipples. Maybe if they had a better view, men would be a little more interested.

She scowled, wrenching the panties off the hanger and dragging them on as quickly as possible, followed closely by the bra. She was overthinking things. She was overthinking all of this. Had been from the moment Chase had walked into the barn. As evidenced by that lapse in the shower.

She had spent years honing her Chase Control. It was just this change in how they were interacting that was screwing with it. She was not letting this get inside her head, and she was not letting hot, unsettled feelings get inside her pants.

She pulled the garment bag away entirely, revealing a tight red dress slightly too reminiscent of what the woman he had been flirting with last night was wearing.

"Clearly you have a type, Chase McCormack," she muttered, beginning to remove the slinky scrap of material from the hanger.

She tugged it up over her hips, having to do a pretty intense wiggle to get it up all the way before zipping it into place. She took a deep breath, turned around. She faced her reflection in the mirror full-on and felt nothing but deflated.

She looked…well, her hair was wet and straggly, and she looked half-drowned. She didn't look curvy, or shimmery, or delightful.

This was the problem with tight clothes. They only made her more aware of her curve deficit.

Where the blonde last night had filled her dress out admirably, and in all the right places, on Anna this dress kind of looked like a piece of fabric stretched over an ironing board. Not really all that sexy.

She sighed heavily, trying to ignore the sinking feeling in her stomach.

Chase really was going to have to be a miracle worker in order to pull this off.

She didn't really want to show him. Instead, she found the idea of putting the coveralls back on a lot less reprehensible. At least with the coveralls there would still be some mystery. He wouldn't be confronted with just how big a task lay before him.

"Buck up," she said to herself.

So what was one more moment of feeling inadequate? Honestly, in the broad tapestry of her life it would barely register. She was never quite what was expected. She never quite fit. So why'd she expect that she was going to put on a sexy dress and suddenly be transformed into the kind of sex kitten she didn't even want to be?

She gritted her teeth, throwing open the bedroom door and walking out into the room. "I hope you're happy," she said, flinging her arms wide. "You get what you get."

She caught a movement out of the corner of her eye and turned her head, then recoiled in horror. It was even worse out here. Out here, there was a full-length mirror. Out here, she had the chance to see that while her breasts remained stunningly average, her hips and behind had gotten rather wide. Which was easy to ignore when you wore loose attire most days. "I look like the woman symbol on the door of a public restroom."

She looked over at Chase, who had been completely silent upon her entry into the room, and remained so.

She glared at him. He wasn't saying anything. He was only staring. "Well?"

"It's nice," he said.

His voice sounded rough, and kind of thin.

"You're a liar."

"I'm not a liar. Put the shoes on."

"Do you even know what size I wear?"

"You're a size ten, which I know because you complain about how your big feet make it impossible for you to find anything in your size. And you're better off buying men's work boots. So yes, I know."

His words made her feel suddenly exposed. Well, his words in combination with the dress, she imagined. They knew each other a little bit too well. That was the problem. How could you impress a guy when you had spent a healthy amount of time bitching to him about your big feet?

"Fine. I will put on the shoes." He held them up, and her jaw dropped. "I thought you were taking me out to dinner."

"I am."

"Do I have to pay for it by working the pole at the Naughty Mermaid?"

"These are *nice* shoes."

"If you're a five-foot-two-inch Barbie like that chick you were talking to last night. I'm like…an Amazon in comparison."

"You're not an Amazon."

"I will be in those."

"Maybe that would bother some men. But you want a man who knows how to handle a woman. Any guy with half a brain is going to lose his mind checking out your legs. He's not going to care if you're a little taller than he is."

She tried her best to ignore the compliment about her legs. And tried even harder to keep from blushing.

"I care," she muttered, snatching the shoes from his hand and pondering whether or not there was any truth to her words as she did.

She didn't really date. So it was hard to say. But now that she was thinking about it, yeah. She was self-conscious about the fact that with pretty low heels she was eye level with half the men in town.

She finished putting the shoes on and straightened. It was like standing on a glittery pair of stilts. "Are you satisfied?" she asked.

"I guess you could say that." He was regarding her closely, his jaw tense, a muscle in his cheek ticking.

She noticed that he was still a couple of inches taller than her. Even with the shoes. "I guess you still meet the height requirement to be my dinner date."

"I didn't have any doubt."

"I don't know how to walk in these," she said.

"All right. Practice."

"Are you out of your mind? I have to *practice* walking?"

"You said yourself, you don't know how to walk in heels. So, go on. Walk the length of the room."

She felt completely awash in humiliation. She doubted there was another woman on the planet that Chase had ever had to instruct on walking.

"This is ridiculous."

"It's not," he said.

"All of women's fashion is ridiculous," she maintained. "Do you have to learn how to walk when you put on dress shoes? No, you do not. And yet, a full-scale lesson is required for me to go out if I want to wear something that's considered *feminine*."

"Yeah, it's sexist. And a real pain in the ass, I'm sure. It's also hot. Now walk."

She scowled at him, then took her first step, wobbling a bit. "I don't understand why women do this."

She took another step, then another, wobbling a little less each time. But the shoes did force her hips to sway, much more than they normally would. "Do you have any pointers?" she asked.

"I date women in heels, Anna. *I've* never walked in them."

"What happened to helping me be a woman?"

"You'll get the hang of it. It's like… I don't know, water-skiing maybe?"

"How is this like water-skiing?"

"You have to learn how to do it and there's a good likelihood you'll fall on your face?"

"Well, I take it all back," she said, deadpan. "These shoes aren't silly at all." She took another step, then another. "I feel like a newborn baby deer."

"You look a little like one, too."

She snorted. "You really need to up your game, Chase. If you use these lines on all the women you take out, you're bound to start striking out sooner or later."

"I haven't struck out yet."

"Well, you're still young and pretty. Just wait. Just wait until time starts to claim your muscular forearms and chiseled jawline."

"I figure by then maybe I'll have gotten the ranch back to its former glory. At that point women will sleep with me for my money."

She rolled her eyes. "It's nice to have goals."

In her opinion, Chase should have better goals for himself. But then, who was she to talk? Her current goal was to show her brothers that they were idiots and she could too get a date. Hardly a lofty ambition.

"Yes, it is. And right now my goal is for us not to miss our reservation."

"You made a…reservation?"

"I did."

"It's not like it's Valentine's Day or something. The restaurant isn't going to be full."

"Of course it won't be. But I figured if I made a reservation for the two of us, we could start a rumor, too."

"A rumor?"

"Yeah, because Ellie Matthews works at Beaches, and I believe she has been known to *service* your brother Mark."

Anna winced at the terminology. "True."

"I thought the news of our dining experience might make it back to him. Like I said, the more we can make this look organic, the better."

"No one ever need know that our relationship is in fact grown in a lab. And in no way GMO free," she said.

"Exactly."

"I don't have any makeup on." She frowned. "I don't have any makeup. At all."

"Right," he said. "I didn't really think of that."

She reached out and smacked him on the shoulder. "You're supposed to be my coach. You're failing me."

He laughed, dodging her next blow. "You don't need makeup."

She let out an exasperated sigh. "You're just saying that."

"In fairness, you did threaten to castrate me with your car keys earlier."

"I did."

"And you hit me just now," he pointed out.

"It didn't hurt, you baby."

He took a deep breath, and suddenly his expression turned sharp. "Believe me when I tell you you don't need makeup." He reached out, gripping her chin with his thumb and forefinger. His touch was like a branding iron, hot, altering. "As long as you believe it, everyone else will, too. You have to believe in yourself, Anna."

He released his hold on her, straightening. "Now," he said, his tone getting a little bit rougher, "let's go to dinner."

Chase felt like he had been tipped sideways and left walking on the walls from the moment that Anna had emerged from the bathroom at his house wearing that dress. Once she had put on those shoes, the feeling had only gotten worse.

But who knew that underneath those coveralls his best friend looked like that?

She had been eyeing herself critically, and his brain had barely been working at all. Because he didn't see anything to criticize. All he saw was the kind of figure that would make a man willingly submit to car key castration.

She was long and lean, toned from all the physical labor she did. Her breasts were small, but he imagined they would fit in a man's hand nicely. And her hips…well, using the same measurement used for her breasts, they would be about perfect for holding on to while a man…

Holy hell. He was losing his mind.

She was Anna. Anna Brown, his best friend in the entire world. The one woman he had never even considered going there with. He didn't want a relationship with the women he slept with. When your only criteria for being with a woman was orgasm, there were a lot of options available to you. For a little bit of satisfaction he could basically seek out any woman in the room.

Sex was easy. Connections were hard.

And so Anna had been placed firmly off-limits from day one. He'd had a vague awareness of her for most of his life. That was how growing up in a small town worked. You went to the same school from the beginning. But they had separate classes, plus at the time he'd been pretty convinced girls had cooties.

But that had changed their first year of high school. He'd ended up in metal shop with the prickly teen and had liked her right away. There weren't very many girls who cursed as much as the boys and had a more comprehensive understanding of the inner workings of engines than the teachers at the school. But Anna did.

She hadn't fit in with any of the girls, and so Chase and Sam had been quick to bring her into their group. Over the years, people had rotated in and out, moved, gone their separate ways. But Chase and Anna had remained close.

In part because he had kept his dick out of the equation.

As they walked up the path toward Beaches, he considered putting his hand on her lower back. Really, he should. Except it was potentially problematic at the moment. Was he this shallow? Stick her in a tight-fitting dress and suddenly he couldn't control himself? It was a sobering realization, but not really all that surprising.

This was what happened when you spent a lot of time practicing no restraint when it came to sex.

He gritted his teeth, lifting his hand for a moment before placing it gently on her back. Because it was what he would do with any other date, so it was what he needed to do with Anna.

She went stiff beneath his touch. "Relax," he said, keeping his voice low. "This is supposed to look like a date, remember?"

"I should have worn a white tank top and a pair of jeans," she said.

"Why?"

"Because this looks… It looks like I'm trying too hard."

"No, it looks like you put on a nice outfit to please me."

She turned to face him, her brow furrowed. "Which is part of the problem. If I had to do this to please you, we both know that I would tell you to please yourself."

He laughed, the moment so classically Anna, so familiar, it was at odds with the other feelings that were buzzing through his blood. With how soft she felt beneath his touch. With just how much she was affecting him in this figure-hugging dress.

"I have no doubt you would."

They walked up the steps that led into the large white restaurant, and he opened the door, holding it for her. She looked at him like he'd just caught fire. He stared her down, and then she looked away from him, walking through the door.

He moved up next to her once they were inside. "You're going to have to seem a little more at ease with this change in our relationship."

"You're being weird."

"I'm not being weird. I'm treating you like a lady."

"What have you been treating me like for the past fifteen years?" she asked.

"A…bro."

She snorted, shaking her head and walking toward the front of the house where Ellie Matthews was standing, waiting for guests. "I believe we have a reservation," Anna said.

He let out a long-suffering sigh. "Yes," he confirmed. "Under my name."

Ellie's eyebrow shot upward. "Yes. You do."

"Under Chase McCormack and Anna Brown," Chase clarified.

"I know," she said.

Ellie needed to work on her people skills. "It was difficult for me to tell, since you look so surprised," Chase said.

"Well, I knew you were reserving the table for the two of you, but I didn't realize you were…reserving the table for *the two of you*." She was looking at Anna's dress, her expression meaningful.

"Well, I was," he said. "Did. So, is the table ready?"

She looked around the half-full dining area. "Yeah, I'm pretty sure we can seat you now."

Ellie walked them over to one of the tables by a side window that looked out over the Skokomish River where it fed into the ocean. The sun was dipping low over the water, the rays sparkling off the still surface of the slow-moving river. There were people milling along the wooden boardwalk that was bordered by docks on one side and storefronts on the other, before being split by the highway and starting again, leading down to the beach.

He looked away from the scenery, back at Anna. They had shared countless meals together, but this was different. Normally, they didn't sit across from each other at a tiny table complete with a freaking candle in the middle. Mood lighting.

"Your server will be with you shortly," Ellie said as she walked away, leaving them there with menus and each other.

"I want a burger," Anna said, not looking at the menu at all.

"You could get something fancier."

"I'll get it with a cheese I can't pronounce."

"I'm getting salmon."

"Am I paying?" she asked, an impish smile playing around the corners of her lips. "Because if so, you better be putting out at the end of this."

Her words were like a punch in the gut. And he did his best to ignore them. He swallowed hard. "No, *I'm* paying."

"I'll pay you back after. You're doing me a favor."

"The favor's mutual. I want to go to the fund-raiser. It's important to me."

"You still aren't buying my dinner."

"I'm not taking your money."

"Then I'm going to overpay for rent on the shop next month," she said, her tone uncompromising.

"Half of that goes to Sam."

"Then he gets half of it. But I'm not going to let you buy my dinner."

"You're being stubborn."

She leaned back in her chair, crossing her arms and treating him to that hard glare of hers. "Yep."

A few moments later the waiter came over, and Anna ordered her hamburger, and the cheeses she wanted, by pointing at the menu.

"Which cheese did you get?" he asked, attempting to move on from their earlier standoff.

"I don't know." She shrugged. "I can't pronounce it."

They made about ten minutes of awkward conversation while they waited for their dinner to come. Which was weird, because conversation was never awkward with Anna. It was that dress. And those shoes. And his penis. That was part of the problem. Because, suddenly, it was actually interested in his best friend.

No, it is not. A moment of checking her out does not mean that you want to...do anything with her.

Exactly. It wasn't a big deal. It wasn't anything to get worked up about. Not at all.

When their dinner was placed in front of them, Anna attacked her sweet potato fries, probably using them as a displacement activity.

"Chase?"

Chase looked up and inwardly groaned when he saw Wendy Maxwell headed toward the table. They'd all gone to high school together. And he had, regrettably, slept with Wendy once or twice over the years after drinking too much at Ace's.

She was hot. But what she had in looks had been deducted from her personality. Which didn't matter when you were only having sex, but mattered later when you had to interact in public.

"Hi, Wendy," he said, taking a bite of his salmon.

Anna had gone very still across from him; she wasn't even eating her fries anymore.

"Are you… Are you on a date?" Wendy asked, tilting her head to the side, her expression incredulous.

Wendy wasn't very smart in addition to being not very nice. A really bad combination.

"Yes," he said, "I am."

"With Anna?"

"Yeah," Anna said, looking up. "The person sitting across from him. Like you do on a date."

"I'm just surprised."

He could see color mounting in Anna's cheeks, could see her losing her hold on her temper.

"Are you here by yourself?" Anna asked.

Wendy laughed, the sound like broken crystal being pushed beneath his skin. "No. Of course not. We're having a girls' night out." She eyed Chase. "Of course, that doesn't mean I'm going home with the girls."

Suddenly, Anna was standing, and he was a little bit afraid she was about to deck Wendy. Who deserved it. But he didn't really want to be at the center of a girl fight in the middle of Beaches.

That only worked in fantasies. Less so in real life.

But it wasn't Wendy whom Anna moved toward.

She took two steps, came to a stop in front of Chase and then leaned forward, grabbing hold of the back of his chair and resting her knee next to his thigh. Then she pressed her hand to his cheek and took a deep breath, making determined eye contact with him just before she let her lids flutter closed. Just before she closed the distance between them and kissed him.

Chapter 4

She was kissing Chase McCormack. Beyond that, she had no idea what the flying F-bomb she was doing. If there was another person in the room, she didn't see them. If there was a reason she'd started this, she didn't remember it.

There was nothing. Nothing more than the hot press of Chase's lips against hers. Nothing more than still, leashed power beneath her touch. She could feel his tension, could feel his strength frozen beneath her.

It was…intoxicating. Empowering.

So damn *hot*.

Like she was about to melt the soles of her shoes hot. About to come without his hands ever touching her body hot.

And that was unheard-of for her.

She'd kissed a couple of guys, and slept with one,

and orgasm had never been in the cards. When it came to climaxes, she was her own hero. But damn if Chase wasn't about to be her hero in under thirty seconds, and with nothing more than a little dry lip-to-lip contact.

Except it didn't stay dry.

Suddenly, he reached up, curling his fingers around the back of her head, angling his own and kissing her hard, deep. With tongue.

She whimpered, the leg that was supporting her body melting, only the firm hold he had on her face, and the support of his chair, keeping her from sliding onto the ground.

The slick glide of his tongue against hers was the single sexiest thing she'd ever experienced in her life. And just like that, every little white lie she'd ever told herself about her attraction to Chase was completely and fully revealed.

It wasn't just a momentary response to an attractive man. Not something any red-blooded female would feel. Not just a passing anomaly.

It was real.

It was deep.

She was so screwed.

Way too screwed to care that they were making out in a fancy restaurant in front of people, and that for him it was just a show, but for her it was a whole cataclysmic, near-orgasmic shift happening in the region of her panties.

Seconds had passed, but they felt like minutes. Hours. Whole days' worth of life-changing moments, all crammed into something that probably hadn't actually lasted longer than the blink of an eye.

Then it was over. She was the one who pulled away and she wasn't quite sure how she managed. But she did.

She wasn't breathing right. Her entire body was shaking, and she was sure her face was red. But still, she turned and faced Wendy, or whichever mean girl it was. There were a ton of them in her nonhalcyon high school years and they all blended together. The who wasn't important. Only the what. The *what* being a kiss she'd just given to the hottest guy in town, right in front of someone who didn't think she was good enough. Pretty enough. Girlie enough.

"Yeah," she said, her voice a little less triumphant and a lot more unsteady than she would like, "we're here on a date. And he's going home with me. So I'd suggest you wiggle on over to a different table if you want to score tonight."

Wendy's face was scrunched into a sour expression. "That's okay, honey, if you want my leftovers, you're welcome to them."

Then she flipped her blond hair and walked back to her table, essentially acting out the cliché of every snotty girl in a teen movie.

Which was not so cute when you were thirty and not fifteen.

But, of course, since Wendy was gone, they'd lost the buffer against the aftermath of the kiss, and the terrible awkwardness that was just sitting there, seething, growing.

"Well, I think that started some rumors," Anna said, sitting back down and shoving a fry into her mouth.

"I bet," Chase said, clearing his throat and turning back toward his plate.

"My mouth has never touched your mouth directly

before," she said, then stuffed another fry straight into her mouth, wishing it wasn't too late to stifle those ridiculous words.

He choked on his beer. "Um. No."

"What I mean is, we've shared drinks before. I've taken bites off your sandwiches. Literally sandwiches, not— I mean, whatever. The point is, we've germ-shared before. We just never did it mouth-to-mouth."

"That wasn't CPR, babe."

She made a face, hoping the disgust in her expression would disguise the twist low and deep in her stomach. "Don't call me babe just because I kissed you."

"We're dating, remember?"

"No one is listening to us talk at the table," she insisted.

"You don't know that."

Her heart was thundering hard like a trapped bird in her chest and she didn't know if she could look at him for another minute without either scurrying from the room like a frightened animal or grabbing him and kissing him again.

She didn't like it. She didn't like any of it.

It all felt too real, too raw and too scary. It all came from a place too deep inside her.

So she decided to do what came easiest. Exactly what she did best.

"I expected better," she told him, before taking a bite of her burger.

"What?"

"You're like a legendary stud," she said, after swallowing her food. "The man who every man wants to be and who every woman wants to be with. Blah, blah." She picked up another sweet potato fry.

"It wasn't good for you?" he asked.

"Six point five from the German judge. Who is me, in this scenario." She was a liar. She was a liar and she was a jerk, and she wanted to punch her own face. But the alternative was to show that she was breaking apart inside. That she had been on the verge of the kind of ecstasy she'd only ever imagined, and that she wanted to kiss him forever, not just for thirty seconds. And that was...damaging. It wasn't something she could admit.

"Six point five."

"Sorry." She lifted her shoulder and shoved the fry into her mouth.

They finished the rest of the dinner in awkward silence, which made her mad because things weren't supposed to be awkward between them. They were friends, dammit. She was starting to think this whole thing was a mistake.

She could bring Chase as her plus one to the charity thing without her brothers buying into it. She could lose the bet. The whole town could suspect she'd brought a friend because she was undatable and who even cared?

If playing this game was going to screw with their friendship, it wasn't worth it.

Chase paid the tab—she was going to pay the bastard back whether he wanted her to or not—and then the two of them walked outside. And that was when she realized her truck was back at his place and he was going to have to give her a ride.

That sucked donkey balls. She needed to get some Chase space. And it wasn't going to happen.

She wanted to go home and put on soft pajamas and watch *Seven Brides for Seven Brothers*. She needed a safe, flannel-lined space and the fuzzy comfort of an old movie. A chance to breathe and be vulnerable for a second where no one would see.

She was afraid Chase might have seen already.

They still didn't talk—all the way back out of town and to the McCormack family ranch, they didn't talk.

"My dirty clothes are in your house," she said at last, when they pulled into the driveway. "You can take me to the house first instead of the shop."

"I can wash them with mine," he said.

Her underwear was in there. That was not happening.

"No, I left them folded in the corner of the bathroom. I'd rather come get them. And put my shoes on before I try to drive home actually. How do people drive in these?" She tapped the precarious shoes against the floor of the pickup.

Chase let out a harsh-sounding breath. "Fine," he said. He sounded aggrieved, but he drove on past the shop to the house. He stopped the truck abruptly, throwing it into Park and killing the engine. "Come on in."

Now he was mad at her. Great. It wasn't like he needed her to stroke his ego. He had countless women to do that. He had just one woman who listened to his bullshit and put up with all his nonsense, and in general stood by him no matter what. That was her. He could have endless praise for his bedroom skills from those other women. He only had friendship from *her*. So he could simmer down a little.

She got out of the truck, then wobbled when her foot hit a loose gravel patch. She clung tightly to the door, a very wussy-sounding squeak escaping her lips.

"You okay there, *babe*?" he asked, just to piss her off.

"Yeah, fine. Jerk," she retorted.

"What the hell, Anna?" he asked, his tone hard.

"Oh, come on, you're being weird. You can't pretend you aren't just because you're layering passivity over your aggression." She stalked past him as fast as her shoes would let her, walked up the porch and stood by the door, her arms crossed.

"It's not locked," he said, taking the stairs two at a time.

"Well, I wasn't going to go in without your permission. I have manners."

"Do you?" he asked.

"If I didn't, I probably would have punched you by now." She opened the door and stomped up the stairs, until her heel rolled inward slightly and she stumbled. Then she stopped stomping and started taking a little more consideration for her joints.

She was mad at him. She was mad at herself for being mad at him, because the situation was mostly her fault. And she was mad at him for being mad at her for being mad at him.

Mad, mad, *mad.*

She walked into the bathroom and picked up her stack of clothes, careful not to hold the greasy articles against her dress. The dress that was the cause of so many of tonight's problems.

It's not the dress. It's the fact that you kissed him and now you can't deal.

Rationality was starting to creep in and she was nothing if not completely irritated about that. It was forcing her to confront the fact that she was actually the one being a jerk, not him. That she was the one who was overreacting, and his behavior was all a response to the fact that she'd gone full Anna-pine, with quills out ready to defend herself at all costs.

She took a deep breath and sat down on the edge of his bed, trading the high heels for her sneakers, then collecting her things again and walking back down the stairs, her feet tingling and aching as they got used to resting flat once more.

Chase wasn't inside.

She opened the front door and walked out onto the porch.

He was standing there, the porch light shining on him like a beacon. His broad shoulders, trim waist… oh, Lord, his ass. Wrangler butt was a gift from God in her opinion and Chase's was perfect. Something she'd noticed before, but right now it was physically painful to look at him and not close the space between them. To not touch him.

This was bad. This was why she hadn't ever touched him before. Why it would have been best if she never had.

She had needs. Fuzzy-blanket needs. She needed to get home.

She cleared her throat. "I'm ready," she said. "I just… If you could give me a lift down to the shop, that would be nice. So that I'm not cougar food."

He turned slowly, a strange expression on his face. "Yeah, I wouldn't want you to get eaten by any mangy predators."

"I appreciate that."

He headed down the steps and got back into the truck, and she followed, climbing into the cab beside him. He started the engine and maneuvered the truck onto the gravel road that ran through the property.

She rested her elbow on the armrest, staring outside at the inky black shadows of the pine trees, and the white glitter of stars in the velvet-blue sky. It was a clear night, unusual for their little coastal town.

If only her head was as clear as the sky.

It was full. Full of regret and woe. She didn't like that. As soon as Chase pulled up to the shop, she scrambled out, not waiting for him to put the vehicle in Park. She was heading toward her own vehicle when she heard Chase behind her.

"What are you doing?" she asked, turning to face him.

But her words were cut off by what he did next. He took one step toward her, closing the distance between them as he wrapped his arm around her waist and drew her up against his chest. Then, before she could protest, before she could say anything, he was kissing her again.

This was different than the kiss at the restaurant. This was different than…well, than any kiss in the whole history of the world.

His kiss tasted of the familiarity of Chase and the strangeness of his anger. Of heat and lust and rage all rolled into one.

She knew him better than she knew almost anyone. Knew the shape of his face, knew his scent, knew his voice. But his scent surrounding her like this, the feel of his face beneath her hands, the sound of that voice—transformed into a feral, passionate growl as he continued to ravish her—was an unknown. Was something else entirely.

Then, suddenly—just as suddenly as he had initiated it—the kiss was over. He released his hold on her, pushing her back. There was nothing but air between them now. Air and a whole lot of feelings. He was standing there, his hands planted on his lean hips, his chest rising and falling with each labored breath. "Six point five?" he asked, his tone challenging. "That sure as hell was no six point five, Anna Brown, and if you're honest with yourself, you have to admit that."

She sucked in a harsh, unsteady breath, trying to keep the shock from showing on her face. "I don't have to admit any such thing."

"You're a little liar."

"What does it matter?" she asked, scowling.

"How would you like it if I told you that you were only average compared to other women I've kissed?"

"I'd shut your head in the truck door."

"Exactly." He crossed his arms over his broad chest. "So don't think I'm going to let the same insults stand, honey."

"Don't *babe* me," she spat. "Don't *honey* me."

Triumph glittered in his dark eyes. The smugness so certain it was visible even in the moonlight. "Then don't kiss me again."

"You were the one who kissed me!" she shouted, throwing her arms wide.

"*This* time. But you started it. Don't do it again." He turned around, heading back toward his truck. All she could do was stand there and stare as he drove away.

Something had changed tonight. Something inside of her. She didn't think she liked it at all.

Chapter 5

"Now, I don't want to be insensitive or hurt your feelings, princess, but why are you being such an asshole today?"

Chase looked over at Sam, who was staring at him from his position by the forge. The fire was going hot and they were pounding out iron, doing some repairs on equipment. By hand. Just the way both of them liked to work.

"I'm not," Chase said.

"Right. Look, there's only room for one of us to be a grumpy cuss, and I pretty much have that position filled. So I would appreciate it if you can get your act together."

"Sorry, Sam, are you unable to take what you dish out every day?"

"What's going on with you and Anna?"

Chase bristled at the mention of the woman he'd kissed last night. Then he winced when he remembered the kiss. Well, *remembered* was the wrong word. He'd never forgotten it. But right now he was mentally replaying it, moment by moment. "What did you hear?"

Sam laughed. An honest-to-God laugh. "Do I look like I'm on the gossip chain? I haven't talked to anybody. It's just that I saw her leaving your house last night wearing a red dress and sneakers, and then saw her this morning when she went into the shop. She was pissier than you are."

"Anna is always pissy." Sam treated his statement to a prolonged stare. "It's not a big deal. It's just that her brothers bet her that she couldn't get a date. I figured I would help her out with that."

"How?"

"Well…" he said, hesitating about telling his brother the whole story. Sam wasn't looking to change the business on the ranch. He didn't care about their family legacy. Not like Chase did. But Chase had made promises to tombstones and he wasn't about to break them.

It was one of their main sources of contention. So he wasn't exactly looking forward to having this conversation with his older brother.

But it wasn't like he could hide it forever. He'd just sort of been hoping he could hide it until he'd shown up with investment money.

"That's an awfully long pause," Sam said. "I'm willing to bet that whatever you're about to say, I'm not going to like it."

"You know me well. Anna got invited to go to the big community charity event that the West family hosts every year. Now I want to make sure that we can extend our contract with them. Plus…doing horseshoes and gates isn't cutting it. We can move into doing details on custom homes. To doing art pieces and selling our work across the country, not just locally. To do that we need investors. And the West fund-raiser's a great place to find them. Plus, if I only have to wear a suit once and can speak to everyone in town that might be interested in a single shot? Well, I can't beat that."

"Dammit, Chase, you know I don't want to commit to something like that."

"Right. You want to continue on the way we always have. You want to shoe horses when we can, pound metal when the opportunity presents itself, build gates, or whatever else might need doing, then go off and work on sculptures and things in your spare time. But that's not going to be enough. Less and less is done by hand, and people aren't willing to pay for hand-crafted materials. Machines can build cheaper stuff than we can.

"But the thing is, you can make it look special. You can turn it into something amazing. Like you did with my house. It's the details that make a house expensive. We can have the sort of clients who don't want work off an assembly line. The kind who will pay for one of a kind pieces. From art on down to the handles on their kitchen cabinets. We could get into some serious custom work. Vacation homes are starting to spring up around here, plus people are renovating to make rentals thanks to the tourism increase. But we need some investors if we're really going to get into this."

"You know I hate this. I don't like the idea of charging a ton of money for a…for a gate with an elk on it."

"You're an artist, Sam," he said, watching his

brother wince as he said the words. "I know you hate that. But it's true."

"I hate that, too."

"You're talented."

"I hit metal with a hammer. Sometimes I shape it into something that looks nice. It's not really all that special."

"You do more than that and you know it. It's what people would be willing to pay for. If you would stop being such a nut job about it."

Sam rubbed the back of his neck, his expression shuttered. "You've gotten off topic," he said finally. "I asked you about Anna, not your schemes for exploiting my talents."

"Not really. The two are connected. I want to go to this thing to talk to the Wests. I want to talk about investment opportunities and expanding contracts with other people deemed worthy of an invite. In case you haven't noticed, we weren't on that list."

"Yeah, I get that. But why would the lately not-so-great McCormacks be invited?"

"That's the problem. This place hasn't been what it was for a couple of generations, and when we lost Mom and Dad…well, we were teenagers trying to keep up a whole industry, and now we work *for* these people, not with them. I aim to change that."

"You didn't think about talking to me?" Sam asked.

"Oh, I did. And I decided I didn't want to have to deal with you."

Sam shot him an evil glare. "So you're going as Anna's date. And helping her win her bet."

"Exactly."

"And you took her out last night, and she went back to your place, and now she's mad at you."

Chase held his hands up. "I don't know what you're getting at—"

"Yes, you do." Sam crossed his arms. "Did you bang her?"

Chase recoiled, trying to look horrified at the thought. He didn't *feel* horrified at the thought. Which actually made him feel kind of horrified. "I did not."

"Is that why you're mad? Because you didn't?"

His brother was way too perceptive for a guy who pounded heavy things with other heavy things for a living.

"No," he said. "Anna is my friend. She's just a friend. We had a slight…altercation last night. But it's not that big a deal."

"Big enough that I'm worried with all your stomping around you're eventually going to fling the wrong thing and hit me with molten metal."

"Safety first," Chase said, "always."

"I bet you say that to your dates, too."

"You would, too, if you had any."

Sam flipped Chase the bird in response.

"Just forget about it," Chase said. "Forget about the stuff with the Wests, and let me deal with it. And forget about Anna."

When it came to that last directive, he was going to try to do the same.

Anna was dreading coming face-to-face with Chase again after last night. But she didn't really have a choice. They were still in this thing. Unless she called it off. But that would be tantamount to admitting that what had happened last night *bothered* her. And she didn't want to do that. More, she was almost incapable of doing it. She was pretty sure her pride would wither up and die if she did.

But Chase was coming by her shop again tonight, with some other kind of lesson in mind. Something he'd written down on that stupid legal pad of his. It was ridiculous. All of it was ridiculous.

Herself most of all.

She looked at the clock, gritting her teeth. Chase would be by any moment, and she was no closer to dealing with the feelings, needs and general restlessness that had hit her with the blunt force of a flying wrench than she had been last night.

Then, right on time, the door opened, and in walked Chase. He was still dirty from work today, his face smudged with ash and soot, his shirt sticking to his muscular frame, showing off all those fine muscles underneath. Yeah, that didn't help.

"How was work?" he asked.

"Fine. Just dealing with putting a new cylinder head on a John Deere. You?"

"Working on a gate."

"Sounds…fun," she said, though she didn't really think it sounded like fun at all.

She liked solving the puzzle when it came to working on engines. Liked that she had the ability to get in there and figure things out. To diagnose the situation.

Standing in front of a hot fire forging metal didn't really sound like her kind of thing.

Though she couldn't deny it did pretty fantastic things for Chase's physique.

"Well, you know it would be fine if Sam wasn't such a pain in the ass."

"Sure," she said, feeling slightly cautious. After last night, she felt like dealing with Chase was like approaching a dog who'd bitten you once. Only, in this case he had kissed her, not bitten her, and he wasn't a dog. That was the problem. He was just much too *much* for his own good. Much too much for her own good.

"So," she said, "what's on the lesson plan for tonight?"

"I sort of thought we should talk about…well, talking."

"What do you mean?"

"There are ways that women talk to men they want to date. I thought I might walk you through flirting."

"You're going to show me how to flirt?"

"Somebody has to."

"I can probably figure it out," she said.

"You think?" he asked, crossing his arms over his chest and rocking back on his heels.

His clear skepticism stoked the flames of her temper, which was lurking very close to the surface after last night. That was kind of her default. Don't know how to handle something? Don't know *what* you feel? Get angry at it.

"Come on. Men and women have engaged in horizontal naked kickboxing for millennia. I'm pretty sure flirting is a natural instinct."

"You're a poet, Anna," he said, his tone deadpan.

"No, I'm a tractor mechanic," she said.

"Yeah, and you talk like one, too. If you want to get an actual date, and not just a quick tumble in the back of a guy's truck, you might want to refine your art of conversation a little."

"Who says I'm opposed to a quick rough tumble in the back of some guy's truck?"

"You're not?" he asked, his eyebrows shooting upward.

"Well, in all honesty I would probably prefer my truck, since it's clean. I know where it's been. But why the hell not? I have needs."

He scowled. "Right. Well, keep that kind of talk to yourself."

"Does it make you uncomfortable to hear about my *needs*, Chase?" she asked, not quite sure why she was poking at him. Maybe because she felt so unsettled. She was kind of enjoying the fact that he seemed to be, as well. Really, it wouldn't be fair if after last night he felt nothing at all. If he had been able to one-up her and then walk away as though nothing had happened.

"It doesn't make me uncomfortable. It's just unnecessary information. Now, talking about your needs is probably something you shouldn't do with a guy, either."

"Unless I want him to fulfill those needs."

"You said you wanted to date. You want the kind of date who can go to these functions with you, right?"

"It's moot. You're going with me."

"This time. But be honest, don't you want to be able to go out with guys who belong in places like that?"

"I don't know," she said, feeling uncomfortable.

Truth be told, she wasn't all that comfortable thinking about her needs. Emotional, physical. Frankly, if it went beyond her need for a cheeseburger, she didn't really know how to deal with it. She hadn't dated in years. And she had been fine with that. But the truth of the matter was the only reason Mark and Daniel had managed to get to her when they had made this bet was that she was beginning to feel dissatisfied with her life.

She was starting a new business. She was assuming a new position in the community. She didn't just want to be Anna Brown, the girl from the wrong side of the tracks. She didn't just want to be the tomboy mechanic for the rest of her life. She wanted…more. It had been fine, avoiding relationships all this time, but she was thirty now. She didn't really want to be by herself. She didn't want to be alone forever.

Dear Lord, she was having an existential crisis.

"Fine," she said, "it might be nice to have somebody to date."

Marriage, family—she had no idea how she felt when it came to those things. But a casual relationship… That might be nice. Yes. That might be nice.

Last night, she had gone home and gotten under a blanket and watched an old movie. Sometimes, Chase watched old movies with her, but he did not get under the blankets with her. It would be nice to have a guy to be under the blanket with. Somebody to go home to. Or at least someone to call to come over when she couldn't sleep. Someone she could talk to, make out with. Have sex with.

"Fine," she said. "I will submit to your flirting lessons."

"All the girls submit to me eventually," he said, winking.

Something about that made her stomach twist into a knot. "Talking about too much information…"

"There," he said, "that was almost flirting."

She wrinkled her nose. "Was it?"

"Yes. We had a little bit of back and forth. There was some innuendo."

"I didn't make innuendo on purpose," she said.

"No. That's the best kind. The kind you sort of walk into. It makes you feel a little dangerous. Like you might say the wrong thing. And if you go too far, they might walk away. But if you don't go far enough, they might not know that you want them."

She let out a long, frustrated growl. "Dating is complicated. I hate it. Is it too late for me to become a nun?"

"You would have to convert," he pointed out.

"That sounds like a lot of work, too."

"You can be pleasant, Anna. You're fun to talk to. So that's all you have to do."

"Natural to me is walking up to a hot guy and saying, 'Do you want to bone or what?'" As if she'd ever done that. As if she ever would. It was just…she didn't really know how to go about getting a guy to hook up with her any other way. She was a direct kind of girl. And nothing between men and women seemed direct.

"Fine. Let's try this," he said, grabbing a chair and pulling it up to her workbench before taking a seat.

She took hold of the back of the other folding chair in the space and moved it across from his, positioning herself so that she was across from him.

"What are you drinking?" he asked.

She laughed. "A mai tai." She had never had one of those. She didn't even know what it was.

"Excellent. I'm having whiskey, straight up."

"That sounds like you."

"You don't know what sounds like me. You don't know me."

Suddenly, she got the game. "Right. Stranger," she said, then winced internally, because that sounded a little bit more Mae West in her head, and just kind of silly when it was out of her mouth.

"You here with anyone?"

"I could be?" she said, placing her elbow on the workbench and tilting her head to the side.

"You should try to toss your hair a little bit. I dated this girl Elizabeth who used to do that. It was cute."

"How does touching my hair accomplish anything?" she asked, feeling irritated that he had brought another woman up. Which was silly, because the only reason he was qualified to give her these lessons was that he had dated a metric ton of women.

So getting mad about the thing that was helping her right now was a little ridiculous. But she was pretty sure they had passed ridiculous a couple of days ago.

"I don't know. It's cute. It looks like you're trying to draw my attention to it. Like you want me to notice."

"Which…lets you know that I want you in my pants?"

He frowned. "I guess. I never broke it down like that before. But that stands to reason."

She reached up, sighing as she flicked a strand of her hair as best she could. It was tied up in a loose bun and had fallen partway thanks to the intensity of the day's physical labor. Still, she had a feeling she did not look alluring. She had a feeling she looked like she'd been caught in a wind turbine and spit out the other end.

"Are you new in town?"

"I'm old in town," she said, mentally kicking herself again for being lame on the return volley.

"That works, too," Chase said, not skipping a beat.

Yeah, there was a reason the man had never struck out before.

She started to chew on her lip, trying to think of what to say next.

"Don't chew a hole through it," he said, smiling and reaching across the space, brushing his thumb over the place her teeth had just grazed.

And everything in her stopped dead. His touch ignited her nerve endings, sending a brush fire down her veins and all through her body.

She hadn't been this ridiculous over Chase since she was sixteen years old. Since then, she had mostly learned to manage it.

She pulled away slightly, her chair scraping against the floor. She laughed, a stilted, unnatural sound. "I won't," she said, her voice too loud.

"If you're going to chew on your lip," he said, "don't freak out when the guy calls attention to it or touches you. It looks like you're doing it on purpose, so you should expect a comment."

"Duh," she said, "I was. That was…normal."

She wanted to crawl under the chair.

"There was this girl Miranda that I—"

"Okay." She cut him off, growing more and more impatient with the comparisons. "I'm old in town, what about you?"

"I've been around."

"I bet you have been," she said.

"I'm not sure how I'm supposed to take that," he said, flashing her a lopsided grin.

"Right," she said, "because I don't know what I'm doing."

"Maybe this was a bad idea," he said. "I think you

actually need to feel some chemistry with somebody if flirting's going to work."

His words were sharp, digging into her chest. *You actually had to feel some chemistry* to be able to flirt.

They had chemistry. She had felt it last night. So had he. This was his revenge for the six-point-five comment. At least, she hoped it was. The alternative was that he had really felt nothing when their lips attached. And that seemed…beyond unfair.

She had all this attraction for Chase that she had spent years tamping down, only to have it come roaring to the surface the moment she had begun to pretend there was more going on between them than just friendship. And then she had kissed him. And far from being a disappointment, he had superseded her every fantasy. The jackass. Then he had kissed her, kissed her because he was angry. Kissed her to get revenge. Kissed her in a way that had kept her awake all night long, aching, burning. And now he was saying he didn't have chemistry with her.

"It's just that usually when I'm with a girl it flows a little easier. The bar to the bedroom is a pretty natural extension. And all those little movements kind of lead into the other. The way they touch their hair, tilt their head, lean in for a kiss…"

Oh, that did it.

"The women that I usually hook up with tend to—"

"Right," she said, her tone hard. "I get it. They flip their hair and scrunch their noses and twitch at all the appropriate times. They're like small woodland creatures who only emerge from their burrows to satisfy your every sexual whim."

"Don't get upset. I'm trying to help you."

She snorted. "I know." Just then, she had no idea what devil possessed her. Only that one most assuredly did. And once it had taken hold, she had no desire to cast it back out again.

She was mad. Mad like Chase had been last night. And she was determined to get her own back.

"Elizabeth was good at flipping her hair. Miranda gave you saucy interplay like so." She stood up, taking a step toward him, meeting his dark gaze with her own. "But how did they do this?" She reached down, placing her hand between his thighs and rubbing her palm over the bulge in his jeans.

Oh, sweet Lord, there was more to Chase McCormack than met the eye.

And she had a whole handful of him.

Her brain was starting to scream. Not words so much as a high-pitched, panicky whine. She had crossed the line. And there was no turning back.

But her brain wasn't running the show. Her body was on fire, her heart pounding so hard she was afraid it was going to rip a hole straight through the wall of her chest and flop out on the ground in front of him. Show him all its contents. Dammit, *she* didn't even want to see that.

But it was her anger that really pushed things forward. Her anger that truly propelled her on.

"And how," she asked, lowering herself slowly, scraping her fingernails across the line of his zipper, before dropping to her knees in front of him, "did they do this?"

Chapter 6

For one blinding second, Chase thought that he was engaged in some sort of high-definition hallucination.

Because there was no way that Anna had just put her hand…there. There was no way that she was kneeling down in front of him, looking at him like she was a sultry-eyed seductress rather than his best friend, still dirty from the workday, clad in motor-oil-smudged coveralls.

He blinked. Then he shook his head. She was still there. And so was he.

But he was so hard he could probably pound iron with his dick right about now.

He knew what he should do. And just now he had enough sense left in his skull to do it. But he didn't want to. He knew he should. He knew that at the end of this road there was nothing good. Nothing good at all. But he shut all that down. He didn't think of the road ahead.

He just let his brain go blank. He just sat back and watched as she trailed her fingers up the line of his zipper, grabbing hold of his belt buckle and undoing it, her movements clumsy, speaking of an inexperience he didn't want to examine too closely.

He didn't want to examine any of this too closely, but he was powerless to do anything else.

Because everything around the moment went fuzzy as the present sharpened. Almost painfully.

His eyes were drawn to her fingers as she pulled his zipper down, to the short, no-nonsense fingernails, the specks of dirt embedded in her skin. That should... well, he had the vague idea it should turn him off. It didn't. Though he had a feeling that getting a bucket of water thrown on him while he sat in the middle of an iceberg naked wouldn't turn him off at this point. He was too far gone.

He was holding his breath. Every muscle in his body frozen. He couldn't believe that she would do what it appeared she might be doing. She would stop. She had to stop. He needed her to stop. He needed her to never stop. To keep going.

She pressed her palm flat against his ab muscles before pushing her hand down inside his jeans, reaching beneath his underwear and curling her fingers around him. His breath hissed through his teeth, a shudder racking his frame.

She looked up at him, green eyes glittering in the dim shop light. She had a smudge of dirt on her face that somehow only highlighted her sharp cheekbones, somehow emphasized her beauty in a way he hadn't truly noticed it before. Yes, last night in the red dress she had been beautiful, there was no doubt about that.

But for some reason, her femininity was highlighted wrapped in these traditionally masculine things. By the backdrop of the mechanic shop, the evidence of a day's hard work on her soft skin.

She tilted her chin up, her expression one of absolute challenge. She was waiting for him to call it off. Waiting for him to push her away. But he wasn't going to. He reached out, forking his fingers through her hair and tightening them, grabbing ahold of the loose bun that sat high on her head. Her eyes widened, her lips going slack. He didn't pull her away. He didn't draw her closer. He just held on tight, keeping his gaze firmly focused on hers. Then he released her. And he waited.

She licked her lips slowly, an action that would have been almost comically obvious coming from nearly anyone else. Not Anna.

Then she squeezed him gently before drawing her hand back. He should be relieved. He was not.

But her next move was not one he anticipated. She grabbed hold of the waistband of his jeans and underwear, pulling them down slowly, exposing him. She let out a shaky, shuddering breath before leaning in and flicking her tongue over the head of his arousal.

"Hell." He wasn't sure at first if he had spoken it out loud, not until he heard it echoing around him. It was like cursing in a church somehow, wrong considering the beauty of the gift he was about to receive.

Still, he couldn't think of anything else as she drew the tip of her tongue all the way down to the base of his shaft before retracing her path. She shifted, and that was when he noticed her hands were shaking. Fair enough, since he was shaking, too.

She parted her lips, taking him into her mouth completely, her lips sliding over him, the wet, slick friction almost too much for him to handle. He didn't know what was wrong with him. If it was the shock of the moment, if it was just that he was this base. Or if there was some kind of sick, perverted part of him that took extra pleasure in the fact that this was wrong. That he should not be letting his best friend touch him like this.

Because he'd had more skilled blow jobs. There was no question about that. This didn't feel good because Anna was an expert in the art of fellatio. Far from it.

Still, his head was about to blow off. And he was about to lose all of his control. So there was something.

Maybe it was just her.

She tilted her head to the side as she took him in deep, giving him a good view of just what she was doing. And just who was doing it. He was so aware of the fact that it was Anna, and that most definitely added a kick of the forbidden. Because he knew this was bad. Knew it was wrong.

And not many things were off-limits to him. Not many things had an illicit quality to them. He had kind of allowed himself to take anything and everything that had ever seemed vaguely sexy to him.

Except for her.

He shoved that thought in the background. He didn't like to think of Anna that way, and in general he didn't.

Sure, in high school, there had been moments. But he was a guy. And he had spent a lot of time with Anna. Alone in her room, alone in his. He had a feeling that half the people who had known them had imagined they were getting it on behind the scenes. Friends with benefits, et cetera. In reality, the only benefit to their friendship had been the fact that they'd been there for each other. They had never been there for each other in this way.

Maybe that's what was wrong with him.

Of course, nothing felt wrong with him right now. Right now, pleasure was crackling close to the surface of his skin and it was shorting out his brain. All he could do was sit back and ride the high. Embrace the sensations that were boiling through his blood. The magic of her lips and tongue combined with a shocking scrape of her teeth against his delicate skin made him buck his hips against her even as he tried to rein himself in.

But he was reaching the end of his control, the end of himself. He reached down, cupping her cheek as she continued to pleasure him, as she continued to drive him wild, urging him closer to the edge of control he hadn't realized he possessed.

He felt like he lived life with the shackles off, but she was pushing him so much further than he'd been before that he knew he'd been lying to himself all this time.

He'd been in chains, and hadn't even realized it.

Maybe because of her. Maybe to keep himself from touching her.

She gripped him, squeezing as she tasted him, pushing him straight over the edge. He held on to her hair, harder than he should, as a wave of pleasure rode up inside of him. And when it crashed he didn't ride it into shore. Oh, hell no. When it crashed it drove him straight down to the bottom of the sea, the impact leaving him spinning, gasping for breath, battered on the rocks.

But dammit all, it was worth it. Right now, it was worth it.

He knew that any moment the feeling would fade and he would be faced with the stark horror of what he'd just done, of what he'd just allowed to happen. But for now, he was foggy, floating in the kind of mist that always blanketed the ocean on cold mornings in Copper Ridge.

And he would cling to it as long as possible.

Oh, dear God. What had she done? This had gone so far beyond the kiss to prove they had chemistry. It had gone so far past the challenge that Chase had thrown down last night. It had gone straight into Crazy Town, next stop You Messed Up the Only Friendship You Hadville.

In combination with the swirling panic that was wrapping its claws around her and pulling her into a spiral was the fuzzy-headed lingering arousal. Her lips felt swollen, her body tingling, adrenaline still making her shake.

She regretted everything. She also regretted nothing.

The contradictions inside her were so extreme she felt like she was going to be pulled in two.

One thing her mind and body were united on was the desire to go hide underneath a blanket. This was definitely the kind of situation that necessitated hiding.

The problem was, she was still on her knees in front of Chase. Maybe she could hide under his chair.

What are you doing? Why are you falling apart? This isn't a big deal. He has probably literally had a thousand blow jobs.

This one didn't have to be that big a deal. Sure, it

was the first one she had ever given. But he didn't have to know that, either.

If she didn't treat it like a big deal, it wouldn't be a big deal. They could forget anything had ever happened. They could forget that in a moment of total insanity she had allowed her anger to push her over the edge, had allowed her inability to back down from a challenge to bring them to this place. And that was all it was—the fact that she was absolutely unable to deal with that blow to her pride. It was nothing else. It couldn't be anything else.

She rocked back on her heels, planting her hands flat on the dusty ground before rising to her feet. She felt dizzy. She would go ahead and blame that on the speed at which she had stood up.

"I think it's safe to say we have a little bit more chemistry than you thought," she said, clearing her throat and brushing at the dirt on her pants.

He didn't say anything. He just kept sitting there, looking rocked. And he was still exposed. She did her very best to look at the wall behind him. "I can still see your..."

He scrambled into action, standing and tugging his pants into place, doing up his belt as quickly as possible. "I think we're done for the day."

She nodded. "Yeah. Well, *you* are."

She could feel the distance widening between them. It was what she needed, what she wanted, ultimately. But for some reason, even as she forced the breach, she regretted it.

"I don't... What just happened?"

She laughed, crossing her arms and cocking her hip out to the side. "If you have to ask, maybe I didn't do a very good job." The bolder she got, the more she retreated inside. She could feel herself tearing in two, the soft vulnerable part of her scrambling to get behind the brash, bold outward version that would spare her from any embarrassment or pain.

"You're…okay?"

"Why wouldn't I be okay?"

"Because you just…"

She laughed. Hysterically. "Sure. But let's not be ridiculous about it. It isn't like you punched me in the face."

Chase looked stricken. "Of course not. I would never do that."

"I know. I'm just saying, don't act like you punched me in the face when all I did was—"

"There's no need to get descriptive. I was here. I remember."

She snorted. "You should remember." She turned away from him, clenching her hands into fists, hoping he didn't notice that they were shaking. "And I hope you remember it next time you go talking about us not having chemistry."

"Do you *want* us to have chemistry?"

She whirled around. "No. But I have some pride. You were comparing me to all these other women. Well, compare that."

"I…can't."

She planted her hands on her hips. "Damn straight."

"We can't… We can't do this again," he said, shaking his head and walking away.

For some reason, that made her feel awful. For some reason, it hurt. Stabbed like a rusty knife deep in her gut.

"I don't want to do it again. I mean, you're welcome, but I didn't exactly get anything out of it."

He stopped, turning to face her, his expression tense. "I didn't ask you to do anything."

"I'm aware." She shook her head. "I think we're done for tonight."

"Yeah. I already said that."

"Well," she said, feeling furious now, "now I'm saying it."

She was mad at herself. For taking it this far. For being upset, and raw, and wounded over something that she had chosen to do. Over his reaction, which was nothing more than the completely predictable response. He didn't want her. Not really.

And she knew that. This evening's events weren't going to change it. An orgasm on the floor of the shop she rented from him was hardly going to alter the course of fifteen years of friendship.

An orgasm. Oh, dear Lord, what had she done? She really had to get out of here. There was no amount of bravado left in her that would save her from the meltdown that was pending.

"I have to go."

She was gone before he had a chance to protest. He should be glad she was gone. If she had stayed, there was no telling what he might have done. What other stupid bit of nonsense he might have committed.

He had limited brainpower at the moment. All of his blood was still somewhere south of his belt.

He turned, surveying the empty shop. Then, in a fit of rage, he kicked something metal that was just to the right of the chair. And hurt his foot. And probably broke the thing. He had no idea if it was important or not. He hoped it wasn't. Or maybe he hoped it was. She deserved to have some of her tractor shit get broken. What had she been thinking?

He hadn't been able to think. But it was a well-known fact that if a man's dick was in a woman's mouth, he was not doing much problem solving. Which meant Chase was completely absolved of any wrongdoing here.

Completely.

He gritted his teeth, closing his eyes and taking in a sharp breath. He was going to have to figure out how to get a handle on himself between now and the next time he saw Anna. Because there was no way things could continue on like this. There weren't a whole lot of people who stuck around in his world. There had never been a special woman. After the death of his and Sam's parents, relatives had passed through, but none of them had put down roots. And, well, their parents, they might not have chosen to leave, but they were gone all the same. He couldn't afford to lose anyone else. Sam and Anna were basically all he had.

Which meant when it came to Sam's moods and general crankiness, Chase just dealt with it. And when it came to Anna...no more touching. No more... No more of any of that.

For one second, he allowed himself to replay the moment when she had unzipped his pants. When she had leaned forward and tasted him. When that white-hot streak of release had undone him completely.

He blinked. Yeah, he knew what he had been thinking. That it felt good. Amazing. Too good to stop her. But physical pleasure was cheap. A friendship like theirs represented years of investment. One simply wasn't worth sacrificing the other for. And now that he was thinking clearly he realized that. So that meant no more. No more. Never.

Next time he saw her, he was going to make sure she knew that.

Chapter 7

Anna was beneath three blankets, and she was starting to swelter. If she hadn't been too lazy to sit up and grab hold of her ice-cream container, she might not be quite so sweaty.

The fact that she was something of a cliché of what it meant to be a woman behind closed doors was not lost on her. Blankets, old movies, Ben & Jerry's. But hey, she spent most of the day up to her elbows in engine grease, so she supposed she was entitled to a few stereotypes.

She reached her spoon out from beneath the blankets and scraped the top of the ice cream in the container, gathering up a modest amount.

"Oklahoma!" she sang, humming the rest of the line while taking the bite of marshmallow and chocolate ice cream and sighing as the sugar did its good work. Full-fat dairy products were the way to happiness. Or at least the best way she knew to stop from obsessing.

Her phone buzzed and she looked down, cringing when she saw Chase's name. She swiped open the lock screen and read the message.

In your driveway. Didn't want to give you a heart attack.

Why are you in my dr—

She didn't get a chance to finish the message before there was a knock on her front door.

She closed her eyes, groaning. She really didn't want to deal with him right now. In fact, he was the last person on earth she wanted to deal with. He was the reason she was currently baking beneath a stack of blankets, seeking solace in the bosom of old movies.

Still, she couldn't ignore him. That would make things weirder. He was still her best friend, even if she had— Well, she wasn't going to think about what she had. If she ignored him, it would only cater to the weirdness. It would make events from earlier today seem more important than they needed to be. They did not need to be treated as though they were important.

Sure, she had never exactly done *that* with a man. Sure, she hadn't even had sexual contact of any kind with a man for the past several years. And sure, she had never had that kind of contact with Chase. But that was no reason to go assigning meaning. People got ribbons and stickers for their first trips to the dentist. They did not get them for giving their first blow job.

She groaned. Then she rolled off the couch, pushing herself into a standing position before she padded through the small living area to the entryway. She jerked the door open, pushing her hair out of her face and trying to look casual.

Too late, she realized that she was wearing her pajamas. Which were perfectly decent, in that they covered every inch of her body. But they were also baggy, fuzzy and covered in porcupines.

All things considered, it just wasn't the most glorious of moments.

"Hello," she said, keeping her body firmly planted in the center of the doorway.

"Hi," he returned. Then he proceeded to study her pajamas.

"Porcupines," she informed him, just for something to say.

"Good choice. Not an obvious one."

"I guess not. Considering they aren't all that cuddly. But neither am I. So maybe it's a more obvious choice than it originally appears."

"Maybe. We'll have to debate animal-patterned pajama philosophy another time."

"I guess. What exactly did you come here to debate if not that?"

He stuffed his hands in his pockets. "Nothing. I just came to…check on you."

"Sound of body and mind."

"I see that. Except you're in your pajamas at seven o'clock."

"I'm preparing for an evening in," she said, planting her hand on her hip. "So pajamas are logical."

"Okay."

She frowned. "I'm fine."

"Can I come in?"

She was frozen for a moment, not quite sure what

to say. If she let him come in...well, she didn't feel entirely comfortable with the idea of letting him in. But if she didn't let him in, then she would be admitting that she was uncomfortable letting him in. Which would betray the fact that she actually wasn't really all that okay. She didn't want to do that, either.

No wonder she had avoided sexual contact for so long. It introduced all manner of things that she really didn't want to deal with.

"Sure," she said finally, stepping to the side and allowing him entry.

He just stood there, filling up the entry. She had never really noticed that before. How large he was in the small space of her home. Because he was Chase, and his presence here shouldn't really be remarkable. It was now.

Because things had changed. She had changed them. She had kissed him the other day, and then...well, she had changed things.

"There. You are in," she said, moving away from him and heading back into the living room. She took a seat on the couch, picking up the remote control and muting the TV.

"Movie night?"

"Every night is movie night with enough popcorn and a can-do attitude."

"I admire your dedication. What's on?"

"Oklahoma!"

He raised his brows. "You haven't seen that enough times?"

"There is no such thing as seeing a musical too many times, Chase. Multiple viewings only enhance the experience."

"Do they?"

"Sing-alongs, of course."

"I should have known."

She smiled, putting a blanket back over her lap, thinking of it as a sort of flannel shield. "You should know these things about me. Really, you should know everything about me."

He cleared his throat, and the sudden awkwardness made her think of all the things he didn't know about her. And the things that he did know. It hit her then—of course, right then, as he was standing in front of her—just how revealing what had happened earlier was.

Giving a guy pleasure like that…well, a woman didn't do that unless she wanted him. It said a lot about how she felt. About how she had felt for an awfully long time. No matter that she had tried to quash it, the fact remained that she did feel attraction for him. Which he was obviously now completely aware of.

Silence fell like a boulder between them. Crushing, deadly.

"Anyway," she said, the transition as subtle as a landslide. "Why exactly are you here?"

"I told you."

"Right. Checking on me. I'm just not really sure why."

"You know why," he said, his tone muted.

"You check on every woman you have…encounters with?"

"You know I don't. But you're not every woman I have encounters with."

"Still. I'm an adult woman. I'm neither shocked nor injured."

She was probably both. Yes, she was definitely perilously close to being both.

He shifted, clearly uncomfortable. Which she hated, because they weren't uncomfortable with each other. Ever. Or they hadn't been before. "It would be rude of me not to make sure we aren't…okay."

She patted herself down. "Yes. Okay. Okay?"

"No," he said.

"No? What the hell, man? I said I'm fine. Do we have to stand around talking about it?"

"I think we might. Because I don't think you're fine."

"That's bullshit, McCormack," she said, rising from the couch and clutching her blanket to her chest. "Straight-up bullshit. Like you stepped in a big-ass pile somewhere out there and now you went and dragged it into my house."

"If you were fine, you wouldn't be acting like this."

"I'm sorry, how did you want me to act?"

"Like an adult, maybe?" he said, his dark brows locking together.

"Um, I am acting like an adult, Chase. I'm pretending that a really embarrassing mistake didn't happen, while I crush my regret and uncertainty beneath the weight of my caloric intake for the evening. What part of that isn't acting like an adult?"

"We're friends. This wasn't some random, forgettable hookup."

"It is so forgettable," she said, her voice taking on that brash, loud quality that hurt her own ears. That she was starting to despise. "I've already forgotten it."

"How?"

"It's a penis, Chase, not the Sistine Chapel. My life was hardly going to be changed by the sight of it."

He reached forward, grabbing hold of her arm and drawing her toward him. "Stop," he bit out, his words hard, his expression focused.

"What are you doing?" she asked, some of her bravado slipping.

"Calling you on *your* bullshit, Anna." He lowered his voice, his tone no less deadly. She'd never seen Chase like this. He didn't get like this. Chase was fun, and light. Well, except for last night when he'd kissed her. But even then, he hadn't been quite this serious. "I've known you for fifteen years. I know when your smile is hiding tears, little girl. I know when you're a whole mess of feelings behind that brick wall you put up to keep yourself separate from the world. And I sure as hell know when you aren't fine. So don't stand there and tell me that it didn't change anything, that it didn't mean anything. Even if you gave out BJs every day with lunch—and I know you don't—that would have still mattered because it's *us*. And we don't do that. It changed something, Anna, and don't you dare pretend it didn't."

No. *No.* Her brain was screaming again, but this time she knew for sure what it was saying. It was all denial. She didn't want him to look at her as if he was searching for something, didn't want him to touch her as if it was only the beginning of something more. Didn't want him to see her. To see how scared she was. To see how unnerved and affected she was. To see how very, very not brave she was beneath the shield she held up to keep the world out.

He already knows it's a shield. And you're already

*screwed ten ways, because you can't hide from him
and you never could.*

He'd let her believe she could. And now he'd
changed his mind. For some reason it was all over
now. Well, she knew why. It had started with a dress
and high heels and ended with an orgasm in her shop.
He was right. It had changed things.

And she had a terrible, horrible feeling more was
going to change before they could go back to normal.

If they ever could.

"Well," she said, hearing her voice falter. Pretending
she didn't. "I don't think anything needs to change."

"Enough," he said, his tone fierce.

Then, before she knew what was happening, he'd
claimed her lips again in a kiss that ground every other
kiss that had come before it into dust, before letting
them blow away on the wind.

This was angry. Intense. Hot and hard. And it was
happening in her house, in spite of the fact that she was
holding a blanket and *Oklahoma!* was on mute in the
background. It was her safe space, with her safe friend,
and it was being wholly, utterly invaded.

By him.

It was confronting and uncomfortable and scary
as hell. So she responded the only way she could. She
got mad, too.

She grabbed hold of the front of his shirt, clinging
to him tightly as she kissed him back. As she forced
her tongue between his lips, claiming him before he
could stake his claim on her.

She shifted, scraping her teeth lightly over his bottom lip before biting down. Hard.

He growled, wrapping his arms around her waist.

She never felt small. Ever. She was a tall girl with a broad frame, but she was engulfed by Chase right now. His scent, his strength. He was all hard muscle against her, his heart thundering beneath her hands, which were pinned between their bodies.

She didn't know what was happening, except that right now, kissing him might be safer than trying to talk to him.

It certainly felt better.

It let her be angry. Let her push back without saying anything. And more than that…he was an amazing kisser. He had taken her from zero to almost-there with one touch of his lips against hers.

He slid his hand down her back, cupping her butt and bringing her up even harder against him so she could feel him. All of him. And just how aroused he was.

He wanted her. Chase wanted her. Yes, he was pissed. Yes, he was…trying to prove a point with his tongue or whatever. But he couldn't fake a hard-on like that.

She was angry, but it was fading. Being blotted out by the arousal that was crackling in her veins like fireworks.

Suddenly, she found herself being lifted off the ground, before she was set down on the couch, Chase coming down over her, his expression hard, his eyes sharp as he looked down at her.

He pressed his hand over her stomach, pushing the hem of her shirt upward.

She should stop him. She didn't.

She watched as his strong, masculine hand pushed her shirt out of the way, revealing a wedge of skin. The contrast alone was enough to drive her crazy. Man, woman. Innocuous porcupine pajamas and sex.

Above all else, above anything else, there was Chase. Everything he made her feel. All of the things she had spent years trying *not* to feel. Years running from.

She couldn't run. Not now. Not only did she lack the strength, she lacked the desire. Because more than safety, more than sanity, she wanted him. Wanted him naked, over her, under her, *in* her.

He gripped the hem of her top and wrenched it over her head, the movement sudden, swift. As though he had reached the end of his patience and had no reserve to draw upon. That left her in nothing more than those ridiculous baggy pajama pants, resting low on her hips. She didn't have anything sexier underneath them, either.

But Chase didn't look at all disappointed. He didn't look away, either. Didn't have a faraway expression on his face. She wasn't sure why, but she had half expected to look up at him and be able to clearly identify that he was somewhere else in his mind, with someone else. But he was looking at her with a sharp focus, a kind of single-mindedness that no man, no *one*, had ever looked at her with before.

He knew. He knew who she was. And he was still hot for her. Still hard for her.

"You are so hot," he said, pressing his hand flat to her stomach and drawing it down slowly, his fingertips teasing the sensitive skin beneath the waistband. "And you don't even know it, do you?"

Part of her wanted to protest, wanted to fight back, because that was what she did. Instead, everything inside of her just kind of went limp. Melted into a puddle. "N-no."

"You should know," he said, his voice low, husky. A shot of whiskey that skated along her nerves, warming her, sending a kick of heat and adrenaline firing through her blood. "You should know how damn sexy you are. You're the kind of woman who could make a man lose his mind."

"I could?"

He laughed, but it wasn't full of humor. It sounded tortured. "I'm exhibit A."

He shifted his hips forward, his hard length pressing up against that very aroused part of her that wanted more of him. Needed more of him. She gasped. "Soon," he said, the promise in his words settling a heavy weight in her stomach. Anticipation, terror. Need.

He continued to tease her, his fingertips resting just above the line of her panties, before he began to trail his hand back upward. He rested his palm over her chest, reaching up and tracing her lower lip with his thumb.

She darted her tongue out, sliding the tip of it over his skin, tasting salt, tasting Chase. A flavor that was becoming familiar.

Then she angled her head, taking his thumb into her mouth and sucking hard. His hips arched forward hard, his cock making firm contact, sending a shower of sparks through her body as he did.

"You're going to be the death of me," he said, every word raw, frayed.

"I might say the same about you," she said, her voice thick, unrecognizable. She didn't know who she was right now. This creature who was a complete and total slave to sexual sensation. Who was so lost in it, she could feel nothing else. No sense of self-preservation, no fear kicking into gear and letting her know that she needed to put her walls up. That she needed to go on the defense.

She was reduced. She had none of that. And she didn't even care.

"You're a miracle," he said, tracing the line of her collarbone with the tip of his tongue. "A damn *miracle*, do you know that?"

"What?"

"The other day I told you you didn't look like a miracle. I was a fool. And I was wrong. Every inch of you is a miracle, Anna Brown."

Those words were like being submerged in warm water, feeling it flow over every inch of her, a kind of deep, soul-satisfying comfort that she really, really didn't want. Or rather, she didn't *want* to want it. But she did, bad enough that she couldn't resist.

But it was all a little too heavy. All a little too much. Still, she didn't have the strength to turn him away.

"Kiss me."

She said that instead of *get the hell out of my house*, and instead of *we can't do this*, because it was all she had strength for. Because she needed that kiss. And maybe, just maybe, if they didn't talk, she could make it through.

Chase—gentleman that he was—obliged her.

He angled his head, reaching up to cup her breast as he did, his mouth crashing down on hers just as his palm skimmed her nipple. She gasped, arching up against him, the combination of sensations almost too much to handle.

Yeah, she did not remember sex being like this.

Granted, it had been a million years, but she would have remembered if it had come anywhere close to this. And her conclusion most certainly wouldn't have been that it was vaguely boring and a little bit gross. Not if it had even been in the same ballpark as what she was feeling now.

There was no point in comparing. There was just flat out no comparison.

He kissed her, long, deep and hard; he kissed her until she couldn't breathe. Until she thought she was going to die for wanting more. He kissed her until she was dizzy. And when he abandoned her mouth, she nearly wept. Until he lowered his head and skimmed his tongue over one hardened bud, until he drew it between his lips and sucked hard, before scraping her sensitized flesh with his teeth.

She arched against him, desperate for more. Desperate for satisfaction. Satisfaction he seemed intent on withholding.

"I'm so close," she said, panting. "Just do it now." Then it would be over. Then she would have what she needed, and the howling, yawning ache inside of her would be satisfied.

"No," he said, his tone authoritative.

"What do you mean no?"

"Not yet. You're not allowed to come yet, Anna. I'm not done."

His words, the calm, quiet command, made everything inside of her go still. She wanted to fight him. Wanted to rail against that cruel denial of her needs, but she couldn't.

Not when this part of him was so compelling. Not

when she wanted so badly to see where complying would lead.

"We're not done," he said, tracing her nipple with the tip of his tongue, "until I say we are." He lifted his head so that their eyes met, the prolonged contact touching something deep inside of her. Something that surpassed the physical.

He kissed her again, and as he did, he pulled his T-shirt over his head, exposing his incredible body to her.

Her mouth dried, and other parts of her got wet. Very, very wet.

"Oh, sweet Lord," she said, pressing her hand to his chest and drawing her fingertips down over his muscles, his chest hair tickling her skin as she did.

It was a surreal moment. So strange and fascinating. To touch her best friend like this. To see his body this way, to know that—right now—it wasn't off-limits to her. To know that she could lean forward and kiss that beautiful, perfect dip just next to his hip bone. Suddenly, she was seized with the desire to do just that. And she didn't have to fight it.

She pushed against him, bringing herself into a sitting position, lowering her head and pressing her lips to his heated skin.

"Oh, no, you don't," he said, his voice rough. He took hold of her wrist, drawing her up so that she was on her knees, eye to eye with him on the couch. "We're not finishing it like that," he said.

"Damn straight we aren't," she said. "But that doesn't mean I didn't want to get a little taste."

"You give way too much credit to my self-control, honey."

"You give too much credit to mine. I've never…"

She stared at his chest instead of finishing her sentence. "It's like walking into a candy store and being told I can have whatever I want. Restraint is not on the menu."

"Good," he said, leaning in, kissing her, nipping her lower lip. "Restraint isn't what I want."

He wrapped his arm around her, drawing her up against him, her bare breasts pressing against his hard chest, the hair there abrading her nipples in the most fantastic, delicious way.

And then he was kissing her again, slow and deep as his hand trailed down beneath the waistband of her pants, cupping her ass, squeezing her tight. He pushed her pants down over her hips, taking her panties with them, leaving her completely naked in front of him.

He stood up, taking his time looking at her as he put his hands on his belt buckle.

Nerves, excitement, spread through her. She didn't know where to look. At the harsh, hungry look on his face, at the beautiful lines of muscle on his perfectly sculpted torso. At the clear and aggressive arousal visible through his jeans.

So she looked at all of him. Every last bit. And she didn't have time to feel embarrassed that she was sitting there naked as the day she was born, totally exposed to him for the first time.

She was too fascinated by him in this moment. Too fascinated to do anything but stare at him.

This was Chase McCormack. The man that women lost their minds—and their dignity—over on a regular basis. This was Chase McCormack, the sex god who could—and often did—have any woman he pleased.

She had known Chase McCormack, loyal friend and confidant, for a very long time. But she realized that up until now, she had never met *this* Chase McCormack. It was a strange, dizzying realization. Exhilarating.

And she was suddenly seized by the feeling that right now, he was hers. All hers. Because who else knew both sides of him? Did anyone?

She was about to.

"Get your pants off, McCormack," she said, impatience overriding common sense.

"You don't get to make demands here, Anna," he said.

"I just did."

"You want to try giving orders? You have to show me you can follow them." His eyes darkened, and her heart hammered harder, faster. "Spread your legs," he said, his words hard and uncompromising.

She swallowed. There was that embarrassment that she had just been so proud she had bypassed. But this was suddenly way outside her realm of experience. It was one thing to sit there in front of him naked. It was quite another to deliberately expose herself the way he was asking her to. She didn't move. She sat there, frozen.

"Spread your legs for me," he repeated, his voice heavy with that soft, commanding tone. "Or I put my clothes on and leave."

"You wouldn't," she said.

"You don't know what I'm capable of."

That was true. In this scenario, she really didn't know him. He was a stranger, except he wasn't.

Actually, if he had been a stranger, all of this would've been a lot easier. She could have spread her legs and she wouldn't have worried about how she looked. Wouldn't have worried about the consequences. If a stranger saw her do something like that, was somehow unsatisfied and then walked away, well, what did it matter? But this was Chase. And it mattered. It mattered so very much.

His hands paused on his belt buckle. "I'm warning you, Anna. You better do as you're told."

For some reason, that did not make her want to punch him. For some reason, she found herself sitting back on the couch, obeying his command, opening herself to him, as adrenaline skittered through her system.

"Good girl," he said, continuing his movements, pushing his jeans and underwear down his legs and exposing his entire body to her for the first time. And then, it didn't matter so much that she was sitting there with her thighs open for him. Because now she had all of him to look at.

The light in his eyes was intense, hungry, and he kept them trained on her as he reached down and squeezed himself hard. His jaw was tense, the only real sign of just how frayed his control was.

"Beautiful," he said, stroking himself slowly, leisurely, as he continued to gaze at her.

"Are you just going to look? Or are you going to touch?" She wasn't entirely comfortable with this. With him just staring. With this aching silence between them, and this deep, overwhelming connection that she felt.

There were no barriers left. There was no way to hide. She was vulnerable, in every way. And normally she hated it. She kind of hated it now. But that vulnerability was wrapped in arousal, in a sharp, desperate need unlike anything she had ever known. And so it was impossible to try to put distance between them, impossible to try to run away.

"I'm going to do a lot more than look," he said, dropping down to his knees, "and I'm going to do a hell of a lot more than touch." He reached out, sliding his hands around to her ass, drawing her forward, bringing her up toward his mouth.

"Chase," she said, the short, shocked protest about the only thing she managed before the slick heat of his tongue assaulted that sensitive bundle of nerves at the apex of her thighs. "You don't have to..."

He lifted his head, his dark eyes meeting her. "Oh, I know I don't have to. But you got to taste me, and I think turnabout is fair play."

"But that wasn't..."

"What?"

"It's just that men..."

"Expect a lot more than they give. At least some of them. Anyway, as much as I liked what you did for me—and don't get me wrong, I liked it a lot—you have no idea how much pleasure this gives me."

"How?"

He leaned in, resting his cheek on her thigh. "The smell of you." He leaned closer, drawing his tongue through her slick folds. "The taste of you," he said. "You."

And then she couldn't talk anymore. He buried his face between her legs, his tongue and fingers working black magic on her body, pushing her harder, higher, faster than she had imagined possible. Yeah, making out with Chase had been enough to nearly give her an orgasm. This was pushing her somewhere else entirely.

In her world, orgasm had always been a solo project. Surrendering the power to someone else, having her own pleasure not only in someone else's hands but in his complete and utter control, was something she had never even thought possible for her. But Chase was proving her wrong.

He slipped a finger deep inside of her as he continued to torture her with his wicked mouth, then a second, working them in and out of her slick channel while he teased her with the tip of his tongue.

A ball of tension grew in her stomach, expanded until she couldn't breathe. "It's too much," she gasped.

"Obviously it's not enough yet," he said, pushing her harder, higher.

And when the wave broke over her, she thought she was done for. Thought it was going to drag her straight out to sea and leave her to die. She couldn't catch her breath as pleasure assaulted her, going on and on, pounding through her like a merciless tide, battering her against the rocks, leaving her bruised, breathless.

And when it was over, Chase was looming over her, a condom in his hand.

She felt like a creature without its shell. Sensitive, completely unprotected. She wanted to hide from him, hide from this. But she couldn't. How could she? The simple truth was, they still weren't done. They had gone only part of the way. And if they didn't finish this, she would always wonder. He would, too.

She imagined that—whether or not he admitted it— was why he had come here tonight in the first place.

They had opened the lid on Pandora's box. And they couldn't close it until they had examined every last dirty, filthy sin inside of it.

Even though she thought it might kill her, she knew that they couldn't stop now.

He tore open the condom, positioning the protection over the blunt head of his arousal, rolling it down slowly.

She was transfixed. The sight of his own hand on his shaft so erotic she could hardly stand it.

She would pay good money to watch him shower, to watch his hands slide over all those gorgeous muscles. To watch him take himself in hand and lead himself to completion.

Oh, yeah. That was now her number-one fantasy. Which was a problem, because it was a fantasy that would never be fulfilled.

Don't think about that now. Don't think about it ever.

He leaned in, kissing her, guiding her so that she was lying down on the couch, then he positioned himself between her legs, testing the entrance to her body before thrusting forward and filling her completely.

She closed her eyes tight, unable to handle the feeling of being invaded by him, both in body and in her soul.

"Look at me," he said.

And once more, she was completely helpless to do anything other than obey.

She opened her eyes, her gaze meeting his, touching her down deep, where his hands never could.

And then he kissed her, soft, gentle. That kind of tenderness that had been missing from her life for so long. The kind that she had always been too embarrassed to ask for from anyone. Too embarrassed to show that she needed. That she desperately craved.

But Chase knew. Because he was Chase. He just knew.

He flexed his hips again, his pelvis butting up against her, sending a shower of sparks through her body. There was no way she was ready to come again. Except he kept moving, creating new sensations inside of her, deeper than what had come before.

It shouldn't be possible for her to have another orgasm now. Not after the first one had stripped her so completely. But apparently tonight, nothing was impossible.

There was something different about this. About the two of them, working toward pleasure together. This wasn't just her giving it out to him, or him reciprocating. This was something they were sharing.

She focused on pieces of him. The intensity in his eyes. The way the tendons in his neck stood out, evidence of the control he was exerting. She looked at his hand, up by her head, grabbing hold of one of the blankets she had been using, clinging tightly to it, as though it were his lifeline.

She looked down at his throat, at the pulse beating there.

All these close, intimate snapshots of this man that she knew better than anyone else.

Her chest felt heavy, swollen, and then it began to expand. She was convinced that she was going to break apart. All of these feelings, all of this pleasure. It was just too much. She couldn't handle it.

"Please," she begged. "Please."

He released his grip on the blanket to grasp her hips, holding her steady as he pounded harder into her, as he pounded them both toward release. Toward salvation. It was too much. It needed to end. It was all she could think. She was begging him inside. *End it, Chase. Please, end it.*

Orgasm latched on to her throat like a wild beast,

gripping her hard, violently, shaking her, pleasure exploding over her. Ugly. Completely and totally beyond control.

And then Chase let out a hoarse cry, freezing above her as he thrust inside her one last time, shivering, shaking as his own release took hold.

They were captive to it together. Powerless to do anything but wait until the savage beast was finished having its way. Until it was ready to move on.

And when it was over, only the two of them were left.

Just the two of them. Chase and Anna. No clothes, no shields.

She remembered the real reason she hadn't had sex since that first time. It had nothing to do with how good or bad it had felt. Nothing to do with what a jerk she'd been after.

It had been this. This feeling of being unable to hide. But with the other guy, it had been easy to regroup. Easy to pretend she felt nothing.

She couldn't do that with Chase. She was defenseless.

And for the first time in longer than she could remember, a tear slid down her cheek.

Chapter 8

He couldn't swear creatively enough. He had just screwed his best friend's brains out on a couch in her living room. On top of what might be the world's friendliest, most nonsexual-looking blanket. With a Rodgers and Hammerstein musical on the TV in the background.

And then she had started crying. She had started crying, and she had wiggled out from beneath him and gone into the bathroom. Leaving him alone.

He had been sitting there by himself for a full thirty seconds attempting to reconcile all of these things.

And then he sprang into action.

He got up—still bare-ass naked—and walked down the hall. "Anna!" He didn't hear anything. And so he pounded on the bathroom door. "Anna!"

"I'm in the bathroom, dumbass!" came the terse, watery reply.

"I know. That's why I'm knocking on the bathroom door."

"Go away."

"No. I'm not going to go away. You need to talk to me."

"I don't want to talk."

"Anna, dammit, did I hurt you?"

He got nothing in return but silence. Then he heard the lock rattle, and the door opened a crack. One green eye looked up at him, accusing. "No."

"Why are you hiding?" He studied the eye more closely. It was red-rimmed. Definitely still weeping a little bit.

"I don't know," she said.

"Well…you had me convinced that I… Anna, it happened really fast."

"Not *that* fast. Believe me, I've had faster."

"You wanted all of that…? I mean…"

She laughed. Actually laughed, pushing the door open a little bit wider. "After my emphatic… After all the *yes-ing*… You can honestly ask whether or not I wanted it?"

"I have a lot of sex," he said. "I don't see any point in beating around the bush there. And women have had a lot of reactions to the sex. But I can honestly say none of them have ever run away crying. So, yeah, I'm feeling a little bit shaky right now."

"You're shaky? I'm the one that's crying."

"And if I was alone in this…if I pushed you further than you wanted to go… I'm going to have to ask Sam to fire up the forge and prepare you a red-hot poker so you can have your way with me in an entirely different manner."

"I wanted it, Chase." Her tone was muted.

"Then why are you crying?"

"I'm not very experienced," she said.

"Well, I mean, I know you don't really hook up."

"I've had sex once. One other time."

He was stunned. Stunned enough that he was pretty sure Anna could have put her index finger on his chest, given a light push and knocked him flat on his ass. "Once."

"Sure. You remember Corbin. And that whole fiasco. Where I kind of made fun of his…lack of…attributes and staying power in the hall at school. And… basically ensured that no guy would ever touch me ever again."

"Right." He remembered that.

"Well, I didn't really get what the fuss was about."

"But you… I mean, you've had…"

"Orgasms? Yes. Almost every day of my life. Because I am industrious, and red-blooded, and self-sufficient."

He cleared his throat, trying to ignore the shot of heat that image sent straight through his blood. Anna. Touching herself.

What the hell was happening to him? Well, there was nothing happening. It had damn well *happened*. On the couch in Anna's living room.

He could never look at her again without seeing her there, obeying his orders. Spreading her thighs for him so that he could get a good look at her. Yeah, he could never unsee that. Wasn't sure if he wanted to. But where the hell did he go from here? Where did they go?

There were a lot of women he could have sex with, worry-free. Anna wasn't one of them. She was a rare, precious thing in his life. Someone who knew him. Who knew all about how affected he and Sam had been by the loss of their parents.

Someone he never had to explain it to because she'd been there.

He didn't like explaining all that. So the solution was keep the friends that were there when it happened, and make sure everyone else was temporary.

Which meant Anna couldn't be temporary. She was part of him. Part of his life. A load-bearing wall on the structure that was Chase McCormack. Remove her, and he would crumble.

That was why she had always stayed a friend. Why he had never done anything like this with her before. It wasn't because of her coveralls, or her don't-step-on-the-grass demeanor. Or even because she'd neatly neutered the reputation of the guy she'd slept with in high school.

It was because he needed her friendship, not her body.

But the problem was now he knew what she looked like naked.

He couldn't get that image out of his head. And he didn't even want to.

Same with the image of all her self-administered, industrious climaxes.

Damn his dirty mind.

"Okay," he said, taking a step away from the door. "Why don't you come out?"

"I'm naked."

"So am I."

She looked down. "So you are."

"We need to talk."

"Isn't it women who are supposed to require conversation after basic things like sex?"

"I don't know. Because I never stick around long enough to find out. But this is different. This is you and me, Anna, and I will be damned if I let things get messed up over a couple of orgasms."

She chewed her lower lip. She looked…well, she looked young. And she didn't look too tough. It made him ache. "They were pretty good ones."

"Are you all right?"

"I'm fine. It's just that all of this is a little bit weird. And I'm not really experienced enough to pretend that it isn't."

"Right." The whole thing about her having been with only one guy kind of freaked him out. Made him feel like he was responsible for some things. Big things, like what she would think of sex from this day forward. And then there was the bone-deep possessiveness. That he was the first one in all this time… He should hate it. It should scare him. It should not make him feel…triumph.

He was triumphant, dammit. "Why haven't you slept with anyone else?"

She lifted a shoulder. "I told you. I didn't really think my first experience was that great."

"So you just never…"

"I'm also emotionally dysfunctional, in case you hadn't noticed."

A shocked laugh escaped his lips. "Right. Same goes."

"I don't know. Sex kind of weirds me out. It's a lot of closeness."

"It doesn't have to be," he pointed out. It felt like a

weird thing to say, though, because what they'd done just now had been the epitome of closeness.

"It just all feels…raw. And…it was good. But I think that's kind of why it bothered me."

"I don't want it to bother you."

"Well, the other thing is it was *you*. You and me, like you said. We don't do things like this. We hang out, we drink beer. We don't screw."

"Turns out we're pretty compatible when it comes to the screwing." He wasn't entirely sure this was the time to make light of what had just happened. But he was at sea here. So he had to figure out some way to talk to her. He figured he would make his best effort to treat her like he always did.

"Yeah," she said, finally pushing her way out of the bathroom. "But I'm not really sure there's much we can do with that."

He felt like he was losing his grip on something, something essential, important. Like he was on a rope precariously strung across the canyon, trying to hang on and not fall to his doom. Not fall to *their* doom, since she was right there with him.

What she was saying should feel like safety. It didn't. It felt like the bottom of the damn canyon.

"I don't know if that's the way to handle it."

"You don't?" she asked, blinking.

Apparently. He hadn't thought that statement through before it had come out of his mouth. "Yeah. Look, you kissed me yesterday. You gave me…oral pleasure earlier. And now we've had sex. Obviously, this isn't going away. Obviously, there's some attraction between us that we've never really acknowledged before."

"Or," she said, "someone cast a spell on us. Yeah, we drank some kind of sex potion. Makes you horny for twenty-four hours and then goes away."

"Sex potion?"

"It's either that or years of repressed lust, Chase. Pick whichever one makes you most comfortable."

"I would go with sex potion if I thought such a thing existed." He took a deep breath. "You know there's a lot of people that think men and women can't just be friends. And I've always thought that was stupid. Maybe this is why. Maybe it's because eventually, something happens. Eventually, the connection can't just be platonic. Not when you've spent so long in each other's company. Not when you're both reasonably attractive and single."

She snorted. "*Reasonably* attractive. What happened to me being a *damn miracle*?"

"I was referring to myself when I said reasonably. I'd hate to sound egotistical."

"Honestly, Chase, after thirty years of accomplished egotism, why worry about it now?"

He looked down at her. She was stark naked, standing in front of him, and he felt like he was in front of the pastry display case at Pie in the Sky. He wanted to sample everything, and he didn't know where to start.

But he couldn't do anything about that now. He was trying to make amends. Dropping to his knees in front of her and burying his face between her legs probably wouldn't help with that.

He could feel his dick starting to wake up again. And since he was naked he might as well just go ahead and shout his intentions at her, because he wouldn't be able to hide them.

He couldn't look at her and not get hard, though. A new development in their relationship. But then, so was standing in front of each other without clothes.

"You're beautiful," he said, unable to help himself.

She wasn't as curvy as the women he usually gravitated toward. Her curves were restrained, her waist slim, with no dramatic sweep inward, just a slow build down to those wide, gorgeous hips that he now had fantasies about grabbing hold of while he pumped into her from behind. Her breasts were small but perfection in his mind. More would just be more.

He couldn't really imagine how he had ever looked at her face and found it plain. He had to kick his own ass mentally for that. He had been blind. Someone with unrefined, cheap taste. Who thought that if you stuck rhinestones and glitter on something, that meant it was prettier. But that wasn't Anna. She was simple, refined beauty. Something that only a connoisseur might appreciate. She was like a sunset over the ocean in comparison to a gaudy ballroom chandelier. Both had their strong points. But one was real, deep. Priceless instead of expensive.

That was Anna.

Something about those thoughts made a tightening sensation start in his gut and work its way up to his chest.

"Maybe what happened was just inevitable," he said, looking at her again.

"I can't really disprove that," she said, shifting uncomfortably. "You know, since it happened. I really need to put my clothes on."

"Do you have to?"

She frowned. "Yes. And you do, too. Because if we don't…"

"We'll have sex again."

The words stood between them, stark and far too true for either of their liking.

"Probably not," she said, sounding wholly unconvinced.

"Definitely yes."

She sighed heavily. "Chase, you can have sex with anyone you want. I'm definitely hard up. If you keep walking around flashing that thing, I'm probably going to hop on for a ride, I'll just be honest with you. But I understand if I'm not half as irresistible to you as you are to me."

Anger roared through him, suddenly, swiftly. And just like earlier, when she'd thrown her walls up and tried to drive a wedge between them, he found himself moving toward her. Moving to break through. He growled, backing her up against the wall, almost sighing in relief when his hardening cock met up with her soft skin, when her small breasts pressed against his chest. He grabbed hold of her hands, drawing them together and lifting them up over her head. "Let's get one thing straight, Anna," he said. "You are irresistible to me. If you weren't irresistible to me, I would still be at home. I never would have come here. I never would have kissed you. I never would have touched you. Don't you dare put yourself down. If this is because of your brothers, because of your dad…"

She closed her eyes, looking away from him. "Don't. It's not that."

"Then what is it? Why don't you think you can have this?"

"There's nothing to have. It's just sex. You mean the world to me. And just because I'm…suddenly unable to handle my hormones, I'm not going to compromise our friendship."

"It doesn't have to compromise it," he said, lowering his voice.

"What are you suggesting? We can't have a relationship with each other. We don't have those kinds of feelings for each other. A relationship is more than sex. It's romance and all kinds of stuff that I'm not even sure I want."

"I don't want it, either," he said. "But we're going to see each other. Pretty much every day. Not just because of the stupid bet. Not just because of the charity event. I'd call all that off right now if I thought it was going to ruin our friendship. But the horse has left the stable, Anna, well and truly. It's not going back in." He rolled his hips forward, and she gasped. "See what I mean? And if you were resistible? Then sure, I would tell you that we could just be done. We could pretend it didn't happen. But you're not. So I can't."

She opened her eyes again, looking up at him. "Then what are we doing?"

"You've heard of friends with benefits. Why can't we do that? I mean, I would never have set out to have that relationship. Because I don't think it's very smart. But…it's a little bit late for smart."

"Friends with benefits. As in…we stay friends by day and we screw each other senseless by night?"

Gah. That about sent him over the edge. "Yeah."

"Until what? Until…"

"Until you get that other date. Until the charity thing. As long as we're both single, why not? You're working toward the relationship stuff. You said you didn't want to be alone anymore. So, maybe this is good in the meantime. I know you're both industrious and red-blooded, and can get those orgasms all by yourself." He rolled his hips again and, much to his satisfaction, a small moan of pleasure escaped her lips. "But are they this good?"

"No," she said, her tone hushed.

"This is possibly the worst idea in the history of the world. But hell, you wanted to get some more experience… I'm offering to give it to you." The moment he said the words he wanted to bite his tongue off. The idea of giving Anna more experience just so she could go and do things with other men? That made him see red. Made him feel violent. Jealous. Things he never felt.

But what other option was there? He couldn't keep her. Not like this. But he couldn't let her go now.

He was messed up. *This* was messed up.

"I guess… I guess that makes sense. You know, until earlier today I'd never even given a guy a blow job."

"You're killing me," he said, closing his eyes.

"Well, I don't want you to die. You just offered me your penis for carnal usage. I want you alive."

"So that's it? My penis has now become the star of the show. Wow, how quickly our friendship has eroded."

"Our friendship is still solid. I think it just goes to prove how solid your dick is."

"With romantic praise like that, how are you still single?"

"I have no idea. I spout sonnets effortlessly."

He leaned forward, kissing her, a strange, warm sensation washing over him. He was kissing Anna. And it didn't feel quite as rushed and desperate as all the other times before it. A decision had been made. This wasn't a hasty race against sanity. This wasn't trying to get as much satisfaction as possible squeezed into a moment before reality kicked in. This was…well, in the new world order, it was sanctioned.

Instantly, he was rock hard again, ready to go, even though it'd been only a few minutes since his last orgasm. But there was one problem. "I don't have a condom," he said, cursing and pushing himself away from her. "I don't suppose the woman who has been celibate for the past thirteen years has one?"

"No," she said, sagging against the wall. "You only carry one on you?"

"Yeah. I'm not superhuman. I don't usually expect to get it on more than once in a couple of hours."

"But you were going to with me?"

He looked down at his very erect cock. "Does this answer your question?"

"Yeah."

"Well, then." He let out a heavy sigh.

"You could stay and watch… *Oklahoma!* with me."

He nodded slowly. He should stay and watch *Oklahoma!* with her. If he didn't, it kind of made a mockery of the whole friends-with-benefits thing. Because, before the sex, he would have stayed with her to watch a movie, of course. To hang out, because she was one of his favorite people on earth to spend time with. Even if her taste in movies was deeply suspect.

Of course, he didn't particularly want to stay now, because she presented the temptation that he could not give in to.

"Unless you have to work early tomorrow."

"I really do," he said.

"Thank God."

His eyebrows shot up. "You want to get rid of me?"

"I don't really want to hang out with you when I know I can't have you."

"I felt the same way, but I didn't want to say it. I thought it seemed kind of offensive."

Strangely, she smiled. "I'm not offended. I'm not offended at all. I kind of like being irresistible."

Instead of leaving, he knew that he could drive down to the store and buy a box of condoms. And he seriously considered it. The problem with that was there had to be some boundaries. Some limits. He was pretty sure being so horny and desperate that you needed to buy condoms right away instead of just waiting until you had protection on hand probably didn't fit within the boundaries of friends with benefits.

"I'll see you tomorrow, then."

She nodded. "See you tomorrow."

Chapter 9

By the time Anna swung by the grocery store in the afternoon, she was feeling very mature, and very proud of herself. She was having a no-strings sexual relationship with her friend. And she was going to buy milk, cheese and condoms. Because she was mature and adult and completely fine with the whole situation. Also, mature.

She grabbed a cart and began to slowly walk up and down the aisles. She was not making sure that no one she knew was around. Because, of course, she wasn't at all embarrassed to be in the store looking for milk, cheese and—incidentally—prophylactics. She was *thirty*. She was entitled to a little bit of sexual release. Anyway, no one was actually watching her.

She swallowed hard, trying to remember exactly which aisle the condoms were in. She had never bought any. Ever. In her entire life.

She had been extremely tempted to make a dash to the store last night when Chase had discovered he didn't have any more protection, but she had imagined that was just a little bit too desperate. She was going to be nondesperate about this. Very chill. And not like a woman who was a near virgin. Or like someone who was so desperate to jump her best friend's bones it might seem like there were deeper emotions at play. There were not.

The strong feelings she had were just…in her pants. Pants feelings. That's it.

Last night's breakdown had been purely because she was unaccustomed to sex. Just a little post-orgasmic release. That's all it was. The whole thing was a release. Post-orgasmic tears weren't really all that strange.

She felt bolstered by that thought.

She turned down the aisle labeled Family Planning and made her way toward the condoms. Lubricated. Extra-thin. Ribbed. There were options. She had to stand there and seriously ponder ribbed. She should have asked Chase what he had used last night. Because whatever that had been had been perfect.

"Anna." The masculine voice coming from her left startled her.

She turned and—to her utter horror—saw her brother Mark standing there.

"Hi," she said, taking two steps away from the condom shelf, as though that would make it less obvious why she was in the aisle. Whatever. They were adults. Neither of them were virgins and they were both aware of that.

Still, she needed some distance between herself and

anything that said "ribbed for her pleasure" when she was standing there talking to her brother.

"Haven't seen you in a couple days."

"Well, you pissed me off last time I saw you."

He lifted a shoulder. "Sorry."

He probably was, too.

"Hey, whatever. I win your bet."

His brows shot up. "I heard a rumor about you and Chase McCormack kissing at Beaches, but I was pretty sure that…" His eyes drifted toward the condoms. *"Really?"*

Dying of embarrassment was a serious risk at the moment, but she was caught. Completely and totally caught. And as long as she was drowning in a sea of horror…well, she might as well ride the tide.

If he needed proof her date with Chase was real, she imagined proof of sex was about the best there was.

She took a fortifying breath. "Really," she said, crossing her arms beneath her breasts. "It's happening. I have a date. I have more than a date. I have a whole future full of dates because I have a relationship. With Chase. You lose."

"I'm supposed to believe that you and McCormack are suddenly—" his eyes drifted back to the condoms again *"—that."*

"You don't have to believe it. It's true. He's also going to be my date to the charity gala that I'm invited to. I will take my payment in small or large bills. Thank you."

"I'm not convinced."

"You're not convinced?" She moved closer to the shelf and grabbed a box of condoms. "I am caught in the act."

"Convenient," he said, grabbing his own box.

She made a face. "It's not convenient. It happened."

"You're in love with him?"

The question felt like a punch to the stomach. She did not like it. She didn't like it at all. More than that, she had no idea what to say. *No* seemed…wrong. *Yes* seemed worse. And she wasn't really sure either answer was true.

You can't love Chase.

She couldn't not love him, either. He was her friend, after all. Of course she wasn't in love with him.

Her stomach twisted tight. No. She did not love him. She didn't do love. At all. Especially not with him. Because he would never…

"You look like you just got slapped with a fish," Mark said, and, to his credit, he looked somewhat concerned.

"I… Of course I love him," she said. That was a safe answer. It was also true. She did love him. As a friend. And…she loved his body. And everything about him as a human being. Except for the fact that he was a man slut who would never settle down with any woman, much less her.

Why not you?

No. She was not thinking about this. She wasn't thinking about any of this.

"Tell you what. If you're still together at the gala, you get your money."

"That isn't fair. That isn't what we agreed on."

He lifted a shoulder. "I know. But I also didn't expect you to grab your best friend and have him be your date. That still seems suspicious to me, regardless of… purchases."

"You didn't put any specifications on the bet, Mark. You can't change the rules now."

"We didn't put any specifications on it saying I couldn't."

"Why do you care?"

He snorted. "Why do you care?"

"I have pride, jackass."

"And I don't trust Chase McCormack. If you're still together at the gala, you get your money. And if he hurts you in any way, I will break his neck. After I pull his balls off and feed them to the sharks."

It wasn't very often that Mark's protective side was on display. Usually, he was too busy tormenting her. Their childhood had been rough. Their father didn't have any idea how to show affection to them, and as a result none of them were very good at it, either. Still, she never doubted that—even when he was a jerk— Mark cared about her.

"That's not necessary. Chase is my best friend. And now…he's more. He isn't going to hurt me."

"Sounds to me like he has the potential to hurt you worse than just about anybody."

His words settled heavily in the pit of her stomach. She should be able to brush them off. Because she and Chase were in a relationship. She and Chase were friends with benefits. And nothing about that would hurt at all.

"I'll be fine."

"If you need anything, just let me know."

"I will."

He lifted the condom box. "We'll pretend this didn't happen." Then he turned and started to walk away.

"Pretend what didn't happen?" She pulled her own

box of condoms up against her chest and held it tightly. "See? I've already forgotten. Mostly because I can't afford therapy. At least not until you pay me the big bucks at the gala."

"We'll see," he said, walking out of sight.

She turned, chucking the box into her cart and making her way quickly down to the milk aisle. Chase wasn't going to hurt her, because Mark was wrong. They were only friends, and she quashed the traitorous flame in her stomach that tried to grow, tried to convince her otherwise.

She wasn't going to get hurt. She was just going to have a few orgasms and then move on.

That was her story, and she was sticking to it.

"I'm taking you dancing tonight," Chase said as soon as Anna picked up the phone.

"Did you bump your head on an anvil today?"

He supposed he shouldn't be that surprised to hear Anna's sarcasm. After last night—vulnerability, tears—he'd had a feeling that she wasn't going to be overly friendly today. In fact, he'd guessed that she would have transformed into one of the little porcupines that were on her pajamas. He had been right.

"No," he said. "I'm just following the lesson plan. I said I was taking you out, and so I am."

"You know," she said, her voice getting husky, "I'm curious about whether or not making me scream was anywhere on the lesson plan."

His body jolted, heat rushing through his veins. He looked over his shoulder at Sam, who was working steadily on something in the back of the shop. It was Anna's day off, so she wasn't on the property. But he and Sam were in the middle of a big custom job. A gate with a lot of intricate detail, with matching work for the deck and interior staircase of the home. Which meant they didn't get real time off right now.

"No," he returned, satisfied his brother wasn't paying attention, "that wasn't on the lesson plan. But I'm a big believer in improvisation."

"That was improvisation? In that case, it seems to be your strength."

The sarcasm he had expected. This innuendo, he had not. They'd both pulled away hard last night, no denying it. It would have been simple to go out and get more protection and neither of them had.

But damn, this new dynamic between them was a lot to get used to. Still, for all that it was kind of crazy, he knew what he wanted. "I'd like to show you more of my strengths tonight."

"You're welcome to improvise your way on over to my bed anytime." There was a pause. "Was that flirting? Was that *good* flirting?"

He laughed, tension exiting his body in a big gust. He should have known. He wasn't sure how he felt about this being part of the lesson. Not when he had been on the verge of initiating phone sex in the middle of a workday with his brother looming in the background. But keeping it part of the lesson was for the best. He didn't need to lose his head. This was Anna, after all. He was walking a very fine line here.

On the one hand, he knew keeping a clear line drawn in the sand was the right thing to do. They weren't just going to be able to slide right back into their normal relationship. Not after what had happened. On the other hand, Anna was… Anna. She was essential to him.

And she wasn't jaded when it came to sexual relationships. Wasn't experienced. That meant he needed to handle her with care. And it would benefit him to remember that he couldn't play with her the way he did women with a little more experience. Women who understood that this was sex and nothing more.

It could never be meaningless sex with Anna. He couldn't have a meaningless conversation with her. That meant that whatever happened between them physically would change things, build things, tear things down. That was a fact. A scary one. Taking control, trying to harness it, label it, was the only solution he had. Otherwise, things would keep happening when they weren't prepared. That would be worse.

Maybe.

He cleared his throat. "Very good flirting. You got me all excited."

"Excellent," she said, sounding cheerful. "Also, I bought condoms."

He choked. "Did you?"

"They aren't ribbed. I wasn't sure if the one you used last night was."

"No," he said, rubbing the back of his neck and casting a side eye at his brother. "It wasn't."

"Good. I was looking for a repeat performance. I didn't want to get the wrong thing. Though maybe sometime we should try ribbed."

Sometime. Because there would be more than once. More than last night. More than tonight. "We can try it if you want."

"I feel like we might as well try everything. I have a lot of catching up to do."

"Dancing," he said, trying to wage a battle with the

heat that was threatening to take over his skull. "Do you want to go dancing tonight?"

"Not really. But I can see the benefit. Seeing as there will be dancing at the fund-raiser. And I bet I'm terrible at dancing."

"Great. I'm going to pick you up at seven. We're going to Ace's."

"Then I'll be ready."

He hung up the phone and suddenly realized he was at the center of Sam's keen focus. That bastard had been listening in the entire time. "Hot date tonight?" he asked.

"Dancing. With Anna," he said meaningfully. The meaning being *with Anna and not with you*.

"Well, then, you wouldn't mind if I tagged along." Jerkface was ignoring his meaning.

"I would mind."

"I thought this was just about some bet."

"It is," he lied.

"Uh-huh."

"You don't want to go out. You want to stay home and eat a TV dinner. You're just harassing me."

Sam shrugged. "I have to get my kicks somewhere."

"Get your own. Get laid."

"Nope."

"You're a weirdo."

"I'm selective."

Maybe Sam was, maybe he wasn't. Chase could honestly say that his brother's sex life was a mystery to him. Which was fine. Really, more than fine. Chase had a reputation, Sam…did not. Well, unless that reputation centered around being grumpy and antisocial.

"Right. Well, you enjoy that. I'm going to go out."

"Chase," Sam said, his tone taking on a note of steel. "Don't hurt her."

Those words poked him right in the temper. "Really?"

"She's the best thing you have," Sam said, his voice serious. "You find a woman like that, you keep her. In whatever capacity you can."

"She's my best friend. I'm not going to hurt her."

"Not on purpose."

"I don't think you're in any position to stand there and lecture me on interpersonal relationships, since you pretty much don't have any."

"I have you," Sam said.

"Right. I'm not sure that counts."

"I have Anna. But if you messed things up with her, I won't have her, either."

Chase frowned. "You don't have feelings for her, do you?" He would really hate to have to punch his brother in the face. But he would.

"No. Not like you mean. But I know her, and I care about her. And I know you."

"What does that mean?"

Sam pondered that for a second. "You're not her speed."

"I'm not trying to be." He was getting ready to punch his brother in the face anyway.

"I'm just saying."

"You're just saying," he muttered. "Go *just say* somewhere else. A guy whose only friends are his younger brother and that brother's friend maybe shouldn't stand there and make commentary on relationships."

"I'm quiet. I'm perceptive. As you mentioned, I am an artist."

"You can't pull that out when it suits you and put it away when it doesn't."

"Sure I can. Artists are temperamental."

"Stop beating around the bush. Say what you want to say."

Sam sighed. "If she offers you more than friendship, take it, dumbass."

"Why would you think that she would ever offer that? Why would you think that I want it?"

He felt defensive. And more than a little bit annoyed. "She will. I'm not blind. Actually, being antisocial has its benefits. It means that I get to sit back and watch other people interact. She likes you. She always has. And she's the kind of good… Chase, we don't get good like that. We don't deserve it."

"Gee. Thanks, Sam."

"I'm not trying to insult you. I'm just saying that she's better than either of us. Figure out how to make it work if she wants to."

Everything in Chase recoiled. "She doesn't want to. And neither do I." He turned away from Sam, heading toward the door.

"Are you sleeping with her yet?"

Chase froze. "That isn't any of your business."

"Right. You are."

"Still not your business."

"Chase, we both have a lot of crap to wade through. Which is pretty obvious. But if she's standing there willing to pull you out, I'm just saying you need to take her up on her offer."

"She has enough crap of her own that she's hip deep in, Sam. I don't need her taking on mine."

Sam rubbed his hand over his forehead. "Yeah, that's always the thing."

"Anyway, she doesn't want me. Not like that. I mean, not forever. This is just a…physical thing." Which was way more information than his brother deserved.

"Keep telling yourself that if it helps you sleep at night."

"I sleep like a baby, Sam." He continued out the door, heading toward his truck. He had to get back to the house and get showered and dressed so that he could pick up Anna. And he was not going to think about anything his brother had said.

Anna didn't want forever with him.

That thought immobilized him, forced him to imagine a future with Anna, stretching on and on into the distance. Holding her, kissing her. Sleeping beside her every night and waking up with her every morning.

Seeing her grow round with his child.

He shut it down immediately. That was a fantasy. One he didn't want. One he couldn't have.

He would have Anna as a friend forever, but the "benefits" portion of their relationship was finite.

So, he would just enjoy this while it lasted.

Chapter 10

She looked like a cliché. A really slutty one. She wasn't sure she cared. But in her very short denim skirt and plaid shirt knotted above the waistline she painted quite the picture.

One of a woman looking to get lucky.

"Well," she said to her reflection—her made-up reflection, compliments of her trip to the store in Tolowa today, as was everything else. "You *are* looking to get lucky."

Fair. That was fair.

She heard the sound of a truck engine and tires on the gravel in her short little driveway. She was renting a house in an older neighborhood in town—not right in the armpit of town where she'd grown up, but still sort of on the fringe—and the yard was a little bit…rustic.

She wondered if Chase would honk. Or if he would come to the door.

Him coming to the door would feel much more like a date. A real date.

A *date* date.

Oh, Lord, what were they doing?

She had flirted with him on the phone, and she'd enjoyed it. Had wanted—very much—to push him even harder. Trading innuendo with him was…well, it was a lot more fun than she'd imagined.

There was a heavy knock on the door and she squeaked, hopping a little bit before catching her breath. Then she grabbed her purse and started to walk to the entry, trying to calm her nerves. He'd come to the door. That felt like A Thing.

You're being crazy. Friends with benefits. Not boyfriend.

The word *boyfriend* made her stomach lurch, and she did her best to ignore it. She jerked the door open, watching his face intently for his response to her new look. And she was not disappointed.

"Damn," he said, leaning forward, resting his forearm on the doorjamb. "I didn't realize you would be showing up dressed as Country Girl from My Dirtiest Dreams."

She shouldn't feel flattered by that. But she positively glowed. "It seemed fair, since you're basically the centerfold of *Blacksmith Magazine*."

He laughed. "Really? How would that photo shoot go?"

"You posing strategically in front of the forge with a bellows over your junk."

"I am not getting my *junk* near the forge. The last thing I need is sensitive body parts going up in flames."

"I know I don't want them going up in flames." She

cleared her throat, suddenly aware of a thick blanket of awkwardness settling over them. She didn't know what to do with him now. Did she...not touch him unless they were going to have sex? Did she kiss him if she wanted to or did she need permission?

She needed a friends-with-benefits handbook.

"Um," she began, rather unsuccessfully. "What exactly are my benefits?"

"Meaning?"

"My benefits additional to this friendship. Do I... kiss you when I see you? Or..."

"Do you want to kiss me?"

She looked up at him, all sexy and delicious looking in his tight black T-shirt, cowboy hat and late-in-the-day stubble. "Is that a trick question? Because the only answer to 'Do I want to kiss a very hot guy?' is yes. But not if you don't want to kiss me."

He wrapped his arm around her waist, drawing her up against him before bending down to kiss her slowly, thoroughly. "Does that help?"

She let out a long, slow breath, the tension that had been strangling her since he'd arrived at her house leaving her body slowly. "Yes," she said, sighing. "It does."

"All right," he said, extending his hand. "Let's go."

She took hold of his hand, the warmth of his touch flooding her, making her stomach flip. She let him lead her to the truck, open her door for her. All manner of date-type stuff. The additional benefits were getting bound up in the dating lessons and at the moment she wasn't sure what was for her and what was for the Making Her Datable mission.

Then she decided it didn't matter.

She just clung to the good feelings the whole drive to Ace's.

When they got there, she felt the true weight of the spectacle they were creating in the community. Beaches was one thing. Them being together there had certainly caused a ripple. But everyone in Copper Ridge hung out at Ace's.

Sierra West, whose family was a client of both her and Chase, was in the corner with some other friends who were involved with local rodeo events. Sheriff Eli Garrett was over by the bar, along with his brother, Connor, and their wives, Sadie and Liss.

She looked the other direction and saw Holly and Ryan Masters sitting in the corner, looking ridiculously happy. Holly and Ryan had both grown up in foster care in Copper Ridge and so had been part of the town-charity-case section at school. Though Holly was younger and Ryan a little older, so she'd never been close friends with them. Behind them was Jonathan Bear, looking broody and unapproachable as usual.

She officially knew too many damn people.

"This town is the size of a postage stamp," she muttered as she followed Chase to a table where they could deposit their coats and her purse.

"That's good," he said. "Men are seeing you attached. It's all part of changing your reputation. That's what you want."

She grunted. "I guess." It didn't feel like what she wanted. She mostly just wanted to be alone with Chase now. No performance art required.

But she was currently a dancing monkey for all of Copper Ridge, so performance art was the order of the evening.

She also suddenly felt self-conscious about her wardrobe choice. Wearing this outfit for Chase hadn't seemed bad at all. Wearing it in front of everyone was a little much.

The jukebox was blaring, and Luke Bryan was demanding all the country girls shake it for him, so Anna figured—regardless of how comfortable she was feeling—it was as good a time as any for them to get out on the dance floor.

The music was fast, so people weren't touching. They were just sort of, well, *shaking it* near each other.

She was just standing there, looking at him and not shaking it, because she didn't know what to do next. It felt weird to be here in front of everyone in a skirt. It felt weird to be dancing with Chase. It felt weird to not touch him. But it would be weirder to touch him.

Hell if she knew what she was doing here.

Then he reached out, brushing his fingers down her arm. That touch, that connection, rooted her to the earth. To the moment. To him. Suddenly, it didn't matter so much what other people around them were doing. She moved in slightly, and he put his hand on her hip.

Then, before she was ready, the song ended, slowing things down. And now she really didn't know what to do. It seemed that Chase did, though. He wrapped his arm around her waist, drawing her in close, taking hold of her hand with his free one.

Her heart was pounding hard. And she was pretty sure her face was bright red. She looked up at Chase, his expression unreadable. He was not bright red. Of course he wasn't. Because even if this relationship was new for him, this kind of situation was not. He knew how to handle women. He knew how to handle sex feelings. Meanwhile, she was completely unsure of what to do. Like a buoy floating out in the middle of the ocean, just bobbing there on her own.

Her breathing got shorter, harder. Matching her heartbeat. She couldn't just dance with him like this. She needed to not be in front of people when she felt these things. She felt like her arousal was written all over her skin. Well, it was. She was blushing like a beacon. She could probably guide ships in from the sea.

She looked at Chase's face again. There was no way to tell what he was thinking. His dark gaze was shielded by the dim lighting, his jaw set, hard, his mouth in a firm line. That brief moment of connection that she'd felt was gone now. He was touching her still, but she had no idea what he was feeling.

She looked over to her left and noticed that people were staring. Of course they were. She and Chase were dancing and that was different. And, of course, a great many of the stares were coming from women. Women who probably felt like they should be in her position. Like she didn't belong there.

And they could all see how much she wanted it. That she wanted him more than he wanted her. That she was the one who was completely and totally out of control. Needing him so much she couldn't even hide it.

And they all knew she didn't deserve it.

She pulled away from him, looking around, breathing hard. "I think... I just need a break."

She crossed the room and went back to their table, grabbing her purse and making her way over to the bar.

Chase joined her only a few moments later. "What's up?"

She shook her head. "Nothing."

"We were dancing, and then you freaked out."

"I don't like everybody watching us."

"That's the point, though."

That simple statement stabbed her straight through the heart. "Yeah. I know." That was the problem. He was so conscious of why they were doing this. This whole thing. And she could so easily forget. Could so easily let down all the walls and shields that she had put in place to protect her heart. And just let herself want.

She hated that. Hated craving things she couldn't have. Affection she could never hope to earn.

Her mother had left. And no amount of wishing that she would come back, no amount of crying over that lost love, would do anything to fix it. No amount of hoping her father would drop that crusty exterior and give her a hug when she needed it would make it happen. So she just didn't want. Or at least, she never let people see how much she wanted.

"I know," she said, her tone a little bit stiffer than she would like.

She was bombing out here. Failing completely at remaining cool, calm and unaffected. She was standing here in public, hemorrhaging needs all over the place.

"What's wrong?"

"I need a drink."

"Why don't we leave?"

She blinked. "Just...leave?"

"If you aren't having fun, then there's no point. Let's go."

"Where are we going?"

He grabbed her hand and started to lead her through the bar. "Somewhere fun."

She followed him out into the night, laughing helplessly when they climbed into the truck. "People are going to talk. That was all a little weird."

"Let them talk. They need something to do."

He started the engine and backed out of the parking lot, turning sharply and heading down the road, out of town.

"Where are we going?"

"Somewhere I bet you've never been."

"You don't know my life, Chase McCormack. You don't know where I've been."

"I do know your life, Anna Brown."

She gritted her teeth, because, of course, he did. She said nothing as they continued to drive up the road. And still said nothing when he turned onto a dirt road that forked into a narrower dirt road as it went up the mountain.

"What are we doing?" she asked again.

Just then, they came to a flat, clear area. She couldn't see anything; there were no lights except for the headlights on the truck, illuminating nothing but the side of another mountain, thick with evergreens.

"I want to make out with you. This is where you go do that."

"We're adults," she said, ignoring the giddy fluttering in her stomach. "We have our own bedrooms. And beds. We don't need to go make out in a car."

"*Need* is not the operative word here. We're expanding experiences and stuff." He flicked the radio on, country music filling the cab of the truck. "Actually, I think before we make out—" he opened the driver's-side door "—we should dance."

Now there was nobody here. Which meant there was no excuse. Actually, this made her a lot more emotional. She did not like that. She didn't like the super-power that Chase seemed to have of reaching down inside of her, past all the defenses, and grabbing hold of tender, emotional things.

But she wasn't going to refuse, either.

It was dark out here. At least there was that.

Before she had a chance to move, Chase was at her side of the truck, opening her door. He extended his hand. "Dance with me?"

She was having a strange out-of-body experience. She wasn't sure who this woman was, up in the woods with only a gorgeous man for company. A man who wanted to dance with her. A man who wanted to make out with her.

She unbuckled, accepting his offered hand and popping out of the truck. He spun her over to the front of the vehicle, the headlights serving as spotlights as the music played over the radio. "I'm kind of a crappy dancer," he said, pulling her in close.

"You don't seem like a crappy dancer to me."

"How many men have you danced with?"

She laughed. "Um, counting now?"

"Yeah."

"One."

He chuckled, his breath fanning over her cheekbone. So intimate to share the air with him like this. Shocking. "Well, then, you don't have much to compare it to."

"I guess not. But I don't think I would compare either way."

"Oh, yeah? Why is that?"

"You're in a league of your own, Chase McCormack, don't you know?"

"Hmm. I have heard that a time or two. When teachers told me I was a unique sort of devil, sent there to make their lives miserable. Or all the times I used to get into it with my old man."

"Well, you did raise a lot of hell."

"Yeah. I did. I continue to raise hell, in some fashion. But I need people to see a different side of me," he said, drawing her even tighter up against him. "I need for them to see that Sam and I can handle our business. That we can make the McCormack name big again."

"Can you?" she asked, tilting her head up, her lips brushing his chin. The stubble there was prickly, masculine. Irresistible. So she bit him. Just lightly. Scraping her teeth over his skin.

He gripped her hair, pulling her head back. The sudden rush of danger in the movements sending a shot of adrenaline through her blood. This was so strange. Being in his arms and feeling like she was home. Like he was everything comforting and familiar. A warm blanket, a hot chocolate and a musical she'd seen a hundred times.

Then things would shift, and he would become something else entirely. A stranger. Sex, sin and all the things she'd never taken the time to explore. She liked that, too.

She was starting to get addicted to both.

"Oh, I can handle myself just fine," he said, his tone hard.

"Can you handle me?" she asked.

He slid his hand down to cup her ass, his eyes never leaving hers as they swayed to the music. "I can handle you. However you want it."

"Hard," she said, her throat going dry, her words

slightly unsteady. She wasn't sure what had possessed her to say that.

"You want it hard?" he asked, his words sounding strangled.

"Yes," she said.

"How else do you want it?" he asked, holding her against him, moving in time with the beat. She could feel his cock getting hard against her hip.

"Aren't you the one with the lesson plan?"

"You're the one in need of the education," he said.

"I don't want tonight to be about that," she said, and she was as sure about that as she'd been about wanting it hard and equally unsure about how she knew it.

"What do you want it to be about?"

"You," she said, tracing the sharp line of his jaw. "Me. That's about it."

"What do you want from me?" he asked.

Only everything. She shied away from that thought. "Show me what the fuss is about."

"I did that already."

Something hot and possessive spiked in her blood. Something she never could have anticipated, because she hadn't even realized that it lived inside of her. "No. Something you don't give other women, Chase. You're my friend. You're…more to me than one night and an orgasm. You're right. I could have gotten that from a lot of guys. Well, maybe not the orgasm. But sex for sure. My coveralls aren't that much of a turnoff. And you could have any woman. So give me you. And I'll give you me. Don't hold back."

"You're…not very experienced."

She stretched up on tiptoes, pressing her lips to his. "Did I ask for a gentleman? Or did I ask for hard?"

He tightened his grip on her hair, and this time when she looked up at his face, she didn't see a stranger. She saw Chase. The man. The whole man. Not divided up into parts. Not Her Friend Chase or Her Lover Chase, but just… Chase.

He was all of these things. Fun and laid-back, intense and deeply sexual. She wanted it all. She craved it all. As hard as he could. As much as he could. And still, it would never, ever be enough.

"Go ahead," she said, "take me, cowboy."

She didn't have to ask twice.

He propelled them both backward, pressing her up against the truck, kissing her deeply, a no-holds-barred possession of her mouth. She hadn't even realized kissing like this existed. She wasn't entirely sure what she had thought kissing was for. Affection. A prelude to sex. This was something else entirely. This was a language all its own. Words that didn't exist in English. Words that she knew Chase would never be able to say.

And her body knew that. Understood it. Responded. As surely as it would have if he had spoken.

She was drowning. In this, in him. She hadn't expected emotion to be this…fierce. She hadn't really expected emotion at all. She hadn't understood. She really had not understood.

But then she didn't have the time to think about it. Or the brainpower. He tugged on her hair, drawing her head to the side before he pressed his lips to her tender neck, his teeth scraping along the sensitive skin before he closed his lips around her and sucked hard.

"You want it hard?" he asked, his voice rough. "Then we're going to do it my way."

He grabbed hold of her hips, turning her so that she

was facing the truck. "Scoot just a little bit." He guided her down to where the cab of the truck ended and the bed began. "Grab on." She curved her fingers around the cold metal, a shiver running down her spine. "You ever do it like this?" he asked.

She laughed, more because she was nervous than because she thought the question was funny. "Chase, before you I had never even given a guy a blow job. Do you think I've ever done this before?"

"Good," he said, his tone hard, very definitely him. "I like that. I'm a sick bastard. I like the fact that no other man has ever done this to you before. I should feel guilty." He reached around and undid the top button on her top. "But I'm just enjoying corrupting you."

He undid another button, then another. She wasn't wearing a bra underneath the top. Because, frankly, when you were as underendowed as she was, there really wasn't any point. Also, it made things a little bit more easy access. Though that wasn't something she had thought about until just now. Until Chase undid the last button and left her completely bare to the cool night air.

"I'm kind of enjoying being corrupted."

"I didn't tell you you could talk."

She shut her mouth, surprised at the commanding tone he was taking. Not entirely displeased about it. He cupped her breasts, squeezing them gently before moving his hands down her stomach, bringing them around her hips. Then he tugged her skirt down, leaving her in nothing but her boots and her underwear.

"We'll leave the boots on. I wouldn't want you to step on anything sharp."

She didn't say anything. She bit her lip, eagerly anticipating what he might do next. He slipped his hand down between her thighs, his fingertips edging beneath her panties. He stroked his fingers through her folds, a harsh growl escaping his lips. "You're wet for me," he said—not a question.

She nodded, closing her eyes, trying to keep from hurtling over the edge as soon as his fingertips brushed over her. But it was a pretty difficult battle she was waging. Just the thought of being with Chase again was enough to take her to the precipice. His touch nearly pushed her over immediately.

He gripped her tightly with his other hand, drawing her ass back up against his cock as he teased her between her legs with his clever fingers. He slipped one deep inside of her, continuing to toy with her with the edge of his thumb while he thrust in and out of her slowly. He added a second finger, then another. And she was shaking. Trembling with the effort of holding back her climax.

But she didn't want it to end like this. Didn't want it to end so quickly. Mostly, she just didn't want him to know that with one flick of his fingertip over her sensitized flesh he could make her come so hard she wouldn't be able to see straight. Because at the end of the day it didn't matter how much she wanted him; she still had her pride. She still rebelled against the idea of revealing herself quite so easily.

She probably already had. Here she was, mostly naked, out underneath the stars. Here she was, telling him she wanted just the two of them, that she wanted it hard. Probably there were no secrets left. Not really. There were all sorts of unspoken truths filling in the silences between them, but she felt like they were easy enough to read, if he wanted to look at them.

He might not. She didn't really want to. Yet it didn't make them go away.

But she could ignore them. She could focus on this. On his touch. On the dark magic he was working on her body, the spell that was taking her over completely.

He swept her hair to the side, pressing a hot kiss to the back of her neck. And then there was no holding back. Climax washed over her like a wave as she shuddered out her release.

"Good girl," he whispered, kissing her again before moving away for a moment. He pushed her panties down her legs, helping her step out of them, then he kissed her thigh before straightening.

She heard him moving behind her. But she didn't change her position. She stood there, gripping the back of the truck. Dimly, she was aware the radio was still on. That they had a sound track to this illicit encounter in the woods. It added to the surreal, out-of-body quality.

But then he was back with her, touching her, kissing her, and it didn't feel so surreal anymore. It was too raw. Too real. His voice, his scent, his touch. He was there. There was no denying it. This wasn't fantasy. Fantasy was gauzy, distant. This was sharp, so sharp she was afraid it would cut right into her. Dangerous. She wanted it. All of it. And she was afraid that in the end there would be nothing of her left. At least nothing that she recognized. That his friendship wouldn't be something that she recognized. But they'd gone too far to turn back, and she didn't even want to anymore.

She wanted to see what was on the other side of this. Needed to see what was on the other side.

He reached up, bracing his hand on the back of her neck, holding her hip with the other as he positioned himself at the entrance to her body. He pressed the blunt head of his erection against her, sliding in easily, thrusting hard up inside her. She gasped as he went deeper than he had before. This was almost overwhelming. But she needed it. Embraced it.

His hold was possessive, all-encompassing. She felt like she was being consumed by him completely. By her desire for him. Warmth bloomed from where he held her, bled down beneath the surface of her skin, hemorrhaged in her chest.

"I fantasized about this," he said, the words seeming to scrape along his throat. Rough, raw. "Holding you like this. Holding on to your hips as I did this to you."

She couldn't respond. She couldn't say anything. His words had grabbed ahold of her, squeezing her throat tight, making it impossible for her to speak. He had fantasized about her. About this.

This position should feel less personal. More distant. But it didn't. That made it… It made it exactly what she had asked for. This was for her. And this was him. What he wanted, not just the next item on a list of things she needed to learn. Not just a set routine that he had with women he slept with.

He slid his hand down along the line of her spine, pressing firmly, the impression of his possession lingering on her skin. Then he held both of her hips tight, his blunt fingertips digging into her skin. He thrust harder into her, his skin slapping against hers, the sound echoing in the darkness. She gripped the truck hard, lowering her head, a moan escaping her lips.

"You wanted hard, baby," he ground out. "I'll give it to you hard."

"Yes," she whispered.

"Who are you saying yes to?" There was an edge to his words, a desperation she hadn't imagined he would feel, not with her. Not over this.

"Chase," she said, closing her eyes tight. "Yes, Chase. Please. I need this. I need you."

She needed all of him. And she suddenly realized why those thoughts about having someone to spend her nights with had seemed wrong. Because at the end of the day when she thought of sharing evenings with someone, when she thought of curling up under a blanket with someone, of watching *Oklahoma!* with someone for the hundredth time, it was Chase. It was always Chase. And that meant no other man had ever been able to get close enough to her. Because he was the fantasy. And as long as he was the fantasy, no one else had a place.

And now, now after this, she was ruined forever. Because she would never be able to do this with another man. Ever. It would always be Chase's hand she imagined on her skin. That firm grip of his that she craved.

He flexed his hips, going harder into her, then slipped his fingers around between her thighs again, stroking her as he continued to fill her. Then he leaned forward, biting her neck as he slammed into her one last time, sending them both over the edge. He growled, pulsing inside of her as he found his release. The pain from his teeth mingled with the all-consuming pleasure rolling through her in never-ending waves, pounding over her so hard she didn't think it would ever end. She didn't think she could survive it.

And when it passed, it was Chase who held her in his arms.

There was no denying it. No escaping it. And she was scraped raw. As stripped as she'd been after their first encounter, she was even more exposed now. Because she had read into all those empty, unspoken things. Because she had finally realized what everything meant.

Her asking him for help. Her kissing him. Her going down on him.

Her not having another man in her life in any capacity.

It was because she wanted Chase. All of Chase. It was why everything had come together for her tonight. Why she'd realized she couldn't compartmentalize him.

She wasn't ready to think the words yet, though. She couldn't. She did her very best to hold them at bay. To stop herself from thinking the things that would crumble her defenses once and for all.

Instead, she released her hold on the truck and turned to face him, looping her arms around his neck, pressing her bare body against his, luxuriating in him.

"That was quite the dance lesson," she said finally.

"A lot more fun than it would have been in Ace's." He slid his hand down to her butt, holding her casually. She loved that. So much more than she should.

"Yeah, we would have gotten thrown out for that."

"But can you imagine the rumors?"

"Are they really rumors if everyone has actually seen you screw?"

"Good question," he said, leaning forward and nipping her lower lip.

"You're bitey," she said.

"And you like to be bitten."

She couldn't deny it. "I guess I should... I mean, I have to work tomorrow."

"Me, too," he said, sounding regretful.

She wanted so badly to ask him to stay with her. But he wasn't bringing it up. And she didn't know if the almighty Chase McCormack actually *slept* with the women he was sleeping with.

So she didn't ask.

And when he dropped her off at her house, leaving her at her doorstep, she tried very, very hard not to regret that.

She didn't succeed.

Chapter 11

The best thing about having her own shop was working alone. Some people might find it lonely; Anna found it a great opportunity to run through every musical number she knew. She had already gone through the entirety of *Oklahoma!* and was working her way through *Seven Brides for Seven Brothers*.

Admittedly, she wasn't the best singer in the world, but in her own shop she was the best singer around.

And if the music helped drown out all of the neuroses that were scampering around inside of her, asking her to deal with her Chase feelings, then so much the better. She didn't want to deal with Chase feelings.

"When you're in love, when you're in love, there is no way on earth to hide it," she sang operatically, the words echoing off the walls.

She snapped her mouth shut. That was a bad song.

A very bad song for this moment. She was not... She just wasn't going to think about it.

She turned her focus back to the tractor engine she currently had in a million little pieces. At least an engine was concrete. A puzzle she could solve. It was tactile, and most of the time, if she could just get the right parts, find the source of the problem, she could fix it. That wasn't true with much of anything else in life. That was one reason she found a certain sort of calm in the garage.

Plus, it was something her father knew how to do. He was his own mechanic, and weekends were often spent laboring over his pickup truck, getting it in working order so that he could drive it to work Monday. So she had watched, she had helped. It was about the only way she had been able to connect with her gruff old man. It was still about the only way she could connect with him.

It certainly wasn't through musicals. It could never have been a desire to be seen differently by other kids at school. A need to look prettier for a boy that she liked.

So she had chosen carburetors.

"But it can't be carburetors forever." Well, it could be. In that she imagined she would do this sort of work for the rest of her life. She loved it. She was successful at it. She filled a niche in the community that needed to be filled. But...it couldn't be the only thing she was. She needed to do more than fill. She needed to...be filled.

And right now everything was all kind of turned on its head. Or bent over the back of a pickup truck. Her cheeks heated at the memory.

Yeah, Chase had definitely come by his reputation honestly. It wasn't difficult to see why women lost their ever-loving minds over him.

That made her frown. Because she didn't like to think that she was just one of the many women losing their minds over him because he had a hot ass and skilled hands. She had known about the hot ass for years. It hadn't made her lose her mind. In fact, she didn't really think she had lost her mind now. She knew exactly what she was doing. She frowned even more deeply.

Did she know what she was doing? They had stopped and had discussions, made conscious decisions to do this friends-with-benefits thing. Tricked themselves into thinking that they were in control of this. Or at least that's what she had been doing. But as she had been carried away on a wave of emotion last night, she had known for an absolute fact that she wasn't in control of any of this.

"Doesn't mean I'm going to stop."

That, at least, was the absolute truth. He would have to be the one to call it off.

Just the thought made her heart crumple up into a little ball.

"Quitting time yet?"

She turned to see Chase standing in the doorway. This was a routine she could get used to. She wanted to cross the space between them and kiss him. And why not? She wasn't hiding her attraction to him. They weren't hiding their association.

She dropped her ratchet, wiped her hands on her coveralls and took two quick steps, flinging herself into his arms and kissing him on the lips. She wasn't embarrassed until about midway through the kiss, when she realized she had been completely and totally enthusiastic and hadn't hidden any of it. But he was holding on to her, and he was kissing her back, so maybe it didn't matter. Maybe it was okay.

When they parted, he was smiling.

Her heart felt tender, exposed. But warm, like it was being bathed in sunlight. Something to do with that smile of his. With that easy acceptance of what she had offered. "I think it's about time to quit," she said.

"I like your look," he said, gesturing to her white tank top, completely smeared with grease and dirt, and her coveralls, which were unbuttoned and tied around her waist.

"Really?"

"Last night you were my dirty country girl fantasy and today you're a sexy mechanic fantasy. Do you take requests? Around Christmas you could go for Naughty Mrs. Claus."

She rolled her eyes, grabbing the end of her tank top and knotting it up just under her breasts. "Maybe more like this? Though I think I'm missing the breast implants."

His smile turned wicked. "Baby, you aren't missing a damn thing."

Her heart thundered harder, a rush of adrenaline flowing through her. "I didn't think this was your type. Remember? You had to give me a makeover."

"Yeah, that was stupid. I actually think I just needed to get knocked upside the head."

"Did I…knock you upside the head?"

"Yeah." He wrapped his arms around her bare waist, his fingertips playing over her skin. "You're pretty perfect the way you are. You never needed a dress or high heels. I mean, you're welcome to wear them if you want. I'm not going to complain about that outfit you wore last night. But all that stuff we talked about in the beginning, about you needing to change so that people would believe we were together… I guess everyone is just going to have to believe that I changed a little bit."

"Have you changed?" she asked, brushing her thumb over his lower lip. A little thrill skittered down her spine. That she could touch him like this. Be so close to him. Share this kind of intimacy with a man she had had a certain level of emotional intimacy with for years and years.

It was wonderful. It also made her ache. Made her feel like her insides were being broken apart with a chisel. And she was willingly submitting to it. She didn't know quite what was happening to her.

Are you sure you don't?

"Something did," he said, his dark eyes boring into hers.

"You know," she said, trying to tamp down the fluttering that was happening in her chest, "I think it's only fair that I give you a few lessons."

"What kind of lessons?" he asked, his gaze sharpening.

"I'm not sure you know your way around an engine quite the way you should," she said, smiling as she wiggled out of his hold.

"Oh, really?"

She nodded, grabbing hold of a rag and slinging it over her shoulder before picking up her ratchet again. "Really."

"Is this euphemistic engine talk?"

"Do you think I'm expressing dissatisfaction with the way you work under my hood?"

He chuckled. "You're really getting good at this flirting thing."

"I am. That was good. And dirty."

"I noticed." He moved behind her, sweeping her hair to the side and kissing her neck. "But if you're implying that I didn't do a very good job… I would have to clear my good name."

"I was talking about literal engines, Chase. But if you really want to try to up your game, I'm not going to stop you."

"What's that?" he asked, reaching past her and pointing to one of the parts that were spread out on the worktable in front of her.

"A cylinder head. I'm replacing that and the head gasket on the engine. And I had to take a lot of things apart to get to it."

"When do you need to have it done?"

"Not until tomorrow."

"So you don't need me to play the part of lovely assistant while you finish up tonight?"

"I would like you to assist me with a few things," she said, planting her hand at the center of his chest and pushing him lightly. The backs of his knees butted up against the chair that was behind him and he sat down, looking up at her, a predatory smile curving his lips.

"Is this going to be a part of my lesson?"

"Yeah," she said, "I thought it might be."

Last night had been incredible. Last night, he had given her something that felt special. Personal. Now she wanted to give him something. To show him what was happening inside of her, because she could hardly bring herself to think it. She wanted… She just wanted. In ways that she hadn't allowed herself to want in a long time. More. Everything.

"What exactly are you going to teach me?"

"Well, I could teach you all the parts of the tractor engine. But we would be here all night. And it would just slow me down. Someday, we can trade. You can give me some welding secrets. Teach me how to pound steel."

"That sounds dirty, too."

"Lucky me," she said, stretching her arms up over her head, her shirt riding up a little higher. She knew what she wanted to do. But she also felt almost petrified. This was…well, this was the opposite of protecting herself. This was putting herself out there. Risking humiliation. Risking doing something wrong while revealing how desperately she wanted to get it right.

But she wanted to give him something. And honestly, there was no bigger gift she could give him than vulnerability. To show him just how much she wanted him.

She swayed her hips to the right, then moved them back toward the left in a slow circle. She watched his face, watched the tension in his jaw increase, the sharpness in his eyes get positively lethal. And that was all the encouragement she needed. She'd seen enough movies with lap dances that she had a vague idea of how this should go. Maybe her idea was the PG-13-rated version, but she could improvise.

He moved his hand over the outline of his erection, squeezing himself through the denim as she continued to move. Maybe it wasn't rhinestones and a miniskirt, but he didn't seem to mind her white tank top and coveralls. He was still watching her with avid interest as she untied the sleeves from around her waist and let the garment drop down around her feet. She kicked it off to the side, revealing her denim cutoff shorts underneath it.

"Come here," he said, his voice hard.

"I'm not taking orders from you. You have to be patient."

"I'm not feeling very patient, honey."

"What's my name?"

"Anna," he ground out. "Anna, I'm not feeling very patient."

"Not enough women have made you wait. You're getting spoiled."

She slid her hand up her midsection, her own fingertips combined with the electric look on Chase's face sending heat skittering along her veins. She let her fingers skim over her breast, gratified when his breath hissed through his teeth.

"Anna..."

"You know me pretty well, don't you? But you didn't know all this." She moved her hand back down, over her stomach, her belly button, sliding her fingers down beneath the waistband of her shorts, stroking herself where she was wet and aching for him. His fingers curled around the edge of the chair, his knuckles white, the cords on his neck standing out, the strength it was taking him to remain seated clear and incredibly compelling.

"Take them off," he said.

"Didn't I just tell you that you're not in charge?"

"Don't play games with me."

"Maybe patience is the lesson you need to learn."

"I damn well don't," he growled.

She turned around, facing away from him, taking a deep breath as she unsnapped her shorts and pushed them down her hips, revealing the other purchase she had made at the store yesterday. A black, lacy thong, quite unlike any other pair of underwear she had ever owned. And she had slipped it on this morning hoping that this would be the end of her day.

"Holy hell," he said.

She knew that she was not the first woman to take her clothes off for him. Much less the first woman to reveal sexy underwear. But that only made his appreciation for hers that much sweeter. She swayed her hips back and forth before dropping down low, and sweeping back up. It felt so cheesy, and at the same time she was pretty proud of herself for pulling it off.

When she turned to face him, his expression was positively feral.

Her shirt was still knotted beneath her breasts, and now she was wearing work boots, a thong and the top. If Chase thought the outfit was a little bit silly, he certainly didn't show it.

She moved over to the chair, straddling him, leaning in and kissing him on the lips. "I want you," she said.

She had said it before. But this was more. Deeper. This was the truth. Her truth, the truest thing inside of her. She wanted Chase. In every way. Forever. She swallowed hard, grabbing hold of his T-shirt and tugging it up over his head. She licked her lips, looking at his body, at his chest, speckled with just the right amount of dark hair, at his abs, so perfectly defined and tempting.

She reached between them, undoing his belt and

jerking it through the loops, before tugging his pants and underwear down low on his hips. He put his hand on her backside, holding her steady as she maneuvered herself so that she was over him, rubbing up against his arousal. "I would never have considered doing something like this before last week. Not with anyone. It's just you," she said, leaning in and kissing his lips lightly. "You do this to me."

He shuddered beneath her, her words having the exact effect she hoped they would. He liked feeling special, too.

He took hold of her hand, drawing it between them, curving her fingers around him. "And you do this to me. You make me so hard, it hurts. I've never wanted a woman like this before. Ever."

She flexed her hips, squeezed him tighter, trapping him between her palm and the apex of her thighs. "Why? Why do you want me like this?"

It was important to know. Essential.

"Because it's you, Anna. There's this idea that having sex with a stranger is supposed to be exciting. Because it's dirty. Because it's wrong. Maybe because it's unknown? But I've done that. And this is… You're right. I know you. Knowing you like this… Your face is so familiar to me, your voice. Knowing what it looks like when I make you come, how you sound when I push you over the edge, baby, there's nothing hotter than that."

His words washed over her, everything she had never known she needed. This full, complete acceptance of who she was. Right here in her garage. The mechanic, the woman. The friend, the lover. He wanted her. And everything that meant.

She didn't even try to keep herself from feeling it now. Didn't try to keep herself from thinking it.

She loved him. So much. Every part of him, with every part of her. Her friend. The only man she really wanted. The only person she could imagine sharing her days and nights and blankets and musicals with.

And that realization didn't even make her want to pull away from him. Didn't make her want to hide. Instead, she wanted to finish this. She wanted to feel connected to him. Now that she was in, she was in all the way. Ready to expose herself completely, scrape herself raw, all for him.

She rose up so that she was on her knees, tugged her panties down her hips and maneuvered herself so that she was able to dispense with them completely before settling over him, grabbing hold of his broad shoulders as she sank down onto his hardened length.

He swore, the harsh word echoing in the empty space. "Anna, I need to get a condom."

She pulled away from him quickly, hovering over him as he lifted his hips, grabbing his wallet and pulling out a condom with shaking hands, taking care of the practicalities quickly. She was trembling, both with the adrenaline rush that accompanied the stupidity of her mistake and with need. With regret because she wished that he was still inside of her even though it wouldn't be responsible at all.

Soon, he was guiding her back onto him, having protected them both. Thankfully, he was a little more with it than she was.

He gripped her tightly, guiding her movements at first, helping her establish a rhythm that worked for them both.

He moved his hands around, brushing his fingertips along the seam of her ass before teasing her right
where their bodies were joined. She gasped, grabbing
hold of the back of the chair, flexing her hips, chasing her own release as he continued to touch her. To
push her higher.

She slid her hands up, cupping his face, holding him
steady. She met his gaze, a thrill shooting down her
spine. "Anna," he rasped, the words skating over her
skin like a caress, touching her everywhere.

Pleasure gripped her, low and tight, sending her
over the edge. She held his face as she shuddered out
her orgasm and chanted his name, endlessly. Over and
over again. And when it was over, he held her to him,
kissing her lips, whispering words against her mouth
that she could barely understand. She didn't need to.
The only words she understood were the ones she most
needed to hear.

"Stay with me tonight."

Chapter 12

They dressed and drove across the property in Chase's truck. His heart was still hammering like crazy, and he had no idea what the hell he was doing. But then, it was Anna. She wasn't some random hookup. He wanted her again, and having her spend the night seemed like the best way to accomplish that.

He ignored the little terror claws that wrapped themselves around his heart and squeezed, and focused instead on the heavy sensation in his gut. In his dick. He wanted her, and dammit, he was going to have her.

The image of her dancing in front of him in the shop…that would haunt him forever. And it was his goal to collect a few more images that would make his life miserable when their physical relationship ended.

That was normal.

He parked the truck, then got out, following Anna

mutely up the steps. When they got to the door, Anna paused.

"I don't…have anything with me. No porcupine pajamas."

Some of the tension in his chest eased. "You won't need pajamas in my bed," he said, his voice low, almost unrecognizable even to himself.

Which was fair enough, since this whole damn situation was unrecognizable. Saying this kind of stuff to Anna. Seeing her like this. Wanting her like this.

She was a constant. She was stability. And he felt shaky as hell right now.

"I've never spent the night with anyone," she blurted.

The words hit him hard in the chest. Along with the realization that this was a first for him, too. He knew it, logically. But for some reason it hadn't seemed momentous when he'd issued the invitation. Because it was Anna and sleeping with her had seemed like the most natural thing on earth. He liked talking to her, liked kissing her, liked having sex with her, and he didn't want her to leave. So the obvious choice was to ask her to stay the night.

Now it was hitting him, though. What that usually meant. Why he didn't do it.

But it was too late to take the invitation back, and anyway, he didn't know if he wanted to.

"I haven't, either," he said.

She blinked. "You…haven't? I mean, I had a tenminute roll in the hay—literally—with a loser in high school, so I know why I've never spent the night with anyone. But you…you do this a lot."

"Are you calling me a slut?"

"Yes," she said, deadpan. "No judgment, but yeah, you're kind of slutty."

"Well, you don't have to spend the night with someone when you're done with them. I guess that's why I haven't. Because I am kind of slutty, and it has nothing to do with liking the person I'm with. Just…"

Oblivion. The easiest, most painless connection on earth with no risk involved whatsoever.

But he wasn't going to say that.

Anna wasn't oblivion. Being with her was like… being inside his own skin, really in it, and feeling it, for the first time since he was sixteen.

Like driving eighty miles per hour on the same winding road that had killed his parents, daring it to come for him, too. He'd felt alive then. Alive and pushing up against the edge of mortality as hard as he could.

Then he'd backed way off the gas. And he'd backed way off ever since.

This was the closest thing to tasting that surge of adrenaline, that rush he'd felt since the day he'd basically begged the road to take him, too.

You're a head case.

Yes, he was. But he'd always known that. Anna hadn't, though.

"Just?" she asked, eyebrows shooting up. She wasn't going to let that go, apparently.

"It's just sex."

"And what is this?" she asked, gesturing between the two of them.

"Friendship," he said honestly. "With some more to it."

"Those benefits."

"Yeah," he said. "Those."

He shoved his hands in his pockets, feeling like he'd just failed at something, and he couldn't quite figure out what. But his words were flat in the evening air. Just sort of dull and resting between them, wrong and weird, but he didn't know what to do about it.

Because he didn't know what else to say, either.

"Want to come inside?" he asked finally.

"That is where your bed is," she said.

"It is."

They made their way to the bedroom, and somehow it all felt different. He could easily remember when she'd been up here just last week, walking in those heels and that dress. When he'd been overwhelmed with the need to touch her, but wouldn't allow himself to do so.

He could also remember being in here with her plenty of times before. Innocuous as sharing the space with any friend.

How? How had they ever existed in silences that weren't loaded? In moments that weren't wrapped in tension. In isolation that didn't present the very tempting possibility of chasing pleasure together. Again and again.

This wasn't friendship plus benefits. That implied the friendship remained untouched and the benefits were an add-on. Easy to stick there, easy to remove. But that wasn't the case.

Everything was different. The air around them had changed. How the hell could he pretend the friendship was the same?

"I'm just—" She smiled sheepishly and pulled her shirt up over her head. "Sorry." Then she unhooked her bra, tossing it onto the floor. He hadn't had a chance to look at her breasts the last time they'd had sex. She'd kept them covered. Something that had added nicely to the tease back in the shop. But he was ready to drop to his knees and give thanks for their perfection now.

"Why are you apologizing for flashing me?"

"Because. In the absence of pajamas I need to get comfortable now." She stripped her shorts off, and her underwear—those shocking black panties that he simply hadn't seen coming, much like the rest of her—and then she flopped down onto his bed. He didn't often bring women back here.

Sometimes, depending on the circumstances, but if they had a hotel room, or their own place available, that was his preference. So it was a pretty unusual sight in general. A naked woman in his room. Anna, in this familiar place—naked and warm and about as inviting as anything had ever been—was enough to make his head explode.

His head, and other places.

"You never have to apologize for being naked." He stripped his shirt off, then continued to follow her lead, until he was wearing nothing.

He lay down beside her, not touching her, just looking at her. This was hella weird. If a woman was naked, he was usually having sex with her, bottom line. He didn't lie next to one, simply looking at her. Right now, Anna was something like art and he just wanted to admire her. Well, that wasn't *all* he wanted. But it was what he wanted right now. To watch the soft lamplight cast a warm glow over her curves, to examine every dip and hollow on the map of her figure. To memorize the rosy color of her nipples, the dark hair at the apex of her thighs. The sweet flare of her hips and the slight roundness of her stomach. She was incredible. She was Anna. Right now, she was his.

That thought made his stomach tighten. How long had it been since something was his?

This place would always be McCormack, through and through. The foundation of the forge and the business…it was built on his great-grandfather's back, carried down by his grandfather, handed to their father.

And he and Sam carried it now.

This ranch would always be something they were bound to by blood, not by choice. Even if given the choice, he could probably never leave. Their family… It didn't feel like their family anymore. It hadn't for a lot of years.

It was two of them, him and Sam. Two of them trying so damn hard to push this legacy back to where it had been. To make their family extend beyond these walls, beyond these borders. To fulfill all of the promises he'd made to his dad, even though the old man had never actually heard them.

Even though Chase had made them too late.

And so there was something about that. Anna, this moment, being for him. Something that he chose, instead of something that he'd inherited.

"I like when you look at me like that," she said, her voice hushed.

"I like when you take control like you did back in the shop. I like seeing you realize how beautiful you are," he said. It was true. He was glad that she knew now. And pissed that she was going to take that knowledge and work her magic on some other man with her newfound power. He wanted to kill that man.

But he could never hope to take his place, so he wouldn't.

"You're the first person who has made me feel like it all fit. And maybe it's because you're my friend. Maybe it's because you know me," she said.

"I don't follow."

"I had to be tough," she said, her tone demonstrating just that. "All my life I've had to be tough. My brothers raised me, and they did a damn good job, and I know you think they're jerks, and honestly a lot of the time they are. But they were young boys who were put in charge of taking care of their kid sister. So they took care of me, but they tortured me in that way only brothers can. Probably because I tortured them in ways that most little sisters could never dream. They didn't go out in high school. They had to make sure I was taken care of. They didn't trust my dad to do it. He wasn't stable enough. He would go out to the bar and get drunk, and he would call needing a ride home. They handled things so that I didn't have to. And I never felt like I could make their lives more difficult by showing how hard it was for me."

She shifted, sighing heavily before she continued. "And then there was my dad. He didn't know what to do with a daughter. As pissed as he was that his wife left, I think in some ways he was relieved, because he didn't have to figure out how to fit a woman into his life anymore. But then I kind of started becoming a woman. And he really didn't know what to do. So I learned how to work on cars. I learned how to talk about sports. I learned how to fit. Even though it pushed me right out of fitting when it came to school. When it came to making friends."

He knew these things about Anna. Knew them because he'd absorbed them by being in her house, being near her, for fifteen years. But he'd never heard her say them. There was something different about that.

"You've always fit with me, Anna," he said, his voice rough.

"I know. And even though we've never talked about this, I'm pretty sure somehow you knew all of it. You always have. Because you know me. And you accept me. Not very many people know about the musicals. Because it always embarrassed me. Kind of a girlie thing."

"I guess so," he said, the words feeling inadequate.

"Also, it was my thing. And… I never like anyone to know how much I care about things. I… My mom loved old musicals," she said, her voice soft. "Sometimes I wonder what it would be like to watch them with her."

"Anna…"

"I remember sneaking out of my room at night, seeing the TV flickering in the living room. She would be watching *The Sound of Music* or *Cinderella*. *Oklahoma!* of course. And I would just hang there in the hall. But I didn't want to interrupt. Because by the end of the day she was always out of patience, and I knew she didn't want any of the kids to talk to her. But it was kind of like watching them with her." Anna's eyes filled with tears. "But now I just wish I had. I wish I had gone in and sat next to her. I wish I had risked her being upset with me. I never got the chance. She left, and that was it. So, maybe she would've been mad at me, or maybe she wouldn't have let me watch them with her. But at least I would've had the answer. Now I just wonder. I just remember that space between us.

Me hiding in the hall, and her sitting on the couch. She never knew I was there. Maybe if I'd done a better job of connecting with her, she wouldn't have left."

"That's not true, Anna."

"She didn't have anyone to watch the movies with, Chase. And my dad was so... I doubt he ever gave her a damn scrap of tenderness. But maybe I could have. I think... I think that's what I was always trying to do with my dad. To make up for that. It was too late to make her stay, but I thought maybe I could hang on to him."

Chase tried to breathe past the tightness in his chest, but it was nearly impossible. "Anna," he said, "any parent that chooses to leave their child...the issue is with them. It was your parents' marriage. It was your mom. I don't know. But it was never you. It wasn't you not watching a movie with her, or irritating her, or making her angry. There was never anything you could do."

She nodded, a tear tracking down her pale cheek. "I do know that."

"But you still beat yourself up for it."

"Of course I do."

He didn't have a response to that. She said it so matter-of-factly, as though there was nothing else but to blame herself, even if it made no sense. He had no response because he understood. Because he knew what it was like to twist a tragedy in a thousand different ways to figure out how you could take it on yourself. He knew what it was like to live your life with a gaping hole where someone you loved should be. To try to figure out how you could have stopped the loss from happening.

In the years since his parents' accident he had

moved beyond blame. Not because he was stronger than Anna, just because you could only twist death in so many different directions. It was final. And it didn't ask you. It just was. Blaming himself would have been a step too far into martyrdom.

Still, he knew about lingering scars and responses to those scars that didn't make much sense.

But he didn't know what it was like to have a parent choose to leave you. God knew his parents never would have chosen to abandon their sons.

As if she'd read his mind, Anna continued. "She's still out there. I mean, as far as I know. She could have come back. Anytime. I just feel like if I had given her even a small thing…well, then, maybe she would have missed me enough at some point. If she'd had anything back here waiting for her, she could have called. Just once."

"You were you," he said. "If that wasn't enough for her…fuck her."

She laughed and wiped another tear from her face. Then she shifted, moving closer to him. "I appreciate that." She paused for a moment, kissing his shoulder, then she continued. "It's amazing. I've never told you that before. I've never told anyone that before. It's just kind of crazy that we could know each other for so long and…there's still more we don't know."

He wanted to tell her then. About the day his parents died. About the complete and total hole it had torn in his life. She knew to a degree. They had been friends when it happened. He had been sixteen, and Sam had been eighteen, and the loss of everything they knew had hit so hard and fast that it had taken them out at the knees.

He wanted to tell her about his nightmares. Wanted to tell her about the last conversation he'd had with his dad.

But he didn't.

"Amazing" was all he said instead.

Then he leaned over and kissed her, because he couldn't think of anything else to do, couldn't think of anything else to say.

Liar.

A thousand things he wanted to tell her swirled around inside of him. A thousand different things she didn't know. That he had never told anybody. But he didn't want to open himself up like that. He just… He just couldn't.

So instead, he kissed her, because that he could do. Because of all the changes that existed between them, that was the one he was most comfortable with. Holding her, touching her. Everything else was too big, too unknown to unpack. He couldn't do it. Didn't want to do it.

But he wanted to kiss her. Wanted to run his hands over her bare curves. So he did.

He touched her, tasted her, made her scream. Because of all the things that were happening in his life, that felt right.

This was…well, it was a detour. The best one he'd ever taken, but a detour all the same. He was building the family business, like he had promised his dad he would do. Or like he should have promised him when he'd had the chance. He might never have been able to tell the old man to his face, but he'd promised it to his grave. A hundred times, a thousand times since he'd died.

That was what he had to do. That was on the other side of making love with Anna. Going to that benefit with her all dressed up, trying to help her get the kind of reputation she wanted. To send her off with all her newfound skills so that she could be with another man after.

To knuckle down and take the McCormack family ranch back to where it had been. Beyond. To make sure that Sam used his talents, to make sure that the forge and all the work their father had done to build the business didn't go to waste.

To prove that the fight he'd had with his father right before he died was all angry words and teenage bluster. That what he'd said to his old man wasn't real.

He didn't hate the ranch. He didn't hate the business. He didn't hate their name. He was their name, and damn him for being too young and stupid to see it then.

He was proving it now by pouring all of his blood, all of his sweat, all of his tears into it. By taking the little bit of business acumen he had once imagined might get him out of Copper Ridge and applying it to this place. To try to make it something bigger, something better. To honor all the work their parents had invested all those years.

To finish what they started.

He might not have ever made a commitment to a woman, but this ranch, McCormack Iron Works…was his life. That was forever.

It was the only forever he would ever have.

He closed those thoughts out, shut them down completely and focused on Anna. On the sweet scent of her as he lowered his head between her thighs and lapped at her, on the feel of her tight channel pulsing around his fingers as he stroked them in and out. And finally, on the tight, wet clasp of her around him as he slid home.

Home. That's really what it was.

In a way that nowhere else had ever been. The ranch was a memorial to people long dead. A monument that he would spend the rest of his life building.

But she was home. She was his.

If he let her, she could become everything.

No.

That denial echoed in his mind, pushed against him as he continued to pound into her, hard, deep, seeking the oblivion that he had always associated with sex before her. But it wasn't there. Instead, it was like a veil had been torn away and he could see all of his life, spreading out before him. Like he was standing on a ridge high in the mountains, able to survey everything. The past, the present, the future. So clear, so sharp it almost didn't seem real.

Anna was in all of it. A part of everything.

And if she was ever taken away...

He closed his eyes, shutting out that thought, a wave of pleasure rolling over him, drowning out everything. He threw himself in. Harder than he ever had. Grateful as hell that Anna had found her own release, because he'd been too wrapped up in himself to consider her first.

Then he wrapped his arms around her, wrapped her up against him. Wrapped himself up in her. And he pushed every thought out of his mind and focused on the feeling of her body against his, the scent of her skin. Feminine and sweet with a faint trace of hay and engine grease.

No other woman smelled like Anna.

He pressed his face against her breasts and she sighed, a sound he didn't think he'd ever get tired of. He let everything go blank. Because there was nothing in his past, or his future, that was as good as this.

Chapter 13

Chase woke in a cold sweat, his heart pounding so heavily he thought it would burst through his bone and flesh and straight out into the open. His bed was empty. He sat up, rubbing his hand over his face, then forking his fingers through his hair.

It felt wrong to have the bed empty. After spending only one night wrapped around Anna, it already felt wrong. Not having her... Waking up in the morning to find that she wasn't there was... He hated it. It was unsettling. It reminded him of the holes that people left behind, of how devastating it was when you lost someone unexpectedly.

He banished the thought. She might still be here. But then, she didn't have any clean clothes or anything, so if she had gone home, he couldn't necessarily blame her. He went straight into the bathroom, took a shower, took care of all other morning practicalities. He resisted the urge to look at his phone, to call Anna's phone or to go downstairs and see if maybe she was still around. He was going to get through all this, dammit, and he was not going to behave as though he were affected.

As though the past night had changed something fundamental, not just between them, but in him.

He scowled, throwing open the bedroom door and heading down the stairs.

He stopped dead when he saw her standing there in the kitchen. She was wearing his T-shirt, her long, slim legs bare. And he wondered if she was bare all the way up. His mouth dried, his heart squeezing tight.

She wasn't missing. She wasn't gone. She was cooking him breakfast. Like she belonged here. Like she belonged in his life. In his house. In his bed.

For one second it made him feel like he belonged. Like she'd been the missing piece to making this his, to making it more than McCormack.

He felt like he was standing in the middle of a dream. Standing there looking at somebody else's life. At some wild, potential scenario that in reality he would never get to have.

Right in front of him was everything. And in the same moment he saw that, he imagined the hole that would be left behind if it was ever taken away. If he ever believed in this, fully, completely. If he reached out and embraced her now, there would be no words for how empty his arms would feel if he ever lost her.

"Don't you have work?" he asked, leaning against the doorjamb.

She turned around and smiled, the kind of smile that lit him up inside, from his head, down his toes. He did his very best not to return the gesture. Did his best not to encourage it in any way.

And he cursed himself when the glow leached out of her face. "Good morning to you, too," she said.

"You didn't need to make breakfast."

"*Au contraire.* I was hungry. So breakfast was needed."

"You could've gone home."

"Yes, Grumpy-Pants, I could have. But I decided to stay here and make you food. Which seemed like an adequate thank-you for the multiple orgasms I received yesterday."

"Bacon? You're trying to pay for your orgasms with bacon?"

"It seemed like a good idea at the time." She crossed her arms beneath her breasts and revealed that she did not, in fact, have anything on beneath the shirt. "Bacon is a borderline orgasmic experience."

"I have work. I don't have time to eat breakfast."

"Maybe if you had gotten up at a decent hour."

"I don't need you to lecture me on my sleeping habits," he bit out. "Is there coffee?"

"It's like you don't know me at all." She crossed the room and lifted a thermos off the counter. "I didn't want to leave it sitting on the burner. That makes it taste gross."

"I don't really care how it tastes. That's not the point."

She rested her hand on the counter, then rapped her knuckles against the surface. "What's going on?"

"Nothing."

"Stop it, Chase. Maybe you can BS the other bimbos that you sleep with, but you can't do it to me. I know you too well. This has nothing to do with waking up late."

"This is a bad idea," he said.

"What's a bad idea? Eating bacon and drinking coffee with one of your oldest friends?"

"Sleeping with one of my oldest friends. It was stupid. We never should've done it."

She just stood there, her expression growing waxen, and as the color drained from her face, he felt something even more critical being scraped from his chest, like he was being hollowed out.

"It's a little late for that," she pointed out.

"Well, it isn't too late to start over."

"Chase…"

"It was fun. But, honestly, we accomplished everything we needed to. There's no reason to get dramatic about it. We agreed that we weren't going to let it affect our friendship. And it…it just isn't working for me."

"It was working fine for you last night."

"Well, that was last night, Anna. Don't be so needy."

She drew back as though she had been slapped and he wanted to punch his own face for saying such a thing. For hitting her where he knew it would hurt. And he waited. Waited for her to grow prickly. For her to retreat behind the walls. For her to get angry and start insulting him. For her to end all of this in fire and brimstone as she scorched the earth in an attempt to disguise the naked pain that was radiating from her right now.

He knew she would. Because that was how it went. If he pushed far enough, then she would retreat.

She closed the distance between them, cupping his face, meeting his eyes directly. And he waited for the blow. "But I feel needy. So what am I going to do about that?"

He couldn't have been more shocked than if she had reached up and slapped him. "What?"

"I'm needy. Or maybe…wanty? I'm both." She took a deep breath. "Yes, I'm both. I want more. Not less. And this is… This is the moment where we make decisions, right? Well, I've decided that I want to move forward with this. I don't want to go back. I can't go back."

"Anna," he said, her name scraping his throat raw.

"Chase," she said, her own voice a whisper in response.

"We can't do this," he said.

He needed the Anna he knew to come to his rescue now. To laugh it all off. To break this tension. To say that it didn't matter. To wave her hand and say it was all whatever and they could forget it. But she wasn't doing that. She was looking at him, her green eyes completely earnest, vulnerability radiating from her face. "We need to do this. Because I love you."

Anna could tell that her words had completely stunned Chase. Fair enough, they had shocked her just as much. She didn't know where all of this was coming from. This strength. This bravery.

Except that last night's conversation kept echoing in her mind. When she had told him about her mother. When she had told him about how she always regretted not closing the distance between them. Always regretted not taking the chance.

That was the story of her entire life. She had, from the time she was a child, refused to make herself vulnerable. Refused to open herself up to injury. To pain.

So she pretended she didn't care. She pretended nothing mattered. She did that every time her father ignored her, every time he forgot an important milestone in her life. She had done it the first time she'd ever had sex with a guy and it had made her feel something. Rather than copping to that, rather than dealing with it, she had mocked him.

All of her inner workings were a series of walls and shields, carefully designed to keep the world from hitting the terrible, needy things inside of her. Designed to keep herself from realizing they were there. But she couldn't do it anymore. She didn't want to do it anymore. Not with Chase. She didn't want to look back and wonder what could have been.

She wanted more. She needed more. Pride be damned.

"I do," she said, nodding. "I love you."

"You can't."

"I'm pretty sure I can. Since I do."

"No," he said, the word almost desperate.

"No, Chase, I really do. I mean, I have loved you since I was fifteen years old. And intermittently thought you were hot. But mostly, I just loved you. You've been my friend, my best friend. I needed you. You've been my emotional support for a long time. We do that for each other. But things changed in the past few days. You're my...everything." Her voice broke on that last word. "This isn't sex and friendship, it isn't two different things, this is all the things, combined together to make something so big that it fills me completely. And I don't have room inside my chest for shields and protection anymore. Not when all that I am just loves you."

"I can't do this," he bit out, stepping away from her.

"I didn't ask if you could do this. This isn't about you, not right now. Yes, I would like you to love me, too, but right now this is just about me saying that I love you. Telling you. Because I don't ever want to look back and think that maybe you didn't know. That maybe if I had said something, it could have been different." She swallowed hard, battling tears. "I don't know what's wrong with me. Unless it's a movie, I almost never cry, but you're making me cry a lot lately."

"I'm only going to make you cry more," he said. "Because I don't know how to do this. I don't know how to love somebody."

"Bull. You've loved me perfectly, just the way I needed you to for fifteen years. The way that you take care of this place, the way that you care for Sam… Don't tell me that you can't love."

"Not this kind. Not this… Not this."

"I'm closing the gap," she said, pressing on, even though she could see that this was a losing battle. She was charging in anyway, sword held high, chest exposed. She was giving it her all, fighting even though she knew she wasn't going to walk away unscathed. "I'm not going to wonder what would've happened if I'd just been brave enough to do it. I would rather cut myself open and bleed out. I would rather risk my heart than wonder. So I'm just going to say it. Stop being such a coward and love me."

He took another step back from her and she felt that gap she was so desperate to close widening. Watched as her greatest fear started to play out right before her eyes. "I just… I don't."

"You don't or you won't?"

"At the end of the day, the distinction doesn't really matter. The result is the same."

She felt like she was having an out-of-body experience. Like she was floating up above, watching herself get rejected. There was nothing she could do. She couldn't stop it. Couldn't change it. Couldn't shield herself.

It was…horrible. Gut-wrenching. Destructive. Freeing.

Like watching a tsunami racing to shore and deciding to surrender to the wave rather than fight it. Yeah, it would hurt like hell. But it was a strange, quiet space. Past fear, past hope. All she could hear was the sound of her heart beating.

"I'm going to go," she said, turning away from him. "You can have the bacon."

She had been willing to risk herself, but she wouldn't stand there and fall apart in front of him. She would fall apart, but dammit, it would be on her own time.

"Stay and eat," he said.

She shook her head. "No. I can't stay."

"Are we going to… Are we going to go to the gala together still?"

"No!" She nearly shouted the word. "We are not going to go together. I need to… I need to think. I need to figure this out. But I don't think things can be the same anymore."

It was his turn to close the distance between them. He grabbed hold of her arms, drawing her toward him, his expression fierce. "That was not part of the deal. It was friends plus benefits, remember? And then in the end we could just stop with the benefits and go back to the friendship."

"We can't," she said, tears falling down her cheeks. "I'm sorry. But we can't."

"What the hell?" he ground out.

"We can't because I'm all in. I'm not going to sit back and pretend that it didn't really matter. I'm not going to go and hide these feelings. I'm not going to shrug and say it doesn't really matter if you love me or not. Because it does. It's everything. I have spent so many years not wanting. Not trying. Hiding how much I wanted to be accepted, hiding how desperately I wanted to try to look beautiful, how badly I wanted to be able to be both a mechanic and a woman. Hiding how afraid I was of ending up alone. Hiding under a blanket and watching old movies. Well, I'm done. I'm not hiding any of it anymore. And you know what? Nothing's going to hurt after this." She jerked out of his hold and started to walk toward the front door.

"You're not leaving in that."

She'd forgotten she wasn't exactly dressed. "Sure I am. I'm just going to drive straight home. Anyway, it's not your concern. Because I'm not your concern anymore."

The terror that she felt screaming through her chest was reflected on his face. Good. He should be afraid. This was the most terrifying experience of her life. She knew how horrible it was to lose a person you cared for. Knew what kind of void that left. And she knew that after years it didn't heal. She knew, too, you always felt the absence. She knew that she would always feel his. But she needed more. And she wasn't afraid to put it all on the line. Not now. Not after everything they had been through. Not after everything she had learned about herself. Chase was the one who had told her she needed more confidence.

Well, she had found it. But there was a cost.

Or maybe this was just the cost of loving. Of caring, deeply and with everything she had, for the first time in so many years.

She strode across the property, not caring that she was wearing nothing more than his T-shirt, rage pouring through her. And when she arrived back at the shop she grabbed her purse and her keys, making her way to the truck. When she got there, Chase was standing against the driver's-side door. "Don't leave like this."

"Do you love me yet?"

He looked stricken. "What do you want me to say?"

"You know what I want you to say."

"You want me to lie?"

She felt like he had taken a knife and stabbed her directly through the heart. She could barely breathe. Could barely stand straight. This was… This was her worst fear come true. To open herself up so completely, to make herself so entirely vulnerable and to have it all thrown back in her face.

But in that moment, she recognized that she was untouchable from here on out. Because there was nothing that could ever, ever come close to this pain. Nothing that could ever come close to this risk.

How had she missed this before? How had she missed that failure could be such a beautiful, terrible, freeing experience?

It was the worst. Absolutely the worst. But it also broke chains that had been binding her for years. Because if someone had asked her what she was so afraid of, this would have been the answer. And she was in it. Living it. Surviving it.

"I love you," she repeated. "This is your chance. Listen to me, Chase McCormack, I am giving you a chance. I'm giving you a chance to stop being so afraid. A chance to walk out of the darkness. We've walked through it together for a long time. So I'm asking you now to walk out of it with me. Please."

He backed away from the truck, his jaw tense, a muscle there twitching.

"Coward," she spat as he turned and walked away from her. Walked away from them. Walked back into the damned darkness.

And she got in her truck and started the engine, driving away from him, driving away from the things she wanted most in the entire world.

She didn't cry until she got home. But then, once she did, she was afraid she wouldn't stop.

Chapter 14

She was going to lose the bet. That was the safest thought in Anna's head as she stood in her bedroom the night of the charity event staring at the dress that was laid across her bed.

She was going to have to go there by herself. And thanks to the elaborate community theater production of their relationship everyone would know that they had broken up, since Chase wouldn't be with her. She almost laughed.

She was facing her fears all over the place, whether she wanted to or not.

Facing fears and making choices.

She wasn't going to be with Chase at the gala tonight. Wasn't going to win her money. But she had bought an incredibly slinky dress, and some more makeup. Including red lipstick. She had done all of that for him. Though in many ways it was for her, too. She had wanted that experience. To go, to prove that she was grown-up. To prove that she had transcended her upbringing and all of that.

She frowned. Was she really considering dressing differently just because she wasn't going to be with Chase?

Screw that. He might have filleted her heart and cooked it like those hideous charred Brussels sprouts cafés tries to pass off as a fancy appetizer, but he *wasn't* going to take his lessons from her. She had learned confidence. She had learned that she was stronger than she thought. She had learned that she was beautiful. And how to care. Like everything inside her had been opened up, for better or for worse. But she would never go back. No matter how bad it hurt, she wouldn't go back.

So she wouldn't go back now, either.

As she slipped the black dress over her curves, laboring over the makeup on her face and experimenting with the hairstyle she had seen online, she could only think how much harder it was to care about things. All of these things. It had been so much easier to embrace little pieces of herself. To play the part of another son for her father and throw herself into activities that made him proud, ignoring her femininity so that she never made him uncomfortable.

All of these moments of effort came at a cost. Each minute invested revealing more and more of her needs. To be seen. To be approved of.

But there were so many other reasons she had avoided this. Because this—she couldn't help but think as she looked in the mirror—looked a lot like trying. It looked a lot like caring. That was scary. It was hard.

Being rejected when you had given your best effort was so much worse than being rejected when you hadn't tried at all.

This whole being-a-woman thing—a whole woman who wanted to be with a man, who loved a man—it was hard. And it hurt.

She looked at her reflection, her eyes widening. Thanks to the smoky eye shadow her green eyes glowed, her lips looking extra pouty with the dark red color on them. She looked like one of the old screen legends she loved so much. Very Elizabeth Taylor, really.

This was her best effort. And yes, it was only a dress, and this was just looks, but it was symbolic.

She was going to lay it all on the line, and maybe people would laugh. Because the tractor mechanic in a ball gown was too ridiculous for words. But she would take the risk. And she would take it alone.

She picked up the little clutch purse that was sitting on her table. The kind of purse she'd always thought was impractical, because who wanted a bag you had to hold in your hand all night? But the salesperson at the department store had told her it went with her dress, and that altogether she looked flawless, and Anna had been in desperate need of flattery. So here she was with a clutch.

It *was* impractical. But she *did* look great.

Of course, Chase wouldn't be there to see it. She felt her eyes starting to fill with tears and she blinked, doing her best to hold it all back. She was not going to smear her makeup. She had already put it all out there for him. She would be damned if she undid all this hard work for him, too.

With that in mind, Anna got into her truck and drove herself to the ball.

"Hey, jackass," Sam shouted from across the shop. "Are you going to finish with work anytime today?"

Okay, so maybe Chase had thrown himself into work with a little more vehemence than was strictly necessary since Anna had walked out of his life.

Anna. Anna had walked out of his life. Over something as stupid as love.

If love was so stupid, it wouldn't make your insides tremble like you were staring down a black bear.

He ignored his snarky internal monologue. He had been doing a lot of that lately. So many arguments with himself as he pounded iron at the forge. That was, when he wasn't arguing with Sam. Who was getting a little bit tired of him, all things considered.

"Do I look like I'm finished?" he shouted back.

"It's nine o'clock at night."

"That's amazing. When did you learn to tell time?"

"I counted on my fingers," Sam said, wandering deeper into the room. "So, are we just going to pretend that Anna didn't run out of your house wearing only a T-shirt the other morning?"

"I'm going to pretend that my older brother doesn't Peeping Tom everything that happens in my house."

"We live on the same property. It's bound to happen. I was on my way here when I saw her leaving. And you chasing after her. So I'm assuming you did the stupid thing."

"I told her that I couldn't be in a relationship with

her." That was a lie. He had done so much more than that. He had torn both of their hearts out and stomped them into the ground. Because Sam was right, he was an idiot. But he had made a concerted effort to be a safe idiot.

How's that working for you?

"Right. Why exactly?"

"Look, the sage hermit thing is a little bit tired. You don't have a social life, I don't see you with a wife and children, so maybe you don't hang out and lecture me."

"Isn't tonight that thing?" Sam seemed undeterred by Chase's rudeness.

"What thing?"

"The charity thing that you were so intent on using to get investors. Because the two of us growing our family business and restoring the former glory of our hallowed ancestors is so important to you. And exploiting my artistic ability for your financial gain."

"Change of plans." He grunted, moving a big slab of iron that would eventually be a gate to the side. "I'm just going to keep working. We'll figure this out without schmoozing."

"Who are you and what have you done with my brother?"

"Just shut up. If you can't do anything other than stand there looking vaguely amused at the fact that I'm going through a personal crisis, then you can go straight to hell without passing Go or collecting two hundred dollars."

"I'm not going to be able to afford Park Place anyway, because you aren't out there getting new investors."

"I'm serious, Sam," Chase shouted, throwing his

hammer down on the ground. "It's all fine for you because you hold everyone at a distance."

Sam laughed. The bastard. "*I* hold everyone at a distance. What do you think you do? What do you think your endless string of one-night stands is?"

"You think I don't know? You think I don't know that it's an easy way to get some without ever having to have a conversation? I'm well aware. But I don't need you standing over there so entertained by the fact that..."

"That you actually got your heart broken?"

Chase didn't have anything to say to that. Every single word in his head evaporated like water against molten metal. He had nothing to say to that because his heart was broken. But Anna wasn't responsible. It was his own fault.

And the only reason his heart was broken was because he...

"Do you know what I said to Dad the day that he died?"

Sam froze. "No."

No, he didn't. Because they had never talked about it. "The last thing I ever said to him was that I couldn't wait to get away from here. I told him I wasn't going to pound iron for the rest of my life. I was going to get away and go to college. Make something real out of myself. Like this wasn't real."

"I didn't realize."

"No. Because I didn't tell you. Because I never told anybody. But that's why I needed to fix this. It's why I wanted to expand this place."

"So it isn't really to harness my incredible talent?"

"I don't even know what it's for anymore. To what?

To make up for what I said to a dead man. And for promises that I made at his grave... He can't hear me. That's the worst thing."

Sam stuffed his hands in his pockets. "Is that the only reason you're still here?"

"No. I love it here. I really do. I had to get older. I had to put some of my own sweat into this place. But now... I get it. I do. And I care about it because I care about it, not just because they cared about it. Not just because it's a legacy, but because it's worth saving. But..."

"I still remember that day. I mean, I don't just remember it," Sam said, "it's like it just happened yesterday. That feeling... The whole world changing. Everything falling right down around us. That's as strong in my head now as it was then."

"How many times can you lose everything?" Chase asked, making eye contact with his brother. "Anna is everything. Or she could be. It was easy when she was just a friend. But... I saw her in my house the other morning cooking me breakfast, wearing my T-shirt. For a second she made me feel like...like that house was our house, and she could be my...my everything."

"I wouldn't even know what that looked like for me, Chase. If you find that...grab it."

"And if I lose it?"

"You'll have no one to blame but yourself."

Chase thought back to the day his parents died. That was a kind of pain he hadn't even known existed. But, as guilty as he had felt, as many promises as he had made at his father's grave site, he couldn't blame himself for their death. It had been an accident. That was the simple truth.

But if he lost Anna now… Pushing her away hadn't been an accident. It was in his control. Fully and absolutely. And if he lost her, then it was on him.

He thought of her face as she had turned away from him, as she had gotten into her truck.

She had trusted him. His prickly Anna had trusted him with her feelings. Her vulnerability. A gift that he had never known her to give to anybody. And he had rejected it. He was no better than he had been as an angry sixteen-year-old, hurtling around the curves of the road that had destroyed his family, daring it to take him, too.

Anna, who had already endured the rejection of a mother, the silent rejection of who she was from her father, had dared to look him in the face and risk his rejection, too.

"I'll do it," Sam said, his voice rough.

"What?"

"I'm going to start…pursuing the art thing to a greater degree. I want to help. You missed this party tonight and I know it mattered to you…"

"But you hate change," Chase reminded him.

"Yeah," Sam said. "But I hate a lot of things. I have to do them anyway."

"We're still going to have to meet with investors."

"Yeah," Sam replied, stuffing his hands in his pockets. "I can help with that. You're right. This is why you're the brains and I'm the talent."

"You're a glorified blacksmith, Sam," Chase said, trying to keep the tone light because if he went too deep now he might just fall apart.

"With talent. Beyond measure," Sam said. "At least my brother has been telling me that for years."

"Your brother is smart." Though he currently felt anything but.

Sam shrugged. "Eh. Sometimes." He cleared his throat. "You discovered you cared about this place too late to ever let Dad know. That's sad. But at least Dad knew you cared about him. You know he never doubted that," Sam said. "But, damn, bro, don't leave it too late to let Anna know you care about her."

Chase looked at his brother, who was usually more cynical than he was wise, and couldn't ignore the truth ringing in his words.

Anna was the best he'd ever had. And had been for the past fifteen years of his life. Losing her...well, that was just a stupid thing to allow.

But the thing that scared him most right now was that it might already be too late. That he might have broken things beyond repair.

"And if it is too late?" he asked.

"Chase, you of all people know that when something is forged in fire it comes out the other side that much stronger." His brother's expression was hard, his dark eyes dead serious. "This is your fire. You're in it now. If you let it cool, you lose your chance. So I suggest you get your ass to wherever Anna is right now and you work at fixing this. It's either that or spend your life as a cold, useless hunk of metal that never became a damn thing."

It had not gone as badly as she'd feared. It hadn't gone perfectly, of course, but she had survived. The lowest point had been when Wendy Maxwell, who was still angry with Anna over the whole Chase thing, had wandered over to her and made disparaging comments

about last season's colors and cuts, all the while implying that Anna's dress was somehow below the height of
fashion. Which, whatever. She had gotten the dress on
clearance, so it probably was. Anna might care about
looking nice, but she didn't give a rat's ass about fashion.

She gave a couple of rat's asses about what had happened next.

Where's Chase?

Her newfound commitment to honesty and emotions
had compelled her to answer honestly.

We broke up. I'm pretty upset about it.

The other woman had been in no way sympathetic
and had in fact proceeded to smug all over the rest
of the conversation. But she wasn't going to focus on
the low.

The highs had included talking to several people
whom she was going to be working with in the future.
And getting two different phone numbers. She had
made conversation. She had felt…like she belonged.
And she didn't really think it had anything to do with
the dress. Just with her. When you had already put everything out there and had it rejected, what was there
to fear beyond that?

She sighed as she pulled into her driveway, straightening when she saw that there was a truck already
there.

Chase's truck.

She put her own into Park, killing the engine and
getting out. "What are you doing here, McCormack?"
She was furious now. She was all dressed up, wearing her gorgeous dress, and she had just weathered

that party on her own, and now he was here. She was going to punch his face.

Chase was sitting on her porch, wearing well-worn jeans and a tight black T-shirt, his cowboy hat firmly in place. He stood up, and as he began to walk toward her, Anna felt a raindrop fall from the sky. Because of course. He was here to kick her while she was down, almost certainly, and it was going to rain.

Thanks, Oregon.

"I came to see you." He stopped, looking her over, his jaw slightly slack. "I'm really glad that I did."

"Stop checking me out. You don't get to look at me like that. I did not put this dress on for you."

"I know."

"No, you don't know. I put this dress on for me. Because I wanted to look beautiful. Because I didn't care if anybody thought I was pretty enough, or if I'm not fashionable enough for Wendy the mule-faced ex-cheerleader. I did it because I cared. I do that now. I care. For me. Not for you."

She started to storm past him, the raindrops beginning to fall harder, thicker. He grabbed her arm and stopped her, twirling her toward him. "Don't walk away. Please."

"Give me a reason to stop walking."

"I've been doing a lot of thinking. And hammering."

"Real hammering, or is this some kind of a euphemism to let me know you're lonely?"

"Actual hammering. I didn't feel like I deserved anything else. Not after what happened."

"You don't. You don't deserve to masturbate ever again."

"Anna…"

"No," she said. "I can't do this. I can't just have a little taste of you. Not when I know what we can have. We can be everything. At first it was like you were my friend, but also we were sleeping together. And I looked at you as two different men. Chase, my friend. And Chase, the guy who was really good with his hands. And his mouth, and his tongue. You get the idea." She swallowed hard, her throat getting tight. "But at some point…it all blended together. And I can't separate it anymore. I just can't. I can't pull the love that I feel for you out of my chest and keep the friendship. Because they're all wrapped up in each other. And they've become the same thing."

"It's all or nothing," he said, his voice rough.

"Exactly."

He sighed heavily. "That's what I was afraid of."

"I'm sorry if you came over for a musical and a look at my porcupine pajamas. But I can't do it."

He tightened his hold on her, pulling her closer. "I knew it was going to be all or nothing."

"I can even understand why you think that might not be fair—"

"No. When you told me you loved me, I knew it was everything. Or nothing. That was what scared me so much. I have known… For a lot of years, I've realized that you were one of the main supports of my entire life. I knew you were one of the things that kept me together after my parents died. One of the only things. And I knew that if I ever lost you…it might finish me off completely."

"I'm sorry. But I can't live my life as your support."

"I know. I'm not suggesting that you do. It's just… when we started sleeping together, I had the same realization. That we weren't going to be able to separate the physical from the emotional, from our friendship. That it wasn't as simple as we pretended it could be. When I came downstairs and saw you in my kitchen… I saw the potential for something I never thought I could have."

"Why didn't you think you could have that?"

"I was too afraid. Tragedy happens to other people, Anna. Until it happens to you. And then it's like… the safety net is just gone. And everything you never thought you could be touched by is suddenly around every corner. You realize you aren't special. You aren't safe. If I could lose both my parents like that… I could lose anybody."

"You can't live that way," she said, her heart crumpling. "How in the world can you live that way?"

"You live halfway," he said. "You let yourself have a little bit of things, and not all of them. You pour your commitment into a place. Your passion into a job, into a goal of restoring a family name when your family is already gone. So you can't disappoint them even if you do fail." He took a deep breath. "You keep the best woman you know as a friend, because if she ever became more, your feelings for her could consume you. Anna… If I lost you… I would lose everything."

She could only stand there, looking at him, feeling like the earth was breaking to pieces beneath her feet. "Why did you—"

"I wanted to at least see it coming." He lowered his head, shaking it slowly. "I was such an idiot. For a long time. And afraid. I think it's impossible to go through tragedy like I did, like we did, and not have it change you. I'm not sure it's even possible to escape it doing so much as defining you. But you can choose how. It was so easy for me to see how you protected yourself. How you shielded yourself. But I didn't see that I was doing the same thing."

"I didn't know," she said, feeling stupid. Feeling blind.

"Because I didn't tell you." He reached up, drawing his thumb over her cheekbone, his expression so empty, so sad. Another side of Chase she hadn't seen very often. But it was there. It had always been there, she realized that now. "But I'm telling you now. I'm scared. I've been scared for a long time. And I've made a lot of promises to ghosts to try to atone for stupid things I said when my parents were alive. But I've been too afraid to make promises to the people that are actually still in my life. Too afraid to love the people that are still here. It's easier to make promises to ghosts, Anna. I'm done with that.

"You are here," he said, cupping her face now, holding her steady. "You're with me. And I can have you as long as I'm not too big an idiot. As long as you still want to have me. You put yourself out there for me, and I rejected you. I'm so sorry. I know what that cost you, Anna, because I know you. And please understand I didn't reject you because it wasn't enough. Because you weren't enough. It's because you were too much, and I wasn't enough. But I'm going to do my best to be enough for you now. Now and forever."

She could hardly believe what she was hearing, could hardly believe that Chase was standing there making declarations to her. The kind that sounded an awful lot like love. The kind that sounded an awful lot like exactly what she wanted to hear. "Is this because I'm wearing a dress?"

"No." He chuckled. "You could be wearing coveralls. You could be wearing nothing. Actually, I think I like you best in nothing. But whatever you're wearing, it wouldn't change this. It wouldn't change how I feel. Because I love you in every possible way. As my friend, as my lover. I love you in whatever you wear, a ball gown or engine grease. I love you working on tractors and trying to explain to me how an engine works and watching musicals."

"But do you love my porcupine pajamas?" she asked, her voice breaking.

"I'm pretty ambivalent about your porcupine pajamas, I'm not going to lie. But if they're a nonnegotiable part of the deal, then I can adjust."

She shook her head. "They aren't nonnegotiable. But I probably will irritate you with them." Then she sobbed, unable to hold her emotions back any longer. She wrapped her arms around his neck, burying her face in his skin, breathing his scent in. "Chase, I love you so much. Look what we were protecting ourselves from."

He laughed. "When you put it that way, it seems like we were being pretty stupid."

"Fear is stupid. And it's strong."

He tightened his hold on her. "It isn't stronger than this."

Not stronger than fifteen years of friendship, than holding each other through grief and pleasure, laughter and pain.

When she had pulled up and seen his truck here,

Anna Brown had murder on her mind. And now, everything was different.

"Remember when you promised you were going to make me a woman?" she asked.

"Right. I do. You laughed at me."

"Yes, I did." She stretched up on her toes and kissed his lips. "Chase McCormack, I'm pretty sure you did make me a woman. Maybe not in the way you meant. But you made me feel…like a whole person. Like I could finally put together all the parts of me and just be me. Not hide any of it anymore."

He closed his eyes, pressing his forehead against hers. "I'm glad, Anna. Because you sure as hell made me a man. The man that I want to be, the man that I need to be. I can't change the past, and I can't live in it anymore, either."

"Good. Then I think we should go ahead and make ourselves a future."

"Works for me." He smiled. "I love you. You're everything."

"I love you, too." It felt so good to say that. To say it and not be afraid. To show her whole heart and not hold anything back.

"I bet that I can make you say you love me at least a hundred more times tonight. I bet I can get you to say it every day for the rest of our lives."

She smiled, taking his hand and walking toward the house, not caring about the rain. "I bet you can."

He led her inside, leaving a trail of clothes in the hall behind them, leaving her beautiful dress on the floor. She didn't care at all.

"And I bet—" he wrapped his arm around her waist,

then laid her down on the bed "—tonight I can make you scream."

"I'll take that bet," she said, wrapping her legs around his hips.

And that was a bet they both won.

* * * * *

"Hopefully everyone will get home safe," she said.

Gabe took in her high cheekbones, the soft roundness of her jaw
and the tilt of her chin. The scent of something subtle but sweet
surrounded her. He forced his eyes away from her and cleared his
throat. "Hopefully," he agreed as he poured a small amount of
champagne into his flute.

"I'll leave you to celebrate," Monica said.

With a polite nod, Gabe took a sip of his drink and set the bottle
at his feet, trying to ignore the reasons why he was so aware of her.
Her scent. Her beauty. Even the gentle night winds shifting her
hair back from her face. Distance was best. Over the past week he
had fought to do just that to help his sudden awareness of her ebb.
Ever since the veil to their desire had been removed, it had been
hard to ignore.

She turned to leave, but moments later a yelp escaped her as
her feet got twisted in the long length of her robe and sent her body
careening toward him as she tripped.

Reacting swiftly, he reached to wrap his arm around her waist
and brace her body up against his to prevent her fall. He let the hand
holding his flute drop to his side. Their faces were just precious

inches apart. When her eyes dropped to his mouth, he released a small gasp. His eyes scanned her face before locking with hers.

He knew just fractions of a second had passed, but right then, with her in his arms and their eyes locked, it felt like an eternity. He wondered what it felt like for her. Was her heart pounding? Her pulse sprinting? Was she aroused? Did she feel that pull of desire?

He did.

With a tiny lick of her lips that was nearly his undoing, Monica raised her chin and kissed him. It was soft and sweet. And an invitation.

"Monica?" he asked, heady with desire, but his voice deep and soft as he sought clarity.

"Kiss me," she whispered against his lips, hunger in her voice.

"Shit," Gabe swore before he gave in to the temptation of her and dipped his head to press his mouth down upon hers.

And it was just a second more before her lips and her body softened against him as she opened her mouth and welcomed him with a heated gasp that seemed to echo around them. The first touch of his tongue to hers sent a jolt through his body, and he clutched her closer to him as her hands snaked up his arms and then his shoulders before clutching the lapels of his tux in her fists. He assumed she was holding on while giving in to a passion that was irresistible.

Monica was lost in it all. Blissfully.

The taste and feel of his mouth were everything she ever imagined.

Ever dreamed of.

Ever longed for.

Don't miss what happens next in
One Night with Cinderella
by nationally bestselling author Niobia Bryant!

Available February 2021 wherever
Harlequin Desire books and ebooks are sold.

Harlequin.com

HDEXP0121

HARLEQUIN
DESIRE

Luxury, scandal, desire—welcome to the lives of the American elite.

One Night with Cinderella

NIOBIA BRYANT

Save **$1.00**

on the purchase of ANY Harlequin Desire book.

Available wherever books are sold, including most bookstores, supermarkets, drugstores and discount stores.

Save $1.00

on the purchase of ANY Harlequin Desire book.

Coupon valid until March 31, 2021.
Redeemable at participating outlets in the US and Canada only.
Not redeemable at Barnes & Noble stores. Limit one coupon per customer.

52616945

5 65373 00076 2 (8100)0 12481

Get 4 FREE REWARDS!

We'll send you 2 FREE Books plus 2 FREE Mystery Gifts.

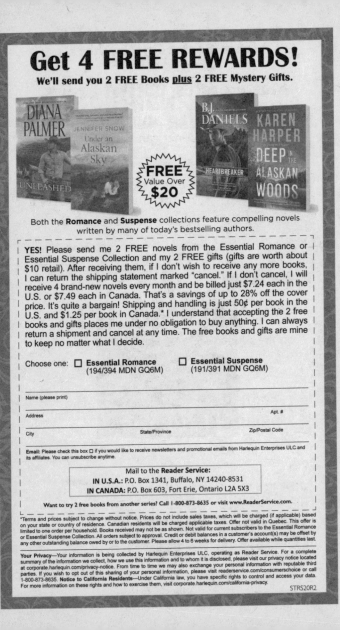

FREE Value Over **$20**

Both the **Romance** and **Suspense** collections feature compelling novels written by many of today's bestselling authors.

YES! Please send me 2 FREE novels from the Essential Romance or Essential Suspense Collection and my 2 FREE gifts (gifts are worth about $10 retail). After receiving them, if I don't wish to receive any more books, I can return the shipping statement marked "cancel." If I don't cancel, I will receive 4 brand-new novels every month and be billed just $7.24 each in the U.S. or $7.49 each in Canada. That's a savings of up to 28% off the cover price. It's quite a bargain! Shipping and handling is just 50¢ per book in the U.S. and $1.25 per book in Canada.* I understand that accepting the 2 free books and gifts places me under no obligation to buy anything. I can always return a shipment and cancel at any time. The free books and gifts are mine to keep no matter what I decide.

Choose one: ☐ **Essential Romance**
(194/394 MDN GQ6M)

☐ **Essential Suspense**
(191/391 MDN GQ6M)

Name (please print)

Address   Apt. #

City   State/Province   Zip/Postal Code

Email: Please check this box ☐ if you would like to receive newsletters and promotional emails from Harlequin Enterprises ULC and its affiliates. You can unsubscribe anytime.

Mail to the Reader Service:
IN U.S.A.: P.O. Box 1341, Buffalo, NY 14240-8531
IN CANADA: P.O. Box 603, Fort Erie, Ontario L2A 5X3

Want to try 2 free books from another series? Call 1-800-873-8635 or visit www.ReaderService.com.

*Terms and prices subject to change without notice. Prices do not include sales taxes, which will be charged (if applicable) based on your state or country of residence. Canadian residents will be charged applicable taxes. Offer not valid in Quebec. This offer is limited to one order per household. Books received may not be as shown. Not valid for current subscribers to the Essential Romance or Essential Suspense Collection. All orders subject to approval. Credit or debit balances in a customer's account(s) may be offset by any other outstanding balance owed by or to the customer. Please allow 4 to 6 weeks for delivery. Offer available while quantities last.

Your Privacy—Your information is being collected by Harlequin Enterprises ULC, operating as Reader Service. For a complete summary of the information we collect, how we use this information and to whom it is disclosed, please visit our privacy notice located at corporate.harlequin.com/privacy-notice. From time to time we may also exchange your personal information with reputable third parties. If you wish to opt out of this sharing of your personal information, please visit readerservice.com/consumerschoice or call 1-800-873-8635. **Notice to California Residents**—Under California law, you have specific rights to control and access your data. For more information on these rights and how to exercise them, visit corporate.harlequin.com/california-privacy.

STRS20R2

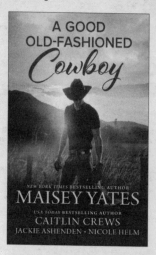

Love Harlequin romance?

DISCOVER.

Be the first to find out about promotions,
news and exclusive content!

Facebook.com/HarlequinBooks

Twitter.com/HarlequinBooks

Instagram.com/HarlequinBooks

Pinterest.com/HarlequinBooks

YouTube.com/HarlequinBooks

ReaderService.com

EXPLORE.

Sign up for the Harlequin e-newsletter and
download a free book from any series at
TryHarlequin.com

CONNECT.

Join our Harlequin community to
share your thoughts and connect
with other romance readers!
Facebook.com/groups/HarlequinConnection

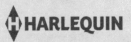

HARLEQUIN

Heartfelt or thrilling, passionate or uplifting—Harlequin is more than just happily-ever-after.

With twelve different series to choose from and new books available every month, you are sure to find stories that will move you, uplift you, inspire and delight you.

HNEWS2021